Land's Breath

by Śivani Howe

office@solaceandshine.ca
www.solaceandshine.ca

This book has been written from the view point of two different paradigms of reality. One is objectification—the "what do I get out of this" mindset prevalent in today's society. The second is interconnection or oneness—expressing the unified relationship that can and does exist between all beings.

These two paradigms are shown through the use of creative capitalization of animals and beings in some chapters but not in others.

ISBN: 978-1-9990541-1-3

10 9 8 7 6 5 4 3

Published by Solace & Shine Publishing
A subsidiary of Solace & Shine Ltd. © 2024

SOLACE&SHINE
PUBLISHING

Acknowledgement

Like anything worthy in life, nothing is created alone and this book is no different.

It has been a 5 year adventure that I will always cherish and I'd like to acknowledge the following souls for adding their heart, kindness, and encouragement to the process.

Firstly, to the Land called 'Niwas situated on the unceded territory of the Ktunaxa people in the foothills of the Purcell Mountains. I am so grateful I get to call you home, especially Ma Ponderosa and Brother Fir. For receiving my tears, then finding my pups, for telling me this story; for asking me to believe….

To my guides and teachers both etherial and in body. I am so grateful for your inspiration, guidance, love, and solace. Thank you for sharing the teachings and holding the light.

Renee, Thank you for stepping up as I was about to give up forever. Land's Breath simply would not have been finished without you. My deepest gratitude for your encouragement, expertise and fastidiousness over timelines and grammer.

Paramjyoti, my beloved, thank you for encouraging me, and believing in this project right from the beginning. I know you don't like reading books, so the fact you got through it multiple times was such a vote of confidence.

For my Babalu, for being the best storyteller I know, and for your ability to make me laugh every single day.

To Mum and David for eagerly reading the very first draft with such care and encouragement that I believed I could actually write.

To Omshanti and Aradhana for your constant encouragement, great eye and most loving friendship. I love you both.

To Tim WJ, Thank you for your expertise and for being patient with my quirks and dislexia you really supported it being a most enjoyable process (not easy) for my first novel. Deepest pranaams.

To David B, thanks for the nudge to get her out of the draw and finish her.

I'm am quite sure there are many more who have held space, encouraged, and supported this project, and to you, I thank you.

A heartfelt thank you to those who came together to support this book being published: Bhakti and Divya, Saumya, Siddhi and 'Niwas members.

*This book is dedicated to
the Land especially
the Trees—forever listening,
forever whispering.
I am forever grateful.*

Prelude

Obituary

Jade Melanie Brennan. Born on 12th August 2005. Died on 5th November 2022. She was born into nothing, and she left nothing behind. She was loved by her mother and equally regretted by her father. Or so she assumed. He had never shown his face in all the years she could remember.

Jade was middle in size; freckled; almost invisible if not for her hair. Hair as red as molten lava and as long and thick as a horse's tail — her crown of fire. It kept people at arm's length. Fear of being burned will do that.

She was average at school, excelling in math and barely scraping by in the rest. But, she was bursting with the potential for something more. Yet, now, on this sad day, that potential would never be actualized. "Such a shame." "Such a waste." Murmurs fell from the lips of the mourners.

This was the obituary she wrote and rewrote in her head while standing in the courtroom. She probably should've been rehearsing an apology to the court (seeing as the victim wasn't present) or, at the minimum, an apology to her dead mother. But, no. She sat there writing her own obituary. Who else would write it? No one else knew her, nor did she think anyone else would take the time to know her. She would have to do it herself, alone, like always. Time was running out. The fall of the judge's gavel would end her life as she knew it.

1 The Courthouse

 and wood-panelled, the courtroom reeks of desperation-caught-red-handed. Buzzing, fluorescent tubes flood the room with glaring accusations as the clerk, a middle-aged woman who looks like she holds onto just a little of every heartbreak that walks through the door monotonously recites wrongdoing after wrongdoing. Her words, while factually accurate, do not acknowledge the despair and shame that lies thick in the air.

The Court hears the deeds of person after person; it notes their pleas and seals their fates. They stand. They sit. They stand. They sit. A perverse game of whack-a-mole with each 'criminal' waiting for the inevitable blow from the judge's hand. The bang of the gavel barely causes the clerk to blink.

The older woman shifts slightly and gently touches the worn pew as memories of childhood confessions flit across her mind—pulling Tommy's hair, eating an extra cookie, fibbing about who fed the dog scraps from the table. Oh, Father Paul, how he must've chuckled over some of her "sins". Her memories fade and she can now view her reason for being here: the two women sitting four rows in front of her.

They resemble a pair of matchsticks sticking up from a navy-blue box. Fine ivory necks capped in bright, red Irish hair. The older of the two has her hair in a French roll and is wearing a navy-blue-no-mess dress. The younger has opted for a bun and a thin, navy-blue cardigan as if being dressed as a school teacher will soften the gavel strike heading her way.

She knows the older one, Carole, is playing double roles today: lawyer and aunt and suspects the role of a hot-shot-Vancouver-lawyer is the more comfortable of the two. At least that was the impression Carole gave during their one brief meeting—family was something to be negotiated and managed, to ensure the least amount of carnage as possible. The younger girl, she has never met. Yet, she feels as if she knows Jade already. After all, Jade is the reason she's here. Well, her mother is the reason—the memory of her that is.

Carole leans over to Jade and whispers something in her ear. Jade shifts uncomfortably in her seat and steals a look around the room as if searching for her escape. It's the first time she has seen Jade's face. Oval and pale. Jade's not wearing any make-up, and she wonders if Carole has forbidden it to have her appear as young as possible for the Court or, if like her mother, the young lady simply forgoes it. She catches Jade's eyes—aquamarine pools upon pale sand that perfectly balances the heat of her red hair—which are the same eyes as her mother's. Jade seems to have the same spattering of freckles across her nose and under her eyes, the same nose, and the same jawline. She is beautiful. Jade looks directly at her, and she is able to hold her gaze, for just a moment, and nods. She sends Jade a thread of calm, hoping the young girl will catch it and hold onto it tightly. But Jade looks away, unaware of the connection, and the thread unravels into nothingness.

She turns her attention to the judge sitting on his pedestal and listening to the proceedings. He is unable to stop himself from glancing at the clock every few minutes. He busies himself by fanning out the reports and statements on the desk before him. Maybe if he arranges them just so, they would conjure themselves into an accurate picture of the case at hand. It doesn't work. He sighs. Removes his glasses and polishes them. Nothing can detract from the look of disillusionment on his face: what a life judiciary service had promised him—and failed to deliver. Authority seeps from his black robe, red sash, and white collar. She wonders if the judge knows the collar looks like an adult-sized spit bib he has forgotten to take off after breakfast. The permanent furrow in his brow seems to be the finishing touch to his uniform. Her thoughts are interrupted by the clerk's monotone voice.

"Case 3254-1KA. Calling upon Ms. Jade Melanie Brennan. Please stand."

Carole and Jade rise in unison. Jade wipes her hands on her skirt, smoothing invisible wrinkles. Her height falls short of her aunt's, but only by an inch.

"Miss Brennan, do you understand the charges brought against you by the Crown at this time?" the judge asks mechanically fanning out another set of papers in front of him. He frowns, rearranges the papers, and glances at the clock.

Jade leans down to speak into the microphone. "Yes, your… Honour," she says. The words catch in her throat. The hand that reaches for the glass of water trembles slightly.

The judge stares at her, as though trying to reconcile the person in front of him with the deeds she's been accused of on the papers before him. "And how do you plea?" he asks finally.

"Guilty, your Honour."

Her words create an immediate flurry of whispers from those gathered in the room. It's as if a gun has been fired and the crows have taken flight to spread the news far and wide. Danger! Danger!

The judge glowers until silence is restored and then shuffles the papers back into the folder. He steals another glance at the clock and sighs. He turns to the Crown attorney sitting at the desk to the right of Carole and Jade. He's a middle-aged man in a suit and tie that look as though they were expensive, once. The seat next to him is empty. The charges laid against Jade were not civil, so there was no need for the boy to be present.

"Crown Council, in light of the charges and of the plea, do you have a recommendation you would like to make before I declare my ruling?"

"Yes, your Honour." He stands to address the court, and Carole takes her seat. Jade follows her aunt's lead. "The Crown and Ms. Brennan's defence council have spoken at length and negotiated a way forward. We would, your Honour, like to make a recommendation for your consideration." He smiles politely and turns toward Carole, acknowledging their proposed agreement; she nods at him in reply. She does not look at Jade. The courtroom is silent, expectant, wondering what sort of deal the guilty party has negotiated. Freedom? Unlikely. But, hope springs eternal.

"Your Honour," the Crown Council says turning back to the judge, "the Crown is asking for leniency as this is Miss Brennan's first offence and she has no prior record. We are suggesting a one-year probation at a full residency program located at... uh...," he looks down at his notes, pin-pointing the answer with his finger, "at Ponderosa Grove."

"Ponderosa Cove?" the judge repeats. "What is Ponderosa Cove?" He looks confused and adjusts his collar and bib. He then leans forward as if a change in position could improve the situation. "Never heard of it."

"Ponderosa *Grove,* your Honour," Carol interjects, half standing. "May I?" She looks questioningly toward the Crown Council. He gestures with an open hand to indicate the floor is hers and takes his seat. Carole nods in appreciation and turns back to the judge waiting for his nod of approval before continuing.

"Ponderosa Grove is a centre for transformation and contemplation. It is based on an ancient Eastern framework of teachings that are known to be very successful for helping people who are... lost." She casts a glance at Jade and continues her speech. "The centre helps them find a purpose. It is a place of healing and…," here her voice almost falters as she wavers between her roles as defence council and aunt. She pauses to collect herself. When she speaks again, it is with her former strength, "… it helps get its residents back on track—with life."

The judge peers over his glasses at Carole before sliding his gaze to Jade and then over to the prosecution. It is the first time that day that he has shown any interest in what is happening in his courtroom. "And the Crown agrees with this recommendation? This, Ponderosa Grove?"

"Yes, your Honour. In light of the circumstances leading up to this… incident, and the subsequent charges laid, we stand by this request."

"And how did you find out about this Ponderosa Grove, Ms. Brennan?" the judge addresses Carole, pointing his finger at her to make clear which Ms. Brennan he wants to answer. Carole hesitates and looks down at the microphone. "Ms. Brennan…," the judge prods.

"Our family has long been connected with this lineage of teachings. This way of life rather. It has served many people for thousands of years, your Honour, and while we understand that it is… unusual, for this to be the course of action sanctioned by the Court, under the circumstances…," Carole pauses for a moment waiting for her words to land. "And, although my niece has never had any direct contact with Ponderosa Grove or its teachings, I believe that in light of her mother's passing, this will give her the best chance of moving forward." Jade shoots a look of surprise at her aunt but remains silent. Carole's gaze remains fixed on the judge and, ever so slightly, she leans away from Jade. No one else likely noticed the gesture, but to her, watching from behind, the distance created speaks volumes.

The judge seems incapable of pulling himself away from Carole's unwavering stare. It is only when someone else in the courtroom coughs loudly, breaking the silence, that he turns to scrutinize Jade. Like her aunt, Jade's gaze does not waver. She waits.

He clears his throat and speaks to Jade as though she is the only one in the room. "Ms. Brennan, listen to me carefully. If I agree to this arrangement and you leave the program, for any reason, before your full year is up, you will violate your probation and you will be arrested. Do you understand that?"

"Yes, your Honour." Jade's voice is barely audible now, childlike.

"If you violate your probation and are arrested, you will come back to this Court for an alternative, and may I be frank here, a much harsher sentencing. Is this understood?"

"Yes, your Honour." Her words are only a faint whisper. Carole leans over to her and murmurs in her ear. "Yes, your Honour," Jade repeats, louder and Carole gives a tiny nod of approval. Her words hang in the air. The judge stares at Jade and her aunt. The futility of his job is temporarily forgotten as something stirs in the depths of his mind—a lost memory. A loud wailing in the hallway breaks the spell, the memory fades, and the judge glances at the clock.

"Very well then. The Court approves this application for a year's residency at Ponderosa Grove starting March 15th." He gathers the papers on his desk and taps them together. "Good luck, young lady. I hope I never see you in this court again."

And without another word, the gavel falls and Jade's shoulders flinch. Another mole whacked.

The light of day momentarily blinds the older woman as she steps out onto the sidewalk. She readjusts the orange shawl around her shoulders to protect herself from the cold breeze and the waves of despair surging past her, buffeting her in every direction as if she were a lone ship in an angry sea. She needs to leave the area before Carole and Jade emerge—this is not the time nor the place for introductions. As she moves along the sidewalk, a flutter of movement catches her eye. She stops and looks up to see a Robin perched on the lowest branch of a Fir tree. She lingers, absorbed in the scene before her: the light, the breeze, the bird, the tree. The fir tree must have been there since before the courthouse was built, or maybe it used to be the courthouse. Its branches stretch as if to offer protection from the harsh light of day, while the breeze moving through the needles creates a soothing sound to ease the pain of the tormented souls leaving the courthouse. The Robin titters. It must have only just arrived that morning for she had not seen one on her arrival yesterday. It is the first Robin of the year. Its presence is Nature's decree that Winter has given notice and Spring will arrive soon to take its place. She must start the long drive home immediately. A new cycle of the seasons is about to begin, and there is much to prepare for the year ahead.

Spring

2 Arriving

The black highway snaked through the expanse of white fields rendering the scene before them into a binary reality. Black on white, white on black. Even the evergreen trees looked black against the monochrome sky.

"Clouds look heavy. Think it will snow?" Carole asked. *They're more like laden with despair,* Jade thought but remained silent.

Nothing inside of Jade felt so definitive as the world passing by outside the window. Right. Wrong. Guilty. Not guilty. Locked up. Free. Alive. Dead. Her world was filled with shades of grey. And as she moved through the fog she felt isolated and lost and betrayed.

The song playing on the radio jangled on about love and happiness. It was nauseating. It was fingernails on a blackboard. Each happy lyric, each "oh baby" and auto-tuned harmony added to the anger building inside of her. Anger that threatened to erupt and destroy the tenuous hold she had over her emotions.

But, apparently, "Ooooh, baby, I love your way…," was perfect road-tripping music for Carole. She hummed along tapping a plain gold wedding band on the steering wheel of the black Jeep she had rented for the journey to Ponderosa Grove—which struck Jade as odd because her aunt wasn't married.

"Why do you wear a wedding ring?" Jade asked in a desperate attempt to distract from the music. "Doesn't that, like, jinx your chances of finding love and marital bliss and all that fucking Hallmark bullshit?"

"Maybe, but it also stops overworked lawyers from flirting with me… Well, most of them anyway." Carole shifted uneasily in her seat as if she wanted to say something more but decided against it. She went back to humming and tapping along to the music. Every once and awhile an "oh, yeah" and an "a-ha" burst forth from her lips in an uncontrolled burst of enthusiasm that turned Jade's stomach.

Unable to feign any more lightheartedness, Jade reached out and clicked the seek button on the radio. Everything sounded happy and upbeat—which only agitated her more. She clicked faster and with increasing force, attempting to bully the stations into submission. Over and over she changed the station, only hearing the first few seconds of a song before moving on to the next.

"There's never any decent music on the fucking radio," she said, half under her breath. Finally, landing on something suitably angry, Jade sat back in her seat and glared out the passenger side window.

"Language, Jade. Seriously," Carole said. "Does every second word out of your mouth have to be an expletive? You never used to speak like that. Not when…," Carole didn't finish the sentence. She didn't have to.

"Not when my mother was alive? Is that what you mean, *Carole*?" Jade spat. "Before she was hit by a *fucking* bus, and I was left on my *fucking* own in an empty *fucking* apartment?"

The radio howled, *I'm becoming this, all I want to do, Is be more like me and be less like you…*

"That's what you wanted!" Carole snapped back no longer able to bite her tongue. She leaned into the vitriol they'd been circling since the trial's end. "*You* begged me to figure out how to let you stay in your apartment and finish your last year of school. *You* pleaded with me not to bring you to Vancouver. I…" The car slid on a patch of black ice and the two women stopped talking as Carole focused on the road. Screaming pain and angst flowed through the speakers doing the communicating for them. Carole slammed off the radio and let out a deep breath that sounded, to Jade at least, very much like a long, drawn out, "Fuuuuuuuuuuuuuuccccck."

"Hypocrite," she said, but silently. Now was not the time to taunt her aunt.

Carole turned off the black, snaking highway and ground to a halt as the road before them abruptly morphed into a white, satin ribbon of unplowed snow. Only a single set of tracks gave any indication that it was a road and not a dead end. Jade hoped it was passable.

Moving at a snail's pace, Carole began to follow the tracks up the hill. Where the snow had been compacted, ice glistened and soon the Jeep's tires started to slip and spin on the slope forcing them to stop and slowly back down to the bottom. Jade shuffled her feet nervously and grasped her armrest.

"Shi… Do we walk from here?" Jade asked looking down at her street sneakers and back again at the snow-covered road.

"Nope, not yet." Carole searched for the 4WD button on the dashboard, pressed it, and took a deep breath. "At least I hope not yet," she muttered. Carole glanced over at Jade and attempted a caring smile. She failed. Gripping the steering wheel until her knuckles started to pale, Carole pressed the accelerator. The Jeep surged forward cutting its own tracks in the snow.

The road sloped upwards until it plateaued at a fork. The tracks they'd been following continued along the table and disappeared into the woods ahead while the sign *Ponderosa Grove* beckoned them down and to the left along a path of unmarked snow. Carole stopped the Jeep and assessed the path without a word. The descent looked ominous.

"This is bullshit," Jade said at last, not fully knowing if she meant the road in front of them or the year ahead. "Bull. Shit."

Carole inhaled audibly and turned the radio back on. "Never gonna give you up, never gonna let you down, never gonna run around and desert you….," filled the silence. Carole turned the radio off. She released both the brake and her breath and started the car on its descent. Jade noticed that the trees seemed to grow densely along this part of the driveway. Large Fir trees with thick trunks and snow-laden branches lined the sides of the drive giving the impression that the trees had gathered together to watch the new arrival make her appearance.

Carole hugged the bank, and Jade hugged her knees. The Jeep moved slowly down the icy slope until the road flattened and both women breathed more easily. As a peace offering, Jade turned the radio back on as they rolled toward the entrance to Ponderosa Grove. A wooden archway that had seen better days spanned the drive and two locked gates prevented anyone from going any farther.

"That looks welcoming," Jade muttered eyeing the visual contradiction of the locked gates and the welcome sign to the side of the gates. Carole pulled up so they could both read it.

Welcome to Ponderosa Grove.
If gates are shut, please park in the designated space to the left.

Carole parked and in the sudden silence, Jade recognized the song "Don't You Forget About Me" was now playing on the radio. It was her mother's favourite song from her favourite 80s movie *The Breakfast Club*.

The music cracked open the floodgates to the memories Jade had so carefully locked away: her mother dancing in the kitchen with a rolled-up tea towel in her hand as a huge mic; her mother making embarrassing flirty faces at her from across the counter as she ate a banana sandwich during the after school recap; them huddled together on the couch under a duvet hugging a huge bowl of popcorn. As each memory surfaced, Jade felt her face flush and her throat burn. She groped for the door handle desperate to escape the ghost of her mother. Feeling as if she may vomit, Jade leaped from the car into the cold February afternoon. Her sneakers sank into the ankle-deep snow. Jade gasped from the shock of the cold and the wetness on her feet, yet she welcomed the distraction from the pressure of tears building behind her eyes. She lifted her chin and faced the oncoming breeze from the small valley, letting the subzero temperatures freeze the flow of emotion before it could carve tracks down her face. Only the trees would be able to see the sparkling at the corner of her eye, the flare of her nostrils, the trembling of her lips.

Jade eyed the closed gates warily knowing that once she crossed that threshold, her year-long incarceration would begin. Jade rubbed her cheeks, wiping the last of her emotion from her face and inhaled deeply. The frigid air froze the back of her throat.

"OK. Jay," Carole declared, trying to sound enthusiastic about the situation, "let's get you up that hill."

Carole opened the trunk, poked around the back of the Jeep, and emerged with a large shopping bag Jade hadn't seen before. "Knowing this place is… let's use the word rustic," Carole said, "I picked these up for you." She had her hand in the bag like a magician searching for a rabbit in a hat. "Ta-da!" Carole pulled out a pair of new winter boots with woollen socks stuffed in the top like festive tissue paper. Jade was suddenly and acutely aware that her feet had gone from helpfully cold to borderline painful. They had been marinating in the snow, and Jade knew from experience that her littlest toes were probably white already.

"Thanks," she croaked, her throat still too full of emotion to speak clearly.

Jade sat on the trunk's lip and kicked off her sneakers. Pulling the new wool socks over her icy toes, Jade realized this was how all inmates prepared for prison—a changing of clothes. She sighed, slid into the new boots, and looked at Carole who was beaming with delight.

"Good, now you'll be able to walk around here without fear of losing your toes."

"Well, there's a f…," Jade bit her lip to stop the word from slipping through and then muttered, "silver lining if ever I heard one." Carole pretended not to hear. Jade stared at the remaining bag in the trunk. She sighed, shook her head to clear her mind, and grabbed the strap. Heaving the too-big-for-her pack onto her shoulders, Jade was instantly transformed into the hunchback of Notre Dame. She staggered under the weight of it, slipping slightly in the snow.

"Want help carrying that up the hill?" Carole asked. "Maybe we can take out a few things and put them into the boot bag, and I can——"

"I got it," Jade cut her off and moved away so Carole couldn't see her discomfort. She jostled the pack into a more comfortable position on her shoulders and cinched the belt that hugged her hips. Better but not great. She leaned forward to offset the weight of her pack and began to walk. Each step required more effort than the one before, and Jade felt like she was forcing herself through a headwind. They crossed the threshold at the side of the gate and started up the hill.

The snow crunched underfoot; their footfalls amplified in the eerie silence of the place. The road was wide enough for a vehicle, but there were no tire tracks. A single set of footprints seemed to be coming down the drive, but they changed direction before getting to the gated entrance and headed straight into the forest in the direction of the highway.

"Someone escaped," Jade said wryly. Her voice seemed to have triggered a silent alarm because a dog started to bark in the distance. The bark grew louder and louder as the dog raced toward them, and the sound of the bark indicated that it was not a chihuahua headed their way. Jade froze. Memories of being chased by the neighbourhood Rottweiler as a kid flashed before her. She had had to climb a tree to save herself then, would she have to do the same now? Her legs twitched as she looked for a suitable tree to climb, but none of the trees had weight-bearing branches lower than twenty feet. It was as if they had all put their hands behind their backs and were standing silently waiting to see how this would play out.

"Shit," she said to herself. "Shitshitshitshitshit."

"It's OK," Carole said coming to stand beside her, "I'm sure it's just coming to greet us. They know we're coming."

The bark was low, urgent, battle-ready. Thoughts of a wolf barreling toward them caused Jade to drop her pack on the ground. It made a muffled thud. She kept hold of one handle in case she needed to lift it, in front of her, in defence. Her eyes strained to see what her ears told her was just moments away.

"Um...," Jade said, but her throat, suddenly dry, failed to finish the sentence.

From around a large tree on the side of the drive, the dog appeared. It took the corner at full speed and barreled toward them. Jade's hand tightened on her backpack as she took a step back leaving Carole out in front. The dog was huge, completely white, and with its teeth bared and hackles raised it looked like a polar bear. Jade closed her eyes, turned her face away, and braced for impact.

"Well, hello there, big boy!" Carole cooed. "Are you taking care of your home? Are you? You're doing such a good job! Yes, you are. Ooooh, do you like that?"

Jade opened her eyes to see her aunt kneeling on the ground, rubbing the monster behind the ears. Its tail wagged side to side, and its whole body quivered with excitement.

Carole looked up at Jade, beaming. "Isn't he just lovely?"

Jade merely looked at her, incapable of speech. Aunt Carole cooing over a dog? She wondered if she had just stepped into an alternate universe. A universe where guard dogs licked instead of bit, and straight-laced lawyers talked in baby voices.

"Sure…uh, lovely," Jade managed to croak out and looked around to see if a human was following the dog, but all she saw were trees, snow, and a pair of ravens flying overhead.

"You going to show us where to go, boy?" Carole said standing up and brushing snow from her jeans. The dog barked as if to say, "Yes, nice lady. I'll show you." Carole laughed and began to follow the polar bear-like dog up the drive.

"You coming?" Carole turned and asked when she noticed Jade was standing, staring at the hill ahead with the strap of the pack still in one hand. Before Jade could muster a reply, Carole was already walking, eager to reach their final destination.

Jade hauled her backpack onto her shoulders again. This time, its weight nearly brought her to her knees. "Do I have a choice?" she mumbled as she steadied herself. No one and nothing offered a reply. With another deep breath and clenched fists, Jade followed the dog and her aunt up the hill.

3 Trees: Prophecy

Huddling together, we watch the black rock roll slowly down the hill and stop.

Whispers of excitement weave between us, the way Nuthatches and Juncos chase each other in the Spring—here, there, flittering from branch to branch and trunk to trunk. Our old friend, you are finally returning! Of course, the shell is different, but your signature is the same: pale, golden yellow like Larch needles in their final song, mesmerizing—unforgettable. We have been waiting a long time for your homecoming. Some beasts will say lifetimes. Yet, it is written in our rings—in the tightest circles of Elders—that the new moon will return and take the pain away; when Sun touches Mother and the heart melts; when the past is honoured but not held; then light will shine once more and remembrance will reign.

All is written, you see, yet all must unfold, for a song must be sung to give Bird's life meaning.

4 Orientation

"*Hello* and welcome!" exclaimed a voice seemingly out of nowhere. Jade had been so focused on putting one foot in front of the other on the icy drive that she had not looked ahead to see the woman walking down to meet them. The woman's cheerful greeting had nearly caused Jade to lose her footing.

"I'm Meera, and you must be Carole and Jade," she said extending her hand to be shaken rather than opening her arms for a new-age hug. Jade hated hugging strangers.

"Hi! Yes, that's us," Carole replied shaking her hand cheerfully; she continued speaking before Jade could muster a simple hello. "We were greeted by your welcoming committee here," Carole said, giving the dog another scratch behind his ear, "and he showed us the rest of the way."

"Ah, great. Yes, that's Sam. Nothing comes on this property that he doesn't know about." Jade saw Meera look from Carole's open and welcoming smile to her own pursed lips and furrowed brow. With kindness, Meera held Jade's gaze as she spoke, "He's all bark and no bite. Unless you're a bear or a coyote that is. But with humans, he's harmless. Aren't you boy?" She turned back to Sam who had trotted over to Meera at the sound of his name and was sniffing her leg to see if it held a clue to where he might find food. He found none and laid down at her feet just in case he had missed it.

"Let's head inside for a warm cup of tea and your orientation." Meera took a step to the side and opened her hand, gesturing up the drive behind her to the big, grey house on top of the hill. "Carole, do you want to join us? Or...," she looked to the west as though listening to something Jade couldn't hear and sniffed, "Are you going to try and beat the snow that's coming our way?"

Jade followed Meera's gaze to the west, where a blanket of snow-laden clouds filled the sky.

"Ummm…," Carole said and scanned the horizon. The threat of snow gave her aunt the escape she wanted but hadn't known how to get. Carole nodded making a decision, and then turned to Jade.

"Alright, Jay, you've got this. I'm not needed anymore, OK?" Jade didn't answer. Instead, she kept her gaze fixed in the direction of the pending weather. Carole grabbed her by the shoulders, ducking and diving until they made eye contact. "I can't think of a better place to spend some time. If I was your age again, I'd be here in a heartbeat." She was lying; they both knew it. Jade faced her aunt but stared straight through her.

Carole turned to Meera and stretched out her hand once more. "Thank you," she said before giving Jade an awkward, one-sided hug and a quick peck on the cheek. "You've got this," Carole repeated to Jade, to herself, or to Meera, Jade couldn't tell; she didn't care. "I love ya, kid," Carole said. The final step in the prisoner exchange was now over, Carole turned and headed back down the drive, back to civilization, back to her hassle-free life.

Jade watched her aunt walk down the hill. It wasn't quite a jog, but it was faster than a stroll for sure. Sam acted as her chaperone, snuffling the ground with his nose as he went, no doubt decoding nature's many messages.

"OK!" Meera said, a little too loudly in an attempt to bring Jade's attention back to her. "Let's go have a cuppa tea, shall we? Get you settled in."

Jade turned to Meera, "OK," she said. Her voice sounded foreign and awkward, even to herself. She shrugged the mountainous backpack higher onto her shoulders, resumed the position of a hunchback, and braced herself for the road ahead.

Jade sat at the island in the kitchen of the main house nibbling on the corner of her middle fingernail, a habit she had been trying to break for more years than she cared to remember, while Meera flitted from the kettle to the sink to the stove to the pantry. She reminded Jade of Tinker Bell: short in stature, almost pixie-like with her cropped, dark hair and long-sleeved shirt layered under a plain yellow t-shirt. She seemed to be a no-nonsense ball of sunshine.

While Meera bustled about, Jade examined her surroundings. From her perch at the island, Jade could see into the open kitchen in front of her, and behind her was a dining area under a large, open, cathedral-styled roof with exposed posts and beams. The wooden posts looked like trees holding up the ceiling. Between the woodwork, the walls were plastered in stone grey, giving the impression that they were secure and safe in a large cave. Only after closer inspection could Jade see the faint outline of straw bales, which had been stacked like huge bricks to form the walls. The centrepiece of the room, where she expected to see a T.V., Jade saw a large wood stove with a glass door. The fire inside burned brightly.

"What kind of tea do you want? Herbal? Caffeinated?" Meera asked holding a box of each in each of her hands and shaking them slightly for effect.

"Um, Earl Grey? If you have it. Thanks," Jade said glancing down at her hands as they started involuntarily to wring themselves red in her lap. She tucked them under her thighs hoping to squish them into stillness.

"Earl Grey it is," Meera said. "Perhaps, after we have settled you in, you would like to go and check out the sheep and the goats? We even have an alpaca. He is a favourite of the people here." Meera's cheery expression faltered for half a second when Jade didn't perk up at the idea of animals like most people did. But, she recovered quickly.

"I thought this place was vegetarian."

"It is," Meera said. "We don't eat the animals."

"Then…what?" she shrugged one shoulder in question, wondering what the point of raising animals on a farm was if you didn't plan on eating them.

"Purpose," Meera said as she got two mugs from the cupboard and placed them on the counter.

"What do you mean, purpose?" Jade's hands started to throb from the lack of circulation. She released them for their temporary imprisonment and leaned forward, her elbows on the counter in anticipation of holding a warm mug.

"Well," Meera said, "She says that when people go through deep states of change, change that makes them want to disappear, one of the most important things for them to have is purpose. It's fundamental to functioning. So, She's got all sorts of animals here because there is nothing more purposeful than the care of an animal that will not survive, let alone thrive, without your care. Animals make you get up in the morning, especially on the mornings when you would rather not."

"Who's 'She'?" Jade asked when Meera paused for a breath.

"Oh! Sorry!" Meera exclaimed. "She's the lady that lives on the hill." She paused to pour the boiling water into a mug with the three hear no-, speak no-, and see-no-evil monkeys on it. "You likely haven't seen her yet, but you will. Sugar or honey?" she asked.

"Honey, please." Meera dolloped a teaspoon of honey into the mug of hot water, dissolved it with a water tornado, and slid it across the counter to Jade. Jade nodded her thanks and asked, "What's her name?"

Meera looked slightly confused and tilted her head to the side.

"Her name? Well, that's not for me to say. She will tell you when She's ready."

"What does it matter if you tell me her name or she does?" Jade leaned back and folded her arms in suspicion.

"What does it matter if I don't?" Meera shot back, not unkindly, and looked at her compassionately. "There are some things here that are challenging to understand at first. They seem almost backward to the way the rest of the world works. But, then, look at the rest of the world. I do think that sometimes having a little "backwards" might actually be an improvement."

The sound of the front door opening and closing stopped their conversation. The thumping of boots and rush of cold air announced someone was coming.

"Right on time!" Meera exclaimed as an elderly gentleman with white, shaggy hair walked into the room. "I swear, Avi, you can hear a kettle boiling from across the valley." Avi nodded in mild agreement at Meera's observation, and then seeing they had a guest, he bowed his head to greet her like a cowboy out of an old western would. He walked over to the kettle with a limp that looked as if it had set in—become part of him—and made himself a cup of tea. He didn't speak.

"Avi, this is Jade. Jade, Avi. She's going to be here for a year's residency." Avi regarded Jade with renewed interest.

"She's just arrived, so be gentle with her, OK?" She handed him the honey and spoon without prompting.

"Yes, ma'am," he replied.

Meera turned back to Jade. "Avi's the night watchman here, so you'll often find him snoozing in the rocking chair in the afternoons. Don't mind him. He is diligently awake most of the night." Jade watched Avi as he took his tea and ambled out the door, back to wherever he had come, thinking he looked remarkably like Sam Elliot.

Jade sipped her hot tea, savouring the warmth of the cup in her hands. She wondered why this place would need a watchman at all. Was it to make sure the residents didn't run away in the night? Or was it to keep the outside world at bay?

As the door shut behind him, Meera leaned in. "Don't look so worried. It's not that we need a night watchman. It goes back to what I was talking about earlier. Purpose. Being a night watchman gives Avi purpose. He needs a place to be, and this is the most suitable position for a man who doesn't like to speak much." She gave a glance toward the door. "He was a veteran in another life," she confided, "and like so many, he is carrying the wounds from that time into this one. Sometimes when he stands his leg shakes. He tries to make light by calling it his tribute to Elvis. But, I'll tell ya, if the sheep ever get loose, you'll see him running like a middle-aged athlete on steroids! It's a sight for sore eyes." She smiled at a memory and left Jade hanging in the present, waiting. After a moment of awkward silence, Jade lifted her mug and slurped trying to get Meera back to the present.

Meera offered a bashful, apologetic smile, quietly took a sip of tea, and continued speaking. "Anyway. He has found sanctuary and purpose in service to the land." She shrugged one shoulder and with the slightest hint of sadness, went on. "We all have found a purpose here that is a balm for the soul. It is why we stay." The two women sat in silence; each lost in their thoughts. Jade chanced a peek at her watch. It was barely 2:00 pm. She had only been here an hour, and it already felt like a week.

"Right." Meera abruptly put down her cup and clapped her hands startling Jade so much that she nearly dropped her mug. "Let's get you settled in. We have chosen a lovely spot for you. Your own private space. It's simple but will fulfill your needs. It's still a little bit cool at night, but we have lots of blankets to offer and a hot water bottle that will keep you warm. The Lady on the Hill herself stayed in this cabin while there was snow on the ground when She first moved here. So, it's considered auspicious to be able to reside in that space. Of all the different housing we have here, I must admit, I have a soft spot for this particular one. I'll give you an orientation sheet to read, and then, if you have any questions, you can ask me at dinner. OK?"

Jade, who was stuck on the idea of using a hot water bottle like it was the 1800s quickly gulped down the rest of her tea and followed Meera to the door. She reached for her jacket and bag.

"Here. Let me help you with that," Meera said as she picked up Jade's back-pack without any hint of struggle and held it so Jade could climb into it. "Wait here a minute. I'll just grab an extra duvet for you, and then we'll be off."

Jade stepped outside and looked at the courtyard. Snow had slid off the roof to form two huge mountains. Someone had shovelled a flat, narrow path between them and sprinkled dark sand on the white snow. It looked like the reverse of a starry night sky, and it made Jade wonder if everything on Earth was the exact opposite of Heaven.

Jade turned toward the building when Meera opened the door and saw a plaque hung above the doorway. She hadn't noticed it before. The words Tat Twam Asi were carved into it. Meera, arms full with an off-white duvet and without a winter coat, followed Jade's gaze to the sign. "Ah, Tat Twam Asi. You'll learn all about that while you're here," she said repositioning her load.

"Now, if you have any questions or need anything, I'll be around at dinner time which is at five o'clock." They walked through the courtyard and back down to the drive. "I saw you have a watch with you," she said and nodded toward Jade's wrist.

"It was my mother's watch," Jade said as she touched the cuff of her jacket sleeve. Her heart ached painfully at the word *was*.

"Well, that's good, then. Phones aren't allowed here, you see." Like a sure-footed forest nymph, Meera walked quickly down the icy drive. She had to stop and wait regularly for Jade, who lumbered behind like an over-burdened elephant.

"Right, then. Here we are. This is Mantra Kutir."

"Mun what?" Jade said, screwing up her face.

"Don't worry, dear, you'll get used to the different names and such." Meera opened the door and put the duvet inside.

Jade surveyed Mantra Kutir, which to her looked like nothing more than a glorified tin can. There was a deck attached to it—a couple of pallets with wood nailed on top to make a floor. The surface had been shovelled clear of snow to make a white, welcoming carpet. Someone had painstakingly scribed Indian words around the metal exterior of the camper in dark brown paint. Prayer flags, like the ones her mum had insisted on putting up in the front window of their apartment, linked the closest trees to the corners of the camper. "Rainbow anchors" her mother called them. Jade looked away noticing the formation of trees. One, two, three… nine trees standing in a circle with the camper at its centre. Nine trees with huge, thick trunks. Nine thick jail bars.

"Your home for the foreseeable future. I'll let you settle in and I'll see you—"

"At five," Jade said.

Meera smiled. "Exactly. There will be a bell at ten-to if that helps. Until then, unpack, rest, and we will see you in…," she checked her watch for the time, "Oh, Ram! I have to go. See you soon!" Her tour guide persona disappeared and a slightly frazzled, behind-schedule-cook persona emerged. She spun on her heels and flew back up the hill leaving Jade alone. The silence was deafening.

5 Home

Once Meera was out of sight, Jade unclasped the buckle of her backpack, took hold of the shoulder straps, and braced herself to hurl it angrily through the camper's door. But before she could unburden herself, something caught her eye and her pack slid off her shoulders and landed again with a thud on the deck.

To the left of the door in the shelter of the camper's wall, where there was less snow than in the open, a single yellow and purple flower wavered in the air. Unassuming, and yet un-ignorable, it sat alone, surrounded by an uninhabitable sea of winter.

"Look at you all alone, defying the odds," she said under her breath. "I know how you fucking feel."

Jade glanced over her shoulder to make sure no one was watching her talk to a flower before she hoisted her backpack onto her shoulder and threw it through the camper door.

"Honey I'm home," She said sarcastically as she stepped inside and slammed the door behind her. The door bounced open in rebuke, making Jade reach out and slam it again, determined to get the last word. It was, aside from using the bathroom, the first time she had been alone since the hearing. The silence was absolute and broken only by her racing heart and shallow breathing. Jade surveyed the interior of the camper, taking stock of her new surroundings. It was, after all, going to be her "home" for the next twelve months.

There wasn't much to look at.

A double bed made up of two separate foam mattresses took up most of the space. Sheets were folded neatly and placed on the pillow. Jade turned to look at the dining table, absentmindedly picking up the duvet and tossing it onto the bed. The table was scratched and scuffed in places but serviceable. The seats were padded and covered in a 1970s, forest-green cloth, which appeared to be holding onto the decade—and its seams—for dear life.

At the far end of the camper were some cupboards, a small kitchen sink, and a counter where a mason jar full of beautiful, dried flowers sat. She picked up the small jar and took a sniff. The lavender and straw flowers that looked like miniature suns—the kind a three-year-old would draw, all spiky and chaotic. She stared at them, head cocked to one side; she didn't think people got welcoming posies in prison.

After wrestling her backpack onto the table, she began the task of "settling in". She started to unzip the main compartment, and the jostled contents, as though gasping for air, spilled out onto the floor. Her pencil case and journal led the charge, followed by assorted clothes and a small brass statue of a grasshopper her mother had kept next to her bed. The journal struck her foot and opened to a page with an old photo wedged inside. She picked up the journal and the photograph and sat on the bed, reading the words on the page, and staring at the image for the millionth time.

I love you.
I love you more.
Not possible. I love you all the way to the Moon and back.
I love you everywhere and back as long as the numbers go.
Well, then me times two, kidlet——me times two.

It was the banter she had had with her mother from when she was a little girl right up until the week she died. The words were always the same—they would roll off her tongue, each word tumbling after the other without the need for thought, as instinctual as breathing. Jade had written them down in her journal the night after her mother's funeral. It was her first night alone, and she wanted to hear her mother's voice—even if it was just an echo. She read them regularly.

Taking the photo carefully in her hand, Jade looked at it. It was a picture of her mother standing with a friend on the banks of a river. She guessed they were in India by the clothes they were wearing and the beads around their necks. Her mother, not much older than she was now, and her friend, who looked quite a bit older than her mum, but youthful in her own right, looked up at her smiling broadly. Happiness exuded from the paper as they hugged each other tightly. Her mother's friend was slightly shorter with blond hair and bright wise eyes. The photo, along with the grasshopper, had always been on her mother's bedside table. Whenever Jade had asked her mother about the lady, she would just say it was her sister; this had confused Jade as a child because the lady looked soft and kind, nothing like her straight-edged Aunt Carole. Placing the photo and the little brass grasshopper on the shelf next to her bed, Jade mused about the life her mother had lived and the long-lost aunt she had never met. After making sure neither would fall, she returned to unpacking her bag.

Casually at first, Jade removed shirts, pants, and pyjamas—the usual items one packs for an extended stay someplace. As the pile on the table grew, so did Jade's unease. She searched for her grey socks, the ones with the yellow toes, and for a split second she thought perhaps Carole had gone through her bag and found them. But then she saw a flash of yellow amidst the jumble of dark fabrics. She snatched the socks and walked backwards until the bed caught her at the back of the knees and forced her to sit. Feeling around between the folds of grey, scratchy wool, her finger caught the sharp edge of a plastic corner. She winced at the warning bite to stay away. Instead of heeding the warning, Jade was comforted by the pain. Carefully she unrolled the pair of socks until she could see the small plastic sheet. Sighing with relief, she gently pulled it out and held it in her hand as though a precious gem. It was her insurance policy. Her *just-in-case*. Just in case things got too hard. Just in case she couldn't sleep. Just in case she started having nightmares. Again. The ones where the floor started to flood with blood, and she kept slipping as she tried to get away from it. Just in case that feeling in her chest came back. The one where she needed to scream but couldn't even breathe. The one where her lungs were crushed by grief.

Staring at the walls of the camper, but not really seeing them, Jade remembered what it was like the day she was told her mother had died and then the days that followed. Jade didn't have the luxury of an illness. Something that could help her ease into what was coming. A long, drawn-out wasting away where death would be a reprieve from the pain. A blessing. No, the impact of an accident is as jarring to the people left behind as it is to the victim.

Jade had felt as if she, too, had been hit by the bus. She couldn't formulate logical sentences. Couldn't move. She was overwhelmed by the simplest of questions: *do you want a cup of tea? Have you eaten?* All she wanted to do was roll up in a cocoon, disintegrate, and wait for the feeling of abandonment or her life-force-energy to leave; she didn't care which one. Every day had been the same as the day before, and nothing seemed capable of penetrating the haze of grief.

A few clear memories of that time did exist: The first was standing in the shower (wondering if she had washed her hair or not) looking at her mother's shampoo and conditioner. She couldn't throw it out; she couldn't use it. Using it would make her smell like her mother, and she wouldn't be able to bear it. If she threw it out, how would she be able to remember the smell of her mother? The water had turned to ice, and still Jade had stood there.

The second memory—hours or days after the shower incident—was of her standing at a bus stop, frozen in place, as the Downtown Express slammed on its brakes and threw open its doors to load and unload passengers. *Was it this bus? Was this guy driving? Jade had wondered.* She was jostled on all sides by people in a hurry to be somewhere else. The driver had yelled—"Shit or get off the pot, kid. You're holdin' us up! Jesus Christ on a cracker..."—his harsh voice finally breaking through Jade's horrified musings; one can only stand, imagining their dead mother's crushed and mutilated body for so long. She had fled "Fucking kids these days" echoed behind her as the driver closed the door and merged into traffic, tears blinding her vision. It had been a long walk home.

The last memory from that horrific week still made Jade cringe. She had been walking through Kimberley's *Platzl*, everyone saying hello to her like they normally would on a beautiful summer day. Jade had had to stop her-self from saying 'My mother died this week' in response to *how are you* and *how's it going* and *what's new?* Once she answered honestly; the news sent the cashier into a tailspin of embarrassment. Flustered and unsure of what to do or say, the cashier refused to charge Jade for the cheese she was trying to buy. Instead, she had made a huge fuss over her by asking questions—prolonging the purchase and deepening the hole, Jade was sure, they both wanted to jump into. When the customer behind Jade started to offer her a hug, Jade ran. Cursing under her breath that not only had she lost her mum, but she had also lost her local grocery, too.

Jade didn't know exactly what she had been expecting by being honest. There was a good chance that the cashier's mother hadn't been hit by a bus, crumpled into an almost unrecognizable pile of mangled bones and flesh. It would have been best if Jade had just kept her mouth shut, said as little as pos-sible, and moved on. They didn't need to be burdened with the knowledge. She didn't need to be burdened with their awkwardness.

Jade fell back on the bed and closed her eyes, lost in the memories. In truth, the words, 'my mother died this week' had felt like a betrayal of the strength her mother had taught her to have. It had felt dirty (still did) to speak of the only thing occupying space in her mind. Weak.

Simultaneously, saying 'my mother died this week' had felt like a lie. Jade hadn't felt like her mother was gone. She had felt the same as she always had when she was out and about the town. It was only, and always, first thing in the morning after the thought "I hope Mum has made coffee" and when she walked through the door at night into their apartment and no one was there to welcome her, Jade felt her mother's absence. Mum wasn't going to make coffee or greet her when she walked through the door. Mum wasn't going to sing into a banana microphone or pretend to Molly Ringwald her lipstick. Her mother was gone. And that harsh wave of reality had crashed into Jade again and again. First thing in the morning and last thing at night. Day after day. Week after week. It hadn't been long before she was floundering, searching, grasping for any means of escape. She turned her head to the side and looked at the package in her hand.

Ten little sunshine-coloured pills were safely housed in their protective case. There was a strict, no non-prescription drug policy at the centre. She knew that. Aunt Carole had told her probably fifty times or so. If they were found, she would be asked to leave and that would mean heading back to court. Carefully, Jade returned the pills to their hiding place inside her socks, put them in the middle of the shelf, and piled her other socks and the rest of her clothes around them making a nest for her precious egg—just in case— and closed the cupboard door.

6 First Dinner

Twelve feet long, four feet wide and three inches thick, the dining table dominated the room the way an altar draws one's gaze in church. "Commence communion," Jade muttered. Big enough to sit twelve people, it looked empty with only four places set all bunched together in the middle. One end of the table abutted the deep-set windowsill which, Jade observed, was filled with dried flowers and pine cones, various kinds of rocks and crystals, and a single photograph of an old man with his eyes closed and his hands folded in prayer. The flickering light from a small candle gave the image life; the old man seemed to be waiting patiently for his guests—a creepy ghost playing host Jade thought.

Jade looked around wondering where everyone else was. It was 5:00. Dinner time. Meera had stressed the importance of being on time, and Jade had made sure to arrive exactly at 5:00. Yet, no Meera. No Avi. A pot sat on the stove and it smelled…earthy. She stood contemplating whether or not she was supposed to feed herself. She looked again at the fourth-place setting and wondered who it was for. Her musings were interrupted by Meera as she came hurrying down the stairs.

"Oh, good! Jade, you're here. Come get your dinner. I'll serve you," she flitted past her and into the kitchen. In one fluid motion, almost as if she were dancing, Meera lifted the heavy pot and placed it on the island counter. She removed the lid with one hand—steam billowed out everywhere—and used the other hand to stir the pot with the biggest spoon Jade had ever seen. Once. Twice. Three times. Meera looked expectantly at Jade. Jade came over to the island, picked up a bowl, and murmured her thanks as Meera went to serve her. But, her thanks were drowned out by the sound of the front door opening and closing.

Jade stood still, empty bowl in her hand, and watched the mudroom door. Avi walked in, and she felt herself relax. Then she realized he was followed by another man—a younger man. She froze like a deer in headlights. Jade had thought the fourth setting was for the lady on the hill or whatever she was called. She hadn't known there was someone else, someone her age, a boy—a man?—here as well.

"Great! Kitchari! I'm starving!" the younger boy said sniffing the air. Jade eyed him warily noting that he was a boy in face only, the rest of his body was that of a man: broad-shouldered, muscular, tall. His long legs carried him into the room in three quick strides as he made a beeline for the food; he didn't notice Jade standing at the counter.

"Now, now, Aaden. Wait your turn," Meera said waving the ladle at him. "You know the rules. Newest guests first."

At the mention of a new guest, Jade seemed to materialize before him. Aaden bounced back half a step realizing at the last second that he was about to bump into her.

"Oh! Hi! I'm Aaden," he said smiling at her, his hand outstretched in greeting and a nod of acknowledgment that Meera had already introduced him. His face was thin, and his skin was weathered and tan. His smile made his face as wide as it was long—a Mick Jagger grin or perhaps the Joker's.

The thought of spending a year with a psychopath almost made Jade shudder. She felt the fight or flight impulse rise from her stomach and her heart began to race. Jade pushed it down, forced a smile, a pursed one, and tried to act normal. "Hi," she said lifting her chin. She willed her teeth to unclench long enough to say her name. "Jade."

She looked from him to Meera who stood waiting with her hand out to take her bowl. Rejecting Aaden's hand, Jade gave Meera her bowl to fill. When Meera handed it back, laden with something Jade couldn't identify, Jade quickly took a place at the table, refusing to look at him again.

She sat with her back to the wall and a clear line of sight to the door, just like the old mob movies had taught her, and looked down at her food. Jade kept her head down while everyone else got their meals and sat down around her. She examined the contents of her bowl and saw it was filled with yellow, mushy rice and topped with a dollop of yogurt—a reverse egg she thought. The image didn't turn her stomach as it normally would have though. She had been so nervous earlier in the day that she had had only a cup of coffee for breakfast and had skipped lunch. She was starving.

Avi sat diagonally across from her, and Jade watched him from the corner of her eye as he enthusiastically mixed the mush and yogurt. Then he added a spoonful of something oily from a jar on the table. He licked his lips in anticipation. He noticed her watching and said, "It's called Kitchari, Jade. It'll cure what ail's ya." He gave a sigh of anticipation and began to eat.

"Have some pickle. It's the best part," Aaden said as he took the seat opposite her. Jade jerked back involuntarily as he slid the pickle jar across the table to her, flashing a Joker/Jagger smile at her when she looked up.

"I would recommend just a piece or two to see if you like it first," Meera said taking her place at the table next to Jade. "It's an acquired taste."

Jade dutifully mixed the yogurt into the rice as Avi had done, and then added a small spoon of what looked to be lemon pieces on top. Cautiously she tasted it, and to her surprise, found that she liked it. She quickly took a second larger bite.

"So, Jade," Aaden said between mouthfuls, "where are you from? What brings you to Ponderosa Grove, and how long are you here for?" She looked up at him, temper beginning to flare, and was met with an innocuous gaze. That startled her. He was either a really good actor or he had no idea what had happened to her or what she had done to land herself in this place. She looked back down at her dinner. "Um…."

Meera came to her rescue, "Give her a moment to settle in, will you? Let the girl eat her dinner in peace, and I'm sure she'll get around to telling you her particulars when she's ready. Right, Jade?" She looked at Aaden trying to communicate with her eyes as well as her words to give Jade some space.

Jade nodded, never taking her eyes off her bowl, and kept eating. The rest of the room followed suit and ate without speaking. Unaccustomed to the silence at the table, Aaden tried again.

"OK, so seeing as it's my turn to choose the topic of conversation tonight, I wanna know where in the world you'd all like to visit one day."

"Can you pass the yogurt please, Avi?" Meera asked.

Aaden ate another spoonful while he waited for Avi to pass the yogurt and for someone to answer his question. When no one did, he continued, "Come on, Meera, you first."

Meera looked at him like a mother resigned to another knock-knock joke and rolled her eyes. "Oh, OK. Ummmm… I'd like to see king penguins in real life doing their penguin thing. So, I guess that means Antarctica. I want to see with my own eyes the male penguins doing their part, you know, with the eggs on their feet, keeping them warm. Like you see on the nature documentaries with… what's that man's name?" she asked. "The English one?"

"David Attenborough," Avi grunted.

"Yeah... him," Meera nodded as she took another bite, and Jade wondered if everyone was playing their version of David Attenborough's voice in their head while they ate, or if it was just her. She almost smiled at the voiceover, "They gathered at the feeding ground, the newcomer cautious and unsettled in her new surroundings. The juvenile male pays little attention to her defensive posturing..." Aaden's voice brings her attention back to the table.

"Avi?" Aaden nudged when no one continued the conversation.

"Well," Avi said, taking the tea towel Meera had used to transport a hot pot of tea to the table and wiped his mouth. Without a word, Meera snatched it from him mid-wipe, stuffed the paper napkin that was beside his bowl into his hand, folded the tea towel with care, and placed it on the chair next to her—out of his reach. Clearly, this was not a new dance between them.

Avi didn't miss a beat. He simply wiped his mouth again with the napkin, not that it needed it after the tea towel, and leaned back in his chair. He seemed to be giving Aaden's question serious thought.

"I've often thought about heading down to Brazil. I've always wanted to see that place where the two rivers meet and make that line."

"You mean where the Rio Negro and the Amazon meet?" Aaden asked as he loaded up his spoon. "We had to do a project on it at school."

"Yeah, that would be the one... or two," Avi said thoughtfully, leaning forward and resuming his dinner without another word.

"Jade?" Aaden asked.

He caught her just as she went to eat another bite. Hearing him say her name made Jade jump and clamp down on the spoon with her teeth. Instinct took over, and she slurped the rest into her mouth. But as soon as it got in there, she realized it was too hot. She sucked in the air trying to cool it, keeping the too-hot food moving around with her tongue before it burned her, all the while fanning her mouth with her hand. She tried to ignore the sounds she was making—like a horse walking through mud—but it was difficult.

Avi and Meera both froze, spoons halfway to their mouths, looked at each other, and then looked at her.

"What?" she said, her face flushing red with embarrassment. Silently, Meera poured a glass of water from the carafe on the table and slid it to her. Meera and Avi exchanged another glance and resumed their meal; Aaden looked intently at his bowl as though trying not to smile.

"What place in the world would you like to visit one day?" he said acting as if the last minute never happened—for which she was grateful.

"Ah, I dunno," Jade said staring straight down at her food, gripping the sides of the chair with her hands so she wouldn't run. "How 'bout you?" Flipping the question back to him without looking up.

"Well, there are many places I'd like to see with my own eyes." Everyone seemed to relax as Aaden's lighthearted voice absorbed the tension in the room and redirected it into his musings—even Jade relaxed enough to pick up her spoon and start to eat again as he spoke. "But, the first place I think I'll go is Paris. I've always wanted to sit outside of this place called Angelina's on the *Rue de Rivoli*", he said in a mock French accent, "and try their *chocolat du chaud* and a *pain du chocolat* while I sit in the sun and people watch. Did you know," he leaned slightly forward, but then thought better of it and leaned back again, "that they melt an entire chocolate bar in each cup? My grandmother used to tell me about it as a kid. They say it's the best in the world. And, well," he said, "I want to find out for myself." He pushed his now empty bowl away from him with satisfaction.

"Well, it's always good to have dreams, Aaden," Meera said. "I hope yours come true." She stood to clear her bowl and headed over to the kitchen.

"Well?" Aaden said to Jade after Meera had left.

Jade stared fixedly down at her plate. Her dinner, which only a moment ago had been nourishing, now looked and smelled like something that had been regurgitated. "I dunno," she murmured.

"Jade… come on. Where?" He wasn't going to quit.

"I said I don't *fucking* know." Her chair legs scraped the floor as she stood up—screeching like a cornered cat—which Jade thought was apt. Aaden and Avi stopped and stared at her. Meera, who was walking back toward the table with tea mugs, paused.

Jade turned and bolted through the front door before Meera could spring into action. "Jade, wait!" she called. "Wait!"

Jade stopped at the second plea just outside the front door and spun around ready for a fight. Her eyes flashed, fists clenched.

"He didn't mean to badger you. He's just excited you're here and wants to get to know you." Meera folded her arms against the cold night coming in through the open door, no mugs in sight. "He doesn't know anything about you—or why you're here."

An uncomfortable silence blossomed and then grew between them as Jade stood and stared through Meera to the door behind her.

"You forgot your jacket," Meera said calmly, reaching and grabbing it off the hook. She handed it to Jade keeping as much distance between them as possible. "And you will need a hot water bottle. I'll put the kettle on and bring it down to you in twenty minutes. OK?"

Jade took the coat and nodded mutely as she put it on. She retreated as fast as her legs would take her back to cell block Mantra Kutir.

Jade sat in bed. After checking the lock on the door twice and putting on every item of warm clothing she owned including her tuque, she burrowed under a mass of blankets and duvets cursing the temperature inside the camper.

Then she took out her journal and began to write.

Day one of incarceration. She crossed out incarceration and wrote *banishment* above it. *Cell—a freezing tin can. If they wanted to kill me they could just take away my blankets. I'd be dead by morning. Place—Middle of fucking nowhere. I can't imagine staying a weekend let alone a year. The people here are... odd. Weird? A silent cowboy, a guy that talks too much (waaaaaaay too much) and a pixie chick that's hard to read. They keep talking about some woman on a hill...nope, LADY on a hill. WTF? Maybe I'll be eaten by a bear and it'll save me the trouble of living in this hick hell.* Then she spent a few minutes sketching a bear standing over a stick figure with a speech bubble that said "Just kill me." She sat back against her pillows and closed her eyes.

Her dinner sat undecided in her stomach, and her elephantine companion of the past year was back, sitting on her chest. Her breathing was becoming shallow, too weak to blow out a candle or call for help. Not that anyone would hear her. She knew this growing feeling all too well since her mother died. It was the one where she hoped she didn't wake up. Her eyes flicked toward the cupboard door. What was only six feet, but felt like a football field away, was the reprieve from her circling thoughts of dinner, of the trial, of why there was a trial, of the last terrifying year, of the terrifying year ahead. Jade closed her eyes again and tried to focus on her breathing. *Do the box* she thought. *Do the fucking rainbow. Name five items you can see.* She went through her litany of how-to-stop-a-panic-attack tricks she had gleaned from the internet, but as usual, they were of little help.

She only had one tab. Ten pills. Not even one per month. *You need help. A good night's sleep will help you start on the right foot tomorrow,* said the little red beast on her right shoulder. *You should try and get through one night alone without it,* the white mist said on her left. *Getting through the first night will be the hardest; take the support. This is why you brought it,* the red beast countered. *You don't...*

Jade jumped out of bed and checked the door was locked for a third time. Before she could change her mind, she dashed across the camper and threw open the cupboard door. She dove her hand into the pile of socks the way a fox dives into the snow to find a mouse. Her fingers grasped the blister pack of pills, and she popped the seal on the dome, throwing the promised circle of relief into her mouth before the white mist could object again. She imagined the red beast nodding with satisfaction and the mist shaking its head in sorrow. But it was done now. Nothing more to talk about.

She returned the tab to its woollen womb for safekeeping. By the time she got back into bed, her breathing had started to slow and her muscles had begun to relinquish their grip on her bones due to the mere anticipation of the chemical mellow on its way. Jade crawled back under the covers and curled her lanky body around the hot water bottle that Meera had delivered as promised. She had also brought warm wishes for a good first night, and to Jade's surprise gave no lecture or remonstration for her earlier behaviour.

Waiting for the pill to take effect, Jade let her mind drift. It landed on a memory of the time the furnace had broken in their apartment. Her mother had insisted they both put on every item of warm clothing they had and jumped about the house exclaiming, "It's colder than a porcupine's bum!" Somewhere between the memory of laughter and the present moment of dread, she fell into a sleep tormented by a porcupine in a white bib repeatedly banging a gavel on the dining table and demanding to know what she was going to do about the blood on the floor.

7 Cleaning

An ungodly, incessant tapping reverberated through her skull like a jackhammer waking Jade only moments after she had fallen asleep. Or that's what she thought until she opened her eyes and discovered it was light out.

She tried to put the pillow over her head to block out the noise, but it was no use. It was as though whoever was tapping had orders not to stop until she emerged from the camper. "Oh my God!" she yelled. "I'm awake!"

The tapping continued.

Jade sat up on the side of her bed and let her feet touch the floor. "Fuuuck. Fuck me that's cold," she growled through gritted teeth as she jerked her feet back up onto the bed. The floor was ice dressed as linoleum. She looked at the cupboard across the camper where she had stacked her clothes the day before. The six feet didn't look any closer in the daylight.

Remembering when she played 'The Floor is Lava' as a kid, Jade decided to straddle the kitchen table and jump onto the dining bench to reach the cupboard door. While not exactly the safest course of action, it worked. She grabbed out her fancy wool socks to put on as a second pair; the ones on her feet weren't going to cut it. Then she pulled her winter coat directly over her sleeping hoodie and decided she would rather look like a fool than strip off her pink pyjama pants. She'd just have to act cool like she wore her PJs out in the world all the time. Grabbing her toque, which had come off her head in the night, she jammed it back on before opening the door to stare down the incessant tapper.

No one was there.

Jade put on her boots, stepped onto the pallet deck, and looked around zeroing in on the direction of the banging. As she walked toward the sound, she saw a single bird clinging to a tree trunk nearly ten feet from the ground.

Despite her annoyance, Jade noticed it was quite beautiful. From her vantage point below, she could see it was mostly tan with black markings and was small—about the size of her palm. The bird had a black bib on its chest and black spots on its belly and wings. Its head was undecorated and plain in comparison, which made the markings all the more striking.

The bird looked right and left, hammered in the centre, and then looked right and left again. Its movements resembled a nervous tick. Then the bird spun its head around and looked directly at her. Jade scowled up at it. How could one relatively tiny bird make this much noise?

"See?" she yelled spreading her arms wide. "I'm up, you stupid bird."

The bird didn't even flinch. Its black, beady eyes seemed to be assessing her. Satisfied with its completed mission, the bird took to the sky. "That's right, bugga off why don't you? Scram you scrawny little….," The sun's morning rays lit the undersides of the bird's wings and tail as it flew away. The sudden flash of bright orange stopped Jade's tirade. She gasped. She had never seen anything like it. So monochromatic on the outside, so flashy and bright on the inside. It was breathtakingly unexpected.

"Ah! Good morning, Jade. You're up. How did you sleep?"

Jade spun around to see Meera walking past her camper up the hill towards the main house. She was puffing frost from her mouth, and Jade immediately thought of little smoke clouds coming from a cold engine on a freezing day.

"Morning, Meera. Fine. Cold. Thanks," she spoke to her boots hoping Meera had not heard her outburst at the bird. Meera looked Jade up and down; Jade suddenly wished she'd dared to change out of her pink pyjama pants. "I hope it wasn't too cold in there for you last night. The weatherman says we are in the last of the freezing temps, and by the end of next week, we will be full speed into spring. So that's good news." Meera followed Jade's gaze, which had resumed watching the little bird drill for its next snack from another tree in the ring. "Ah, I see Brother Flicker has made his acquaintance with you this morning. He's not one for sleeping in, as you can tell. He's a wonderful alarm."

"If you say so."

"Come now. Let's get a nice cuppa and some hot porridge into you. You've missed morning chanting and breakfast. Everyone else is already onto their morning duties."

And so it began. The daily routine for the first few weeks was as dependable as the soft up and down movement of a ship upon the water. Well, it would have been if Jade had been on the same ship as everyone else. Instead, it was more like two ships sailing too close to one another. The ripples from one making turbulence for the other. Avi, Meera, and Aaden rose early, chanted, and prepared breakfast. They ate quickly to move on to their morning duties. Jade rose late, missed breakfast, and took her time getting to the main building. When she arrived, Meera would be in the kitchen cleaning, and she'd greet Jade cordially—either not caring or silently disapproving of Jade's habitual lateness. At first, Jade couldn't tell which.

Jade would eat her breakfast, leftover and set aside from that morning, and then clean the dining area and communal spaces while Meera prepared lunch. Her job was to sweep the dining room floor, restock the firebox, and clean the bathroom, toilet and bathtub (that nobody ever seemed to use). None of these tasks were particularly arduous or demanding except one. And that one she just couldn't, just wouldn't, do: clean the bathroom floor. Every day she could see the cream tiles getting progressively dirtier and dirtier. Yet, every day when it came time to wash the floor, she simply closed the bathroom door behind her and hid in her camper until the lunch bell tolled.

She could sense Meera's kind and patient demeanour wearing thin, but no matter how hard Jade tried, she couldn't make herself clean the floor. Her journal was filled with various drawings of herself standing in front of the judge with him asking her, "Why did they send you back?" Cartoon Jade replied, "Because I refused to clean the bathroom floor, your Honour."

Avoiding everyone at lunchtime was not an option, so Jade intentionally arrived late each day knowing Meera and the boys would already be focused on eating so nothing would be said about her lack of cleaning. Jade knew that as everyone finished eating, Meera would begin doling out afternoon tasks, and she'd have survived another meal. Aaden would nod enthusiastically at whatever Meera would assign, occasionally adding other tasks to the list, and Jade would wait for Meera to tell her what her afternoon tasks were. Usually, she would be instructed to help Avi with anything too physical for his old bones. He would grunt and mutter at Meera that he didn't need any help from anyone. She'd just look at him, and then, begrudgingly, he would let Jade tag along. He never gave her clear instructions and ignored her questions, but Jade didn't mind. She found being around him somewhat comforting. He didn't expect anything from her; she didn't feel like a disappointment. Until one day she did.

After a terrible night of no sleep, Jade decided to lie down for a quick nap after lunch. She awoke to Avi banging on her camper door, and the groggy, stupid feeling one gets from being jarred awake prevented her from doing anything more than wiping the dried drool from her cheek as he snarled something about lazy kids with no work ethic and walked away. Avi, not exactly a loquacious man on a good day, barely spoke to her for the remainder of the day. Jade followed him around trying to anticipate his needs, and she felt for sure she was going to be in trouble. Avi was bound to say something to Meera, his anger over her tardiness nearly palpable throughout the afternoon. But when Jade got to dinner, Meera was her usual polite and cheerful self. Jade realized her mistake had been just between the two of them. And mistakes can be fixed. She hoped.

The next day Jade made sure she was at the post waiting for him when he arrived after lunch—she had eaten quickly to avoid needless conversations as well as any conversation about the bathroom's current state. When he saw she was already there, he looked pleasantly surprised, gave her a nod, and handed her the tools to carry down the hill. Although nothing was said, Jade understood something had changed between them, and afternoons with Avi quickly became a highlight of her day. Only when Avi's tasks had been completed did she hide in her camper to read, journal, or nap until the dinner bell tolled.

Jade didn't see much of Aaden, except at meal times. But when she did see him, he talked, usually in an upbeat, dreaming-of-the-future-never-of-the-past kind of way that she came to depend on for mealtime distraction. Jade learned quickly that when Aaden looked like he had finished talking about something, she just needed to ask him another question and he would start up right on cue like a music box that just needed winding. Aaden's babbling wasn't nonsense though. He was smart and passionate about learning "what it was to be human" as he called it. As the days passed, she learned Aaden's smile was definitely more Jagger than Joker's. He was a kind, gentle soul and also a bit goofy, too. Yet, there was something forlorn about him. A private side Jade couldn't quite pin down. She'd seen a flash of something race across his face—there and gone again—that hinted at solemnity, seriousness. Its fleetingness, a direct contrast to Jade's constant broodiness lurking below the surface of her skin. Still, she didn't ask questions, mainly so she wouldn't have to answer questions.

One day, with the snow finally gone, (which she learned was officially called mud season), Meera asked everyone to leave their boots outside to save the mud room from having to be cleaned, by Jade, multiple times a day. Jade was only too happy to comply, and although she'd never say it, grateful. She "yes-ed" and "uh-huh-ed" her way through another lunch wondering what she would be up to that afternoon. She finished her meal, brought her dish to the sink to wash, and still lost in thought made her way to the front door. She was startled to find Aaden waiting for her with a piece of an unimpressive plant in his hand.

"Hey, Jade?" He said tentatively, not entirely sure how she'd respond.

"Yeah?" she said pulling on her filthy boots and trying to hurry inconspicuously.

"Meera told me that the reason you're here was because your mother died and you needed some time."

Jade froze for a moment, wondering if that was all Meera had told him. If that was all Meera knew? She lifted one eyebrow—a signature Brennan family move—signalling that she was willing to listen but not about to give anything away.

"So, I wanted to give you this." He handed her the plant. "I know what it's like to feel trapped in experiences that… suck."

"Uh… thanks?" Jade said and looked at the fuzzy leaves and long stalk covered in little flowers that had not yet bloomed. "Is that why you're here? Because you were trapped in an experience that…sucked?"

"Yeah, but show me someone who isn't, eh?" He tried to smile, tried to make light, but that something flashed across his face and for a moment he looked burdened. For a split second, she almost asked a follow-up question but decided against it. He pointed to the plant. "It's Mullein. Not maybe the prettiest of plants," he admitted as he scratched the back of his head and self-consciously shifted his weight from one foot to the other as if suddenly feeling uneasy, "but traditionally it was smoked to relieve grief in the heart."

"Oh," Jade said. "I didn't think we were allowed to smoke here."

"Well, no. We're not. I figured you could dry it, and then, seeing as you're here for a year, you'll likely end up with a herb pouch, and then you could add the Mullien to your offerings." Another wave of uncertainty crossed his face, as he saw hers fill with skepticism. "The posy of dried flowers in your camper, I did those too," he said sheepishly, "You could put those in a pouch too, when you get one, if you liked them."

"Cool. Yeah. OK. I'll… um, dry it then?" she said trying to put his mind at ease. She attempted a smile, but it felt forced; she thought it made her look like she was grimacing, so she stopped.

"Yeah, OK. Well, have a nice day, Jade. I'd better head off to my, um, tasks, for the afternoon. So, ah, see ya at dinner."

"OK," she said as they both stepped onto the path, heading in their usual, opposite, directions.

The only other person at the centre Jade knew of, was the illusive "Lady on the Hill". Jade still didn't know her name and everyone seemed content with that. From what Jade could tell, Meera, Avi, and Aaden all seemed quite ready and happy to jump if she would only tell them how high. Jade hadn't even met this woman yet, and she was already intimidated by her. Despite her illusiveness, the Lady on the Hill had a hand in every aspect of the centre. Nothing happened that she didn't know about. Jade tried to find out more about her, probing gently, but all anyone would say about The Lady (capital T, capital L, no hill, was what Jade called her in her mind) was that she was remarkably kind. Jade found herself daydreaming about what it would be like to meet The Lady while actively avoiding the classes and programs, like morning chanting, where she knew The Lady would be in attendance.

And then one day, she saw the old woman walking up the drive with her two dogs following obediently at her heel. Jade dove behind one of the big water cisterns and waited for The Lady and her dogs to pass. Jade knew it was childish, but she could not bring herself to step out and face her. *Next time,* Jade thought. When the woman and her dogs were close enough for Jade to see them clearly, the dogs stopped and looked her way. Jade stayed crouched as the woman stopped as well.

Perhaps it was the fact The Lady wore rust-coloured flowing robes like the Swami's Jade had seen on TV, or perhaps it was the way her grey hair was piled on the top of her head, exposing a kind, grandmotherly face like the ones in her fairytale books, but the old woman looked familiar. Very familiar. Jade searched for a recollection of where or how she could have met this woman before, but she couldn't. She nibbled on her lower lip in quiet contemplation, scrutinizing the Lady on the Hill.

The old woman bent down and patted one of the pups on the head. She said something to them both, and then together they turned and continued walking. Jade was sure The Lady had known that she was there but had chosen not to look her way. Jade didn't know what to make of it at first, but the amount of relief she felt when she realized the old woman had kept moving without calling her out of her hiding place was palpable. And well, what could she call it, if not kindness?

8 Burdens and Beasts

"*Jade!* Wait a minute, would ya?" Meera called. Jade, who was doing her duck-out-for-the-night-before-anyone-could-realize-she-was-gone routine, stopped and watched three geese fly west honking to each other like trucks, while she waited for Meera to catch up.

"Did you have a good day today?" Meera asked when she reached her. Jade turned, and unable to make eye contact, stared at the ground in front of Meera's feet.

"Sure. If cleaning day in and day out, smattered with a little hanging out with grandpa is your idea of good. Then, yeah. I guess I did. Great day!" Jade glanced up at Meera to see how that landed, but Meera hadn't even flinched. Jade retreated to looking at the ground, focusing on the stones stuck in the frozen mud, and shivered.

She clutched the hot water bottle she'd prepared a little tighter. Her winter jacket was draped over her shoulders as she hadn't planned on loitering, so the sleeves hung useless at her sides. The night air suggested a second winter, the one just before spring fully commits. She thought of a meme she had seen: first winter, false spring, second winter, spring, the fuckening. She was definitely in second winter. Spring might be OK, everyone talked like it was. She knew "the fuckening" part of the meme meant pollen and allergy season and all the misery that entailed, but Jade thought it pretty much summed up her daily existence, too. The fuckening Jade realized was her every day. She snorted. She was sick of it. She was sick of being cold. Sick of cleaning. Sick of taking instructions. Sick of being asked if she was OK. She wasn't OK. Nothing was OK. She wanted to escape. She needed to escape. She had even stopped complaining in her journal. Each page just said the same thing, over and over, like *Groundhog Day*—but without even Sonny and Cher to mark the occasion.

Dear diary, today was hell. Guess what, diary? More cleaning today! Just a modern-day slave. This place sucks. I'm in jail. Hell…cleaning….slave…jail. Repeat.

Jade scuffed the ground with her boot as Meera gathered her thoughts.

"You've been here for a month or so now," Meera said calmly. "Cleaning is where everyone starts, but they usually balance it with the rest of the program. Perhaps now is a good time to come more into the flow of the place. Join us for chanting in the morning, why don't you?" She tried to make it sound like an invitation to a party rather than the directive it was. "It will help you feel the energy of the place. Help you to feel more at home."

"This isn't my home," Jade said and looked down the drive at her cabin. Begging it to move closer so she could escape the conversation. Defiantly, the tin can just sat there playing dumb, ignoring her silent plea.

"Home is not a physical place where you reside, Jade. It's a place inside of you," Meera tapped her breastbone. "The centre, simply mirrors what's inside you. So, it can be heaven, or it can be hell. It can be a prison, or it can be complete, unadulterated freedom." Meera took her hand from the pocket of her coat and gestured to the acres around them before quickly returning it. "Places like this are designed to show you what's on the inside. So, the more you can be here, immerse yourself in the flow of the place, the more you'll feel at home—physically and mentally." She rocked onto her tiptoes and then back onto her heels. "Or, it's going be a very long year—for the both of us." Her last words caught Jade by surprise. Reflexively, she tried to catch Meera's expression to see if there was anger or resentment, but Meera just looked contemplative as she stared at something over Jade's shoulder.

Meera took her hands from her pockets and breathed into them, her words hung in the air, waiting for Jade's reply. Jade, still not wanting to make eye contact, looked up to see a single pinprick of light shining in the full expanse of the cloudless sky. She let the words fall.

"Soooo…, we will see you at chanting in the morning then. Six am start. Please be five minutes early. That way I won't have to save breakfast for you, and you'll get a full day in. OK?" Meera turned to go back inside without waiting for an answer.

"Do I even have a choice?" Jade muttered refusing to let Meera have the last say. Meera stopped, turned, and sighed. She put her hands back into her pockets and looked to the stars.

"You always have a choice, Jade. Our choices are what have brought us to this moment." Meera paused, searching for the right words. "Sometimes though, when we have made a series of choices that have created a reality of chaos, or drama if you will, we have to choose to surrender our decision-making in hopes that we can experience a different kind of reality. But even surrendering is a choice." They stood, billowing frost into the night air between them like posturing dragons.

"Goodnight, Jade," Meera said almost sadly. "Tat Twam Asi."

Too deep in her thoughts to realize that Meera had gone, Jade whispered "Goodnight" to the bare ground where Meera had been standing. The ground said nothing.

Jade shifted her hold on the hot water bottle and was about to head down to her camper when she heard a soft whispering of feathers. She looked behind her to see six eyes glinting in the shadows. Three peafowl had silently observed the exchange from the rafters of the hay shed. They were huddled together against the cold night air, heads hunched back into feathered shoulders. Jade had seen these birds around, haughty and proud in the daylight. Before this moment, she had never in her life thought about where they slept or how. They didn't look quite so full of themselves now in the dark of night. They looked like turkeys. Beautiful, neckless turkeys, but turkeys all the same.

While her eyes were cast high on the roosted fowl, something leaned against her leg. The Jade of four weeks ago would've screamed in alarm at being touched in the dark unexpectedly. But, stuck-in-this-prison-for-a-month-Jade merely looked down at the honey-coloured cat. A tabby with a faint brown and black pattern was rubbing its muscular body against her. Chewie Chewbacca mewed mournfully hoping for a sympathetic handout. Jade had none to give. In place of food, Jade bent down to pet the cat. She let its lithe little body undulate between her leg and her hand. *A furry python*, Jade thought and snorted laughter. *A mythical, magical, furry, purring python.* She quickly followed that thought up with, *My god, I'm losing my mind.*

"Goodnight to you, too, Chewie, " she said with a sigh. Standing up, she once again sought the warmth of the hot water bottle. "Stay warm, OK?" she murmured, wondering if she could somehow convince Chewie to bunk with her. His warm little body becoming her heat source; his companionship making the night a little less lonely. Jade resumed her walk down the drive to her sleeping quarters. As she approached the camper, it no longer felt like a cell, but it wasn't exactly a place of solace either, and her body began to recoil in revulsion. Her ears began to ring and her vision to tunnel. She couldn't stand the thought of going inside and being cooped up for another night. She was utterly sick of her own company. She thrust her arms through the sleeves of her jacket and zipped it closed, sealing in the hot water bottle, and kept walking.

She didn't know where she was going. She wasn't running away, she was just walking… away. Cradling her now pregnant-looking stomach to keep her hands warm, she matched her pace to the rapid beating of her heart. After the initial rush of defiance and adrenaline passed, her heart and feet slowed, and she began to take note of her surroundings—low bushes and tall trees surrounded her.

As she ambled, she remembered Meera speaking of Sam's great dislike for bears and coyotes on her first day. She glanced behind her, making sure she knew the fastest route back to the camper. Although she had fantasized about being eaten by a bear to end her misery, she didn't want to come face to face with one. Satisfied, she continued to walk through the towering columns of trunks until she reached the top of a knoll. There she noticed a movement at the far side. She froze mid-step, terrified. *Don't run, don't move—hide,* she thought. She ducked behind the closest tree and carefully peered around its trunk, going only far enough to see what had caught her eye.

Scratching at the barren ground near the base of some trees was a beast. Bigger than a deer and smaller than a moose, it stood with two, no, three others. Jade had watched enough nature programs to know she was looking at one male and three females. She let out a breath she didn't realize she was holding and marvelled at their beauty. Her fear abated; surely if these beasts were calm, then there was nothing else in the area to be afraid of.

Slowly, she stepped out from behind the tree. The animals didn't scatter at the sight of her, so she moved another step closer. She didn't want to scare them away, but she couldn't help herself. She was drawn to them. The closest one without antlers lifted its head and looked at her as though it had never seen a human up close and didn't know what to make of her. Something tickled Jade's forehead enough to make her abandon her hold on the hot water bottle and extend her arm to scratch it. The beast snorted and resumed foraging. Jade noted, however, that it kept one cupped ear swivelled in her direction. The largest beast was crowned with huge, spiked antlers, *like something you see in a postcard* Jade thought. It took a step toward her, exposing a limp in his front leg that seemed to stem from a wound just below his right knee.

He sniffed the air and looked directly at her. Unafraid. Curious. They stood like statues regarding each other. She didn't dare take another step forward because she knew that if she did the magic would be broken. Instead, she crouched down, leaned against a tree for comfort, and scratched her head again. Seeing her settle put the male at ease, and he went back to eating. Jade saw he placed his body between her and the rest of the group. She watched them graze, moving silently and delicately over the still mostly frozen ground. Even though they were large and powerful, they seemed vulnerable.

The chittering of a squirrel broke the silence. To Jade, it seemed like nothing out of the ordinary, but to the beasts, it was a warning of some sort: danger approaching! The females turned in unison, fleeing down the hill to the river; the male remained behind a moment longer, his eyes locked on Jade's—a silent communion of souls—and then he, too, turned and lumbered to safety.

Jade watched until the last white rump was out of view and then stood up. She looked around, listening to hear what could have startled them, but all was silent. It was almost full dark now, and she was tired. The thought of getting up early to chant filled her with dread. She knew the Lady on the Hill would be there. She also knew, in front of The Lady, she wouldn't be able to hide.

Jade walked back the way she had come, hurrying to keep warm and eager to get her hot water bottle into her bed. As she opened her camper door, she stopped and looked up into the infinite night sky. There were more stars now, but the majority of them were barely visible, as though they too were on the fence about showing their faces too early.

"If I wake, then I'll go," she said to them, "and if I sleep through, I sleep through. How 'bout that?" The stars above her didn't respond, they just twinkled down at her, bearing witness to her every move.

9 Chanting

Dong... Dong... Dong...

Jade woke to the call of the bell. Like the flicker on her first morning, it seemed hell-bent on not letting her roll over and go back to sleep. "Oh my fucking God, I hate you!" she called out from under the covers, but the bell didn't care; it just kept chiming. Was it always this loud in the morning she wondered, and if it was, how had she slept through it all these weeks?

She pushed back the covers and briefly congratulated herself for sleeping in her long johns and socks so she wouldn't be discouraged by the cold when it was time to get up. She fumbled for the headlamp she had placed under her pillow (it had migrated between the mattress and the wall during the night) and positioned it on her head. She put on her jacket, braced herself for the damp cold of the pre-dawn air, and opened the door. She yearned for the hot water bottle from the night before—zipping it into her jacket had been a great idea. As she started to stomp up the hill to the main house, the bell stopped. Her boots' crunch on the thin layer of frozen mud seemed overly loud in the sudden silence, and her ragged breathing (her throat trying and failing to heat the air on its way to her lungs) drowned out any morning bird song.

When she reached the teaching house, she was met by the smell of incense. Her mum had burned incense in their apartment, and Jade never figured out if she was doing it to cover something up or usher something in. She hadn't liked it then, and she didn't like it now. However, the smell held a visceral memory of her life...before. She shook her head, dislodging the memory, and exhaled. She didn't want to be reminded of her mother this morning. Or her old life. Not today.

She took her boots off, noisily throwing them so that those inside would know she had made it, and opened the door. The room was dark. What little light there was came from small mason jars placed in the windows. The jars weren't holding tea lights, like Jade expected, but were filled with oil and floating wicks. Tiny, delicate flames illuminated photos and statues; the flickering lights made the shadows dance and the whole room felt full of ghosts.

As her eyes adjusted to the dimness, she found Aaden and Avi already there. They were sitting still and facing the altar. They seemed almost a little too still like they were trying not to turn and look at her. Jade noted she was the only one without a shawl, guess that wasn't part of the welcome package, Jade thought.

Meera on the other hand, upon hearing the door, looked over and smiled. She patted the empty cushion next to her. It wasn't a welcoming pat, but more of a you-will-sit-here-and-learn pat. Jade did as she instructed and sat down on the cushion.

She tried to sit like everyone else, legs criss-crossed like a kindergartener's with knees resting comfortably on the floor. But her knees stuck up at awkward angles and made her feel like she was falling backwards. Meera handed her a red book that was already opened to the correct page, and the Lady on the Hill started to chant. It took Jade about two seconds to realize there was no way she was going to keep up with the others who knew what they were doing. The book was written in a foreign language, and as Jade looked closely at the page, she saw some words had more letters than the English alphabet. How could she chant at the same pace as everyone else if she couldn't even read what she was supposed to say? "What the ever-loving fuck," Jade mouthed silently, hoping her moving lips matched the mumbo-jumbo she was hearing. She knew she could mouth "watermelon" from a long ago Google search when she had been trying to avoid singing in the choir. But, "what the ever-loving fuck" felt more satisfying.

They weren't even on the second chant before Jade's legs started to ache and her back began to hurt. She glanced around the room at the others. They looked so peaceful. Focused. She shut her book and leaned back on her hands. She tried not to think about the precious minutes of sleep she had lost and focused on easing the ache in her back. She settled her neck into the valley of her hunched shoulders. *Be like the peafowl*, she thought, *be the peafowl*. She closed her eyes wondering if she could sleep sitting up and had decided to give it a try when Meera tapped her on the leg and earnestly tried to show her where they were in the book. Jade opened her book again and pretended to care. *What a colossal waste of my fucking…,* The next chant started and stopped Jade's train of thought in its tracks.

The new chant had the same tune as a song her mum used to sing to her as a child—a song to the ancestors. She was shocked to her very core. Completely unprepared for the reminder of her mother. Sadness began to overwhelm her, and Jade felt the heat rising in her cheeks. As everyone began to sing in unison, her mother's voice seemed to join them. Jade opened her eyes to see if anyone was looking at her, but thankfully they were all focused on their chanting—calm, joyful expressions on their faces.

Fuck, fuck, fuckity-fuck-fuck, replaced Jade's earlier mantra, and she tried to focus on her breath, tried to push her feelings down. She didn't want to make a scene by running out like she had done on her first evening.

A door hinge squeaked, and Jade welcomed the distraction. The pressure building inside her was momentarily redirected toward the newcomer. She tried to see who it was, but the door was in the darkest corner of the room. Meera, seeing Jade distracted, tapped her leg again. When Jade looked at her, Meera pointed out the page they were on in the book—a bit more emphatically this time. Jade looked at the words; they swam across the page. She gave up and closed her eyes once more, hoping no ghosts had arrived, hoping no one saw her tears, hoping no one heard her heart pounding in her chest.

By the time the chanting finally ended, Jade had regained her composure. She opened her eyes to see the room awash with the pale light of morning and beside her, as close as possible but not touching, lay one of the Lady's dogs. The pup looked like she was trying to become one with the floor with its body prostrate and front paws outstretched. It had its chin lowered to the ground between its paws. Everyone turned and looked at them. Aaden, his mouth hanging open, looked from the Lady on the Hill to the dog, waiting for her to reprimand the pup for entering the sacred space.

"Really, Lola?" The Lady said half-smiling. She gave a gentle nod, and much like the bell that had called them to chanting, her nod released them to their duties. Everyone silently picked up their cushions, folded their shawls, and walked to the shelves at the back of the room to return them. As Aaden walked past, he looked at Lola and then at Jade and gave one of his wide-mouthed smiles and winked. Jade reached out and brushed her fingers through the dog's fur. She hadn't known she was going to do it until it was already being done; normally Jade avoided dogs at all costs. The dog rolled onto its side—its heavy weight pressing against her—groaned with pleasure, and offered Jade its warm belly in case she wanted to keep doling out pets.

"Come," Meera whispered as she glanced at the dog getting a belly rub. "Let's get some breakfast." Jade didn't know if Meera was talking to the pup or her, so they both, reluctantly and stiffly, made their way to the door. Each of the four residents sat where they always did since Jade's arrival—Avi opposite Meera, Aaden opposite Jade, Meera on Jade's left. The Lady, and the pup, had quietly left before breakfast was served.

Avi, predictably, was dressed in his usual faded, stonewashed jeans and white collared shirt. Why he wore white on a farm continued to confound Jade. He sat, silent as ever, holding a steaming cup of tea in one hand and using the other to spoon porridge into his mouth. Meera, noticing droplets of porridge in his moustache, pushed a napkin across the table and removed the tea towel from around the pot; she placed it out of sight.

Dressed in a long-sleeved, purple cotton top with a single string of wooden beads around her neck, Meera sat quietly eating her porridge. She seemed deep in thought. Aaden wore the same green t-shirt he had on the day before, and his hair was all sorts of dishevelled as if a chimp had searched his head for nits while he slept. Jade wasn't sure why she was so fixated on what everyone was wearing this morning. The lack of sleep and emotional whiplash of the morning had set her on edge, and she knew focusing on things she could see and feel would help to ground her and keep the panic at bay.

She watched Aaden prepare his porridge with butter and honey, his head bopping to a song only he could hear. She followed Aaden's lead and stirred a knob of butter into her porridge, along with a big spoonful of honey and a sprinkle of salt. If she pretended hard enough, maybe the mush would taste like pancakes. It didn't.

"Did you sleep well, Jade?" Aaden asked once his breakfast had been prepared to his liking. He sounded overly cheerful and upbeat in a room of introversion and melancholy.

"OK thanks," Jade said. She wasn't in the mood for Aaden's cheerfulness. She had not been able to shake the sadness that had risen after hearing the ancestral chant and smelling the incense—both strong reminders of her mother and their lives together.

"Any good dreams?" he prodded.

Jade stared at him, allowing the silence to spiral for a few seconds longer than usual, a warning, and then slowly said, "No." Meera cleared her throat and must have backed it up with a look because Aaden didn't say another word for the remainder of his meal.

"Avi, are you able to be in the garden this morning? We've got to get those beds prepped for the radishes to be planted. Ground should thaw out pretty quickly by 10:00 this morning." Meera's reviewing of the day's tasks was a clear attempt to diffuse the tension building in the room.

"Yes, ma'am," Avi said, as he wiped his moustache with the napkin. "I noticed a fir down the hill was taken by winter. I'm planning on bucking that up and getting started on next winter's firewood this afternoon." He pushed his empty bowl away and pulled his mug of tea closer, cradling it in both hands as though he was holding a baby chick not yet comfortable outside the confines of its egg.

"Sounds good," Meera said. "Then in the afternoon, why don't you and Jade split it and get it stacked?" No one responded; they knew it wasn't a question. Meera was already moving on to Aaden's tasks anyway. "Aaden, what have you got going on in the garden this morning?" she asked him waiting patiently for him to finish his mouthful.

"I gotta whole lot of transplanting to do. Onions, broccoli and spinach are all ready for their second trays. Which is great. Means we'll be able to get them into the ground in a month. Right on schedule." He ran his fingers through his hair, looking suddenly self-conscious. "Then, this afternoon, once everything thaws out a bit, I hope to turn the compost. Get'er steamin'." He grinned.

Meera turned to Jade, and before she could speak, Jade said, "Let me guess, I'm on cleaning." She delivered this with the carefully honed snark of her teenage years and abruptly stood up. Before leaving the table, she noticed the faint twitch of a smile cross Avi's face. She grabbed her bowl and headed to the kitchen to wash up.

"Great! Well, if everyone's clear about their morning duties I'll see you all back at noon for lunch. Tat Twam Asi"

The men, sensing the brewing storm quickly washed their dishes and ducked out the door, leaving the two women to bring the kitchen back to order.

The room was pregnant with unspoken words. Each woman absorbed in their tasks yet completely aware of the other. The kettle protested its need to heat water, letting out little screams and hisses that sounded like a distant animal being tortured. Meera busied herself organizing the teas in the rustic wooden tray, first alphabetically and then by size. Jade grabbed the long, red-handled broom, and except for a few flecks of dust here and there from people's socks, started to sweep an already clean floor.

"Are you OK?" Meera spoke in the calm, soothing voice Jade was starting to loathe. It was the one she used when some dumb animal got stuck in something. Jade stopped sweeping and looked at her.

"Did you enjoy the chanting this morning?" Meera tried again.

Jade scoffed, "Honestly? I'd rather slit my wrists than have to sit through that again." Meera winced at her words and switched her attention back to the teas. Jade resumed sweeping the clean floor.

Finally, having drawn out the organizing of the tea box as long as she possibly could, Meera pushed the box against the wall and turned to face Jade. "What's going on, Jade? What's upset you?"

Jade stopped sweeping, squared her shoulders, and looked Meera in the eye. "What's going on, Meera? I'll fucking tell you what's going on. I'm a god damned slave around here. I've been here for over a month, and all I do is clean up everyone else's shit. The boys can't aim into the fucking toilet to save their lives. And you? You cook in the kitchen like the meal won't taste as good if you don't use every fucking utensil and bowl on the premises. Jesus Christ, would it kill you to reuse a spoon?" Jade's voice rose in pitch as she gathered steam, voicing her frustrations without considering, or caring, about which words she used. She expected to see Meera recoil at the vehemence of her accusation, but she just stood there calmly. Jade continued, "This place is supposed to help people, be a haven. But, it's Hell. All it is is a free labour camp. It's bullshit. When I got here, I wondered why there weren't more people. But, now I know why. It's because as soon as they see what you're on about, they all get up and leave! I'd leave, too, except I can't, Meera," She spat out Meera's name as though it soured her tongue. "I can't leave. Which means you get to dump on me all the shit jobs you don't wanna do yourself because you know I have no choice!" Jade was elated to finally be able to say exactly what she had written in her journals. She took a deep, steadying breath, preparing herself for Meera's retaliation, but she just stood there listening deeply to every word Jade said. Meera's refusal to engage disarmed Jade, and she stood there, exposed, elation rapidly fading.

"I can see why you would have this perspective. It must feel terrible to believe yourself enslaved. I could assure you you're not, but I don't think you'd hear me. However," Meera took a deep breath, "I do want you to know that everyone here started where you are now. Both in duty and mindset. Me. Avi. Aaden." Jade felt her righteousness falter a bit. Meera kept talking, her eyes never leaving Jade's face.

"The cleaning never stops," she continued. "But, it's not the floor you are getting the dust from. It's the internal dust. The dust that stops you from seeing straight. That's what you're cleaning up, Jade. So, keep going. Watch your mind; witness your emotions. By the force that is coming up in you this morning, I would say you're right on track. What comes up while you are cleaning is what needs to be cleaned out of you." Jade stared at her mutely. "Now, I'm going to the garden to check on Aaden; then I have my morning meeting with the Lady on the Hill. I'll come back after that to prepare lunch and check in. I'll see you soon. OK?" She turned to the stove and shut off the screaming kettle. Turning back to Jade she said, "Oh, and please give the bathroom floor a decent scrub. I don't know if it's getting missed or if elves are dancing in there with muddy shoes in the night, but it's… disgusting."

Meera had left for the garden before she could object; the kettle sat quietly steaming.

10 Reason for Being

When Meera walked in, Jade was sitting on the bathroom floor, scrubber in hand, staring blankly at the tiles.

"Oh dear. What happened?" Meera murmured discretely taking a strapless watch face out of her pocket to check the time. Then she knelt beside Jade.

Jade turned her face away from her. "I hate this place."

"The bathroom is…"

"No, this whole fucking place."

"Ah."

"It's stupid. It's a fucking cult *serving* some 'old lady on the hill' who I haven't even met properly yet! This morning was the first morning I've even been close to her since I got here, and she didn't even say hello! What the fuck is that? She said it would be better than prison, but it's worse!"

"Who said?" Meera asked.

"My aunt!"

"Carole?"

"Yeah. I swear to God! If I didn't think you'd call the cops the moment I left, I'd be out of here!" Meera nodded in agreement or understanding; Jade was too wrapped up in herself to notice.

"What happened, Jade?"

"What do you mean, 'What happened'?" Jade could feel Meera treading lightly with her, but couldn't match her with vulnerability so opted for vitriol.

"What happened that you ended up here instead of prison?" Meera said more clearly.

"Don't ask me like you don't already know. I'm sure everybody here knows."

"Well, no, actually. I don't know. Nor does Avi or Aaden. I told you that."

"Right!"

"The Lady on the Hill knows—nothing happens here that she doesn't know about. All *I* was told was that your Aunt Carole contacted her and that you were coming for a year—not exactly of your own free will."

Jade continued to stare at the floor, a look of revulsion on her face. She was so tired of pretending to be fine, of not having anyone to talk to.

"So why are you here, Jade?" Meera asked as she moved off her knees and sat on the floor beside her—with her.

Jade scanned her face, trying to decide which version of the truth she should tell, and although every bone in her body was telling her to rattle off the hardened don't-give-a-shit version of events, her mouth craved honesty.

"After Mum died," she began, "my aunt took custody of me 'cause I was only sixteen. She has money; she's a lawyer. Anyway, she said she'd keep paying Mum's rent so I didn't have to move *if* I kept going to school and getting good grades. I'm not stupid you know, it's just school was…"

"What?"

"Boring."

Meera nodded and gave her an I-know-exactly-what-you-mean smile.

"At first I was doing well. But I missed Mum. And coming home every day to an empty place was depressing. So, I started to stay out later and later with my friends from school. There's a certain "crowd" that stays out later, you know?" She glanced at Meera and then looked back at the floor. "So, I started hanging out with 'em. God I fucking hated walking into that apartment every day. Seeing that absolutely nothing had changed since I'd left that morning. I used to love coming home. Mum would always have some corny music playing on the radio, and she'd be cooking something that only she liked—usually something spicy—but she would be so excited about it that I would try to eat it anyway. Ya know? So as not to hurt her feelings. It was almost always terrible. I didn't realize how much I'd miss her awful cooking. But I did." Jade used the bottom of her shirt sleeve to wipe her nose.

"So, uh, my friends were bored, too. They didn't have dead parents, just parents that worked a lot and didn't notice, or care, if their kids were home or not. They'd just tell their parents they were playing video games at a friend's place, and they'd believe 'em. Sometimes though, the boredom'd be so bad that we'd end up daring each other to do stupid shit. We were so stupid. Some nights we'd shoot a pellet gun at the road signs with the animals crossing. Other nights we'd go to Timmy's and get coffee and donuts and then run out before paying."

Meera nodded in encouragement for her to keep going. She did.

"Once in a while, someone would get caught, but I always seemed to get away." She said this with, not exactly pride in her voice, but something close to it. She went to wipe her nose on her sleeve again, but Meera stopped her, gesturing to the roll of toilet paper. "But one of my friends, Katie, had this older boyfriend, Dave, who worked at the oil change place in town. He was trouble. He started bringing his buddies around, and then the drugs started showing up. Up until then, it had been stupid kid shit. But then it became this…you're not *in* unless you're trying the harder stuff. So we would sit around and get stoned, or high, or whatever. Being high…," she stopped, pausing to stay calm, and collected, "Being high was the only time I didn't miss Mum. It felt so good to not feel anything. One of Dave's buddies kinda liked me, so we started to hang out some. Movies, mall meals, that sort of thing. Anyway, one night I invited him back to my place and we were, you know…" she tipped her head to one side in hopes of not having to spell it out.

"Yep," Meera said with a knowing sigh and a nod. Jade swallowed a few times, gathering her courage for the part that came next.

"So, we were getting pretty involved, but I wanted to stop. He didn't. I told him to leave, and he got upset with me. But he left. I'd never kicked someone out before, but I didn't think too much of it. We hadn't had sex. Just fooled around in the movie theatre a couple of times, but he was really pissed off, ya know. Like *really* pissed off…"

Oh, yeah. Meera knew. "Slighted?" she asked.

"Yeah, That's it. Slighted." Jade sighed and looked down at her fingernails, whittled stumps, gnawed to the point of bleeding. "About a week later I was at home. I wasn't feeling great, and I was still laying low after kicking Steve out—that was the guy's name. Steve. I didn't want anything to start back up again. I'd been sorta ghosting him. Fading away. Anyway, there was a knock on my door, and I answered it thinking it was Katie. But it wasn't. It was Dave. As soon as I opened the door, he pushed his way past me. At first, I was surprised, and then I was kinda annoyed. He started off saying Katie was worried about me, and that he told her he'd check in on me after work. Put her mind at ease. But then he started walking towards me in that sleazy kinda way, ya know?" Meera nodded and rolled her eyes; every woman in the world knows that walk. "Then he tried to kiss me. He tried to kiss ME! I swear I never led him on. I was wearing fluffy pyjama pants and a tank top with a raspberry jam stain dribbled down the front for fuck's sake." Jade stopped, realizing she had shredded toilet paper all around her, decided she didn't care all that much, and kept going. "Then he was all over me. I tried to push him off, but he was so much bigger and stronger than me. He said Steve hadn't appreciated how last week went. Said I was a cocktease and needed to be taught a lesson. Said he was there to show me what happens to little girls who tease boys like that. I could see in his eyes where he was going and I just—"

She stopped. A rush of fear prevented her from uttering what came next as if voicing it aloud would cause Dave to appear in front of her.

"Keep going, Jade, it's OK." Meera offered her hand, palm up, in case holding it would help Jade have the courage and the energy to continue. Jade didn't take it, but Meera left it there, all the same, an open invitation.

"I finally managed to get away from him, and that made him even more angry. I ran across the room to the bathroom and grabbed the kitchen knife out of the linen cupboard next to the bath."

Confusion flashed across Meera's face. "Why was there a knife in the linen cupboard?" Jade laughed, not because it was funny. It wasn't. But because it was a question all the male cops had asked her; the female ones hadn't needed to. They knew. "Well, living by ourselves, Mum had always taught me to have one surprise in every room."

"Aaaaaah," Meera exhaled.

"So, we had a knife in the bathroom, another one under the couch cushion, and since Mum's been gone, I've been sleeping with one under my pillow." Jade looked at Meera hoping for reassurance that this was normal behaviour; she was met with a creased forehead and a sad nod. She didn't know how to read that expression. Jade took some more deep breaths, and continued—it was easier now that she had started.

"Anyway, he ran into the bathroom just as I grabbed the knife. I held it at stomach height, the blade perpendicular to me just like Mum had taught me." Jade demonstrated for Meera. "Mum said they either run into it or it's at the perfect height and position for you to be able to defend yourself." Again, Jade demonstrated what her mum had meant. Meera nodded. "He was so focused on my face—he was getting off on how scared I was—he thought I just had my hands out in front of me." She paused, took Meera's hand, and squeezed it tightly.

"I yelled at him to stay away, but he rushed at me. And with the knife where it was, he ran right into it. He kept trying to hit me, so I didn't know if it had worked or not. So I pulled my hand back and stabbed him. That time he doubled over and collapsed on the bathroom floor, but not before he punched me in the face, knocking me to the floor, too." Jade raised her hand to her cheekbone at the memory. "There was blood everywhere," she whispered. "It spread over the tiles and into the grout. I don't remember what he said to me then. I don't remember the look on his face. I just remember laying on the floor and watching his blood run down the lanes of the grout straight towards me."

With her free hand, Jade traced a line of grout on the floor in front of them, her finger turning this way and that until she reached her leg.

Snapping out of the memory she looked at Meera with tears in her eyes. "I didn't mean to. I didn't want to hurt him. But he was going to rape me or beat me… maybe… even kill me and I just…"

She dropped Meera's hand and wiped her palms on her jeans like she was trying to rid them of blood. Then she bent her knees and wrapped her arms around her legs. She rested her forehead on her knees suddenly looking years younger than seventeen.

"It's OK," Meera said taking back her hand and leaning against the cupboard. "So what happened?" she asked gently. "Did he die? Why did you end up getting charged? Surely they could see it was self-defence?"

Jade shook her head. "He didn't die. The first stab was only a flesh wound and the second cut into his intestine. He had surgery and is fine, but he's going to have one of those bags for a while." Jade let go of her legs and let them relax. "He told the police he was there to check on me for his girlfriend. And that when he arrived, I freaked out. He was just trying to get me to calm down when I stabbed him. You know, I finally snapped because of my dead mother. Katie backed up his story, and I was charged with 'assault causing bodily harm'." She said the last part in an official tone. "But, because I was under eighteen at the time, I was going to be sentenced to a state attendance program for a year. The judge said I was getting off easy because I had no record and Dave had a history of drugs and violence against him. So, Aunt Carole flew in from Vancouver, did her lawyer thing, and convinced the Crown to let me come here for a year instead of doing the state program." She wiped her eyes. She wasn't sure when she had started crying, again. Then she looked at Meera. "*That's* why I can't leave."

Meera nodded and held Jade's eyes with her own. "And that's why you refuse to clean the bathroom floor," she said. Jade nodded.

"I went back to the apartment only once after that. Aunt Carole had had the place cleaned, but I could still see the faint marks on the grout. Where all the blood had been. If you didn't know, you wouldn't know it was there. But I knew. She moved me to Vancouver until the trial and…"

"And then you came here. To us."

Jade nodded; she felt raw, empty, and to her surprise, better. She was glad that she had told Meera everything, but also embarrassed. "You probably don't want anything to do with me now. Now that you know that I'm capable of 'assault causing bodily harm'." She wiped her nose again with her sleeve even though the toilet paper was close at hand. Meera didn't move. She sat in silence, listening to some unknown force for guidance as to what to do or say next. Finally, she said very softly, "I'm so sorry. No woman should have to experience that, go through what you did, and then be forced to defend herself."

"I still get nightmares. That's why I don't always wake up early. I don't sleep."

"Ah," Meera said. Jade could tell a lot of things were suddenly making sense. "Well, I hope that your time here proves to be the healing you need. That it heals your heart, eases your mind, and helps you let go of the grief of your mum's passing. You never forget a loved one's passing, but in time it does become less painful. At least it did for me." There seemed to be no judgment behind Meera's words. They were just... kind. "I'm always willing to listen if you are willing to talk." She squeezed Jade's knee, once, quickly, and let go.

Meera checked the time again. Jade could tell their conversation had thrown the morning routines out the window but Meera hadn't rushed her. She returned the watch to her pocket and said, "Come now, let's finish up in here. It's getting close to lunchtime." She started to stand up.

"You want me to finish?" Jade said, confused. "You want me to keep cleaning the tiles? After everything I just told you?"

Meera crouched back down, being sure to stay balanced on her toes to show she was not staying, and looked Jade in the eye. "I'll go put the kettle on... then I'll come back and help you, OK?" She put her hand on Jade's shoulder. "Once it's cleaned up, you can have a cuppa while I prepare lunch for everyone." Seeing her words made no impact on Jade's emotional state, she sighed and tried a different tactic. "Jade, hon, it's a tiled floor in a bathroom at a meditation centre in the forest. I'll help you, just this once, but if you don't finish cleaning this floor, today, then all the tile floors for years to come will loom over you—have power over you. And every time you see one, every time you clean one, you will be thrown back into that horrible night. You will live it over and over and over. But you have spoken your story today and discharged its power. So, in this moment, clean the floor. The next time you clean it, likely tomorrow, you won't be able to say 'The *last time I saw a floor like this something horrible happened.*' You will be able to say '*The last time I saw a floor like this, I cleaned it and I cried. But, I did not let the past ruin my present. I cleaned the damn floor!*' OK?" She stood up and started to walk out the door. "I believe in you. Now, let's go."

"Meera?" Jade called out to her, suddenly feeling naked, exposed. Meera now knew so much about her, and she knew nothing about Meera. "What brought you here? How did you find this place?"

Meera smiled. "I'll tell you. Not today, but I promise I'll tell you when the time's right. For now, clean. Like I was trying to say this morning. Clean—"

"Clean the outside, like you are cleaning all the crap on the inside."

Meera's smile brightened. She nodded. "Do you know what a *tabula rasa* is?"

"A clean slate?"

"Exactly. Clean so you get that."

11 A Rose by Any Other Name

"*PAL*" the text message reads. It doesn't need elaboration. She has been waiting patiently for Jade to peel a layer ever since she arrived; it has taken her almost a month. Longer than she had hoped, but Jade is stubborn. Just like her mother had been. Always holding it together. Putting on that brave Brennan face. Keep the exterior rock-solid to protect the more delicate interior. It's why she has not pushed for an introduction. She wants Jade to feel comfortable here, safe in her own right, without leaning on another motherly figure.

It is not surprising to her that the day Jade finally joins them for chanting is the same day she breaks down. Lola feels it, too. The mantras have a way of piercing the toughest of exteriors; they reach beyond the mind and connect to the soul.

Wrapping her softest shawl around her shoulders, she starts to walk down from her house on the hill and then up the other side of the valley to where the centre is. Lola, her oldest pup, falls in at her heel. They walk the path together. She smiles fondly at the thought of 'pup' and Lola in the same sentence—Lola is almost ten and Pebbles is four. But, much the same way mothers refer to their adult children as always being their babies, she will always think of her dogs as pups.

The warm spring Sun is teasing everything back to life—its warmth helping to unfurl one budded leaf at a time. The honey bees buzz with fervent purpose seeking the dandelion flowers that bloomed just this morning along the southern face of the hillside. However, it is not yet quite warm enough for her bones, and she pulls the wrap tighter as she walks. Her eyes sweep across the landscape, noting the way the earth vacillates between wakefulness and slumber. Here a few dusty green tulip leaves poke through the dark, fecund soil. There the gardens bask in sunlight, earth is turned over in preparations for planting. The northern parts of the path, those shadowed by trees, still cling to bone-chilling winter with a mix of frost and snow on the ground; those trees are not yet ready to put forth their buds. Everything in its own time and on its schedule of growth she thinks, and not for the first time.

As she enters the courtyard, she finds Jade sitting on a boulder with her back to Father Sun, examining her pruned fingertips. Jade's frame looks delicate in her oversized hoodie and baggy jeans. The expression on her face looks raw, stunned, like she has been to battle, and now is sitting alone in its aftermath, unsure of who has won. Jade doesn't look up as her footsteps and Lola's nail-tapping on the cobblestones announce their approach. Jade just keeps staring at her shrivelled fingertips.

"Hello, Jade," she says softly trying not to startle her. "May I sit with you for a moment?"

Jade's eyes slowly move from the pathway to her face, taking in her rust-coloured dress, shawl, and hair piled high on her head. When Jade finally meets her gaze, she offers a smile. Jade's eyes narrow slightly in confusion, like she is trying to place her but can't, and she wonders if Jade recognizes her from the courthouse.

Jade doesn't answer, only shifts over on the boulder until there is room enough for the both of them and resumes looking at her hands, elbows on her thighs, head down. It is a position of profound defeat and exhaustion. Rose's heart aches to see her like this.

"I am pleased to see you sitting here. I'm sorry it has taken so long for us to connect." She sits down next to Jade; Lola lays across her feet and prepares for a nap. "I was hoping to speak with you this morning after chanting, but I got an urgent message that called me away before I had the opportunity to say hello. Anyway," her eye catches a Red Breasted Nuthatch hopping head-first down old Fir's trunk. "I was glad to see you there this morning."

Jade, now examining her fingernails, simply nodded.

"Have you had a challenging morning?" the old woman asks.

"Yeah," Jade says quietly, "you could say that."

"Hmm." The old woman reaches down to pat Lola between the ears, hoping her pup's contentment will help Jade relax. "Challenges are hard, and…," she searches to find the right words: nothing too preachy, something tangible. Words Jade can hold on to as she rides the waves of emotion beginning to break through the dam she has built to keep them at bay. "This centre," she says softly, "is a very powerful place for change. The challenge, however, is the pain inside holding us down. It is making us stuck. The pain must come to the surface and be acknowledged for change to happen."

Jade shifts uneasily on the boulder; the old woman sits and waits for Jade to speak again, comfortable in the silence.

"Be acknowledged," Jade echoes, with a hint of a sarcastic smile. "You don't want to see how my pain wants to be acknowledged." It's a warning shot—a cornered cat flashing its claw. But Jade doesn't realize she is still a kitten, and the old woman is not afraid of kittens.

Jade looks up at her as pain flashes across her features. For a moment, the woman catches her breath. It is not Jade she sees, but rather her mother, Angelica's, face. She is transported back in time to the days before she…

"How do you… *acknowledge…?*" Jade doesn't finish her sentence, but she senses the words bouncing around inside. She waits until they settle before speaking.

"The key is to witness an emotion. Speak of it. Name it. But not be it."

Unable to hold the old woman's gaze, Jade looks down at her hands, or perhaps through her hands, to the cobbled pathway before speaking. Then, "Isn't witnessing your emotions a little… dissociative?"

Her words are edged with judgment, a challenge. Jade will not blindly accept these words of wisdom and is letting the old woman know. Jade is touting one of the labels the West uses to lock people in their pain, just so they can finally belong. Jade's lack of understanding does not surprise her. She loves that Jade is not afraid to speak to her honestly. Her words and her feelings match in frequency. So many others fake politeness while reeling on the inside, and they are the ones who dissociate. The irony makes her smile.

"It's the difference between feeling or experiencing anger and being angry. One is a transient emotion and the other defines you," she explains.

Jade, raises half an eyebrow in skepticism.

"That's OK," she says, "I realize it's a new way of looking at experiences. But, believe me when I say, it's a very powerful practice. It will change your whole outlook on life. Just start small. Every time you experience an emotion say to yourself: *I'm experiencing joy; I'm feeling sadness; I'm experiencing anger; I'm feeling fear; I'm feeling OK.* Instead of being sad or being angry or being afraid, saying those words to yourself will help you to shift the energy so it doesn't take hold of you. It doesn't have to come through so… violently, Jade." Jade flinches at the sound of her name and shifts uneasily in her seat again. "And then when the waves come, and they *will* come, you won't have to feel so shattered, so raw and empty every time you peel back a layer." Jade's eyes widened not expecting the old woman to know exactly how she felt.

"Everyone starting on this path has felt like you do now. Do you have any questions that I can help you with?" Father Sun's warmth has reached through her wrap now, and she can feel the muscles around her old bones begin to soften and relax.

Jade looks back down at her hands, as though preparing to speak. "Ah, actually. I do," Jade says. "Why does everyone here call you the Lady on the Hill? Why don't you have a name?"

Direct; unabashed. Oh, how she has missed this. She smiles at Jade, who has turned her attention to patting the sleeping Lola at their feet. While she contemplates how to answer her questions, she considers telling her about her mother but decides against it. Not yet. Telling her now will hit her too strongly—she is still reeling from this morning. But soon. To wait much longer runs the risk of adding another layer of betrayal. She cannot risk that. So instead she answers, "When we name someone or something, we create separation, individuality, and other-ness." She pauses, wetting her lips before continuing. "When there is no name, the lack of language creates an energetic connection between souls to use as a thread of remembrance. It creates awareness that we've been together before rather than a push and pull between separate beings. That is the premise for why Avi, Meera and Aaden call me the Lady on the Hill."

Lola looks up at the old woman as though asking if they have finished, then groans softly and puts her head back on her paws as she starts to speak again.

"But, if there needs to be a name," she reaches down and strokes Lola's honey-coloured fur, "Then the name should resonate as the potential for that person—or the person using it. It should be a beacon of light to move toward so that they can use the name as a tuning fork to calibrate to."

"But *the lady on the hill* sounds so, so… stupid." Jade glances at her to see how her words land, but love is all she feels for this fiery girl before her, so she smiles in return and gives a low chuckle to show she is not offended.

"Very well. If you insist on having a name for me, you may call me Rose. Not because my name is Rose, mind you," she says flattening out the linen of her dress, "but because the scent of a rose is the frequency of trust, of faith. The foundation of life. If you are to use your time here to truly heal, Jade, you will need to come into a willingness to let go of the fear and anxiety and learn to trust. To trust the centre, to trust the Divine, to trust me, and most importantly, to trust yourself." She leans toward Jade a little more with each mention of trust, emphasizing the importance each one carries. "But I'm telling you now," she stands up and slides her feet from under Lola signalling it is time to go, "this is only a temporary label. At some point, you will need to hear for yourself what my true name is, and perhaps one day, learn what is yours."

"Now," she cuts Jade off as she sees her about to speak, "it's time for lunch. I think Meera has prepared something nice and grounding. Something nourishing for you." She reaches out and places her hand on Jade's shoulder. Jade's body tenses momentarily at being touched, but then relaxes as she takes a full, deep breath. "Tat Twam Asi," Rose says before turning to Lola, who has stood up, stretched, and is patiently waiting to move on to their next destination.

She drapes her wrap over one shoulder, warm now, and heads back along the path. "Come now, little one, it's time we go."

Lola takes one look at Jade, wags her golden tail, and then trots after Rose. Neither looked back in Jade's direction.

Jade breathed deeply and noticed her whole body had become calmer, fuller somehow. The nausea she had felt while cleaning the tile floor—vanished. She watched until Lola and Rose could no longer be seen and then looked at the door to the house realizing (surprisingly) that she had an appetite. Jade looked back to where Rose and Lola had disappeared half expecting some evidence of sorcery: golden footprints rising like steam from the cobbles, flowers blooming in the cracks of the path, a rainbow. But everything looked the same as before. The sun still shone, the birds still twittered, and the insects buzzed. Tiny bits of green could be seen at the tips of tree branches and tender shoots were trying to escape the sea of sleeping mud in the garden. But inside Jade, something felt different. Like a seed inside was germinating.

Meera poked her head out the door. "Lunch is ready, Jade." She went to move back inside, but something made her hesitate. "Are you OK, Jade?" she asked.

"Yeah, I'm OK," Jade replied. "Wait. No, I'm feeling OK." And she got up and headed in for lunch.

12 Trees: Earth

Little Sister, remember now, how our two-legged ancestors kept their hands in the ground and thus their hearts in sync with the pulse of Gaia.

Always giving, tending, before receiving.

Harvesting only what was needed, never more.

But now, most two-legged have forgotten Gaia's pulse, they have lost their place in a reciprocal existence.

Standing tall, they ooze pride; stepping forward with a false sense of separation, of independence; stumbling in shadow.

They want, they demand, they take. They no longer offer, and no longer can receive.

They seek freedom—freedom from what we are not sure.

So many two-legged move through the world now like children, though their child-hoods are long past.

Stomping and splashing in earthen pools of tears. They spend their days chasing a moment's joy; making messes, and leaving a swath of destruction behind them. They have no interest in walking in the steps of Brother Fox—lightly, silently, gently.

They want to move uninhibited upon Earth and want to soar in clouds, untethered. They forget the laws of Gaia. Be Earthbound or Skyward. You can't have both, lest you are a messenger of God.

There is a place we await you.

In our celebration of existence, linked by light—connected by more than blood, communicating without a common language.

The journey to remove the 'I' from I-solation and return to Gaia's solace is before you now.

13 Vultures and Sage

Jade looked down at her journal as she had her breakfast at the kitchen island. Doodling over her lists helped her to float in the morning silence. At one
end of the book, she had lists of duties, with notes and protocols suspended
in bubbles in the margins. At the other end her private thoughts and poetry.

Since her breakdown in the bathroom, Jade's level of responsibility and
engagement at the centre has ramped up considerably. Spring was no longer
creeping along. It had arrived in all its splendour, and Meera responded to the
growing demands of the farm by piling on extra duties. Jade's days started
earlier than she had ever experienced before, and she was so tired. She sometimes felt she would fall asleep standing up. Mid-day naps were a thing of the
past, and Jade longed for them—desperately.

On top of the cleaning, she was now caretaker to all the animals: cats,
peafowl, sheep, goats, and the cantankerous alpaca. Although she was not
expected to go to chanting every morning, she was expected to feed, water,
and graze the animals—all before breakfast, which meant that sometimes,
like today, she was late to breakfast. At first, she was intimidated by the
Angora goats. The bullish shoves they gave each other with their long horns
and their unnerving, starvation-is-imminent bleats rattled her. But after the
first few times that they came running when she called (and shook the grain
bucket), she was hooked.

As Jade got up to wash her breakfast bowl, Meera rushed in. She moved
haphazardly, jumping from one side of the kitchen to the other and muttering
to herself as though unsure which task needed doing first. She looked up, surprised, as Jade's presence broke her trance. "Jade, love, be a darlin' and grab a

toonie's worth of chives out of the garden for me would ya? Now. If you can."

"OK." Jade looked at the dirty breakfast bowl in her hand and back at Meera debating whether she should wash it first or drop it and run.

"I'll do that," Meera said taking it from her. "But grab the chives before you start your morning cleaning, OK? I need them for lunch prep."

"Sure, Meera." She handed over the bowl, "I'll be right back." She hurried from the kitchen, amused to see Meera flustered as she always seemed so even-keeled. It was nice to see this side once in a while. Yet, it unsettled her a bit, too, and Jade wondered about it until she reached the garden where all thoughts of Meera vanished. Jade loved being in the garden. Seeing new growth taking hold in what was once just plain dirt gave her satisfaction she didn't know she was missing.

Jade latched the chain on the garden gate behind her and turned to find Rose standing next to the chives. She had her back to Jade, and with her hands on her hips staring up at the sky—watching the weather on the horizon maybe—Jade thought she looked like a captain plotting a course on the high seas. Jade stood still for a moment, uncertain of her next move. Was it a coincidence that Rose was in the garden at the same time she needed chives, or did Rose know Meera was going to send her out for chives? Jade tiptoed towards the chives hoping to grab them and go without disturbing her.

She liked Rose but preferred to keep her distance. Each time they had exchanged a few words since that day on the boulder, Jade was left feeling self-conscious and eerily transparent. Rose herself, was quite lovely—kind, gentle, soft-spoken, and gave the impression she was listening when you spoke. But, Jade felt that when Rose looked at her, the old woman's gaze was seeing straight through to her broken, fragile, motherless soul. She'd be fine, initially, but then Jade would find herself swimming in shame, all her confidence gone as if it had been picked off her like lint from a sweater.

"Good morning, Jade," Rose said without turning around.

Jade's heart dipped. She was not going to be able to avoid the conversation as she had hoped. "Good morning, Rose," she replied.

"Have you seen sibling Birds this morning?" Rose asked still focused on the horizon.

"No," Jade said as she bent down and grabbed a handful of chives an inch above their base—just as Meera had taught her.

"It's important to know every bird in your surroundings, Jade. Very impor-tant." Rose turned to look at Jade as she felt a mix of wariness, disbelief, and mild curiosity flush through her.

"Why is it important? Aren't they just birds being birds?" She hated the way she sounded like a child with a chip on her shoulder, but she couldn't help asking these questions.

Rose half smiled and looked at Jade the way a mother lovingly looks at her toddler who doesn't yet understand how the world works.

"Why? Because they are the messengers. They bring news of the present and the future. They tell us when something in nature is changing: weather, fire, the arrival of Springtime, sunrise, danger, and even death. They are constantly giving us an update on what is happening in the bigger picture, in this realm, and sometimes, other realms too." Rose looked across the valley. "Like newsies calling out the headlines on the corner of a New York City block back in the day. The birds are interested in all that is happening and therefore are interesting themselves."

Jade looked up, way up, in the direction that Rose was staring and saw some large birds circling at the bottom of the hill from where they stood.

"You only need to learn how to listen. And that, my dear, takes a quieted mind. For when the birds speak, they are talking to your soul." Rose looked at the birds again and then turned to Jade. "Now, I will take those chives into Meera, and I would like you to find Avi. Go and investigate what is happening down the hill."

"OK. Um…do you know where I'd find Avi?"

"Right here," he said from behind her. Jade almost leaped out of her skin. "You called?"

"Yes, I did," Rose replied, looking at Jade, who was looking from one to the other trying to figure out how exactly she had "called him" when neither of them had phones or walkie-talkies.

Rose smiled at her but spoke to Avi. "I'd like you to take Jade and see what has happened in the valley, and then let me know. If a friend has passed, please make sure you do the last right Mantras and smudge the area." Avi looked up to the circling birds and nodded. "Be careful, for we don't know who or what has created the disturbance down there. Bears have not been awake long and are hungry. "

"Hmm," Avi said before he turned around and walked away. Jade watched him exit the garden and head down the drive.

Rose leaned in and said, "You might want to catch up to him. He's not inclined to wait for people." She said the last part softly as though imparting a secret.

"Oh, um. Yeah. OK." Jade murmured and looked vacantly at the chives in her hand. Then she glanced toward Avi's receding—she was still processing the words "bear" and "hungry".

"I'll take those. Stay with Avi and you will be fine." Rose reached for the chives and peeled them out of Jade's hand. At their brief contact, Jade felt a surge of energy run through her body. It was almost like being shocked by static electricity, but far less painful and didn't require dragging stocking feet across carpets or rubbing balloons on her head.

"Quick now," Rose said.

Jade let go of the chives and jogged after Avi.

She caught up to him halfway down the hill, panting, limbs flopping all over the place, and a stitch in her side.

"OK, so…,"

"SHH!" Avi hissed and stopped walking so abruptly that Jade nearly walked into him.

"No talking?" Jade asked.

He nodded. "No. Talking. I need to be able to listen to what's happening. And so do you." He said the last bit as an afterthought. "We want to hear what they are talking about. We don't want to hear them talking about the two humans bumbling down the hill."

For a split-second, Jade wondered who "they" were and how exactly Avi would know what "they" were saying, but decided to keep her mouth shut and do as she was told. She was used to Avi's bark, but this was different. There was an urgency in his voice she had never heard before. Jade felt like they were on a dangerous adventure—a matter of life and death. At least the conversation around the dinner table tonight won't be boring Jade thought.

She looked at Avi, noting his uniform—white shirt, blue jeans—had some extra "flair" today. A can of Bear spray was clipped to his belt on his right hip and a small purse hung from his left shoulder. He walked with one hand on each so they wouldn't bounce.

At the bottom of the hill, the temperature dropped noticeably as they were no longer in the sun's direct rays. Here, winter still wasn't willing to relinquish its hold, although its grasp was weakening. Avi had stressed the importance of silence—especially after Jade had stomped on a branch to hear its crack beneath her foot. The look he had given her promised a long and painful death if she did that again. Hoping to gain back his favour and prove she wasn't a lost cause, Jade faithfully inserted her foot into each invisible print Avi left behind. She found that she had to bend her knees just like he was in order not to lose her balance. It was awkward and slow going, but Jade knew better than to complain.

They walked up a short rise and into a clearing. Jade inhaled deeply; the air smelled of spring. She looked around marvelling at how everything was so green. A city girl since birth, Jade still hadn't adjusted to the smells and richness of the earth. There was a secondary track that headed to the left and a sign with some sort of round symbol on it that she didn't recognize. At the end of the path, Jade could see a single pink object perched in the middle of a clearing. Jade wanted to ask Avi what it was, but he hadn't even glanced in the pink object's direction.

Once they reached the clearing's opposite edge, they stopped for a moment at a man-made strip, long and straight and about 20 feet wide. She couldn't tell what it was for. She thought it might be some sort of firebreak or perhaps a gas line. She was about to ask Avi, she'd been quiet long enough in her opinion, when she felt the energy of the place shift from life to death. She looked around nervously.

Avi slowed his pace.

A breeze whipped past them bringing with it a foul stench.

"Aw, gross!" Jade said, covering her mouth and nose with her hand.

"Shhhhhhh!" Avi said. Drawing it out so that his voice joined with those on the breeze. He closed his eyes.

As she watched him, Jade was paralyzed by conflicting impulses: disgust and curiosity. What was making that *smell?* And *What* was making that smell? She made quiet, gagging noises as Avi stood scenting the air.

He looked at her and narrowed his eyes. "If you need to go, child, go."

She clenched her jaw in defiance. She was no child.

She took the bandanna that was wrapped around her head and wrapped it around her nose and mouth. It wasn't a perfect solution, but it did the job. She no longer felt on the verge of vomiting, and when Avi began to walk, she did, too.

He veered to the left, moving silently through the trees and made his way down to a ledge. There he stopped and crouched low to the ground next to a tree. Jade copied him. When his eyes moved to the vultures and ravens circling overhead and then to the murder of crows perched in the neighbouring trees, so did hers. She listened to them squabbling, loud and raucous, like politicians arguing over important legislation. They cawed over each other, arguing so feverishly to be right that she wondered if the birds had forgotten what it was they were fighting over.

Using the two groups of birds as compass points, Avi adjusted his position by moving a few steps to the right; he crouched low once more. Jade moved with him. Suddenly, a loud cry pierced the air startling Jade with its proximity. An answering caw from behind them answered the call. Their presence had been announced. Avi continued his slow trek down the hillside, Jade scanned the sky, the underbrush, and the trees taking note of the birds, and looking out for anything unusual.

Avi had only taken a few steps when he froze and motioned for Jade to do the same. She peered over his left shoulder to see what had caused him to pull up so suddenly and gasped. She could see an elk lying on its side with a turkey vulture crouched at its belly. The vulture had the carcass to itself; its head buried neck-deep in the elk's soft underbelly. Avi looked around, and seeing no bigger predators, visibly relaxed.

"Get out of it, ya feathered mongrel!" Avi bellowed, jumping to life. He waved his arms at the vulture who had removed its head from inside the elk's belly at the sound of Avi's voice. It looked at Avi, confused by his presence. Choosing not to fight such a strange creature, the vulture leisurely spread its wings and, in a single downward thrust of feathers, took flight to join its companions circling in the sky above. The crows cheered Avi's victory and moved in a little closer.

"An elk," Avi said softly. "Well, that explains it now doesn't it?"

Jade came to stand next to him. They looked down at the lifeless body.

The front half of the elk's body was still basically intact, minus the vulture's head hole in the hide and the missing right eye. Its back half was decimated— a ripped-apart concoction of flesh, bone, skin, and guts.

Jade stared closely at the carcass, her eye taking in the details of what it had been and what it was now. Her breath caught in her throat when she saw the partially healed wound just below its front knee. It was the antlered male! She gave a soft cry of recognition and felt Avi look over at her, but she couldn't return his gaze. Instead, she just stared at the shredded pelt and tried to reconcile it to the beautiful beast she'd seen eating at dusk with his family. The soulful presence she had witnessed—and had witnessed her—had fled at the time of death, leaving behind this horrific sight of putrid, rotting flesh and exposed offal.

"Look there?" Avi pointed to the perfectly round hole from which the vulture had removed its head. "It's exactly halfway between the front and hind legs. He knows exactly where to dive in for the best treats in a limited amount of time. A true master of anatomy."

He knelt beside the elk's head and pulled his purse to the front. His long frail fingers gently removed a smaller handmade leather sack. Now that she could see it up close, Jade realized "purse" wasn't the right word for the bags, they were both pouches, just different sizes. Everyone seemed to have some version of this pouch, but Jade still didn't know its purpose. She supposed she was about to find out. Maybe.

She knelt beside Avi and watched him tip a concoction of dried herbs into his hand before replacing the smaller pouch inside the larger one. He cupped his hands together, the herbs inside, and blew as though he were playing a harmonica. Then, he sprinkled the herbs around the elk's head all the while muttering unintelligible words under his breath. Reaching back into his bag, Avi carefully retrieved a smudging stick like the ones her mum used to have. He set that aside and once more reached into his pouch. This time he removed a lighter and a feather. Jade couldn't tell which bird had donated its feather, but it was beautiful.

He picked up the three items, and Jade could see the yellow staining inside his index and middle fingers between the top and middle knuckles; Avi had been a smoker back in the day.

"See here," Avi said gently touching the tip of an antler with his stained finger. "He has five points on its antlers. That means he was five years old." Jade nodded but she couldn't stop looking at the empty eye socket. She remembered her mum used to say that the eyes were the windows to the soul, and she wondered at what point in the ordeal it had been removed. Had the elk seen what was to become of him; what he was about to endure? Or had he been blind to his fate? She shuddered, careful to hide it from Avi, and pushed the memory of the elk standing watch, majestically, over his herd. *He's dead,* she told herself. *Nothing more. Circle of life. Hakkuna Matata. Ashes to ashes and all that bullshit.*

"Shouldn't we be afraid of a bear or a cougar attacking us?" Jade asked, looking over her shoulder at the dense forest behind them.

"No, lass. They might not be too far off, but they're likely to wait for us to leave. They cannot afford to be injured so early in the spring, and we humans are unpredictable with guns and the like."

The crows above were growing impatient, and Jade looked up to see even more spectators now. Eagles had joined the vultures and were circling the skies above them, biding their time, waiting to feast before dusk brought the coyotes.

"I do think it is likely he was killed by a black bear, though. Hungry after its winter sleep." Avi continued while surveying the carnage. He was looking at the scene like a detective, mentally cataloguing every detail, piecing together a murder scene. "See how whatever killed it started eating from back to front?" He pointed to the bull's missing hindquarters. "That's a sign of a black bear. A cougar," he said eyeing the swirling vortex of black wings above them "would start at the neck."

"Why do you say a black bear and not a grizzly?" Jade asked.

Avi nodded and smiled, acknowledging the quality of her question. "See how no sticks or branches are covering the carcass?" She nodded. "If this was a grizzly's kill, he or she would have tried to bury it, and it would be covered with sticks." He looked around and sniffed the air. "Still, we shouldn't dally."

Placing the feather on his lap, he picked up the lighter with his right hand. The left held the smudging stick level with his heart. He inhaled slowly, reverently, and set it alight. Carefully, Avi blew on the bundle, coaxing the embers to life so they could release the column of swirling white smoke. The sweet smell of burning sage began to replace the putrid smell of death.

Satisfied that the smudging stick was burning correctly, Avi stood up and with the feather in his right hand started to fan the smoke over the carcass with delicate flicks of his wrist. He began at the head and worked his way down the elk's back before returning to the head. Then he repeated the process. This time moving down the elk's underside and finishing where its tail once was. Jade watched, mesmerized by the strange ritual, comforted in a way she could not fully articulate. Avi was chanting as he walked around the dead animal, and she was surprised to recognize the chant as one of their morning mantras.

Om tryumbakum… the words running into one another like a sentence lacking punctuation. There were no moments to breathe, to pause, to take stock. The words just repeated over and over in an endless loop of murmured sounds. Avi circled the elk three times, as though allowing the mantras and the smoke to work in tandem to balance the sudden shift that had been experienced in the clearing. His words were barely audible, just whispers carried on smokey currents of air, and Jade followed along silently in her mind, unsure of her place in this ritual. The contrast between the elk's grisly death and the tenderness of this elderly man chanting and smudging its body caused her senses to become overwhelmed.

Her mind flashed back to the memory of her mother, battered and bloodied from the crash, lying cold on a stainless-steel table surrounded by men and women dressed in the sterile garb of the morgue. There had been no tenderness, just clinical detachment. And as the two events collided within her, she did the one thing the elk couldn't do. She got up and walked away.

Laying in bed that night, Jade replayed the dinner conversation in her mind. She had not eaten much and only watched the banter at the table as though she was watching TV. How she could have thought that that night's dinner conversation was going to be interesting was beyond her imagination now. Aaden had asked about the carcass with boyish fascination, wanting to hear every gory detail. He rattled off his questions, one after the other, "How big was the vulture head hole, Avi? Were there any claw marks? How many? Definitely a bear you think, huh?" He had finally paused to take a bite of food when he had asked Jade's question. "Were you looking over your shoulder every two seconds, Avi? In case there was something out there? Something coming back for the feast?"

"Like what?" Avi had asked.

"Well, like a bear or something. You know it would kill you with one swipe of its paw if you looked to be getting between it and a free meal."

"Aye, I can think of worse ways to go than death by bear... can't you?" At this, Aaden had continued prattling on about all the other ways that were better or worse than death-by-bear. "Yeah, like getting smashed by a bus," Jade had thought and then had asked Avi to pass the sauce. Avi had held onto it just long enough to make her look at him and then flashed her one of his rare smiles. His grandfatherly one. It was like he was trying to tell her:

I get it, they have no idea what we went through today. What you went through. And that's OK.

Jade sat up in bed at the sound of the coyotes announcing their arrival to dinner. She hadn't realized she had been waiting for their song made of yips, hoots, and screeches until their voices shattered the evening quiet. Her imagination conjured up a pantomime worthy of an award: the alpha coyote snarling and holding the others at bay while they danced around him vying for their piece of the elk carcass; the youngsters frolicking and dancing in the moonlight staying just out of reach of the bigger, stronger pack members; snouts glistening with blood after having finally sated their hunger. She tried to put the pillow over her head so she didn't hear them, but it didn't stop the phantom images from playing over and over in her mind. She didn't even realize she was hyperventilating until she was past the point of no return.

She had two choices—call Meera for help or take an Ativan. Well, one choice really. Calling Meera meant swallowing her pride and asking for help. She grimaced. It wasn't like Meera would hear her cries for help anyway. Avi, maybe. But what would she say to him? "The coyotes are eating the elk, Avi. I'm scared." Nope. Not gonna happen she told herself and sighed. Ativan it was. She'd only taken one pill since her arrival, and that was pretty good she told herself as she peeled herself out of bed and dug through her clothes in the cupboard searching for the woollen socks. She dry swallowed the pill and sat on the edge of the bed, waiting. Waiting for the drugs to take hold, waiting for her lungs to slow down, waiting for the sweet reprieve of sleep.

Finally, with the coyotes still yipping distantly in the background, she was able to lie down and close her eyes. Her imagination continued to offer different variations of the coyotes feasting on elk. She drifted off to sleep following the alpha male along the forest path. Shadows swirled around them like smoke as they raced. She smelled her mother's shampoo in the air and thought she heard a voice whispering to her through the trees. She dreamed of life and death and the line, thin and straight, that separates the two.

14 Meeting Ma

Jade stood with her hands soaking in the hot dishwater before washing her breakfast bowl. Lingering. Relaxing. Enjoying the hot water on her skin. The warm, six-inch, bucket baths she'd been taking didn't have the same ability to satiate emotions the way long, steaming hot showers did. She was desperate for a shower. It was one of her top three things she missed about town life—and the list was long.

"Morning, Jade." Meera walked into the kitchen, and by her cheerful greeting, Jade knew she had a spring in her step.

"Morning," Jade replied. "What's, ah, what's new with you?" She quickly grabbed her bowl that had been soaking unnecessarily and washed it while she awaited Meera's reply.

"Glad you asked. Today we are going to switch things up a little. First things first, no cleaning." Meera paused just long enough for her words to soak in. Jade turned to her, unable to stop the smile spreading across her face. Meera continued pretending she hadn't noticed, "First, you and I are going to take a walk, so I hope you're wearing your comfy shoes. Then, you have something else to attend to this morning, which I'll tell you more about later. But, it's going to be a fun-filled day—I can tell you that."

Jade had not seen Meera excited before. Joyful, yes. Kind and considerate, yes. Focused, annoyingly so. But, excited? No. This was new.

"OK. That sounds… wait. Really? No cleaning?" Jade asked as she dried her hands on the tea towel. "Why?" She looked quizzically at Meera.

"Because the Lady on the Hill—Rose—said so." Jade didn't move. She wanted more than blind obedience as a reason for such a drastic change in the schedule.

"She didn't give me a reason." Meera sighed when she saw Jade wasn't budging. "She rarely does. But, I can tell you that days like today are an acknowledgment of the effort on your part and stem from positivity. Now," she said ushering Jade out of the kitchen, "go and get your shoes on, use the loo, do whatever you need to do, and I'll meet you by your camper in…," she glanced at her pocket watch, "ten minutes." Still skeptical of the whole thing, Jade moved. She wasn't about to give up the chance to skip cleaning.

Jade followed Meera down the same path she and Avi had walked the week before. They were headed towards the clearing with the elk. Jade shook her head trying to dispel the unwanted images threatening to surface in her mind. Meera wasn't nearly as stealthy as Avi, birds and chipmunks alike were sounding the alarm of their passing. Meera hummed as she walked, and she seemed to be more interested in looking at the sky and the trees around her than where she was walking.

"Where are we going?"

"You'll see," she called back without slowing.

Jade grumbled silently to herself—why all the mystery? Why couldn't the people here just come out and say what they meant directly? She welcomed the notable dip in temperature at the bottom of the hill and marched up to the clearing on the other side, her thoughts swirling alongside the breeze. Meera was waiting for her in the clearing, and she turned when Jade reached her.

"Right," she said, "Here we are. This is Ma Labyrinth." Her voice was softer now, hushed, and Jade took immediate notice of her surroundings—scanning the trees, bushes, and nearby grasses as Avi had taught her. Whispered voices usually meant danger.

"What's *Ma Labyrinth*?" Jade asked.

"Follow me. She's just over here." Meera veered toward the path on the left Jade had been curious about. The path with the round symbol on it.

The two women walked slower now that they had turned off the main trail and made their way toward the clearing. The pace felt sacred, like walking down the central aisle of a church rather than into a clearing in a forest.

The pink object Jade had seen from the trail with Avi was clearly visible now. It was a huge piece of Rose Quartz set as the centrepiece in an elaborate stone maze. Jade looked closely and saw the maze was constructed of rocks varying in size—some as small as a fist and others that would be better described as small boulders. Each stone was touching its neighbour creating circular lines swirling toward the chunk of quartz.

"Wow," Jade whispered.

"Isn't she beautiful?" Meera asked.

"She?"

"Yes. She. Let me make the formal introductions. Ma Labyrinth, this is Jade," Meera gestured to Jade, "and Jade, this is Ma Labyrinth, also affectionately known as just Ma."

"Ma?" Jade looked at Meera, completely lost in the one-sided conversation.

"Yes. Ma." Meera smiled. "Labyrinths are a symbol of the Divine Mother. They are a place of contemplation. A place to seek answers, to walk, and some even say to connect to and feel held by the divine feminine energy."

Jade refrained from making a woo-woo joke. She'd been here three months now (89 days, but who's counting) and knew better. Still, this mystical stuff took her by surprise now and then. She diverted her gaze back to the swirling lines that were supposed to represent some enigmatic woman. Her mother, Jade thought, would have loved this shit.

"So, it's a maze," Jade said as she tried to get her eyes to track a path to the centre, failing each time. "What if you take a wrong turn?"

"What? No, no, no. She's not a maze, and you can't get lost in Ma's Labyrinth," Meera said trying to hide a smile. "A Labyrinth doesn't have options. Even when you think you're getting farther away from the centre, you just have to trust putting one foot in front of the other, and eventually you'll get there—to her heart."

They both stood silent for a moment. The only sound was the faint breeze sliding between the needles of the trees.

"So, what do we....do?" Jade asked.

"Well, first we offer—always—whether it's to Ma, or to a plant we want to harvest from, or like Avi did, I'm sure, when he met the elk." Meera pulled out that little leather pouch everyone had and dug her fingers around inside until they emerged with a pinch of something between them.

"These herbs are from the land, some cultivated here at the centre and others gathered from the wild," Meera said as she handed the pouch to Jade. "The mixture includes plants like Yarrow flowers, Lavender, Arnica petals, Rose petals, Cornflowers, and of course Tobacco—grown from a strain dating back over a thousand years." She spoke softly, reverently, as she handed Jade the pouch. Jade took a pinch and examined the tiny flecks of different coloured plants in her palm. "The frequency of each of the flowers holds a narrative of place and purpose, a medicine if you will," Meera said. Jade watched her carefully, preparing her offering just as Meera directed.

"So, about your offering and how it's done. First, you take the herbs into the palm of one hand making a cup like this." Then she put her other hand on top so the pinch of herbs was between her palms, hands clasped firmly but gently. "And then, you blow on them like this. So your life force energy coats each part of the plant." She blew in the hole by her thumb knuckles and then opened up her palms. She blew again until all the herbs were sprinkled on the ground at the opening to the labyrinth… to Ma.

"OK…," Jade said trying to keep an open mind, "and, we do this because why?"

"Because when you work with the Divine, the Holy in Nature," Meera looked at her, creased her forehead slightly, and began again. "When you want something, what do you do?"

"I dunno?" Jade said, "Go and buy it?"

Meera smiled. "Well, sort of. You go and find what it is you want. You check its price, you pay, and then you get it, right?"

"Yeah," Jade said looking over at the lines of rocks.

"When you work with the Holy in Nature, your soul is wanting something. And so first, you must offer something of yourself, a heartbeat, a thought, prayers, gratitude, a song, your breath… you put yourself in a position to re-ceptivity, by first coming into reciprocity—you've got to give to get." Meera smiled.

"OK," Jade said, not convinced, but still she followed Meera's lead and blew on her pinch of herbs. Then she offered them to the ground at the entrance. She felt foolish. Like Tinkerbell blowing pixie dust.

"Great!" Meera said. "And now we walk." Meera took off her shoes and socks and placed them to the side. "Hold a question in your mind, or don't— it's up to you. But whatever you do, try not to let your mind wander too far. Keep it on the here and now."

Rather reluctantly and not too keen to be standing on the cold, damp ground, Jade removed her shoes and socks. She looked at her feet, almost the colour of snow, and wondered when the last time they had seen the light of day. Not since before her arrival for sure, but when before that?

She started to walk, following Meera as she had followed Avi. Walking solemnly, looking this way and that all the while trying to keep a respectful distance from Meera. She examined the labyrinth itself as she ambled along. The path was wide enough for two people to cross if both turned sideways and roomy if one was walking alone. The ground was covered with animal prints. She recognized the deer and dog prints, but not the others. Together the footprints created an intricate pattern on the earthen ground. A worn path of bare ground showed her where walkers had stepped before her, and the edges of the path were speckled with little plants waking from their winter sleep. Little trinkets were nestled in between the rocks or draped over them. Treasures people had left behind. Each one, Jade could tell, had a story: the gold necklace with a crystal pendant, the little cherub figurine, the multiple heart-shaped rocks.

A tinkling sound like an old doorbell announcing your arrival in a country store startled Jade from her musings. She saw that Meera had bent down to ring a tiny brass bell—its sound was much larger than its size indicated. Meera offered no explanation over her shoulder; she just continued on her way. Perhaps, Jade thought, you rang it to announce to Ma that you were here. So, when she arrived at the place where the bell was a few steps later, she also picked up the delicate handle and rang it. But to the best of her knowledge, no one showed up to ask her what it was she wanted or how they could be of service.

Meera reached the Rose Quartz. She bowed down and placed her forehead on it briefly. Then stood up and started walking back towards Jade and presumably the exit of Ma. Jade stood still, unsure of proper maze etiquette, but Meera, simply turned her shoulder to shuffle past Jade and kept walking—her eyes never lifting from the ground in front of her. Jade continued along the path to the quartz stone.

When she got to the centre, she took a moment to look around. Meera was right. There were no other options or dead ends along the way. Even when the lines circled away from the centre, they weren't taking you amiss. Returning her attention to the Rose Quartz, she saw a crystal angel standing at its base, sparkling in the sun. Jade put her hands on the Quartz just as Meera had, but she lowered her head too quickly and smacked her forehead against the crystal with a thunk. She stood up and rubbed her head, feeling a slight indentation and a rush of embarrassment. She patted her forehead a few times checking for blood, found none, and looked back at Meera to see if she had witnessed the collision. Thankfully, Meera was still walking, muttering something to herself, and looking fixedly at the ground before her. Rubbing her head once more, Jade turned and walked out much faster than she had walked in. Meera was sitting on a wooden bench waiting for her when she finally emerged from Ma.

Before Jade could say anything, Meera made a spinning motion with her finger and said, "Now you turn and offer your head to the ground in gratitude."

Jade got down on her hands and knees and placed the now throbbing part of her forehead on the cool ground. The song lyrics to "Kiss the Rain" flitted through her mind, although she replaced the word rain with ground.

"How was that?" Meera asked.

"OK, I guess," Jade said, unsure of how it was supposed to be. "A nice walk for sure."

Meera nodded. She had a piece of cloth in her hands Jade hadn't seen earlier.

"This," she said, as she unfolded the cloth into a long silken scarf, "is called an Angavastra. It is a sacred scarf, a symbol of a meeting, of attending a sacred act." Jade stared at the scarf with interest. The cloth was a brilliant blue and made of silk. It reminded her of the white Tibetan one her mother had received when she had travelled to Buddhist monasteries before Jade was born. Meera reached up and placed the blue scarf around Jade's neck. "This one is for you. To acknowledge your first meeting with Ma." She then took a step back and smiled. "That looks beautiful on you, with your red hair and Irish skin."

Jade held the ends of the scarf in her hands. The cloth was thin and creased easily, but Jade loved the way the colour looked in the sun. It was the colour of the sea. It was the colour she had always thought happiness looked like. It was the colour of the doors and windows on the white buildings covering the Greek island her mother had had a painting of. "Someday we'll go together darlin," floated up from the depths of her memories. She swallowed the lump in her throat and took a slow, deep breath, "Thank you, Meera."

Meera, in that way she had of always knowing what Jade was thinking, smiled gently at her and said, "You're welcome. Now, go find Avi and Aaden. They're waiting for you in the meadow."

"Why?" Jade asked, worried another dead carcass waited for her.

"You'll see," she said, sitting back down on the wooden bench. "I'm going to sit here for a bit. Try to take Ma with you into the rest of your day, OK? And perhaps you will see things start to change."

15 Skills

Jade could see the men sitting in the meadow. Their two, thin forms were sitting on the ground, hunched over something that was too far away to identify. As she got closer, she could see they were sitting on a blanket working on something with their hands. They were surrounded by grasses: some green and barely above the ground and some from the previous fall sticking up every which way like morning hair—surviving the winter had taken its toll.

She felt a momentary flash of pride that she was able to get close enough to quietly say hello before they noticed her. Avi greeted her with a soft grunt and a nod of the head and Aaden with his wide-mouthed smile. She could now see what was in their hands. Avi held scissors and Aaden a needle and thread.

"Come and sit," Aaden said as he moved over to make space for her on the blanket. "We're making offering pouches as part of my ecology studies."

"Cool," she said sitting down to join them thinking of Meera's pouch from earlier this morning.

Avi held a piece of leather in his hand and lovingly rubbed his thumb against the soft hide as he spoke. "Many Native cultures made and used these pouches. Here in North America as well as in South and Central America, India, and Asia. Probably Africa, too. They're universal." He brought the leather to his nose and inhaled deeply as if he were smelling the sweetest flower. "The pouches were made of different materials in different places, but they all had the same purpose: to hold the medicine, the offering, to support the teaching."

After one last gentle caress, Avi handed Jade the leather. She nodded her thanks and took them carefully, turning over the two identically shaped tan pieces. He continued, "The Lady taught me when I came here and offered me my start. I believe she received her start from her teacher in India. And now it's time for me to pass the knowledge to you."

He pointed to some tools on the blanket beside Aaden. "Grab the leather hole punch—the awl it's called—from beside Aaden. Aaden, you show her how to line up the two pieces and poke them through so they're ready for stitching."

"OK," Aaden said, handing Jade the awl.

She moved a little closer to Aaden and watched as he showed her how to prepare the bag for stitching. He pierced the leather with care, each hole the same distance apart, the same distance from the edge. He worked slowly, and patiently, and seemed to be mouthing something, but Jade figured he was just bopping along to his soundtrack as usual. The leather was soft and warm in her hands—not quite alive, but not exactly dead either. She started to punch holes along the edge, working her way clockwise as Aaden had done. The leather did not want to be pierced and resisted each hole punch. Over and over she felt like it was trying to tell her that skin wasn't meant to have holes pierced into it and that she should give up. Nevertheless, she kept at it, trying not to jump each time the awl punched through the skin in sudden victory.

"Motherfu…" Jade muttered as the awl pierced through the hide and jabbed her in the calf. Again.

"The Lady on the Hill says she utters a prayer of intention with each hole," Aaden said without looking up, "and a thank you with each stitch. That way the bag's creation holds the energy of reciprocity." He looked up then. His eyes briefly held hers and smiled. She looked back at the leather pieces in her hands and nodded.

"What kind of intention?" Jade asked still focusing on punching each hole evenly. *Motherfucker* probably wasn't going to be on Rose's list of approved intentions she thought.

"Well," Aaden said enthusiastically, "my intention is to learn to be in the right relationship with the land. So, I'm hoping each time I use my pouch I'll get a little closer to that."

"And yours, Avi? What's the intention for your pouch?" Jade asked.

"Well, lass, I'm not making a pouch for myself today—I have mine already," he said tapping the bag that was always on him whenever he was outside. "This one's a gift. But, my intention is to remember," he said, as he unwound a strange type of thread from a small ball into arm-length strips. It looked like string, but dead. "Always to remember." Jade almost asked, "To remember what?" but held her tongue.

Jade continued piercing holes along the border of her offering pouch, setting the intention of happiness. It wasn't as profound as to remember or as useful as connecting to the land maybe, but the only thing she seemed to have forgotten was how to be happy, so she went with that. She began to mouth "happiness" over and over. Sometimes it was "fucking happiness" or "goddamn happiness" and on a few occasions "fuck you, happiness" when the awl jabbed into her skin, but she figured the general thought was what counted.

Once she had all the holes punched, Avi showed her how to stitch the two pieces together with the strange string he had measured out earlier.

"What's the string made of, Avi?" Jade asked as she wove it in one hole and out another.

"That would be sinew."

"Sinew? Like….flesh you mean?"

"The tendon of a deer, not its flesh."

Jade stopped sewing and looked at Avi. "Gross!" she said, dropping the needle and "thread" to the ground.

Neither Avi nor Aaden lifted their eyes at her outburst—their attention fully focused on what they were doing. Jade returned her gaze to the pouch on the blanket in front of her and contemplated her progress—the holes carefully punched and evenly spaced. She thought about what she had learned in school about the First Nations and how out of respect for the animal's life, nothing was wasted. "Well," she murmured, "I guess the bag is made out of the skin of a deer, so…," her voice trailed off and she continued working. Avi and Aaden smiled into their laps. The three of them settled into a silent rhythm of hole-punching and stitching, prayers and thank-yous, breaths in and breaths out. It was comforting, companionable, and calming. When the stitching was complete, she threaded a thin braided leather lace around the top of it so it would close. She held the completed pouch in her hand and felt a burst of pride. It wasn't perfect, but it was hers.

"Here, Jade," Aaden said when she had finished admiring her handiwork. "Have a pinch of the herbs from my pouch to get yours started." He leaned forward to put a couple of pinches of herbs in her bag and left behind a smell of soap and a spice she couldn't quite place.

"And here, lass, let me make an offering to your start as well," Avi said as he opened his pouch.

"Thank you," Jade said. "Guess I'll check to see if my dried Mullein is ready, and if so, I can add some of that, too. Right?" Aaden looked up from his bag and smiled.

"For sure!" he said.

Avi clapped his hands once and then rubbed them together—the universal teacher sign that indicates one lesson is over and another one is about to commence. "Let's get this packed up and start on our second skill for the day," Avi said.

Aaden stood up and began packing away the tools they had used to assemble the pouches.

"What's next?" Jade asked.

"Fox walking and rifle shooting," Aaden said and pulled a bag of something out of his pocket. He handed her two chocolate-covered almonds. When she raised her eyebrows to ask where he got this from, he only winked in reply.

"You're gonna teach me how to shoot a gun?" Jade said through a mouthful of almond.

Avi frowned. "No, not you, lass. Rifle shooting is on Aaden's list today," he said taking off his shoes and socks. He balled up his socks and put them back in his shoes for safekeeping—a leftover habit from his army days.

"And why not?" Jade demanded. "It's 'cause I'm a girl, isn't it?" She watched Aaden take off his shoes and socks.

Avi shrugged and said, "I'm here to teach who and what I'm told. I don't make the rules. Now, take off your shoes and put them over there." He said pointing to an old lone fir standing in the meadow.

Jade did as she was asked and took off her shoes.

"Now, listen up you two. Fox Walking, I learned back in the seventies by a man named Brown, who learned from his teacher, an Apache elder."

"Umm….isn't that like appropriation or something?" Jade asked sucking the chocolate from around the second almond. Avi paused and looked at her, thinking about her question.

"There's a difference between appropriation and honouring, lass. Appropriation claims to own or have invented something ancient and honest. Honouring is sharing or embodying what is ancient. Being honest by holding tight and praising the line of its lineage so that the truth can sing for itself." Avi looked north towards Rose's cabin.

"Oh," Jade said, following Avi's gaze to the cabin to see if Rose was visible. She wasn't.

"Truth teachings are not of race or creed, but of lineage and soul. You must know the line of teachers, of ancestors, and offer up praise to that line. Always." Avi looked at Aaden. "And this practice has come through Brown."

"I've heard of that guy," Aaden said. "So cool, you got to meet him."

"Aye, I did. He's who got me started on my path. I'm forever grateful. Now," he said stepping off the blanket and onto the cold ground. "Fox Walking is a way of maneuvering so that you can listen to the land, see the big picture, and track an animal all at the same time." He took ten steps in one direction and then turned and walked back to them. He looked like a burglar from an old *Inspector Gadget* cartoon. Jade had to look away to stop herself from laughing. "It lets you walk quietly so you can look at what you're stalking and not where you're walking." He took another few steps to demonstrate. "It lets you become part of the land," he said checking to make sure they both were watching. He slowed down and exaggerated his movements even more. He bent his knees and kept his body over his left foot as he stepped with his right. He kept the right foot out and front of him and then slowly lowered it to the ground. He placed the outside edge of his foot on the ground first, before rolling onto the ball, then putting the heel of his foot on the ground and finally transferring his weight to his right foot.

Aaden tried to mimic the process but lost his balance and stumbled sideways. Jade hadn't even bothered to try.

"You got to keep your balance, lad. Bend your knees quite a bit, more than you think you should, ya see? Walk in a way that confirms your step before your weight commits." He took a few more steps, demonstrating again, and then gestured to the both of them to practice.

"Outside of your foot, then roll onto the ball, place your heel, then move your weight. Four stages, then repeat," he said.

Aaden and Jade tried to do as he said. He watched them critically.

"Make sure your foot is fully on the ground before you move your body forward, Jade. In case you step on a sharp stick or a thistle, you want to move your foot to a new spot before you put weight on it. Trust me on that."

Jade nodded; she felt ridiculous but kept it to herself.

"That's it, Aaden! Now shorten your gait and go twice as fast. Don't look at the ground in front of you, but look a hundred steps ahead at all times. There's a squirrel on the right—can you see it?" Both Jade and Aaden looked to the right. Sure enough, a squirrel was sitting on a branch just out of human reach watching them. Jade was sure it was mocking them. "And how 'bout whatever is making the grass move at ten o'clock? See the grass waving? You aren't going to see those things if you're looking at your feet."

Jade tried to spot the grass moving in any special way over to her left, but she couldn't see anything.

"Right, very good. Now turn around and count a hundred steps westward. Then come back again. Do it without looking at your feet if you can."

Jade turned with Aaden and started to walk towards the west, knees bent, looking forward, rolling from the outside to the inside of her foot, trying to remember to place her heel before moving her weight. She constantly felt like she was leaning backward and would fall at any moment. Aaden started to make a funny sound, and Jade glanced in his direction. He had his arms tucked in beside him, hands held at chest height. She burst out laughing.

Aaden stopped, his arms still hooked up beside his body. "What?"

"You. You look like a T-Rex trying to sneak up on something."

He lowered his hands and looked at her with an expression she had not seen before.

"What?" she said. "Why are you looking at me like that?"

"That's the first time I've heard you laugh, Brennan—or seen you smile even."

She liked the way he said her last name, formal yet familiar.

"It's been a while," she said. With that, she turned and started Fox Walking back to Avi tucking her arms like a T-Rex; she could hear Aaden chuckling behind her.

They practiced on the grasses and then graduated to the woods. Twigs and branches were strewn everywhere, highlighting the need for careful foot placement. A sharp jab between the toes and thorns plucked from tender flesh were better teachers than Avi's instructions and four-step-chant. Jade and Aaden tried to sneak up on a robin and then a flock of pine siskins, but both times they stumbled before they could get close enough for Avi to deem their stalking successful. As the sun peaked in the sky, they returned to where Avi was sitting in the shade of an old fir, his back against its thick trunk. "That was good, you two. You've got much still to learn, but you should be satisfied with your beginnings." He rose from his seated position and dusted off his pants.

"It's lunchtime now. After lunch, Aaden, you are with me, for shooting. Jade, you report to Meera for instructions. OK?"

"Why can't I learn to shoot?" Jade asked again hoping that he'd somehow changed his mind since the last time she'd asked.

"Ah, I don't think so," said Avi, his moustache twitched as he looked at her. "As I said before, lass, those weren't my instructions."

"Well, who do I speak to to get the instructions changed? 'Cause if Aaden is learning, then I'd like to learn, too." Jade placed her hands on her hips as she spoke, indignant and defiant. For a brief moment, she wondered if they didn't want her to know how to shoot based on the damage she'd already done with a knife, but she quickly dismissed the thought. She waited for him to answer.

Avi tried to stare her down but relented before too long. "Alright. I'll go and talk to the Lady while you're at lunch. But, whatever she says is final.

OK?" Jade hesitated for half a second, stunned by Avi's quick retreat, and nodded. "OK," she said. "Deal."

Jade and Aaden started to walk back to the centre for lunch. They hadn't gone more than a few feet when they noticed Avi wasn't with them. Aaden and Jade turned back to see what was keeping him. "You coming Avi?" "Don't worry about me for lunch, lad. Apparently, I've got some things to attend to. I'll eat later, don't fret." He said with a wave and then started in the opposite direction to them, toward Rose's cabin.

And for the second time that day, Jade smiled.

16 Beryl

Jade and Aaden walked down to Foxwalk Valley, as they had named it over sandwiches, just as Avi was walking down from Rose's cabin on the other side of the valley. They had debated calling it T-Rex Training Grounds, but Foxwalk Valley fit better with the centre's vibe. And it didn't dissolve them into giggles each time they said it. Avi had a rifle slung over each shoulder and something cradled in his arms. They met up with him at the valley bottom and the three of them continued down to the back of the property, meandering over the land the way streams run down to the river.

Jade still couldn't believe her good fortune. Meera had stepped away to take a phone call halfway through lunch, and when she returned she let Jade know she had received the go-ahead to learn to shoot. Jade and Aaden had cheered at the news. Then Meera handed Aaden a sandwich for Avi and shooed them out the door. "Don't make that man wait for you, especially on an empty stomach!" she had called to their receding backs.

Avi led the way through the thicket of baby firs to where a lone, rickety old picnic table sat on the edge of a boggy clearing. There were no trees—only knee-high shrubs, some spiky grasses and a smattering of wildflowers here and there. The air was still.

"Right. Now, Jade, you take these cans," Avi said uncradling them from his arms, "and line 'em up on the box you see over there."

Aaden and Jade looked in the direction he was pointing and saw a wooden crate nearly overgrown by shrubs about a hundred feet away.

"And, Aaden, you take these," he said, giving him a small handful of balloons from his pocket. "Blow them up and then put two every ten feet or so towards the cans."

When they had finished their tasks and returned to Avi, they saw he had laid out the rifles on the old picnic table and was sitting there looking contemplative. Jade resisted the urge to make some cowboy joke as she walked up—*Allllllright, pardner. This town ain't big enough fer the both of us*—and instead waited patiently for Avi to begin the lesson. After a few moments, he slapped his hands on his thighs, stood up, and said, "Right, now. First lesson. Always hold a gun facing the sky or facing the ground." He grabbed the closest gun on the table and demonstrated.

"Makes sense," Aaden said in a low, joking voice to Jade. She pursed her lips and tried not to giggle.

"This is a .22 bolt action rifle with a scope," Avi said. "It's good for small game like rabbits and such. And this," he said placing it back on the table and picking up the one that looked like an antique with its wooden butt and steel barrel, "is a Winchester 30-30 named Beryl. This model of rifle has been around awhile, more than a hundred years or so and used for deer and elk. It's old. The open sight isn't very accurate, but it always works. It's also dangerous as hell and really easy to go off. So *don't* muck around." He put Beryl back on the table. "Any questions so far."

"Yeah," said Aaden, "Um, why's the gun named Beryl?"

"'Cause, my dear boy, this is *my* rifle, and Beryl was my late wife's name." He touched the rifle laying inert on the table. "And just like she was, Beryl here is sturdy. She'll always feed you if you treat her right, and if you don't, it'll hurt… a lot."

A buzzing punctuated Avi's speech as his phone started to vibrate from the pouch at his hip. It amused Jade to see him pull out a flip phone like the one she used to play with as a child when she pretended to work or call an auntie. Seeing who it was, Avi put his finger up to them—asking for quiet and privacy while also offering an apology for the interruption—and then walked a few steps away.

Aaden turned to Jade while Avi took the call. "Alllll-righty then," he said doing his best Jim Carrey impersonation, and he looked at her with his eyebrows raised questioningly, "Did you know?"

Jade just shrugged and shook her head. It had never occurred to Jade that Avi could have been married. She hadn't thought past the little information Meera had given her about his past. Before she could say anything to Aaden, Avi ended his call and rejoined them.

They started with the .22. Avi, showed them how to load the clip, using bullets much smaller than Jade would have imagined them to be. When he was finished, he handed the rifle to Jade, and she stood holding it in her hands. How many people had been killed by rifles, she wondered. It seemed so easy—too easy—to kill something. She did her safety check and then loaded the bullet into the chamber using the bolt action Avi had shown them: click-click.

"OK," Avi said from behind her, "Steady does it."

Jade lifted the cold rifle and went through Avi's instructions in her mind: stock against cheek, butt locked into shoulder, index finger out straight along the body of the rifle, line up your shot. Avi grunted his approval of her positioning and said, "Put your front foot a little more forward, lass, not that you need it for this one, but it's a good habit for bigger pieces."

She moved her foot forward and found the yellow, smiling emoji balloon looking back at her from the grass. She always thought shooting a gun would feel more badass, or exhilarating. Instead, it just felt like any other skill that needed to be done, like driving a car or building a fire. One careless slip-up and they could kill you or someone else, but in the right hands and used correctly, they were tools—life skills—nothing more, nothing less.

She fumbled her hand to find and release the safety; lined up the yellow, cartoonish grin looking at her with unblinking eyes; curled her finger around the trigger; and—

BAM!

No more grin.

"Ha! I hit it!"

"Yeah, ya did. Great shot!" Aaden crowed.

"Nice shot," Avi said, taking the gun from her and handing it to Aaden for his turn. Aaden fired three times before he hit the balloon staring him down. Jade cheered and congratulated him. Then, one by one they took out the rest of the balloons, each shot progressively farther away from the last until they were nearly at the cans. When the last balloon met its demise, Avi took back the.22, and they returned to the picnic table.

"Now, Beryl has been used for hunting for many generations. She's simple. No bells and whistles. She's not overly accurate at long range because she uses an open sight rather than a scope, but she works. Rain or shine. Whether it's warm out or freezing. She always works," Avi said fondly. Then just as he had with the.22, he showed them the steps for loading, sighting, safety (if you could call it that), and shooting.

Having completed his tutorial, Avi took a step towards Jade with the rifle; she instinctively took a step back.

"I'm good, thanks anyway," she said as she put her hands up to pass. A rifle that's been in use for over a hundred years sounded to her like a disaster waiting to happen. Yet, Avi would not be deterred.

"If you handle her with the care and respect that she is owed, then you will do alright," he said. But the look he gave her said: *You demanded I teach you to shoot, so pick up the gun and stop wasting my time.* "Here," he reached the rifle out to her, "It's not loaded."

Jade took the rifle. Its weight felt almost double that of the.22, and its ammunition seemed gargantuan. After some reassurance and a little coaxing, Avi guided her through how to load a single bullet. "First, pull the handle down and then snap it back into place." When she'd done that, he said, "Now look, the hammer is back. So it's cocked and ready to fire. Hold the hammer with your thumb and then slowly pull the trigger halfway. You'll feel it release the hammer, but the hammer's not firing 'cause of your thumb. Now, slowly lower the hammer." Jade did as she was instructed, resisting the urge to just hand it back to him, certain she was going to screw up and kill them all.

"When the hammer is in its neutral position, that's its safety position. If you cock the hammer back again, it's live. Got it? Good. You're ready. Line up that bubble at the top of the pin into the bottom of the V here," Avi said as Jade brought the stock up to her check again; this time she felt anxious and unsure. "Aim for the bottom of the can."

Jade closed her left eye and focused on her breath. She breathed in and out a few times as she found her aim. Then she lowered and cocked the hammer again. Avi's voice floated in over her shoulder, "It's live now. You touch that trigger, it's going off. Easy does it."

She lined Beryl back up and—

BAM!

Jade brought the rifle down, pointing at the ground, and looked at the cans. All three still stood on the box, mocking her.

"Now, open up the hammer again and discharge the casing," Avi instructed from behind her.

"Boo," Jade said, opening up the hammer and ejecting the case.

"That was a good shot. You were close. A bit more practice and you'll have it."

Jade handed Avi the rifle with the hammer open and stepped aside to allow Aaden to have his turn.

Aaden missed his first shot at the cans as well, but his second was a hit. The can jumped in surprise and tumbled off the crate to the ground. Jade tried three more times to hit a can but missed each time. By her final shot, her shoulder was sore from Beryl's kick.

"Alright, you two. I think you have a solid grasp of things. Just remember, there's a big difference between taking your time and aiming for a can and shooting at something in self-defence. That," he said nodding in agreement with himself, "is a whole other ball game." He slung the rifles over his shoulders and said, "Go and get the balloon pieces and the cans, and I'll see you at dinner."

"Thanks, Avi, sir," Aaden said as the old man turned and started to head back.

"Yeah, thanks, Avi," Jade called out as he got further away.

"Tat-Twam-Asi," they heard from beyond the thicket of baby firs.

Jade and Aaden just looked at each other and laughed. They quickly gathered up the bits of balloons, the cans, and the shell casings—double-checking that the area was clean before they, too, headed back toward the centre. On the walk, they revisited the events of the day—events so fresh in their minds that they could hardly be called memories. The conversation flowed. No awkward pauses or feelings of unease. Each shared their experiences with the pouches "Punching all those holes was fucking hard!"—"No kidding! You should've seen my first attempt…" and the rifles "I thought the whole thing was going to backfire, blow my face off"—"Like the old-timey Westerns?! Tell me about it…". They dissected the process of loading and firing the.22 and Beryl, reciting the steps and reminding one another of anything missing—both eager to perform flawlessly the next time Avi took them out. In no time at all, they were chatting like old friends, sprinkling in tidbits from their past lives. Every time they locked eyes, Jade felt more at home.

17 Fires of Freedom

Although Rose is sitting facing the altar in the main meditation room with her back to the door, she knows it's Jade who clamours into the room by the timbre of her movements: the sliding of her stocking feet across the floor, the colliding bucket and broom against the door frame as she tries to carry everything at once, the mild curses muttered under her breath. She smiles at the "mother fruit snacks" when Jade's elbow catches the corner. *She's trying at least,* Rose thinks, *she's trying.*

Rose has been waiting for Jade to land, waiting for her to stop resisting the space with objections. And now, after hearing reports of laughter and connections being made, she wants to see where Jade sits. Who she is when she's not being a scared child locked into a constant battle between fight, flight, and freeze. Rose wants to know if Jade is ready for the truth.

She hears the door shut with a thud, and then all noises cease as Jade must now realize she's not alone in the room. Rose can tell the girl doesn't know what to do: leave again or start cleaning. She feels her standing there, indecision emanating from her in waves.

"It's OK, Jade," Rose says. "I'll only be a minute more."

The bucket is placed as quietly as possible on the floor, and she hears Jade lean the broom handle against the wall. The water finishes sloshing against the sides of the bucket, and the room returns to its previous state of tranquillity.

Rose looks down at the framed picture in her hand. It takes her back to a time that is only measured in years, yet feels like lifetimes ago. Her teacher sits in the middle of the frame. His body is elderly, delicate rather than frail, but his presence is commanding—even in two dimensions.

In the picture, he is surrounded by four fires. His light cocoa-coloured skin is smeared in ash, and a bun of grey hair is piled high on his head. Around his neck hang multiple strands of thumb-sized beads and black thread tied into bulbous knots. At the time she had taken the photo, she hadn't understood all the symbology of each item, each gesture. It was likely her innocence, her naïveté, that allowed her to do her duty of making sure he had what he needed without imposing her presence on him. It was an art she had learned well over the years: how to be present without being intrusive.

"Perhaps you could first wipe these for me, Jade," she says turning slightly with the frame in hand so Jade can see which cloth to bring. "Come sit. We can do this together." She pats the cushion next to her, and after a few seconds, she hears Jade coming in her direction, sliding across the cork floor. The young girl kneels beside her, and then perhaps feeling too close, she slides to create a bit more distance between them. It's not much, but the inches speak of her uneasiness.

Rose hands the picture to Jade to clean and then reaches for another frame from the altar. But Jade is not dusting it. Instead, she is just sitting there, looking at the picture with slightly squinted eyes as she studies the photograph. She appears to be trying to take it all in, every crumb of information the photo provides, one piece at a time.

"That was my teacher," Rose says preemptively. "He was a kind man, almost grandfatherly. You could feel the most exquisite frequency of unconditional love emanating from him. But he was also a fierce man. Disciplined. Courageous. And he suffered no fools. He required obedience and sincerity, but in return, he offered the keys to your soul's freedom."

"Is he still alive?" Jade asks.

"No, he left his body many years ago now, but still, he is with me," Rose says tapping her chest.

"What's he doing?" Jade asks, her eyes never moving from the photo.

"He is doing something called an Anusthan. A discipline that enables great calibration, or great…" Rose searches for a word that the girl can understand. "… purification."

"By sitting in front of some fires?"

"Yes. It looks like that. But it's more. Much more. The heat of those fires gets up to 90 degrees Celsius. Yes, 90 degrees," she says again at Jade's I-call-bullshit-face. She continues, "It is by grace and endurance, by the purity of his mind and of his heart, that he was able to sustain so many hours, day after day, year after year. Sitting. Chanting. Shedding all the layers that he no longer needed."

"What do you mean 'shedding'?" Jade asks. "Do you mean sweating?"

Rose smiles warmly; Jade does not see as she has not taken her eyes off the delicate man in the frame. "The five fires—the four here," Rose points to each one, "and the Sun in the sky, represent the five fires or afflictions of the mind. He was able to feel, witness, and disconnect from the frequencies…"

At this word, Jade looks up at her, and Rose can see she doesn't understand, that she can't yet comprehend what she is saying.

"Think of it like this," Rose offers. "Your thoughts create your reality. When your mind is full of anger, greed, jealousy, and so forth, then that is the reality you create. Through this Anusthan," Rose says taking the frame from Jade's hand and picking up the cloth to lovingly dust it herself, "he no longer identified with those aspects in his mind. He no longer lived in a reality that experienced those afflictions in the way we do."

Jade's gaze follows the picture as Rose returns it to the altar. "Cool," she says. "So, if you can weed out the… anger and…" she swirls her hand to continue the list without words, "from your mind, you'll never feel anger again?"

"Exactly. And then you can dream your world into form. You are… free."

"Free…," Jade whispers.

"Uh, sorry to interrupt," Meera says from the doorway. "But, there's a phone call for you, Rose. Do you want me to take a message or…?"

Rose looks again at the picture on the altar. She swears she can hear him speak directly to her some days, most days actually.

"Yes. Thank you, Meera. I'll be right there." She hands Jade the cloth. "Have a good day, Jade. Tat Twam Asi."

"Yeah, um, you too," Jade says, her eyes still looking at the man who offered his life to the fires and emerged free.

Summer

18 Letters

"I have been waiting for the right time to give these to you." Jade jumped at Rose's sudden appearance. It was as if she had sprung from the centre of the old tree by the drive rather than from behind it. Jade had been humming one of the morning chants while she tied her shoes on the little pallet deck in front of her camper. She was getting ready for the morning graze, and mulling over Aaden's behaviour at breakfast the day before. He had seemed distant, distracted. Like he had retreated to someplace no one else could get to. She had called him on it. And he had done his best to mask up with joy, said he was just nervous about the quest he was about to start, but she had seen through it. After all, she was the queen of masking up.

Rose sat down next to her and waited for her to finish tying her shoes. They were both silent, lost in their worlds and thoughts, waiting for the moment of convergence. When Jade had finished, Rose handed her an envelope. She turned it over several times, examining it curiously. The envelope was old and the address was a place in India. Jade looked at the neat handwriting on the front and frowned. Rose sat quietly, waiting. The moment Jade's fingers reached inside to remove its contents, Rose started to speak; her words stopping Jade mid-movement.

"Many years ago," she started "when you were two, your mother wrote to me." Jade was unprepared to hear Rose speak of her mother. She shifted uneasily in her seat and looked from the envelope to Rose. "I was still in India at that time," Rose went on. "Your mother and I had been together in India years before. We were close…family—she was like a little sister to me."

The last words—so weighted—made Jade stop breathing. The photo!

That's where she had seen Rose before. Her mother's photo. The sister she always talked about but who never visited. She opened her mouth to say something, but Rose continued speaking before she had the chance.

"But when our teacher left unexpectedly, your mother felt abandoned. She left without warning and returned to Canada. The letter in that envelope was the first piece of correspondence I received from her since her disappearance 7 years prior. I replied to her, as you will see," she nodded to the envelope in Jade's hands, "but I never heard from her again."

Jade held the envelope gently. It had faded over the years and felt soft, like it had been handled, and held. She peered inside and saw two folded pieces of paper—their folds worn, frayed from the need to read and reread the words within—to remember.

"When your mother passed, your aunt found my letter to her among her things. She contacted me to let me know what had happened," she paused, "When you got into trouble…," she paused again, the silence that followed, an acknowledgment that Rose knew everything, then she continued, "Carole asked to meet me in person. She asked if we would take you in for a year. She needed an answer right away so that she could make a proposal to the Crown Council. That is when she returned to me, my letter to your mother. She asked me to give it to you when the time was right." Rose stopped speaking and waited.

Jade, reeling from the unexpected connection to her mother, tried to focus on the red robin bouncing around on the ground looking for worms in the thawing earth. Sergeant Tibs—one of the many young cats at the centre—was off to the side, stalking the bird from behind a mound of sand, camouflaged. Tibs rolled her shoulders and crept silently along the ground, imperceptibly closing in on the unsuspecting bird. She paused, tail twitching as she readied herself to pounce. Jade moved her legs out straight and crossed her ankles startling the bird enough to make it fly to the nearest tree. Tibs sulked off and went to find a patch of morning sun; there she sat licking her paws in defeat.

"So, why now?" Jade asked. "Why do you think the time is right, now?" With no distraction of birds and cats to hold her attention, she noticed her chest was tense with suppressed emotion. Her words were sharp and biting.

"Because I feel that if you are going to make the most of this year, then you need to know that you were not discarded here. That you were not dumped, abandoned… or banished." Roses's words stung like lemon juice on an un-healed wound. Once again, Jade felt Rose had seen to her very core. She began to ask a question, but Rose's words stopped her short.

"I believe, in the light of the circumstances, that this is exactly where your mother would want you to be. Even without your legal troubles. You'll see for yourself when you read the letters." She leaned forward and turned to face Jade, her sunflower eyes locked onto Jade's aquamarine ones. "Read them when you're ready. Take your time. And I'm here if you have any questions."

Jade nodded her understanding and looked back at the envelope, entranced. The letters felt warm in her hand, almost alive. Realizing she was alone, Jade looked up and saw that Rose had started to make her way down the hill back to her cottage.

"Rose!" Jade called, standing up and taking a few steps towards her, making sure she had not disappeared into the trees. Rose stopped and turned to face her. "Um," Jade croaked. She lifted the envelope, its off-white reflecting like a beacon in the sun, signalling her thanks. Her throat was too choked with emotion to get the actual words out.

Rose smiled again, and Jade marvelled at how she hadn't seen the similarities between the woman in the photo that she looked at every day and the Lady on the Hill that she *also* looked at every day. Rose put her hands together at her heart and then continued on her way. Sam appeared next to Jade and leaned his weight into her leg. His big, white, fluffy coat—a grounding cloud she thought—welcomed her hand in for a pet. She felt like she might lose all control, but his solid form grounded the swirling questions and emotions inside her. Together, they stood in the cool morning sun watching Rose as she walked away.

Completely forgetting about the duty of grazing the goats, Jade sat cross-legged on her bed with the contents of the envelope in front of her. The sun streamed through the open door; its bright light splayed across the coverlet illuminating them as though nothing else in the world existed. With every bone in her body, she wanted to rip open the letters and devour her mother's words, Rose's words, and whatever had been created between them. But experience had taught her that the moment of connection would be fleeting. It would dissipate once she read what was written, never to be that first sweet contact again. And so she waited, replaying the morning's conversation with Rose over in her head.

Aunt Carole had known all along but never said anything. *Why*, Jade wondered, She recalled what Carole had said in the courtroom: that her family had a history with this lineage.

Finally, her desire to know outweighed her desire to wait, and she picked up one of the letters. It was on paper discoloured by time, and fingerprints smudged the outside folds—a letter that had been read and reread many times. *My dearest sister Angelica*, she read. No, no. This was from Rose to her mother. She quickly put it down, wanting to read the letters in order. Jade picked up the other one. Its paper was whiter, thicker. She scooted back and leaned against the wall. She braced herself to see her mother's handwriting as well as the words on the page and the spaces between them.

Beloved Sister,

I cannot believe it has taken me this long to write.

I guess that's what happens when guilt mixes with fear and marinates in time. Needing some time morphs into giving some time, and finally lands in not knowing how to take the time. For this I'm sorry. I never should've left without saying goodbye. Forgive me.

Jade had never known her mother to ask for forgiveness. She had seen her mother ferociously sidestep the opportunity to do so. She wondered what it would have felt like to have heard her mother say those words to her now.

Forgive me, Jade. Forgive me for dying. Forgive me for leaving. Forgive me for leaving you alone. Jade wiped her nose with her sleeve.

Since I last stood on the ground of Mother India on that fierce monsoon day, my world has changed in many ways—on the outside at least. I now reside in Canada and have a beautiful two-year-old baby girl named Jade. While her father and I have gone our separate ways—since before she was even born—I can say wholeheartedly that she is my gift from God.

Jade mouthed the words, *my gift from God,* and tried to imprint them physically into her body. She knew her mother loved her. She had told her all the time, in that annoying, eye-rolling way that mothers do, but *gift from God?* She had never even considered that her mother thought that much about God in general. She was into the Divine, the Great Spirit, and other woo-woo things—as she called them—but she had never heard her mother use the G word.

She has my fiery hair and looks as though she will be keeping my blue eyes as well. She knows what she wants when she wants it (I guess the apple really doesn't fall far from the tree?) and I can unequivocally say that her smile coaxes flowers to bloom.

As if on command, Jade smiled to herself. She paused a moment, trying to remember the last time she had genuinely smiled. Fox Walking she realized.

Fox Walking with Aaden. The thought made her smile widen.

Every time she giggles, I have to close my eyes and try to commit it to memory. I never knew birthing a child would simultaneously bring me so much closer to the experience of God, and drive me so crazy at the same time… I jest… sort of.

Ha! That's more like it! There's the mother she knew.

Jade is an old soul who has not yet forgotten who she is. She seems to live with much more clarity than I do 90% of the time. She is bright, funny and fierce, and I pray that her spark helps her to fly high when she is older. Not to crash and burn as it did me. May she learn from my many mistakes.

Ah… sorry, Mum. Guess not. Jade sighed and wiped her nose on her other sleeve. Crashed but not burning yet.

Sometimes I dream about bringing her back to India with me to see you and everyone there. Sharing that world with her; her with that world. Do you think it might be possible one day? Would you embrace her as your own the way I was embraced when I first arrived there? I think this is my one, true heart's desire. When at the end of the day I lie beside her and listen to her breathing, too afraid to get up and go back to the lounge for fear she will wake up—and wake the dead along with her—I long for India. Sometimes I just lie there and wonder what it would be like to live together again, with you, with her, at the feet of the teachings, in the lap of the Divine.

I want you to know that I have thought of you every day. Every single day. And I pray with all my heart that I will be blessed to see you again before our path in this life is done.

With all my heart,

Angelica

Jade tilted her head back and closed her eyes, momentarily unable to exhale. She felt as if her chest was about to burst, either from gratitude or grief, she could not yet tell which. Her mind spun with the phrases and words her mother had written about her: *a beautiful two-year-old baby girl—Jade, wholeheartedly that she is my gift from God… Would you embrace her as your own?*

Jade sat completely still, trying to commit the letter to memory. Five minutes passed, maybe ten. Only when she felt the words reach every part of her, head to toe, did she reach out for Rose's reply.

My Dearest Sister Angelica,

I am overwhelmed with joy to receive your letter. When I saw your hand's script amongst the mail the other day I had to sit down on the spot. I found myself staring at the envelope, long past a reasonable duration, trying to divine what it said without opening it to this world.

I am thrilled to hear that you are well and are now on the path of Motherhood. What an amazing soul she must be to have chosen you as her mother.

I am well. Content—most of the time. The monsoon season still being my most challenging time of year. The last few years more so, having been compounded by the echo of your departure. But I forgive you. How can I not? To hold you out of my heart would be to rip my own heart in two.

While I do not have my own child, (surprise surprise) we have been collaborating with a local orphanage over the past year. So I can empathize with you over navigating the fierce wisdom of a two-year-old who knows what they want and how to get it. I have deep respect for any parent who navigates the gauntlet of child-rearing on a constant day-to-day basis.

Of course, it goes without saying that you and Jade will always be welcome here, or wherever I am. It would give me tremendous joy to see you again and meet your little one. If there is anything you ever need, please do not hesitate to reach out to me.

Eternally yours.

Jade read it through twice for good measure. And then once more just so she could linger on the lines that made pieces of her broken world fall into place. *Jade will always be welcome here. If there is anything you ever need, please do not hesitate to reach out to me.*

She folded the letters, returned them to the envelope, and opened up the cupboard to her clothes. She dove her hand into the sea of cloth, feeling her way to the slightly scratchy cloth of her socks. Holding them in her hands, she felt inside the folds for the familiar sharp edge of the tab of Ativan and pulled them out. She curled the envelope to fit within the tube of the sock and slid it into the place where the pills had been. It was the safest place she had. For the most precious objects she had.

She sat back on her bed and looked at the rows of her little *just-in-case* beads of sunshine with two domes empty. She realized she didn't want them here anymore. But she didn't know what to do with them either. Perhaps she should give them to Rose....

"Miss Jade, the goats...," Avi's voice reached her a split second before the look on his face did. She tried to tuck the pills under her leg so he wouldn't see, but it was no use closing the gate after the horse had bolted. "What are those?"

"They are…" She looked down at the tab of Ativan, trying to decide if Avi would back off faster if she went defensive or decided to be truthful.

He stood calmly at the door, waiting for her to decide her course of action. He held his cards close to his chest.

"They're something I brought with me, and I was just sitting here trying to figure out how to give them to Rose without getting kicked out." She said, opting for the truth.

"Hmmph," Avi said, nodding slowly. He looked like he was weighing how much of that he believed. "And…?"

"And what?"

"And what is your plan?"

"I don't know. That's what I was trying to figure out."

He looked at her a moment longer and then said, "You had better go and feed the goats. They are getting very vocal about their neglect. They'd like you to know they haven't been fed in years."

"Oh, yeah. Sorry, um." She got up, looked at the tab, and then glanced back at Avi. She put the pills in her jean's pocket. "As soon as I see Rose, I'll hand them over." She turned and straightened up her bed, removing the last trace of the letters from the outside world. "You're not going to say something to Meera, are you?" she asked, feeling too vulnerable to say it directly to his face, but when she turned back to the door, he had gone.

She promptly removed the packet from her pocket, opened her cupboard once again, and nestled the blister pack in next to the letters. She turned back to see Sergeant Tibs, sitting in her doorway watching disapprovingly.

"You don't say anything either, OK?" she stated before shooing her out the door.

Indignantly, the cat turned and walked away, making no promises.

19 Meltdowns

Jade sat perched on her goat-grazing stump, staring out across the meadow, watching the land drink in the golden light of morning. She should have been seeking out the flitting movements of birds among the stillness of the trees and matching them to the identification book Avi had loaned her, but instead, her eyes were drawn across the pasture to the long strides of Aaden coming out of the outhouse. He didn't see her watching him. His attention was focused on the meditation area in the garden. He had been engaged in a week-long practice of self-inquiry and firekeeping—his quest—and Jade had been instructed not to bother him in any way. He had only mentioned it at the breakfast right before it began. Even then it was vacant statements that gave nothing away, save his brewing anticipation.

All Jade knew, was Aaden's quest seemed like a big deal. Like a milestone birthday or getting your first car kind of big deal. And not only to Aaden but to Avi and Meera as well. Avi was taking up more of the duties in the garden so Aaden could put his full attention on his quest, and Meera was helping, too. Jade had not yet been asked to help, but she had volunteered all the same. She turned back to the goats and watched them meander along the fenceless hillside, engrossed in their task of eating the spring growth before it had a chance to bloom into its fullness.

"OH MY GOD! NO! No! No-no-no-no-no-no-no. Noooooooooo!" a voice cried out. Each word pierced the still morning air.

The animals stopped and looked toward the disturbance, grass hanging from their mouths. Jade jerked her head up and followed their gaze. Together they tried to decide if they needed to employ freeze, fight, or flight. So far, freeze was winning.

"FIRE!" Avi's voice came bellowing from up the hill.

Jade jumped up, letting her book fall to the ground, and started to run towards the garden. Her long legs carried her quickly across the grazing area. At the last second, she remembered the goats. She stopped in her tracks, spun around, and stared at them. They returned her gaze, still frozen in indecision. "Don't you *dare* go anywhere," she said pointing a finger at them, and then she turned and ran without waiting for a reply.

Jade arrived at the garden's boundary fence, out of breath and clutching at the stitch in her side. She was momentarily mesmerized by the flames licking the air at chest height as they consumed the sleeping bag and blankets Aaden had laid out beside the fire pit. The smoke smelled like burnt marshmallows. The air shimmered with the heat.

Aaden had spent the last two days and nights sitting by that fire. Jade had stolen glances at him as she walked past multiple times a day. Even though each time there had not been much to see: Aaden sitting, Aaden staring into the fire, Aaden muttering something from a book in front of him as his finger traced along the lines as though they were written in braille.

Except now. Now he was clutching his head; his two hands buried in his hair. He paced back and forth like a caged lion, moaning and whimpering while he watched his bed go up in flames.

Jade caught movement out of the corner of her eye and turned to see Avi hauling the garden hose over. His long legs stepped over the newly planted wheat sprouts like Roald Dahl's BFG. By the time Jade ran around to the gate and into the garden, the fire was out. Nobody moved. They all just stood there staring at the soggy mess. Jade looked from Avi to Aaden. She was shocked at the anguish on his face—he looked as if he had just killed someone. She wanted to speak comforting words but was at a loss to find any.

"It's okay, Aaden," Avi said in a soothing voice. "It's not a big deal. You can try again."

"But it IS a big deal, Avi. It is! I failed!" He started to pace again. "I've been waiting and preparing for this for months. MONTHS! And… and…," he looked down at the fire pit. Steam and smoke danced together from the pile of half-burned wood that lay undecided as to whether it should burn or rot. Whatever Aaden was going to say next refused to be spoken and remained caught in his throat. He gave an anguished moan and then turned and ran.

"Aaden!" Jade called out in vain. "Come back!"

She watched him run down the garden path, stumbling through the gate and almost colliding with Meera and a young man Jade did not recognize, before disappearing westward into the forest.

"Let him go," Avi said dishearteningly.

Jade sighed. She and Avi stood silently, staring at the carnage that remained of Aaden's dream—now a shit pile of charred and soggy cloth, paper, and wood. Jade's heart broke for him.

Avi took a deep breath, "Give me a hand will you, Jade? Help get this mess cleaned up," he said as if the task needed clarification.

"Of course," she replied, bending down to grab the remnants of the book. Its pages no longer contained words of wisdom but slivers of silken ash that fell to the ground like grey snow when she lifted it.

They sorted through Aaden's things: compiling items that needed to go to the dump and items that could be salvaged. With each passing moment, Jade felt more and more emotional. It was as if the fire had released the fear and the shame and the despair that had been trapped in Aaden's belongings. And as Jade touched them, she felt each emotion as if they were her own.

She looked up at Avi, sadness and disappointment written across his face, too.

"Do you remember that song, the chant, the we do in the mornings?" he asked. "The one I chanted with you down at the elk?" Jade nodded. "Try and focus your mind on that. Let everything else pass through you."

They continued cleaning in silence; her mind now focused on words she did not understand but calmed her anyway. By the time they finished, only the faint smell of smoke lingered in the air and on their clothing. Avi declared that it was time for a cuppa, but first, they should get changed and Jade should check on the goats.

The word 'goats' had the same effect on Jade as a starter gun has on an Olympic sprinter. Eyes wide, she sprinted out of the garden and down to the field where she had been minding the goats before Aaden's cry drove everything from her mind. There were no goats to be seen. They, like Aaden, had disappeared into the forest.

20 Trees: Water

Home, sweet sister, is where we all stand tall. Not in spite of our neighbours, but because of them.

Because we understand the delusion of ME must be turned on its head.

For all existence births from connection, and to commune is to communicate with the 'other' as Self.

For all faces are but different facets of Mother.

No longer a-lone, but all-one.

Flowing with the waters of life, yet never wet.

To live in this way is to come home.

21 Steve

Jade could do nothing about the missing goats, and she had no energy to get worked up about them after what had transpired with Aaden's fire. What she needed, she decided, was a cup of tea and a chance to mull the morning over. A lot had happened. She would tell Avi about the goats as soon as she saw him, and he could relieve her of the burden of trying to decide what to do.

She changed her smoke-infused clothes and started to walk back up to the main house. Jade could see Avi talking with Meera near his cabin, and Meera looked concerned. Jade couldn't hear the conversation from afar, but when she got close enough, Meera turned and headed in the direction that Aaden had run. Avi turned towards Jade, attempting to conceal his concern, and started to follow her up the drive, likely on his own quest for tea.

"Ah," Jade started hesitantly, slowing her stride so they could walk together. "The goats have… um… kinda gone missing," she said wincing with one eye closed.

"What do you mean, lass?" he said as he caught up to her.

"I mean, I went back down to the pasture, and they were gone," she replied—trying not to use her stating-the-obvious tone.

"Ah." A flicker of a smile crossed his face as he walked beside her, but he quickly squashed it. They stopped just before the goat pen came into view, and he turned to her. "Missing might be too strong a word. Because they put themselves away while we were cleaning up, and I shut the gate when I went to get changed," he said. Incredulous and needing to see with her own eyes, Jade looked past Avi to see Newton and Esse craning their necks at the gate and watching them talk—no doubt hoping the discussion was about them getting more food. Relief coursed through her whole body. "Goats don't like drama. They run home at any sign of danger—unlike sheep," Avi said with more than a little disdain for the centre's small but trouble-making flock. "Not to worry..." he said as he walked away from the goats and toward the tea.

Jade stayed where she was, staring at the little faces framed in ringlets, but could hear Avi talking to her as though she were still walking next to him. She peeled her eyes off the timid yet capricious beasts and hurried to catch up to him before he realized he was talking to himself. "... have a cuppa, and throw the goats some hay to keep them happy seeing as their graze got cut short." She caught up to him just as he opened the door to the main house and stood back, gesturing for her to walk in first.

Inside the kitchen, sitting on the same stool she received her orientation on and sipping a cup of tea, was the man who had been with Meera when Aaden had run past them. He looked as she had felt when she first arrived: out of place, uncertain, aggressive.

"Hi, I'm Steve," he said jumping off the stool and startling Jade with his unexpected movement. He walked past her to shake hands with Avi and then turned back to her, with outstretched arms intending to wrap her in a hug. Jade stepped back, crashing into the pantry door and making it bang; the cups stacked inside rattled in protest. Steve bounced off the hand Avi had shot out as a barrier and took a step back with his arms up in mock defence, "Sorry!... Sorry!" he said, before awkwardly shoving his hands into the pockets of his shorts.

"Hello," Avi said slowly, drawing it out so that it was more of a question than a greeting. He stepped in front of Jade and ushered Steve back to his seat, "I'm Avi, this is Jade." He nodded in her direction as he walked over to the kettle. In an effort to conceal her fear, Jade went to the tea tray to choose what she wanted. She was so distraught she was unable to think straight and stood staring blankly at all the colourful square packages stacked in the tray. She focused on her breath, trying to feel tree roots growing out of her feet— all the things Meera had been trying to teach her—when finally, the light blue and white packet came into view. Earl Grey. Decaffeinated. Her nerves didn't need any more stimulation today.

She plonked her mug on the counter in front of Avi and stood significantly closer to him than she'd ever done before as he poured his tea. To her relief, he didn't move away. While Avi filled Jade's mug, she focused on the hot water pouring over the teabag to avoid making eye contact with Steve, who was sitting opposite them. He kept trying to catch her eye and smile. He's like a puppy who had been told off and wants to squirm back into my good books, she thought. Her breath caught in her lungs, and she was unable to move. She hoped his proposed stay was short.

"So, where are you from, Steve?" Avi asked still not moving from Jade's side.

Steve, Jade thought as she reached for her mug. *If there was one name that she had no time for it was—Steve. Are all Steve's assholes? Poor bastard doesn't have a chance.* She gave Avi a small, grateful smile and went to curl up in one of the comfy chairs. What she wanted to do was go outside and drink her tea, but she did not want to be perceived as *dramatic.* And besides, she was a little curious as to what this man was doing here. Jade chose a chair across the room—clearly showing she was "leaving the men to chat"—but close enough to allow her to watch and listen without straining. She tucked her feet underneath her, wrapped her hands around the warm cup, and settled into her best I'm-not-interested-but-really-I'm-hanging-on-every-word position.

"Oh, I'm from Hamilton… Ontario."

"Ontario?" Avi said. "I spent some time there in the late sixties, haven't been back since then though." Jade could tell Avi was trying hard to chat, perhaps trying to keep the attention away from her, but he looked like he would rather chew off his leg than continue to converse over his morning tea, which was ritualistically drunk in silence. "What's brought you all the way out to BC?" he asked after a brief pause.

"Well," said Steve, shifting in his seat as though getting comfortable for a long story. Jade watched Steve from the safety of her chair in the corner of the room while he talked, and talked, to Avi. From behind, Steve looked unassuming. His newly cut auburn hair exposed a thick, freckled neck. Its size implied that the rest of his body was physically strong, but the slight bulge protruding at his waist and the dark patch of sweat spreading between his shoulder blades suggested otherwise. Apparently sitting upright took most of the strength he had. He was wearing khaki shorts, the type that had too many pockets, and socks that were pulled halfway up his shins. He reminded her of an oversized Boy Scout.

Jade scrutinized Avi's facial expression as he turned away from Steve and began to wash the dishes that usually waited until after lunch to be cleaned.

"I started meditating when I was around twelve, with my Dad, after I was diagnosed with ADHD. And then…," he paused and took a sip of his tea, "when I was sixteen, I started to go to this yoga studio. I found it helped me calm my mind enough to study for school, you know?" Jade watched Avi nod. Not to agree, Jade thought, but to give Steve enough encouragement to keep talking, to get the story over and done with.

Steve placed his elbows on the bench and leaned forward, "My yoga teacher back then knew of the woman that runs this place. Said she was an amazing guru and that if I was serious about meditation then I should come and study with her. So," Steve said sitting back slightly and getting comfortable again, "here I am! I'm hoping to be her assistant so that I can immerse myself in the way she lives. Get to know her. Understand her. Know what I mean?" Avi didn't nod this time. Instead, he took the tea towel in his hands and carefully dried them, picked up his tea, and leaned back against the kitchen counter. Putting as much space between himself and Steve as the space would allow. Jade focused on drinking her tea in a series of connected sips and tried not to laugh.

"Well," Avi said. "It's true. The Lady on the Hill is a very special teacher. She's not one for assistants though. She has her own style of teaching. She's...," Avi took another sip of tea. Jade could see him searching for the right words, perhaps hoping they were floating in his mug along with the stray tea leaves. She looked to see if there was any wisdom floating in her mug but found only her distorted reflection in the water.

"... pretty hands-off," Avi said at last. "She has set this place up so that the activities here—the mere act of living—are what teach you, rather than sitting in front of a teacher all day, every day." He finished his tea in one large gulp.

Steve looked unperturbed. "Ah, well...I was pretty clear in my application for residency that I was hoping to learn directly from her. So, we'll see what happens when she meets me." At this, Jade couldn't resist. She looked directly at Avi and smiled, hoping to catch his eye. He was looking into his empty mug still searching for the right words.

"That's a good plan," he finally said, moving to the sink to rinse his mug after having found nothing better to say. "Let's see what happens. Until then," he said, "let me show you where you'll be staying and get you settled in." Then he turned to Jade and added, "Meera asked if you could please finish grating the cheese and making the hash browns for lunch, and, ah, don't forget to give those goats some hay. OK?"

"Sure. No problem," Jade said. She unfurled from the chair and headed to the kitchen, giving Steve a wide berth, to rinse her mug.

"You start down that path," Avi said to Steve as he ushered him and his huge pack outside. "I'll be right there."

Avi walked back in. "I have been meaning to ask," he said quietly, "did you give those things to Rose yet?" His eyebrows raised hopefully.

It was Jade's turn to search the mug for the right words. Finding none, she said, "No, not yet. I've been a bit… I haven't seen… I'll do it by the end of the week." She turned to the sink, avoiding Avi's gaze, but she could feel his eyes burning into her, weighing the sincerity of her words.

"One of man's main virtues of wealth is the honour of his word, Jade. Without that, we have nothing." He turned and walked out leaving Jade to make a plan.

22 Now or Never

Now or never, now or never, Jade kept repeating to herself as she headed down the path. It had been a week since Aaden's fire; since Steve's arrival. A week full of not-right moments. This one wasn't either, but she could tell Avi was growing impatient so it was now or never.

She kept her eyes focused on Rose's cabin. She was scared that if her gaze broke, for even a moment, she would lose her conviction and turn back.

The old trees that lined the path she walked along felt solid, dependable, and watchful, which only served to amplify her unsteadiness. The spring sun, already summer warm, made Jade's hoodie seem like overkill. But she felt safer hiding behind the extra layer of protection, even though she could feel a single drop of sweat tracing its way down her back.

She walked with her hand wrapped tightly around the tab of little yellow pills inside her hoodie's front pocket. She could hear them screaming at her to take them back to the dark of her hiding place; that she would need them; that she would be sorry if she didn't keep them with her *just-in-case*. She was so fixated on her mission that she didn't notice Meera closing in behind her.

"Jade," Meera called.

Jade spun around, stopping just short of lifting her hands above her head as though Meera had yelled *freeze!*

"Oh, hi!" she breathed, desperately hoping she didn't sound as nervous as she felt.

"Jade, I have something I need to talk to you about," Meera said seriously as she caught up to her.

Guilt coursed through Jade's body with such force, that she almost pulled the contraband out of her pocket and confessed to Meera on the spot, certain that Avi had grown impatient waiting for her to act and had taken it upon himself to rectify the situation.

"Aaden has gone," Meera said.

Taken aback by these unexpected words, Jade stared mutely at Meera trying to comprehend what she was saying. But she was unable to do so. Her vision began to tunnel. And the more Meera talked, the smaller her head became until it was the size of a lemon. This always happened when the stress became too much to handle or when she couldn't take on any more information. *See this is why you need us, just-in-case*—said the pills from her hoodie pocket. Meera the Lemon was gesturing with her hands—explaining something—but the trees had started to spin, blurring into a dark green cyclone with Jade and Meera standing at its centre. Jade began to sway and the day began to fade. Meera reached out, gently putting her hand on Jade's shoulder, grounding her. The trees stopped spinning, the day brightened, and Meera's head returned to its usual size.

"I promised him I would tell you that as soon as I saw you," Meera said. Jade started to comprehend Meera's words. "He left late last night."

Jade stood, glaring at her—wondering how she was going get Meera to repeat his message without admitting she had nearly spiralled out of control. "He... he wasn't coping, Jade," Meera mumbled looking down at the ground unable to face Jade's scowling expression.

"I thought you said he was just feeling unwell and not to worry," Jade said feeling the heat in her body begin to intensify. "You *said* you would let me know if anything changed."

Meera removed her hand from Jade's shoulder. "I did, and I am," she said patiently. "I'm sorry, Jade. I know that you two were friends—are friends," she corrected herself. Moving a few steps back to give Jade some space, Meera looked around, taking stock of where they stood. "What are you doing down here?"

"Oh, um," Jade's cheeks flushed with heat, and her heartbeat quickened, "I need to talk to Rose," she said, now the one who was burdened and unable to maintain eye contact.

"Oh? Can I ask what about?"

"No," Jade said, "I'm sorry Meera, it's... it's private."

"OK. Well, I am heading to the house on the hill now. I'll ask the Lady, Rose, when's a good time for her to meet with you. You do know that we don't just walk up unexpectedly, right?"

"Yeah, I know. It's just... it's important. She'll understand," Jade said, resisting the urge to check that the pills were still there. She didn't trust her hands not to puncture the blister pack and free a little, yellow, just-in-case.

"OK. Come with me then. Wait by the gate. I'll go and talk to her, and then we'll see about a time that's good for you to meet with her."

Jade leaned against the large tree standing guard by the gate at the bottom of the path. A thin, three-rung fence created a boundary between Roses's cabin and the rest of the centre. It was both delicate and functional. Jade found the simplicity of it charming. From the gate a crooked path wound itself through a terraced garden full of lavender, sage, roses, and other plants Jade did not recognize, ending up the hill at the front door. The path was made of old bricks; the steps of flat stones. All were laid by hand in a way that felt antique like the path had been there long before any building. Rivulets of creeping thyme flowed in the gaps between the bricks trying to find their way to an ocean that didn't exist. Too anxious to stand still and wait, she sat down on the side of the path and traced her finger along a line of green thyme. Soft, delicate, and resilient, she thought, as the tiny leaves bounced back into place after her finger had passed. Its sharp, earthy aroma filled her nostrils, and she breathed deeply letting it calm her nerves.

To pass the time, Jade looked around and saw that there were birdhouses on all the large trees surrounding the cabin. A huge bird feeder hung from a shepherd's hook on the deck, acting like a hub on a wheel. The birds flew back and forth, from their homes to the feeder, creating invisible spokes. Nuthatches, from every direction, honked in alarm at her presence. One brave soul cautiously eked its way, head first, down the trunk of the closest tree to get a better look at her. Jade couldn't quell her anxiety and the tremors that shook her body once in a while. Yet, she sat as still as she could, watching and being watched. The bird closed the gap to six feet between them before it decided she was no threat, honked once in acknowledgment of its discovery, and flew off in search of food.

Behind her, a woodpecker tapped on a tree. She turned around to see what she guessed to be a downy, simply because it wasn't a pileated woodpecker or a flicker. It was a small bird. Its body is painted in black and white and sporting a small red dot on its head like a bullseye. She watched it spread its wings, and fly past her flaunting its white polka-dots. Jade smiled. Apparently, her bird identification studies had been making more of an impression than she realized.

"She said you can come up now, Jade," Meera said from behind her.

Jade jumped. "Christ, I wish you people would stop doing that!" she said spinning around to face Meera, her heart pounding in her chest.

"Do what?"

"Creep up on people."

"I wasn't creeping, I was just walking," Meera replied. "Not everyone has to announce themselves and disturb nature with every step." Her words stung; Jade looked away. "But, I'm sorry I startled you. That was not my intention," Meera said, smiling down at her. "Anyway, the Lady will see you now."

Jade stood up. And unable to help herself, she tucked her hands back into her pocket making sure the purpose of the visit was still present and accounted for.

"Go up, and then knock on the door. She will call out to you when you can go in," Meera instructed. "Good luck," she added and then continued on her way, past Jade, and down the path leading back to the main building.

Jade looked up at the small log cabin on the hill before her. Now or never she thought and put one hand on the gate.

Jade braced herself for the usual tsunami of anxiety to overwhelm her, but it never came. Standing there in the sun, she felt grounded in a way she had not felt in a long time. Instead of seeing the trees as guards, she felt they were her allies, encouraging her to stand tall and carry on. She pushed the gate open and walked through. Step by step she made her way up the path. With each footfall, the nervousness she had been feeling the past week loosened, and a feeling of something sacred took its place. She felt as though she was walking into a church that had long ago been abandoned by the agenda of Man; a shell that had been left to nature—to praise and to pray—as her mother would have said.

By the time she reached the front door, Jade felt like she had walked into another time; a place residing somewhere between the past and the present.

Jade stood on the deck and looked over her shoulder to gather strength from the trees once more. *Now or never* she whispered to herself again. *Now or never* the breeze whispered. She knocked.

"Come in!" Rose's voice sang out from within.

Jade opened the door and was immediately greeted, not by Rose, but by the heady aroma of incense and the palpable sound of silence. She entered cautiously. Her shoes' thud on the wooden floor startled her. The sound was loud in the quiet of Rose's home. "Shit!" she mouthed. She should have taken her shoes off outside. She hastily removed them, using her toes to pry them off and kick them out the door before fully crossing the threshold. She turned back to see if Rose had witnessed her fumbled entry, but The Lady was nowhere to be seen.

Jade stood surveying the room, taking in the domicile of Rose. How many times had she looked up at the cabin on the hill and wondered what it was like inside, wondering what amenities Rose would have that the rest did not? Internet? Running water? Electricity? Looking around the kitchen and dining area, Jade noted that the life of luxury she had fantasized about did not exist.

Everything seemed to be designed to use more effort than a normal house. The sink was set on a wooden countertop and had a red cast iron hand pump next to it instead of taps. The wooden dining table hovered only eight or so inches off the floor and was surrounded by cushions covered in hand-woven cases instead of chairs.

"I'm through here," Rose called from an alcove beyond the dining area and to the left.

"OK, I'm just taking off my shoes," Jade called, hoping to buy some time before she had to follow Rose's voice.

An old rocking chair was by the front window. Next to it sat a rustic side table that was home to an oil lamp and a book. Jade glanced curiously at it to see what Rose was reading and saw that the title was not in English.

A huge batik of the elephant-headed god hung on the wall. In front of the hanging, a statue of a blue man with a snake around his neck sitting on a tiger skin was placed on a narrow table. Other smaller statues and trinkets were placed around him; each object had its own unlit candle to gaze upon. They sat there waiting patiently for the light. Jade poked her head into the bathroom as she walked past—no bells and whistles in there either she noted. In the place of a bath was an animal trough and a wooden box with a toilet seat on it stood in the place where she would have expected to see its porcelain equivalent. The mirror on the wall was barely big enough for her whole face to fit in at once.

Jade continued another few steps forward, past the snake-wearing statue to an alcove where Rose sat on the floor looking up at her, smiling.

"Welcome!" she said to Jade. "I'm very glad to see you."

Jade tucked her hands into her hoodie pocket. "Hello."

"Please come and sit down. There's a cushion just there," Rose said pointing to a tidy stack of multicoloured cushions leaning against the wall, "then we can chat comfortably." She turned her attention back to weaving a basket made of pine needles while Jade chose a cushion to sit on. Blue. *I always choose blue* her mother had told her once. Jade had forgotten the reason she'd given her, but ever since her mum's death, choosing blue had helped her feel connected to her. And she needed a connection now more than ever.

Jade placed the cushion in front of Rose and sat down. Her hand returned to feeling the foil and the hard-edged plastic of the pills against her skin. Its sharpness felt out of place in a space covered in softness—from the tapestries and cloths on the walls to the Persian rug that cushioned them on the floor. The pills didn't belong here—hell, she barely felt like she did.

Jade watched Rose as she wove. There was a rhythm to her movements: add needles to the existing cord, wrap-around thread, hold and pull the thread through tight holding the needles in place. Each repetition adds one inch to the basket in an ever-expanding spiral. Jade sat quietly, mesmerized by Rose's movements, by the simplicity of taking something from the forest floor and creating something practical, something beautiful.

"Have you seen a pine needle basket being made before?" Rose asked.

"No," Jade said barely above a whisper so as not to disturb the space.

"It's a very old practice. It's held sacred by the Native people who have cared for this land for centuries," Rose said as she threaded and pulled another inch of basket into form. "The needles speak to you as you weave if you listen carefully. In fact, all trees do." Rose spoke in time with the rhythm of her weaving. "Pine is the heart of this land. It speaks of the past as if it is the present. For time, as we think of it, moves much slower to a tree." Rose paused and searched for the next batch of needles. Wanting to keep the rhythm going, Jade spontaneously reached for some that were particularly long and a beautiful shade of pale moss green. She offered them to Rose, who smiled at Jade in thanks as she took them before she continued speaking, "In fact, Jera, which is the Rune depicted in that tapestry on the wall there," Jade followed Rose's gaze to a honey-coloured glyph on a charcoal background that looked like two interlocking hands forming a sort of S in its centre, "... means a year. Not in our human sense with calendars and clocks, but as a full cycle of the seasons. A Jera," Rose went on as Jade stared at the symbol on the wall, "is one full cycle. It's one inhale and exhale of the Land's breath." Having finished weaving Jade's batch of needles, Rose placed the incomplete basket and assorted materials beside her, leaving nothing but the Persian rug between them. She picked up her mug of tea that had been sitting beside her. "Trees are the wisdom keepers of this land, of any land. They are the keepers of everything." She took a sip, her long bony fingers wrapped around the pottery like she was holding something precious. "Trees are the ones who record the Land's story in the rings of their trunks. Trees witness, and they remember. Two skills we need to master if we are to live fully as humans. They hear us, not in our words, but in our vibration, and in our tears. They hear our heart's call and they help us to remember. For when we remember, dear Jade, we are whole."

"Have the trees ever heard your—heart's call?" Jade asked feeling almost silly saying such words.

"Many times. Once, I asked the trees for help. I had lost something in the forest, something very dear to me. Knowing how the birds and the trees communicate with each other, I thought perhaps the trees could help. Help get the birds to show me the way."

"And?" Jade asked, "What happened? How did you ask? Did you find it?"

"Well, I asked with my tears and with my words, and with my heart. I poured everything I had inside me out to the biggest Ponderosa I could find," Rose said, "and I'm not sure if it was the trees, or the birds, or the fact that I emptied myself and surrendered to the land, but the next day as I walked on the same path I had walked a million times before, I found what I had lost. It had not been there the day before."

Jade stared at the pine needles on the rug trying to imagine having a conversation with them. "Do you think the trees—the birds—put it there for you to find?" Rose didn't answer, she just looked out the window; reminiscing of a time and place Jade couldn't see. So, she sat quietly, alone, waiting for Rose to return to the moment.

"Now, dear Jade," Rose finally said, "what brings you here?"

Jade, who had been swept away by Rose's words of trees and wisdom and of seasons and pine needles that could speak to you if you knew how to listen, suddenly remembered why she was there, and the reality of it came crashing down. Her mind started to race, trying to decide whether to abort the mission, to make up something trivial, or to…

"It's OK, Jade. You can give it to me," Rose said with her hand out.

Jade looked at her and realized Rose knew all along why she was there. How could she have? Had she noticed her fist tightly wound around something in her pocket? Had she heard the crackling of the plastic domes on the tab? Had Avi spoken to her and not Meera? Was it Tibs? Maybe she talks to cats, too, she thought. Regardless of how she knew, Jade was relieved that she knew. She pulled the tab of Ativan from her pocket and placed it in Rose's hand.

"Do you want to tell me why now? After all these weeks?" Rose asked gently.

"It was the letters," Jade said looking down at her empty hands. Empty hands that wanted to snatch the pills back. Empty hands she decided to sit on.

"The letters?" Rose prompted.

"Yeah. I read them, and when I went to put them away, I realized the most precious place I had was the place I had been keeping those." She nodded to the packet that lay on the floor beside Rose's knee. "I had those because sometimes I would get really upset and my anxiety would get out of control—heart racing, feeling like I couldn't breathe. And I'd want to just die. I missed my mum so much. The pills would help me forget. They would put me to sleep." Rose nodded empathetically. "But the letters, they made me feel like my mum was in the room again, in a good way. A way that I didn't want to forget. And I realized how connected you were to her—her sister. And *then* I realized I needed to make this year count. I want to do the work, as you put it. I don't want to do or have anything here that is going to push her or me away. And so, the only thing I could think of doing that would show you my sincerity was to bring these to you." Jade let out a deep sigh of relief when she finished talking.

"Thank you, Jade," Rose said after Jade's words stopped swirling around the room, and the space returned to its previous calm state.

"For what?"

"For your honesty."

Jade just looked down and nodded. "I just… I just miss her." The words sounded too simple for the depth of grief Jade felt.

"I know," Rose said quietly. "I know you do." Again, they waited for the room to settle. Rose looked deep in thought, or maybe she was listening to the needles she had picked up and was now fondling between her fingers.

"Have you told the bees?" Rose asked just as Jade was going to get up and leave, figuring their conversation had come to an end.

"The bees?" Jade repeated. "Have I told the bees…what?"

"About your mother's passing."

"Ah, no? I mostly avoid the bees."

"I'll mention it to Avi when I see him. He can introduce you."

"OK." Jade stood up to leave. She didn't know what Rose was talking about at all, but she was sure she would find out.

"And, Jade?" Rose tapped the pills that looked out of place like a lie in a room full of truth. "Your mother would be proud of you."

Jade tried to smile, but her lips quivered. "I hope so," she mouthed, unable to risk the sound of the words themselves; unable to look at Rose directly. Still, the words were offered from her heart and they echoed into the sound of silence nonetheless. *I sure hope so.*

23 Go Tell the Bees

Jade dug her fingers into the warm, damp ground making a home for one of the hundred bean saplings that needed to be transplanted that morning. Like her, it wasn't going to get a choice where it lived. It had to thrive where she put it—or die. It didn't matter particularly much to her. After all, it was just a bean.

While she worked, she replayed Aaden's fire over and over in her mind's eye: the way he grabbed his hair as he paced; the sight of him running into the forest; Rose's concerned face when Jade saw Meera talking to her before lunch; the trays of food that started to appear at meal times, and then just as seamlessly, stopped appearing. He was gone, and she missed him.

"I hear you met with the Lady on the Hill," Avi said as he knelt beside her. She had been so deep in thought, that she hadn't noticed the gate squeak or the shadow of his body sliding along the ground towards her.

Without a word, he held his hand out to her. She handed him one of the delicate seedlings—its heart-shaped leaves and spindly roots desperately trying to cling to any soil it could.

Avi pulled out a section of a bone from his back pocket and went to work. The section of bone had been cut lengthwise to create a channel that cradled his thumb. It was flared at the joint end and filed to a point at the other making it look like an odd hairpin. He skewered the ground with it, and using the bone as a lever, he made an empty wedge of space in the earth for the seedling to go. Jade marvelled at the pointed end sinking into the rich dirt like a hot knife into butter. Avi lowered the seedling into the hole behind the bone and then gently removed the bone tool. He flipped the bone around, the pointy side held in his palm, and handed it to Jade.

"You will need this, with the amount of transplanting to be done in the next month."

Jade took the bone in her hand; the sharp edges had been smoothed by the friction of soil, skin, and time.

"Thank you," she said. "What type of bone is it?

"Deer."

"Where did you get it?" Jade asked.

"The ground," Avi said. "A few years back now."

"Thank you," she said again as Avi handed her a seedling. Jade skewered the ground to plant it, mimicking his technique. She smiled. Avi's tool had just saved her hours.

"So...?" Avi said once Jade had the hang of her new tool and they had a rhythm going that allowed space for conversation.

"So what?"

"The Lady on the Hill?"

"Oh, yeah," Jade said as she put out her hand for another seedling. "I did. I did it."

Avi carefully peeled apart two seedlings that had tangled themselves together and handed her one, "I take it went well?"

"Yeah, I guess. I mean, I'm still here," she said patting down the soil around the fragile stem.

"Don't do that," Avi interjected, reaching out toward her hands.

"Don't do what?"

"Pat it. Don't compress the soil around the stem. You don't want it to have to work so hard for its fine roots to plow through the soil. It needs air to move and to grow." He explained, demonstrating the proper technique of using his fingertips to flick the dirt around the plant stem without pushing the soil down. Jade mirrored him—it felt like being a child and playing sand-mud-cake kitchen on the beach. A bit of this, a bit of that, a flick of the wrist, and *voila!* Dinner.

"Good," he said as he stood up and helped her move the transplanting board so the next row could be planted. "Once this bed is done, I'll take you over to the bees. I've been asked to make the introductions."

Jade picked up a seedling that was lying on the board. Its stalk had been pinched; the wound, a discoloured thread, barely held the healthy base and top together. She could see it was going to die. It just didn't know it yet. She laid it down gently, covered it with dirt anyway, and put her hand out to Avi for another one.

"What is this whole thing with the bees?" she asked.

"I'll explain it when we get there."

"Can't you tell me now?"

"No." He smiled at her, knowing she had just bitten back a thousand retorts and how hard it had been for her to do so. "I'll explain when we get there."

They finished the rest of the transplants in silence and stood up. Solemnly, they looked down at the new life poking out of the ground. What was to become of them was now out of their hands. Jade bowed her head respectfully, wishing the seedlings good luck.

Behind them, Jade could hear Meera using her instructional voice. She turned to see her showing Steve the procedures for grazing the animals safely.

"Why is Meera showing Steve the routine for the animals? He's only been here a week! Shouldn't he still be scrubbing floors?" Jade said to Avi unable to suppress her snark and her indignation at his speedy ascension in the ranks.

"Ah, yes. Well, with Aaden… gone… and the garden being so busy, we have needed to move things in a different order than usual. Not to worry, lass. He's still cleaning. I heard Meera say something about digging manure out of the goat shed and making compost piles this afternoon." His face was serious, nothing more than a debrief of the day's proposed activities, but Jade felt the compassion behind his words and a little satisfaction: Steve was going to be shovelling shit for the rest of the day. "Let's go and introduce you to the bees," he said as he turned and headed for the hives. Jade fell in step beside him.

"It's an old custom. Celtic in its roots I believe," he said as though her red Irish hair automatically gave her some insight as to what he was talking about, "Some say it's superstition, but I think it's more than that."

"What's the superstition?" Jade asked, eager to know more.

"To believe that when someone dies, you should go and tell the bees."

"Tell the bees what?"

"About the person that has died."

"Why?" Jade said, screwing up her face at the ridiculousness of it. "So they don't go looking to sting that person anymore?"

"No," Avi said trying to hide his impatience. "Because grief lives in the heart, lass." Avi stopped at the first of a long line of hives that were all buzzing with the hum of bees doing their bee things. "The Lady taught me, when I first got here—still all distorted from the war—that the collective hum of a hive, the buzzing, resonates at the same pitch as the human heart when there's no grief in it." He reached out and lovingly placed his hand on the top of the closest hive. "Therefore, spending time at the hives, and talking to them about your grief, helps to shift the heaviness of the heart. It helps you feel better. I know it helped me." He looked at her with such vulnerability that she had to look away.

Jade examined the apiary. There were three rows of hives, arranged like white squares on a chessboard. She counted 13 hives in total. Each hive had bees coming and going like little planes on short runways. She imagined a little bee manning the hives' equivalent of an air traffic control tower and snorted. Partly at the image in her mind, and partly at the ridiculousness of talking to flying, stinging insects to make her heart less heavy. However, she had told Rose she was all in, so all in she would be.

"OK. Introduce me."

"I just did," Avi said as he turned to leave.

"Wait! Where are you going? What do I do?"

"Sit down and talk to them. And if you get stung, leave and go see Meera," he said, raising his voice just enough to compensate for walking away.

Jade turned back to the hives. Almost immediately, one bee flew a few laps around her head—perhaps checking to see if she was a friend or foe. Jade had to fold her arms and close her eyes to stop herself from shooing it away. Halfway down the row, there was a stump. It was positioned in such a way that it reminded Jade of a conductor's rostrum. This time she smiled as the image of Rose conducting the bees flashed into her mind. They probably rehearse intricate dance numbers, too, Jade thought. She walked over, checked the stump for sap, and sat down. She picked a piece of grass from the ground beside her so that her hands would have something to twirl, wrap, to play with, while she sat.

"So," she looked around to make sure no one was listening. She already felt foolish; she didn't need an audience. She allowed the word to hang in the air, teetering like a diver standing on the edge of a cliff, readying herself for the plunge into the water below. Three, two, one. "…my mum died. You probably already know that. I mean," she wrapped the blade of grass around one finger, undid it, and wrapped it around the next, "I bet you can feel that, from me—from my… heart." The bees didn't directly reply, but they didn't leave either, so she continued. "I can't breathe deeply most days. I thought it was 'cause of the cigarettes I started smoking after she died—but I guess it could be grief, too. Don't you get smoked? It's disgusting really. But it's the only thing that would relax my chest enough, you know? So that I could breathe. That, and… these pills. Anyway," The majority of bees kept coming and going from the hives like she wasn't even there; a few circled her and went on their way; one landed briefly on the blade of grass she held in her hands.

"It's just," she said, but then she stopped. She sighed, hoping her breath could say everything that she couldn't bear to speak out loud. She looked down to see that she had tied a knot in the grass. She couldn't tell if the knot was now a point of strength or a point of weakness.

"It's just that I miss her. No one else in this world knew me or understood me like she did. I don't even know myself as well as I think she did." Jade almost cracked a smile—almost. More bees started to take an interest in her. They kept their distance, but they circled the way a plane does at an unfamiliar airport, trying to decide which direction to attempt a landing. Their change in momentum moved her to continue. "She said to me once *'Nobody loves you like your mum'* and, well, I think she was right." A tear started to track its way down her face. Surprised, she wiped off the single droplet that had dared to escape with her finger. She looked at it, searching for her reflection, but found only the distorted grooves of her fingerprint magnified by the water.

Jade transferred the tear onto the blade of grass in her hand and returned the grass to the ground in front of her. "Now… I just think that nobody… nobody…" her shoulders started to tremble, and then her whole torso began to shake. She was no longer able to speak and slipped into the universal dialect of a sob.

The world disappeared as she cried. The bees held her without actually touching her. Their hum wrapped her up in a blanket of sweet nothings, giving her the cover and the courage to let go. And she did. She cried for her mother. She cried for herself. She cried for the child she no longer was and would never be again. She cried into her hands both to hide and to catch her tears. She cried to prove to herself that she was able to *go there*, to the place she had been trying to avoid since the funeral. A single thought flashed across her mind—perhaps now was the time to break apart the shell of protection she had built. Disassemble the pieces. She had needed it in the beginning, but maybe she didn't need it now. She felt safe here. Safer than she had felt since she had been left in the world. Alone. Tears streamed down her cheeks, liquefying the dried soil on her hands from transplanting the seedlings that morning. When she came back up for air, she saw that her hands were covered in mud. *My face must look like I've been on a battleground,* Jade thought. *I feel like I have.*

She showed her palms to the hives, and a single bee flew past them, turned around, and landed in the centre of her left hand. Its tiny feet tickled as it moved about in figure eights along her palm. It wagged its little body back and forth, clearly trying to communicate something to her. What, exactly, she did not know, but it did make her mud-streaked face break out into a smile filled with wonder. Wonder at both the bee and the sudden lightness in her heart. The bee walked up her hand and stopped at her wrist where a lone tear sat suspended. It looked at the droplet and then seemed to lick, perhaps drink the tiniest amount. Satisfied with its sampling, the bee turned to face her briefly and then took off. Jade watched as it landed at the slotted entrance of its hive. There, it was greeted by its fellow bees and escorted inside. Jade wrapped her arms around her legs, rested her chin on her knees, and thought: *I guess it's going home to tell the others that the human's heart cracked open and inside nectar flowed—just like a flower.*

24 The Hell of North North West

Jade sat down to lunch and ate like the food might be taken away from her at any moment. She never realized gardening could be such hard, hot, and physical work. Between seeding, weeding, and transplanting and then weeding around the transplants—like she had done that morning in the bean patch—Jade seemed to barely make it to lunch or dinner without being completely ravenous. It felt good though, to see that the beans had survived being transplanted and had sent out new little leaves in celebration.

Lost in her thoughts, she devoured her curry and bread as Avi, who was sitting opposite her, did the same. She had felt a silent kinship growing with Avi. First with the dead elk incident and then a deepening with the bees. Although his outward speech and dealings with her had not changed, she could feel that he no longer flinched when she walked into a room. Instead, he seemed to be relieved at her presence.

Just as they had both settled into happily eating, alone but together, Steve ran into the main house as if being chased by a bear or something equally as dreadful. He was panting and red in the face from either exertion or embarrassment—Jade was uncertain, but thought it was likely both. The energy shifted in the room, and she began to eat even faster than she already had been.

"Avi, sir! You've… got… to come." His speech was broken up as though each word took too much energy to string together. Avi didn't move. He had barely even twitched when Steve burst into the room calling his name. He sat wiping up the gravy from the curry with bread slathered in butter.

"What is it, boy?" he said calmly, choosing not to turn and face him. Jade dropped her eyes to her plate, willing herself to focus on the meal so she wouldn't choke. She tried not to crack a smile, secure in the knowledge that Steve had screwed something up and the drama about to ensue—for once—wasn't hers.

"The… the sheep…," he said, his hands pressing into his knees while he dry-heaved from the effort of running up from the grazing areas, "they're… gone!"

Avi inhaled deeply, as though trying to ingest as much calm and patience as possible, but his face was flushed with annoyance. He looked up to see Jade watching him with equal parts amusement and dread. She remembered Meera's sheep speech when she first took over the duty of the animals: "Sheep are wonderful animals. They are also a pain in the backside. Intelligent as hell, but not smart. They are redeemed by the beautiful wool they produce and the fact that they are so innocently cute and fluffy—well, at least their babies are. But. Sheep are the worst. DO. NOT. TRUST. THEM. Ever. Sheep have a habit of pretending you don't exist. They stand there with their backs to you. Waiting for the one moment your guard is down and you forget the gate. Then, as soon as you are out of earshot, BOOM! They push it open and laugh at you all the way to greener pastures, or the highway."

Looking now at Steve's face, he had received the same speech. Jade had learned the hard way that she couldn't trust them to make the right decision, but, they had never gone missing on her watch, she thought smugly.

"How long, boy?" Avi asked, still locking eyes with Jade's. *You were annoying like this not so long ago* he seemed to be saying. Mortified at the thought, she looked down at her plate.

"How long is what, sir?" he asked as if Avi had asked him to measure something with a ruler.

Avi pushed his plate away, resigned to the fact that he was going to have to spoon-feed Steve every little bit of common sense he was lacking.

"How long have the sheep been gone? How long since you saw them last?"

"Oh! About fifteen minutes. I was filling their water and then…" Steve started to glow red again, realizing his mistake. For a brief moment, Jade felt sorry for him, but Avi's voice made her sympathy bubble pop.

"You had better come, Jade. They can cover a lot of ground in fifteen minutes. Steve, you go east towards the highway. If you don't hear their bells or see them within thirty minutes you come right back, ya hear? I don't need to spend the rest of my day looking for you, too. Jade, you go northwest out towards the pond but no farther and I'll get Meera to cover west and south of the pond. I'll go north towards old Elbert's. You come back in thirty minutes if there's no hide or hair of them. If you don't, I'll be coming to find you. And you do not want me coming to find you. Got it?"

"Got it," she said as she looked longingly at the rest of her uneaten lunch.

"Got it," Steve whispered. His face looked like he was imagining the sprawled carcasses of his missing charges strewn across the highway.

Fuming, Jade walked to the pond without seeing any signs of the walking mutton. Her undigested lunch sat upon a ball of indignation that was growing with every step. It was hot and humid, and she had other things to do. "They're not my fucking mistake," she muttered under her breath as she stood looking at the dried-up pond. Not that long ago, it had been a body of cool water. Now it was just a huge mud pie covered with animal tracks. The tracks crisscrossed its surface; each set a road map of one animal's journey to find relief. "Why do I have to fix his stupidity?" she asked, but the mud offered no reply.

As she turned to head back, she thought she could hear a single sheep's bell chime from just south of where she stood. The sound surfed the breeze, coming from just beyond the boundary of where she was instructed to go. Avi's words echo through her head—*go to the pond but no further*—and then the disgruntled troll that sat on her right shoulder told her that if they were right there, why turn back? She could save the day AND put Steve in his place.

A thread of anger wove its way through her nervous system. The troll's voice grew louder. "Fuck you, Steve. You had one stupid fucking job to do. Ten-year-old kids in Scotland manage this job. It's the job they give the dumb kids in town. Sit and watch sheep."

A warm wind whipped her face, fueling the fire that was rising inside. The oppressive weight of so many rules and regulations, of where she could and couldn't go, of having to leave her meal for an errand she didn't sign up for mixed with the heat of the summer sun—the midday sun—it was too much. She was left wanting to burst out of her skin, to rebel, to do what *she* wanted to do. She tilted her head back and screamed defiantly—but silently in case the sheep were nearby—at the clouds.

Incensed, she took a few steps to the west and heard another chime. At the same time, a huge raven glided overhead in the direction of the bells—drawing her attention back to the sky. Jade shielded her eyes from the sun to catch a glimpse of its majestic wingspan (its body so dark it seemed to absorb the light around it) as it swooped along the trees tops above her.

Jade hurried to follow it, carelessly moving down the path, more intent on keeping the bird in sight than where she was putting her feet. A downed fir tree that was slowly returning to the earth, one decaying particle at a time, tripped her up, and she fell. Hard. She landed with a grunt, body slamming into the ground, and her hands splayed out in front of her—they had done nothing to stop her fall. Her head resting on the earthen floor, she sighed and could have sworn she saw a tiny puff of smoke. *My inner dragon has woken up* she mused. Harsh cries came from a nearby tree, and when Jade located the sound, she saw the raven watching her with almost human-like curiosity.

"What the hell are you looking at?" she demanded, wincing as she sat up. The fall had knocked the wind out of her, but she was unhurt. Thankfully. The raven cocked his head to the side as if Jade was some sort of entertainment to help pass the day.

"Stupid bird," she muttered as she stood up.

Again, the bell sounded just around the mound to the west.

"Stupid fucking sheep," she muttered. "We should eat you. Then we wouldn't have to deal with your bullshit." She brushed herself off to release the memory of the fall before heading towards the sound. She stepped over the rotting tree and followed a deer track to get around the mound in front of her rather than clamber over it.

She wasn't more than twenty feet from where she had fallen when she came face to face with a wooden door inserted into the side of a hill. It was made of flat planks and faced north-northwest. Its dark wood contrasted greatly with the moss-laden hill in which it was set. It resembled a Hobbit house, but one cast in shadow—a place mushroom spores might be poised to erupt at the next fall of rain rather than a beautiful garden.

She stood like a statue. Silent and immobile. She half expected someone—some kind of little person—to step out of the door and greet her, to click their heels together and offer her a cup of tea or some candy. Feeling uneasy, she glanced around, searching the woods for eyes watching her. Looking up, she found them. The raven had flown closer—eager to witness the events unfold. The sheep's bell rang again, closer this time, towards the north. They taunted her, teasing her to stay on track, to come and find them. But she decided she would deal with them later.

Jade crept cautiously towards the door, unsure of why she was being so quiet but knowing it was the right course of action. A feeling of foreboding came over her as she reached the entrance and raised her hand to knock. She hesitated, fist raised inches from the door. *Turn back! Turn back!* the little white angel whispered in her mind. *Knock, you coward. Knock! You know they won't tell you what it is if you ask* the other voice countered. The raven cawed, and Jade made her decision.

She gave a tentative knock on the door. "Hello?" she called, her voice just above a whisper. No one answered. Despite the hot sun, a shiver ran through Jade's body, and she shook her shoulders and arms to rid herself of the sensation. She scanned her surroundings. Sheep bells were still tinkling in the distance, birds still sang in the trees, and the sound of buzzing insects continued to fill the air. In short, no audible sounds of danger. She turned back to the door and bit her lip, thinking about her next move. *I'll knock one more time and open the door for a quick look around if no one answers,* she thought.

She knocked again, waited for a response—there was none—and then grabbed hold of the cold, iron handle. It was rudimentary but functional. She braced her body against the weight of the door and turned the handle.

"Hello?" she called softly into the darkness. She was assaulted by an overwhelming stench of filth and shit that stopped her in her tracks.

"GET OUT!" a voice cried from inside. "GET OUT! DON'T COME IN HERE!"

The words hit her with such force that she fell backwards and landed on the ground. She sat, too stunned to move, and stared at the doorway, wondering if something or someone was about to fly out and kill her on the spot.

"GET OUT!" the voice screeched again from the darkness, riding another wave of stench that made Jade gag.

She thought of fleeing, of finding Avi and Beryl and having him take care of the situation. He'd been to war. He could handle this… whatever *this* was. She was certain of that. She started to scramble to her feet but stopped. She should have been dead by now. Opening a creepy door in a hillside and having a voice scream "Go away!" is Horror Movie 101. The next scene is always a grisly murder, the victim's remains are left behind as a warning to others not to venture any closer.

Yet, here she was. Still alive. Still breathing. Not murdered. Something wasn't right.

She started to inch toward the door again. "It's OK. I'm not going to hurt you," she called out to the voice in the dark.

"Jade! I SAID GET OUT!" The voice bellowed in anguish.

Jade froze. Stunned into immobility. She had known at the first 'Get out', she realized, but her mind hadn't wanted to believe it. She shoved the door all the way open, allowing the sunlight to pour in, and waited while her senses adjusted to the stench, to the darkness, to the silence. She found herself in a subterranean abode that was home to something that smelled like a rotting corpse. A corpse that could talk. A corpse that knew her name.

Warily, she looked around. Her eyes were now sufficiently acclimated to the dim light, and she tried to make sense of what she was seeing. Two solar tubes instead of windows brought in the sun's rays illuminating the interior. Unlit candles in varying states of deliquesce were everywhere. It was a cozy space. There was a bed, a small table, a few bookshelves, a rug on the adobe floor, and a vessel for water and washing up. Jade gasped. Tucked against the earthen wall, as far from the light as possible, a huddled figure sat. This was no happy Hobbit. This was Gollum. Poor, sad, wretched Gollum. He looked at her, unblinking, and Jade stood transfixed by the unmistakable gaze of Aaden.

"Oh my God! Aaden?" She breathed and rushed towards him. He recoiled at her presence and turned his face toward the wall. "Jesus Christ! What happened? Holy fucking shit, Aaden. What is this?" she whisper-screamed at him—her voice quiet so as not to attract the attention of whoever had done this to him. She knelt before him and saw he was chained to the wall, cuffs on each wrist. Little spools of chain lay beside him like pythons curled up having a nap. There was length enough to move to the bed, but not enough to move to the door. Next to him was a metal bucket. Its contents were responsible for the odour permeating the room. "Fuck! We have to get you out of here." She looked frantically around the room hoping to find something—anything—to free him from his shackles. Seeing nothing, she turned back to Aaden, "What the fuck have they done to you and why?"

"They…" Aaden's voice was just barely a whisper as if his yelling at her to stay outside had exhausted his quota of sound for the day. "They…"

His eyes shot up, and he looked past Jade towards the door. They widened, and Jade could see the outline of another human in their reflection. Jade spun around on her knees and threw her arms out, trying to block Aaden from view, to protect him.

Meera stood rooted to the spot, her face mirroring the horror that Jade felt. She held a tray in her hands laden with food—today's curry and some plain white bread.

"What the fuck, Meera?" Jade's heart was racing, her palms clammy. "What the fuck is going on here?"

"Let me explain," Meera said in her best de-escalation voice, as though Jade was pointing a gun at her. Meera walked slowly inside and put the tray of food down on the chair. Then she returned to her original spot blocking the doorway.

"Did you do this? Did you chain him up?" Jade shrieked.

"No, Jade. Why in the world would I chain him up?" Meera said inching closer to them both. Aaden sat, bug-eyed, mute, watching.

"How could you all do this to him? You're… you're… monsters!" Jade said, bordering on hysteria.

"Look at his chains, Jade," Meera said. "Look at them!"

"I saw his fucking his chains, Meera. Can't miss 'em. He's chained to the fucking wall! Sitting in his filth! Shitting in a bucket!" Jade was torn between running for her own life and protecting Aaden.

"Listen to me, Jade. No, listen," she said as Jade started to interrupt. "You saw his chains, but did you ask him how they got there? Did he tell you that he installed them himself after that horrible day in the garden?" Meera looked past Jade to Aaden, silently asking him for corroboration, but he just sat there with a vacant expression on his face as if he were watching a show on TV. "Did he tell you that he didn't think he should be free? That he didn't *deserve* freedom, so he installed the chains himself?"

Jade looked over her shoulder, expecting Aaden to deny everything, to scream that she was lying. But instead, he looked at the ground, tears streaming down his cheeks. Each one made little indentations in the dirt as they hit the floor. She turned back and looked at Meera as though she had three heads. Calmly, Meera took another half a step forward.

"Did you see the handcuffs on his wrists, Jade? Did you see them?" she asked.

"Of course, I saw them! His wrists are rubbed raw from them!" Jade spat back pointing to the angry red marks that branded Aaden's skin.

"Yes. But look closely." Meera pointed to Aaden's hands which were clasped together, fingers interlocked. He looked like every prisoner Jade had seen portrayed on TV. He just needed the orange jumpsuit.

"They're not even locked," Jade said to herself. She searched Aaden's face for answers but found none. She looked down at his wrists again in disbelief.

"They have never been locked," Meera said. "No one chained him, Jade. He chained himself." Meera's words were full of sadness.

Jade looked again at the handcuffs. They were loose enough that Aaden could slide his hands through if he wanted to and walk out the door. Yet, he stayed. Chained. Immobile.

"He believes he is imprisoned, and his *belief* is the only thing that is keeping him trapped," Meera explained.

Jade stood up slowly, shakily, and took a step back. She stared down at Aaden, trying to reconcile what she was hearing and what she was seeing. None of it was adding up. Every one of her senses was at capacity, and systematically they started to shut down. Shock washed over her, and Jade's vision tunnelled; the scene before her started to fade as she sank to the earthen floor no longer capable of standing.

"Jade!" Meera's voice seemed to come from a great distance. Quickly, Meera put the food tray down in front of Aaden and rushed to Jade's side. She knelt beside Jade's limp form and firmly took hold of her upper arms. Then, she shook Jade gently until she opened her eyes and looked directly into Meera's.

Neither of them blinked.

Time became soft and Jade could feel Meera's eyes bore into her subconscious. A wave of energy washed over her. This time it was filling her up rather than knocking her to the floor. Understanding began to move through the back door of her mind.

"Everyone is chained in some way, Jade. Holding themselves back. Preferring to be trapped in a story that keeps them in bondage. In suffering." Meera's words wrapped softly around Jade.

The two women sat on the floor in silence. Only the sharp clanking of steel colliding against itself could be heard as Aaden picked at the food Meera had brought him. He seemed oblivious to the fact that the women were still in the room.

Meera followed her gaze. "He's angry, Jade," she said, "and he doesn't know what to do with all that fire inside, so he implodes. He gets depressed. Self-destructs. And then he holds himself hostage—as the victim. He's not yet able to believe that he can walk away from that story, from… this," she gestured at the room, "at any time of his choosing."

"We need to get him to a hospital," Jade said. "A real hospital. Where they know how to deal with things like this." She looked directly at Meera, her eyes pleading, wanting to have this entire experience erased from her reality.

Meera took a deep breath. "Come," she said to Jade. "Let's sit outside in the fresh air. We can talk more there. OK? Can you do that? Can you come and talk to me without running off?"

Jade looked at Aaden. He was staring fixedly at his meal, slowly bringing the food to his mouth, barely registering what he was eating. Some curry dribbled onto his shirt, and he didn't bother to wipe it off or even acknowledge that it fell. The spoon returned to the bowl, and the slow process started over again. Jade turned back to Meera and nodded; it was too painful to sit and watch Aaden suffering in the dark.

Meera smiled gently and helped her to her feet. Then they walked to the door, turning only once to make sure Aaden was still eating. Meera held out her hand as Jade stepped into the sunlight, and together they took a moment to let their eyes adjust to the blinding sun. Jade watched Meera reach to close the door, hesitate, and then decide to leave the door ajar. Jade tried to breathe deeply to calm her nerves, but the heat of the day and the stench of the hovel swirled around her. She bent over and threw up her lunch. Meera brushed the wayward strands of Jade's hair out of her face and waited quietly for her to recover.

"Are you okay?" Meera asked

"Yeah—no—I guess," she wiped her mouth with the back of her hand. "Gah! I hate puking." They walked away from the puddle of vomit and sat down on a log that was slowly decaying in the shade of the hill. Meera leaned forward with her elbows on her knees, clasped her hands in prayer, and then returned to the conversation they had started inside.

"What do you think the hospital is going to do, Jade?"

Jade's mouth fell open and she muttered, "Oh, well… uh…," before realizing the question was rhetorical as Meera answered her question.

"They don't care about him, Jade. They don't care about who he is, who he could be, who he *will* be. They care about liability. They care about *optics*." Her tone was calm, loving as ever, but her words were sharp and honest. Spoken with an understanding of how the system works. "Sure they *want* to help everyone. But they are so wrapped up in bureaucracy that they rarely help anyone. The staff is burnt out and half of them need as much help as the patients themselves. To them, Aaden is a bundle of symptoms that can be drugged away. And then, when he has no outward symptoms for as little as forty-eight hours, they will send him back out into the world to figure it out. Alone. Only to come back—worse…," she sighed a breath burdened with remembrance and whispered, "… or even dead."

Jade was looking at Meera's hands clasped so tightly her knucks were turning white so she offered her hand and Meera took it. Meera turned and looked at the open door to the Hobbit's house.

"Here, he is safe. Yes, he's in hell. But it's his hell. He is not in the hell that is the system, bouncing around like a pinball on a bonus round. He's offered three meals of fresh food a day. He has clean water. We cannot point out to him that his chains are not locked. *That* he has to figure out for himself. If we constantly point out to him that he has chosen this, then he will lose trust in us and retreat even further. We can only love him. Be kind to him. Remind him that we are here and take care of his basic needs."

"Who's we?" Jade asked

"Me, Rose, and Avi."

Jade snatched back her hands and glared at Meera. "Avi? Avi knows about this as well. Am I the only one that doesn't know what's going on here?"

"Of course, Avi knows what's going on here. We've been looking after Aaden every day since the incident in the garden." Meera turned away from Jade, leaned forward, and rested her elbows on her knees again. She picked at her fingers as she spoke, "He will get well, but he has to face what is holding him back. He has to face his fear of losing control. His fear of not being good enough. His anger." Meera seemed to be both talking to Jade and planting the seeds of her words into the earth at his doorstep, in the hope they would sprout and bloom when he was ready. "He has to learn that the anger that once kept him safe is now holding him hostage. The stories he tells himself keep him captive. Keep him victimized. Tortured." She turned back to Jade and looked her in the eye. "And only when he faces those will he be able to see that he has put himself in hell. And that he has chosen to stay there."

Jade absorbed Meera's words and felt her heart break just a little under the weight of them. "How can anyone do that to themselves?" She waved her hand at the door. "Is his reality so distorted that this is truly what he feels he deserves?" she asked. But she already knew the answer.

In the two years since her mother had passed, she had seen people chained to drugs, chained to abusive relationships, held captive by crippling anxiety, imprisoned by depression. And in that moment, she could see how she was still chained to her own story of grief. She could see how holding onto her pain, as though it was a lifeline to her mother, had made her a victim, too: a victim of her circumstances.

"I guess everyone that is depressed is imprisoned in one way or another," Jade said.

Meera reached out and took hold of Jade's hands again. "Depression is a bitch. It plays with the mind. It is all smoke and mirrors until you don't even know which way is up anymore. And you definitely can't find the way out. Whether Aaden's here in the centre or out there," she gestured to the outside world, "he'd still be moving through this. It's better to be here. Safer. Surrounded by love. Not isolated. Not just a number. Something to be fixed."

"Well… what can I do? How can I help? I want to help." Jade looked up at Meera, tears pooling in her eyes.

Meera, suddenly looking ten years older and completely exhausted replied, "As I said, we just keep loving him and making sure he's safe until the energy that's torturing him has run its course. Or something—a word, an action— breaks through the spell he's under and sets him free. Shows him there's another way, another reality, that he can step into."

"But how long does it take? I mean, has this happened before?"

"It takes as long as it needs to. Rose, Avi, and I, have all committed to being here for him for as long as we need to. We will not give up on him. Even when it seems he has given up on himself."

"So, this has happened before?" Jade said, sensing that Meera was skirting around the question.

"Well, not exactly like this. Though I have seen this pattern before." Once more she turned, leaned forward, and pressed her hands into the ground. This time, as though summoning courage from the earth itself to keep speaking. "I know the pattern that he is moving through. I know the hold it can have. A hold so strong that there seems like only one way out. Only one way to get some relief." Slowly, Meera rolled up the sleeve of her right forearm and exposed it to Jade.

"Oh…," Jade breathed.

Then Meera rolled up the sleeve of her left forearm. "And I have seen what patience and kindness and clarity… and grace… can do."

Jade looked down at Meera's arms and willed herself not to recoil. Pink ridges snaked from the wrist up the middle of each arm. The scars looked angry. Out of place. Signposts of a tormented and tortured past carved into her otherwise pristine skin. Prying her eyes away from the sight, Jade looked up at Meera who was watching her, gauging how much to say.

"But… when? How? *You?*" Jade said in disbelief.

"This," she said, her right index finger tracing the jagged scar on her left forearm, "was my second attempt. My first one was a drug overdose. I was sent to the hospital. They pumped my stomach and put me on medication. Anti-depressants. Then they sent me home. In the car, between the hospital and my apartment, I had already figured out what I was going to do next." She stared down at her arms. The look on her face was the same as Avi's when he had looked at the elk carcass. It was tender, compassionate, and resigned. It said: what was done was done, and we move forward.

"My friend, Carlos, bless his soul… he found me. Wrapped up my arms and brought me here. The Lady on the Hill, Rose as you call her, she stayed with me. Day in and day out, until my wounds recovered, my fever passed, and my delusions subsided. She saved my life. She was the only one who could see the roots of what I was trying so desperately to escape. She understood why I would choose to bleed out on the floor rather than battle with my mind another minute. Why the hell in here," she tapped a finger against her head, "was worse than any physical suffering I could put myself through." She paused for a moment before continuing. "She helped me get well. She didn't apply a Band-Aid and send me on my way. She didn't fix me. But, she helped me understand why I experienced such suffering in the first place. And then she empowered me to choose to live my life fully rather than settling for survival."

She pulled her sleeves down and glanced back towards the open door. Jade wondered if Aaden was listening—the hovel was completely silent. Perhaps he had fallen asleep after all the excitement, or perhaps their words were reaching a part of him that their presence couldn't.

"Now that you know, if you want to, you can help with the duties of supporting him through this. But if you don't—if you don't think you're up for it—I completely understand, and I will give you updates as you ask for them. We are not trying to keep you from him, or this," she waved her hand at the hill, "but it was not our place to bring you into this if you were not meant to be part of it."

"Yes! Yes, I… I want to help."

There was a screech from the trees.

Jade looked up to see the raven leap from its perch and take off towards the northeast—toward Rose's.

"Ok, then. I will teach you the systems that are in place and why. And with grace on our side, and each of us surrounding Aaden in light when he decides to come back to us he will be welcomed home."

"Oh, there you are, Meera," Avi said, stepping out from around the side of the hill. Jade jumped at the suddenness of his arrival. "I was starting to worry when you didn't come back from dropping off -." He stopped when he saw Jade. He looked at the women sitting on the log and then looked at the open door. When he looked back at Jade, he said, "The sheep are back. The neighbour called to say they were grazing on his south pasture, so I jumped in the truck and got them."

He paused waiting for Jade to say something, to explain why she had gone farther than he had told her. Jade's lips twitched with the effort it took to hold back the excuses for her blatant disregard of his instructions. Unable to look him in the eye she looked down.

"After I found Meera, my next plan was to come and find you." He paused, letting the words hang in the air, "But I can see that I don't need to do that now."

Jade looked at Aaden's door and then met Avi's eye, dishing out her own dose of judgment.

"She knows everything," Meera said, feeling the tension growing between them. "No use in keeping quiet. We need to bring her closer. She can help." Avi looked at her with his chin slightly down and his eyebrows slightly raised, telepathically asking about the obvious wrinkle in her new plan. "Yes, I will talk to the Lady on the Hill." Avi shrugged as though the weight of any part of the decision had been lifted from his shoulders, and looked back to Jade.

Meera stood up signaling the conversation had come to an end and time was wasting. "Why don't you and Jade walk back and get the iced tea out and ready? I'll make sure that Aaden's OK."

Jade's feet felt like blocks of lead too heavy to move. She looked at Meera, searching her face for a trace of malice or manipulation but saw only kindness and vulnerability.

"Come on now," Avi said softly. "Let's go. Meera will make sure he's OK, and then we can make a plan for tomorrow."

"And, Jade," Meera called after them. "Not a word to, or in front of Steve, OK?"

"Like you can get a word in any way," she muttered, the words tumbling from her mouth before she could stop them. Avi nodded his head in silent agreement as he started to walk.

Jade inclined her head toward Meera, acknowledging the seriousness of it all, and stole one more glance through the door into Aaden's hell. Then she turned and followed Avi. Together they walked silently back to the main house.

25 Points of Kindness

The days following Jade's discovery of Aaden developed a predictable rhythm of discreetly tending to him, while everything else at the centre continued as usual—Steve being none the wiser. It wasn't difficult to keep what they were doing from Steve as his tendency to be interested only in himself left little room for him to think of others. The three of them divided the tasks necessary to care for Aaden among themselves: taking food and retrieving leftovers (there were always leftovers), cleaning the makeshift toilet, tidying the space by sweeping the floor and dusting the surfaces, and looking after Aaden's hygiene. Avi usually took the role of bathing, and Meera made the first connection when she delivered breakfast in the morning and the last connection at night. So, it became Jade's duty to deliver lunch and dinner, dust the tables and bookcases, and sweep the earthen floor.

It was hard to say if any of their efforts were making a difference. He did not seem to be making progress in Jade's estimation, but she didn't believe him to be getting worse either. Most days when she visited him he did not speak—he simply sat on the floor in his chains, staring vacantly beyond what was in front of him. Sometimes she sat next to him, trying to see what he saw. Other times she just stood nearby, busying herself with her tasks—shooting glances at him whenever he shifted. She cataloged everything about him, storing information away to pour over later in her attempts to assess his progress or lack thereof.

It was his eyes she noticed the most during her moments with him—celestial blue and grey with green flecks. Sometimes his eyes would slightly squint and his brow would furrow as though trying to remember something.

Occasionally he would look at her and a flash of recognition would dance across his face before it was quickly chased away by embarrassment. Mostly he looked at her as if she were a stranger. But his eyes were always striking, almost otherworldly. She wondered why she had never noticed them before. Perhaps, she thought, they were reflecting the world where he was while his body was trapped here.

One afternoon, a week or so after Jade had started caring for Aaden, Meera took her for a cup of tea in the garden by the bees. Their gentle hum was calming, and Jade realized her heart was a little less heavy as she sipped her tea in companionable silence alongside Meera.

After a few moments of serenity, Meera spoke, "What we have here, with Aaden, is as much our opportunity for growth as it is his." Jade continued to sip her new favourite tea—bergamot lavender—nodding for Meera to continue. "Don't put pressure on him to change or to get better. Up your own game instead. Shift the energy."

Jade frowned a little, mulling over Meera's words. "You mean to focus on how he experiences me when I'm there, rather than how I feel when I'm with him?" Saying it out loud made it seem so obvious, but she'd been so fixated on making Aaden better she hadn't realized she'd made it about her. She needed to make it about him.

"Yes! You have the power to affect the space—his space, his experience. So, explore what that means within yourself."

The next day, and each day that followed, Jade used her walks to Aaden's cottage as a time to practice what she was going to say. To get clear on what topics might be suitable to chat about—or monologue about. She made it a point to talk about their day-to-day activities, how the garden was growing, the animals, and the things she observed. She tried hard not to bitch about Steve, but when he did something particularly asinine she couldn't help herself. She kept it short though; it's not like Aaden knew the guy.

She would remember the careless yet well-meaning things people said to her when her mother had passed and tried to figure out what exactly didn't work about them. Sometimes it was the person's awkwardness at her situation, and sometimes their lack of awareness or consideration. *Oh, you poor dear, who's going to look after you?*—was her least favourite; *If there's anything I can do, I'm here for you.* Drove her crazy 'cause the few times when she did call on them for something they were never available. She tried to practice saying things to herself to see how she might receive them before trying them out on him.

Walking back to the centre was her time to review and reflect on the experience, making a plan for the following day—tweaking and adjusting as needed. Jade discovered she could listen to Aaden with more than her ears, and he was listening to more than her voice. She played with her body language, her humming, and her thought patterns in his presence trying to shift the energy of the space as Meera had suggested. She noted that if she was feeling off, Aaden would not even look up, but when she felt calm and joyful he would often interact in some slight way or another.

On one of her return trips from Aaden's, she thought about the different acts of kindness she had received over the years. Reminiscing on some more than others, she realized true acts of kindness, the ones given unconditionally, were the moments that her mind kept revisiting. Her most recent memory was the simple dried posy inside her camper in the middle of winter. The bright spot in her bleak prison cell. She smiled. Aaden himself had prepared it.

The next morning, Jade quickly finished her morning duties in the garden while also scanning to see what was in bloom that day. Maroon and yellow marigolds and bright orange calendulas glowed in the morning sun. They seemed to be standing particularly tall in the hope of being chosen. She picked a posy worth—not too many as to be missed—and cradled it in baby kale from the second planting that had just come up in abundance. She turned and looked at it from every angle, admiring her handy work.

"You had better work your magic on him," Jade said looking the flowers straight on—they seemed to be smiling silently back at her.

She wrapped a wet paper towel around the bottom of the posy and tied it securely with a strip of flax. Then she went inside the main house to get Aaden's lunch tray from Meera. She left the little posy lying on the table outside the front door—so as not to draw attention to it, or her. But when she walked into the room, her eye immediately went to the little glass vase filled with water on the tray next to Aaden's vegetable broth soup. Jade shot a furtive glance at Meera and caught the hint of a smile on her face. Meera was focused on cutting the carrots the rest of the residents would have with their lunches; she never looked up. Quickly and without a word of thanks to Meera, Jade picked up the tray and headed for Aaden's Hobbit hole.

She arrived and a feeling of déjà vu washed over her. Everything was the same as the day before, which had also been the same as the day before that. Setting the tray down in front of him, she stood back to catch his reaction to the flowers. There was none. He picked up the spoon and started to eat. His chains slithered across the floor as he reached for the bowl and clanked onto the side of the ceramic lip as he scooped. *Slurp—clank—scrape.*

Slurp—clank—scrape.

Jade's heart fell. She had unknowingly built up high hopes that her posy would be the magic bullet. The cure. That Aaden would snap out of it at the sight of her flowers. She turned and started to fuss over the bookshelf. She re-arranged the books to form a triangle. She put the tallest book in the middle, and then on either side she placed the books in diminishing size order ending with the pocket-sized ones. It was futile, but it was all she could manage so that she wouldn't cry in front of him, or worse, run out altogether.

When he had finished eating—slurping—Jade picked up the tray. Balancing it on her hip, she searched for a spot to leave the flowers. She hoped to use them as a point of connection. A way to have the kindness, the friendship, between them linger in the room after she left.

She initially thought to put them on the bedside table to his right, but it was too far away. Then she had a moment of inspiration. Putting the tray down, she crouched down beside him and scanned the room from his level.

"I'm going to put these up here. OK, Aaden?" she said, standing up and walking over to the little bookshelf with the newly arranged books. "That way they'll catch some light from the solar tube." She looked to see if he was watching her, but he was picking at his fingernail, oblivious. She tried to keep the sting from his lack of interest out of her voice. "I'll see you before dinner."

Jade took one more look at the radiant array of oranges, reds, and golds standing out against the dark greens and purples of the kale. She offered a silent prayer for them to shine brightly before she turned to go. She had lost the battle, but not the war. Tomorrow she would bring another one—bright pink fireweed with fir—and the next day, another. She would not give up. Perhaps he would look at it, perhaps he wouldn't. But she knew if he did, he would have to look up.

26 Sandlewood and Rose

Rose stands silently in the doorway allowing her eyes to adjust to the darkness within the room. Concern wells up inside her, but it's pity that flashes across her face. She enters Aaden's hell and walks carefully across the floor as though to pick up a shattered vase and dead flowers. Instead, it is Aaden she finds sitting broken on the floor.

She knows there is no point in rationalizing with him, so she murmurs simple pleasantries while she wipes his face with a cool cloth. She tells him about the inch Newton, the miniature goat, seems to have grown and how Jade has almost transplanted the last of the 3rd round of green onions. She shares other garden tidbits and comments on the weather. He murmurs and nods in all the right places, but she can see he is distracted, disconnected from this reality. His body sits in the room, but his mind is elsewhere: suspended in limbo between life and death and doesn't remember which one is which.

Rose lovingly touches his hand with her fingertips. "Aaden, may I put my hand on your chest? I want to see something and then to show you something. Do you trust me?"

He doesn't respond to her question beyond a flickering of his fingers against her hand—a silent gesture of acknowledgment perhaps? She takes it as one and gently places her left hand on his chest. She can feel the heat of his skin through the T-shirt he's wearing. It is warm to her touch. Almost hot. Not as sharp as a fever but more of a prolonged, slow burn. Ever so slightly, she feels him lean forward and press his chest into her hand. She bows her head, grateful for this simple connection.

She anchors into her being; purposefully slowing her breathing until she feels each exhalation grow roots into Mother Earth below them. Fully grounded, she breathes deeply pulling Aaden's energy through her hand.

Now she can see the room as he perceives it: dark, damp; filthy. She sees the stark interior and the isolation. She feels the futility of trying to leave due to the chains that bind him. Death waits at the door, patient, promising freedom if it is let in. She senses Aaden's helplessness, his shame, his unworthiness. A box has been built around his heart; it is padlocked, and the key is missing.

He is not completely lost to the dark yet. A posy of flowers sitting atop the bookshelf in front of him glows. The single point of light is beautiful and radiant, but it is not enough to banish the darkness.

She removes her hand from his chest and looks at him, but he refuses to meet her eyes. He stares intently at his fingers gently making dents in the floor, turning the earth to dust with his relentless scratching. Clink, clink. The chains keep time. She waits. Gathering her light, preparing to shift his reality.

When she's ready, she holds out her right hand. It hangs in the air. For a moment she thinks he will not take it. Without shifting his gaze from the floor, he lifts a finger higher than the others—inviting her to take his left hand. Ever so gently, she does.

She places his hand on her heart (with hers over the top for good measure) and again breathes deeply. She focuses on the pure life force flowing in from the light outside, moving through her, and filling him up. His eyes flicker, and he looks into her face for the first time. Surprise flashes across his features as if he's only just realizing she's here. He breathes, nose twitching as he searches for something. Locating the source, he lifts the end of the silken scarf she has scrolled around her neck and sniffs it. A hint of peace crosses his face.

Rose continues to focus on the thread of light moving through her as Aaden looks around. She can tell it's working. He can see the room as she sees it. The bones of the room—the objects, the furniture—are essentially the same, but the quality of the light, the energy in the room, is completely different. The *feeling* is completely different. Isolation and dampness have been replaced with coziness and warmth. Objects that looked dark and inanimate now look beautiful and cared for. Sitting in its little vase on the shelf, even the posy of flowers looks as though it is closer to life than it had been a minute earlier.

Rose never stops watching Aaden's face as he perceives the room through her eyes. His free hand gently rubs the end of her scarf between his fingers. The friction on the fibre releases echoes of Nature. He closes his eyes and inhales, drawing in her signature scent of roses and sandalwood. He softly exhales, "Thank you."

"Don't thank me," she says without rebuke. "This is not an enchantment, Aaden, This is reality. Believe…"

She slowly lifts the hand covering his and touches his face; cupping his cheek the way a grandmother does as she wonders at the rapid growth of her grandchild. "All I need for you to do is believe. Believe that you can see it, always, as you do now." His eyes begin to fill with tears.

She is pleased to see that the energy is flowing; that it's bringing emotions to the surface. It is all she can do for now. He nods, and she lets go of his hand. His fingers linger on her chest for a second longer and then trace an invisible line through the air from her heart to his—a silent gesture of gratitude—before they return to his lap. His gaze follows them, and the gentle clanking of chain links folding onto themselves marks the only sound in the room.

"See if you can remember what this feels like… try to remember what you saw… you're not done yet." Her voice is kind, sweet, and commanding. "Tat Twam Asi, sweet Aaden, Tat Twam Asi." Rose studies his face, looking for any hint that he would, or even could, achieve what she's asking of him. She sees none.

Rose gets to her feet and places her hand on Aaden's shoulder. She gives it a gentle squeeze and then turns and walks through the door. She doesn't close it behind her. A shaft of light spills into the darkened room illuminating the way out.

27 Into The Light

"Jade, can I talk to you for a minute please?"

Jade stopped digging and turned towards the voice to see Meera standing quietly by the oats. Her face was serious. Jade noticed she was gently brushing the delicate heads of the grain back and forth with her palm. Jade knew the feeling—the simultaneous tickling and softness against her hand like hundreds of tiny high-fives with each pass.

Steve shot Jade a look. "Someone's in trouble…," he singsonged with his brows raised and a half smile on his face.

"You wish," she said handing him her shovel. "I'll be back in a minute. You keep digging."

"Aye, aye, Captain!" Steve said giving her a mocking salute with his spare hand.

Jade walked towards Meera and rolled her eyes. She could see Meera biting her lip trying to suppress a smile.

"Hi," Meera said. "You good?" she asked flicking her eyes in Steve's direction.

Jade exaggeratedly inhaled while holding Meera's eye, "I'm great." She flashed a fake smile and exhaled noisily through her nose.

"Well," Meera said turning her back to Steve just in case he was gifted at lip reading from afar. "The Lady on the Hill came to me a moment ago."

"Oh, yeah?" Jade said, taking half a step closer so she could hear better.

"Yes. She would like you to go to Aaden early today and take a bucket of hot water with you."

"OK? Uh…isn't that, Avi's duty?" Jade said slowly. She scrutinized Meera's face hoping it would provide context for the request.

Meera shrugged one shoulder. "I don't ask. I just convey." She gave Jade a knowing look. "I find more magic happens when I just surrender." She was suggesting Jade do the same.

"OK. So… uh… like, now?" Jade said glancing back at Steve who had abandoned the shovel (and his task) and was patting one of the cats.

"Yeah. Now," she replied, looking towards the feline love fest. "You go. I'll take care of this." Jade strolled away, smiling, as Meera called out to Steve to, essentially, stop fucking around and get back to work—not that she said it that way, but Jade was listening to the subtext.

Walking slowly along the Elk track to Aaden's, Jade tried hard not to spill the bucket of hot water. Each drop was like liquid gold—rare and cumbersome to acquire.

She could hear some type of woodpecker in the distance hammering on a trunk and chickadees sending a "dee dee dee" alarm call that something scary was coming through the forest. She stopped for a moment and listened, concerned that she would come across a bear up ahead, but then realized the birds were probably sounding the alarm about her.

She stepped carefully over the downed fir tree (now a landmark rather than a tripping hazard) and turned the last bend around the pine that led to the Hobbit hole. She was not prepared for what she saw, and the sudden stopping caused the bucket to bump into her leg. Water sloshed over the sides.

Aaden's wrists were raw but unchained. He looked thinner out in the open air than he had inside hiding from the light. He was kneeling, palms face down on the earth, oblivious to her presence. He looked like he was trying to grow roots into the ground, or perhaps use his arms as straws to bring the throbbing beat of the earth's heart into his body. Maybe both.

Jade put down the bucket and walked over to him, stopping a few feet away so as not to startle him with her presence. She knelt and mirrored his posture. Then she followed his gaze to a single, tiny sprout that was making a run for it—emerging from the darkness and moving towards the light.

He looked over at her with tears in his eyes and his signature smile on his face. Realizing he was coming back to the living, Jade's face burst into a reflection of his: smiles and tears, tears and smiles.

They hugged, murmuring half sentences to each other that didn't need finishing. They spoke of gratitude, of fear, of worry—of kindness. Aaden whispering incoherently about something to do with sandalwood and shafts of light; Jade whispering of magic, powerful posies. She kept leaning back to drink in his face. Each time his eyes looked at her—not through her—she embraced him again.

Once the tears finally subsided, Jade sat back on her heels and looked at him. "Right," she said, wiping her face with the back of her hand. "You need to get cleaned up and put on new clothes. Those…are… gross." She smiled at him and then wrinkled her nose.

Aaden looked down at himself, as though discovering he had a body for the first time.

"Ah, yeah… I guess so." He looked up at her surprised. His voice was weak but audible.

"Okay, um," Jade got to her feet. "I'll start with your face, arms, and legs, and then I'll go inside and straighten up. I'll get some clean clothes for you while you wash… you know… everything else." She waved her hand in the direction of his torso.

"Okay," he said.

He crawled over to a mossy patch which was as comfortable to sit on as it was absorbent. Jade brought over the bucket of hot water and then went inside to grab a facecloth and towel.

Together they worked to get him cleaned and dressed.

"That looks better," she said. "Does it feel better?"

"Yeah. It does. It really does. But I'm pretty tired."

"I bet," Jade said, casting a glance back into the dark hole he had sat in for the last month. "How 'bout we take it slow, but we get you to the main house. I don't think it's a good idea to go back…."

"In there," he said, finishing her thought. "Yeah," he sighed, "I agree." Unable to even bring himself to look into the space that had been his hell.

Jade supported Aaden as he stood up. He stumbled at first, swooning like a sapling in a gale despite there being no wind. The forest, like Jade, was holding its breath.

"Alright?" Jade asked arms and legs akimbo like a mother with her toddler who's about to take its first steps, "Do you want to try and walk a little, without help?"

"It's now or never," Aaden said. He fixed his gaze on a tree several yards away to aid his balance, and he took one, two, three unassisted steps—shuffles—forward. Jade slid his hand into hers and picked up the empty bucket. Slowly and steadily they walked; Jade pointed out places Aaden needed to lift his foot so he would not trip and fall.

Barely halfway back Aaden began to wane. The link of their hands became taught, and he pulled her back. She turned. What little colour he'd had in his face had drained away. They needed to stop. Jade helped Aaden lower himself onto a sun-drenched log to rest and then sat beside him.

For a few minutes, they listened to the forest's murmur—enjoying the sun's warmth on their faces.

"Are you sure you're ready?" She regretted the words even before she had finished speaking—worried about what the answer might be.

"No," he responded honestly, "But I might never be. So we—I—I need to try this now." His words were barely audible.

She nodded "OK, then." And stood up. She quickly brushed the fragments of bark from the seat of her jeans and took his hands, pulling him up to stand again.

"CAW!"

Out of nowhere, a raven swooped towards their heads. His harsh cry echoed through the trees. Aaden squeezed her hand; Jade ducked. The raven soared up to a branch in the next tree. They looked up to witness a single, black feather floating down. It landed at Aaden's feet. He gingerly reached down, picked it up, and sat back down on the log. Jade returned to her position next to him, glared up at the raven, and silently cursed the bird for impeding their progress. The bird cocked his head to the side to intently stare her down with one eye.

Jade looked at Aaden who was turning the feather over in his hands and brushing the barbs into form between his fingers. Then he swept it across his cheek. Several emotions raced across his face—incredulity, relief—hope. He closed his eyes and breathed deeply.

"What?" she asked smiling, pleased to see him flirt with something that looked almost like joy. "What are you thinking about?"

"It was, ah…," he smiled softly, "something Avi said to me some time ago."

Jade looked at the raven again. It was now preening—seemingly unbothered by the lost feather.

"What did he say?" she asked. And then thought it might be private so hastened to add, "If you wanna tell me…," but he had already started to speak.

"He told me about an old custom. Well, more a belief, I guess, from the old tribes who lived… live… in the traditional ways. He said they believed that after a vision quest, or a triumph, the ones who see the bigger picture—the birds—would gift the victor a feather. An acknowledgment of sorts."

Jade smiled. "Perhaps the raven feels you've earned one."

"Perhaps." Aaden looked up at the black beauty and lifted, saluting him. "Thank you, ancestors!" he said and then tucked the feather behind his ear. It stuck up like a black antenna. "Okay. Let's go."

"Let's go," Jade echoed, relieved to see a renewed energy in him. She sent a silent apology to the raven as he took flight, to the Northeast. Then she took Aaden's hand once more, and together they made their way to the main house.

Jade opened the door to the main house and the usual cacophony of lunch washed over her. Plates clanking, Steve talking loudly about some out-of-body experience he'd had once, Meera trying to direct them to get their food and sit down and eat. The only thing Jade couldn't hear was Avi's internal grumblings. She would bet money they were there though.

Aaden's grip suddenly tightened on Jade's hand as the reality of what he was about to do came crashing down on him. Doubt rolled off him smelling sour and pungent. It overpowered the fresh, just-clean scent that had been there only a moment before. The sudden death grip on her hand and change in energy caused Jade to turn toward him. "You don't have to," she whispered. "But I don't know what the alternative is." She glanced behind her into the dining room. "You can't hide again. We've come too far. *You've* come too far. Besides, you don't have the energy to walk back even if you wanted to."

She saw her words registering on his face, the truth of the situation. His hand started to sweat against hers, and he tried to pull her back from the doorway.

"Just try," she said seriously, "and if you scratch your nose, I'll get you out of there." Jade's face broke into a grin. "I'll reenact my first meal with you all—take a bite of something too hot and then try and talk through it. Guaranteed distraction. A real show stopper." He snorted. Not quite laughing, but it was enough to ease his anxiety. She smiled encouragingly, and his grip shifted back to holding her hand rather than trying to remove all feeling in her fingers.

"Like this?" he said, raising his free hand and giving his nose a delicate scratch.

"Yeah, like that." Now it was her turn to squeeze his hand.

"OK," he said. His gaze held hers for just a moment longer than she expected. "OK."

They walked quietly into the room, hand in hand.

"Any chance of an extra place at the table, Meera?" Jade called out.

Meera looked up. "Jesus, Mary, and Joseph!" she exclaimed, dropping the ladle back in the pot, and leaving Steve holding an empty bowl. "Of course! Don't be daft. There's always space. Avi, move over." She hugged Aaden with such force he looked like he might snap in two.

Avi slid down the main bench and tapped it with his hand, inviting Aaden to sit as Meera put a bowl of gazpacho in front of the freshly vacated spot.

Jade guided Aaden over to the table, and he leaned on Avi's shoulder while he swung his legs over the bench to sit down. "Thanks, old man," he murmured as he landed with a thud.

"Anytime," Avi replied, not missing a beat as the next spoonful made its way to his mouth.

Jade sat next to Aaden and watched Steve walk his bowl around to the other side of the table never once taking his eyes off Aaden.

"Aaden, this is Steve. Steve, this is Aaden," Meera said as she put a bowl of soup in front of Jade. "Aaden here has been unwell." She offered no further explanation. "Steve has been here for about, what? A month now?" She looked to Steve who nodded, still staring at Aaden. He was looking at the feather sticking up from behind his ear.

"Nice to meet you," Aaden said, but Jade could tell Steve's unrelenting stare was making him extremely uncomfortable.

"Steve, did you get the digging finished?" she asked, trying to distract him from Aaden.

"Uh, most of it. A little bit more needs to be done. I'll, um… I'll finish it after lunch." He looked at Meera as though the line had been rehearsed between them and then resumed looking at Aaden as if he were from another planet. Jade stared back at him with eyes flashing, daring him to say anything.

"Okay, good," she said, once Steve stopped staring and began to eat.

For the rest of the meal, everyone tried to act casual. They ate mostly in silence although they did not avoid conversation. But, no one could deny the elephant in the room—the emaciated elephant. They all kept casting furtive glances at him as he slowly sipped his soup. Only Meera shuffled uncomfortably in her seat when he politely declined the offer of bread and butter.

Meera pushed her bowl to the side and cleared her throat. Afternoon tasks were about to be reviewed and assigned. Jade and Avi began to quickly finish their meals. Steve had already finished and was now trying to look anywhere but at Aaden.

"As you already said, Steve, you'll be finishing the digging so that Jade can get the last round of Bokchoi in the ground. Those seedlings can't wait another day." Steve flushed at the rebuke but said nothing.

Meera continued speaking, "Aaden, you'll be bunking in with Avi for a little bit, OK? Get yourself settled this afternoon, and then you'll be back on animals. Steve will help you with the heavy lifting until you're ready to take it over again yourself."

Then she turned to Avi. "Avi, what's your afternoon plan?"

"I was going to do a load of firewood, but it can wait," he replied.

"Good, can you get Aaden settled in before you start the wood?"

"Yes, ma'am," Avi said. "I'll go and tidy up the place first before I get started on the stack. Create some space. Give me twenty minutes, young man, and she'll be ready for you." He stood and put his hand briefly on Aaden's shoulder. It seemed like a nothing-much gesture to someone who didn't know Avi. But, Aaden's eyes widened at his touch.

"Thanks, Avi," he said softly.

Everyone began to move. Everyone that is except Steve. He just sat in his seat. Silent for once. His whole world had just been turned upside down at Aaden's arrival, and he didn't bother to hide the disapproving look on his face.

Jade and Aaden headed down to Avi's cabin after lunch, pausing to feed some sunflower seeds to Newton along their way. Aaden smiled when he saw the miniature goat.

"He's grown," he said.

"Yeah, well with the amount he's been eating, I'm surprised he's not double in size," She said trying to sound overly upbeat, but then added more solemnly, "I'm pleased you're up and about," Jade kept her focus on Newton's nimble lips as they delicately took the little black seeds out of her hand.

"Me, too," Aaden said trying to sound stronger than he looked. "Do you think…," he paused and looked around to make sure no one could overhear what he was going to say next. "Do you think I'll be able to look at this as my quarter-life crisis?"

Without even looking at him, she knew he was grinning at her. "Too soon, Aaden," she said shaking her head and patting Newton's at the same time, "Too soon." But still, she couldn't contain her smile.

"Come on. Can you give me a hand to Avi's cabin? I'm tired, and the last thing I need is to fall and break something. I've had enough excitement for the foreseeable future."

"Amen to that."

"Meh," Newton agreed.

28 Her Words Are Not In Jest

Tap tap-tap-tap-tap-tap-tap

"Morning, Thumper," Jade groaned groggily. "I'm up. I'm up."

Morning had come too quickly after a night of nightmares that intermingled Aaden's hell and bathroom floors until she opted to lay awake in the dark. She felt discombobulated and looked more dishevelled than usual as she rolled out of bed and opened the door to her camper to prove to the woodpecker that she was, in fact, up.

"It's Sunday, Thumper," she said as she rubbed a piece of crusted sleep out of her eye. "I don't need an alarm on Sunday."

It cocked its head to look at her and then flew off looking quite pleased with himself.

She looked down onto the deck to see a piece of paper anchored in place with a cup of steaming tea. Aaden, she thought, and her heart skipped a beat. She wrapped her hand around the warm mug, inhaling the sweet smell of lavender and honey, and read the note.

Jade,

Elbert's wife is ill. Needs a meal delivered (it's on the counter in the basket). Fill the basket with huckleberries by the stream for dessert.

Take Steve with you, and flip phone.

Meera

"Crap," she muttered. The uplifting feeling she first felt when seeing the note plummeted when she saw Steve's name. The rapid turnaround of emotions made her feel slightly seasick. She moaned—a petulant, 13-year-old girl-being-asked-to-do-something-she-doesn't-want-to-do moan—and trudged back inside to get dressed. This was not the Sunday she had been expecting.

Jade walked up to the main house, giving herself a pep talk along the way: Elbert's wasn't that far—just follow the stream. She knew the way better than Steve did—she'd be able to stay ahead of him. The huckleberries will be delicious—it'll go twice as fast with his help.

She entered the kitchen (still grumbling) and spied the basket Meera had prepared. It held two jars of warm soup wrapped in a red and white tea towel, an envelope with Lucy and Elbert written on the front, and the centre's flip phone. She looked around for something to eat and saw that Meera had left two breakfast sandwiches—one for her, and one for Steve. She ate hers greedily and then eyed his. Maybe he won't want it, she thought.

She walked out of the house, holding Steve's sandwich and the basket, and saw Steve striding towards her. A smarmy grin plastered on his face. She felt her eyebrows narrow and tried not to look disgusted at the prospect of spending the day with him.

"Well, hello there, little lady," he said on his approach and he tipped an imaginary cowboy hat at her. "I hear we have an adventure ahead of us today."

Jade froze for the briefest moment calculating her response the way a deer does when it senses danger. Then she did the thing most women learn to do far too early on in life, she flipped her fear into fake confidence and marched up to him. She thrust the breakfast sandwich at him and then brushed past.

"We have a task to do, and don't call me little lady," she called over her shoulder.

"Hey! Wait up! Did you wake up on the wrong side of the bed this morning? Assuming it was your bed..." He muttered the last part low enough that Jade could pretend she didn't hear it.

"Keep up, or stay here," she said without turning around. She continued to stride indignantly down the hill. She headed towards the path that would take her to the stream where the huckleberries grew and Elbert lived with his wife.

She expected to hear Steve's voice behind her spewing constant nonsense and polluting the air with his voice. But it was Rose's voice she heard. She stopped and turned, flushed with embarrassment.

"Jade! Steve! Where are you two going?" she asked.

"We, ah, got a note from Meera….," Jade started.

"To deliver some soup to Elbert's wife," Steve interjected, cutting Jade off. "Shouldn't take us long. We'll be back before lunch."

Rose looked first at Jade and then at Steve. Her expression was thoughtful. Jade couldn't look at her without pleading with her eyes to NOT spend the morning with Steve. She focused her attention on the ground between them instead.

"Right. OK. Well, make sure you go River's Way and not Stream's."

"But," Jade said, "Meera has asked us to fill the basket with huckleberries on our way back for dinner."

Rose merely looked at Jade and said nothing. Jade wondered if she was waiting for her to simply say 'OK', or if Rose was listening to something unseen.

"So...," Jade said slowly, "You want us to walk all the way down to the river, then up to Elbert's, go past Elbert's to get the huckleberries, and then walk back down the river and cross at the bridge when we could just cut across the stream where the huckleberries are?"

"That's right," Rose said. Her smile was benevolent, but her voice indicated that she did not understand what the problem was.

"That will add, like, another hour of walking there and back," Jade said. She tried to stop the whine that accompanied her words but couldn't. She didn't want Steve to see her acting like a child, but she also didn't want to spend that much time alone with him. It took all her self-control not to kick a stone in frustration.

"Excellent. I'll ask Meera to save lunch for you both and you can have it when you return." Rose said. "We will expect you around 2 pm."

"Sounds good! See you then." Steve started to walk down the hill. "Come on, Jade we'd better hustle," he called through a mouthful of food, having finally taken a bite of his breakfast.

Jade caught Rose's eye one last time and pleaded with her, just a little. Rose didn't budge. Instead, she said, "See you at two."

Jade turned, annoyed that she was following Steve and not the other way around. She jogged to catch up and then kept moving as fast as she could towards 'River's Way'. She didn't look back.

Old Elbert opened the door slowly and then held onto it like it was the only thing holding him up. "Thank you, children," he said after Jade explained the reason for their visit.

"You're welcome, sir." Steve cut in before Jade could respond.

She rolled her eyes, and for a brief moment thought Elbert had seen her, but he simply said, "Please tell that kind lady over there that we are very grateful. The last time she sent us soup we were up and feeling twenty years younger within a day." His knuckles were turning white as they grasped the handle of the basket Steve had handed him. Steve had picked it up when she'd put it down to knock on the door. He hadn't offered to carry it the whole walk but had no problem acting like he was giving the gift of restorative soup himself when the old man opened the door. Jade wondered exactly how old he was—ninety-something?

"Hold here a minute while I get you your jars." Elbert shuffled down the hall and into the kitchen to get a container for the soup. "Well, let's hope this has the same effect," Jade said calling after him, trying to sound optimistic. Elbert mumbled something incoherent and busied himself emptying the jars into their containers while Jade and Steve waited at the front door. He returned to the door and handed her the basket with the empty jars. Jade thanked him and began to say, "You, um…"

"Take care now. Tat Twam Asi" Steve cut in.

Elbert nodded his gratitude and gently shut the door, leaving them standing in the hot sun.

"Why do you always do that?" Jade spat as soon as they stepped off the stoop. She had resisted engaging with Steve's constant chatter the entire walk and held her tongue despite bursting to tell him to shut up. But grabbing the basket and interrupting her again was too much for Jade to ignore.

"Do what?" Steve asked.

"Cut me off. Try and finish my sentences. Constantly talk like someone is interested in what you have to say! I don't give a shit about what you have to say!" Her voice was filled with emotion and her face was red.

"Whoa! Little lady," he said as he backed away with his hands up.

"And don't fucking call me little lady!" she snapped.

"Man, what did the last guy do to you?" he said with a hint of amusement in his voice. "Or better yet, I wonder what you did to the last guy."

She spun to face him. Her rage coalesced into a ball of fury in her stomach. She looked at him with narrowed eyes and her anger flowed toward him. Steve involuntarily took another step back.

"I stabbed him."

She turned away and walked up the hill to the berry patch.

Steve was silent as he followed Jade to the huckleberry patch. So silent in fact that it crossed her mind that he might have left. Might have walked back River's Way after deciding to leave her to pick the huckleberries alone. She almost went to look for him, but soon realized she didn't need to. She heard him crashing through the woods like a deranged bear. She sighed.

By the time Steve reached her, she had somewhat calmed down. She almost felt badly about her outburst. Almost. But not quite. She picked another few berries, musing to herself: she could hardly ask the plant to share its bounty, offer a meaningful thanks, and then lovingly pick the little plump fruits—that reminded her of new moons—and implode with anger at the same time. Jade frowned and then sighed again. *Shit*, she thought. *I'm gonna have to apologize to that fucker.*

She had half the basket full before Steve dared to approach her. He had a few cups worth of berries cradled in his t-shirt. The fabric was stained with specks of purple, and his pasty, overweight belly was exposed. Jade could see tiny beads of sweat clinging to the hairs on his stomach. Silently she held out the basket so he could add his berries, and then turned away—the image of his moist, hairy belly was seared into her memory.

"I'm sorry," he said, in such a whisper that for a moment she thought she had imagined it. But he didn't turn away. He waited for her to look at him, and when she did, his face was different, it looked… sincere.

She tried to say, "It's OK.—I'm sorry too," like she had planned. But the words got stuck in her head and ricocheted back and forth in her skull. She simply nodded instead. It was the first time she had not been repulsed by his presence. She didn't know what to make of the change in narrative, so she kept picking.

Working separately meant they were able to finish their task quickly. Just as the sun peaked in the sky, Jade called it quits. The basket was near to overflowing. She wiped her brow carefully, trying not to smudge her purple fingers across her forehead—she had already learned that particular lesson. With her feet in the stream's cool water, she sat in the late July sunshine drinking in the smell of summerland.

"We've made good time," Steve said unloading his harvested berries into the basket. Jade noticed his shirt was completely stained now and wondered if he noticed or even cared. He plopped down at the stream's edge and eyed her warily. He scooted over to ensure there were at least ten feet between them before taking off his socks and shoes. Satisfied, he stretched his arms above his head, cleared his throat and tried to speak casually, "If it's going to take us an hour to walk back, and Rose said she would expect to see us by two, then I say we have time for a well-earned Sunday nap under a tree. Whaddya say, li—, Jade?"

Jade didn't say anything at first, just waited to see if he would come closer. When he didn't, she reached into her pocket for the phone to check the time. She had forgotten to put on her watch in the fray of change of the normal Sunday morning routine. The phone's screen read: 12:01 pm. Battery 6%. She flipped it open to set the alarm.

"Um, yeah. Ok. But I'm setting the timer for 1 pm, and I'm not waiting for you to wake up. When the timer goes off, I'm leaving."

"Okey-doke," he said and disappeared through the bushes to the sun-laden mound just beyond.

Jade looked around for her spot to rest in—something that offered a little privacy. She didn't want Steve watching her sleep. She saw a fallen tree lying in the sun. It was in the opposite direction of where Steve had lumbered off to and would hide her from sight. Despite her annoyance in general with Steve, she had to admit the nap was a good idea. She walked over to the spot, barefoot, trying to imitate Avi's fox walk in the long grasses. She was pleased with herself when she managed to walk under a crow sitting on a low branch without it flying away. Jade settled herself in the little hollow behind the tree—her body half in the sun, half in the shade. She sighed, this time with contentment, and felt the warm ground take her weight. She closed her eyes and relaxed, sandwiched between safety and sunshine.

It was her arm that woke her. Well, it was the cool touch of a shadow on her arm that woke her. Her first thought was that Steve was standing over her, so she bolted upright ready for a fight. It wasn't Steve. It was the shadow of a tree twenty feet away that had eked its way closer to her while she napped. Its growing shadow marking the passing of time. Disorientated, Jade took a moment to realize where she was and that she wasn't in imminent danger. An incessant buzzing sound came from nearby. Panic washed over her.

"Shit," she said grabbing the phone vibrating on the grass beside her. 1:45 pm. 1% battery the screen read. "Shit! Shitshitshitshitshit," she said with the same urgency as the buzzing. She flipped it open and dialled the retreat's number, but the battery went dead before it could ring twice. "Fuck!" she said standing up. "STEVE!!"

He gave a startled yelp; her shout had woken him from a deep sleep. "Over here!" he yelled back.

"WE'RE LATE! HURRY!" she cried hastily putting on her socks and shoes. She stood up and began to run down the hill, "Dammit," she muttered, skittering to a stop. "The *fucking* berries!" She raced back to her hidey-hole and grabbed the basket. "HURRY!" She called running towards the stream.

"Jade! Wait!" Steve called out running down the hill behind her. "Where are you going?"

"Where do you think? Back to the centre."

"But we can't go that way. Rose said—"

"I know what Rose said, but we don't have an hour. It's nearly 2:00! We're supposed to be back. We don't have an hour to—"

"But… she told us to take River's Way," he said taking a step in that direction. "Not the stream."

They stood facing off. Each waiting for the other to give way. To drop their end of the tug-of-war rope.

"If we take the stream, we'll be back in fifteen minutes. Which is *hopefully* before they send out the search party." Jade said calmly, trying to stay cool and collected. "If we go back River's Way, we won't be back 'till almost 3:00. And by then, there will definitely be a search party for us. Do you want Meera and Rose to think we're incapable of fulfilling a simple, off-property task?"

"Well, no," he conceded. "But…," he looked in the direction of the river and then back towards Jade standing by the stream. "Fine. But only because I don't want you to go alone."

Jade glared at him but didn't have the time to come up with a retort. "Come on. Hurry!" she said, sounding like a broken record, and jumped the stream in a single bound. She started to run back to the centre trying carefully not to spill too many huckleberries along the way.

Jade rehearsed over and over what she was going to say to Rose upon her return. Absorbed completely by the imaginary conversation—trying out phrases, changing them, trying to guess Rose's replies—she didn't give much consideration to the trail. She was so focused on staying ten steps ahead of Steve and not getting caught on the large log that blocked the trail that she didn't notice the crows in the trees calling out in warning. She didn't see the bald eagle and vultures circling impatiently above her head. She didn't hear the warning sounds of the effort it takes to rip a limb from a torso until she turned the corner and came face to face with a bear—ripping apart a deer.

She stepped back just as Steve jumped the log, and he crashed into her. She dropped the basket of berries on the forest floor and gave a startled yelp.

The bear stopped eating and jerked its head up at the sound of Jade's cry. It turned to face them. In that moment, time slowed. Jade had three thoughts: the bear looked beautiful with its light brown fur catching the sunlight; with its hackles raised on the hump between its shoulder blades, it looked even bigger than in any pictures she had ever seen; and apparently she *was* going to be mauled to death by a bear just like she'd wished for in her journal.

The bear put its head down menacingly and woofed a warning at them as it pawed the ground. "Whoa, bear!" Jade said putting her hands up and taking a step back. Its long, bloodied nails scraped the earth and gouged deep tracks in the dirt.

"WHOA BEAR!" Steve called as Jade heard him stumble his way back over the log. She took another step back knowing if she turned to run, it would chase her down in a matter of seconds. The back of her legs bumped against the timber; she had nowhere to go. The bear lurched forward and reared up. Towering over them, the bear looked almost twice their height. Steve's arm wrapped around Jade's waist and yanked her backwards, putting the log between them and the bear. She growled and dropped onto all fours readying to charge them.

Steve and Jade stepped backwards in unison and stumbled to the ground. They tried to scramble to their feet, terror etched across their faces. Just as the bear reached the log, a cannon went off and a white streak flew through the air crashing into its side. Surprised, the bear stumbled sideways but quickly regained its balance. Jade and Steve were temporarily forgotten.

The bear stood up again; its sheer size cancelling out the sun. It swiped at the snarling, white mass trying to bite it. BANG! Another shot was fired. This time the bear spun around and disappeared into the forest. Leaving behind its kill. For now.

Jade strained her ears—finally listening to the forest around her. The sound of crashing paws grew faint as the bear retreated further into the woods. Steve panted. Her breath came in harsh, ragged gasps. A gentle whimper came from the other side of the log. There were no other sounds. The trees were silent, solemn, watchful.

"Everybody all right?" Avi asked as he stepped out from behind a tree with the shotgun cocked and braced against his shoulder—ready to fire if the bear came back.

Jade nodded, unable to speak. Steve, now beside her, nodded, too.

Avi knelt next to the log, his forehead creased with concern.

Jade got to her feet and peered over to find Sam lying on his side. A sticky, burgundy black oozing from his shoulder.

"Sam!" Jade called as she leaped over the log and crouched beside him. "Oh my God, Sam! I'm so sorry. I'm so sorry." Tears started to stream down her face.

"No point crying now. Save it for later," Avi barked. Jade had never heard him speak with such anger in his voice. "I thought you were told not to cross the creek?"

Jade knew he didn't want an answer. And her reasoning now seemed pathetic in light of what had happened to them and Sam. She glanced in Steve's direction, knowing full well where the fingers pointed. *I'm sure he'll make certain they know *he* hadn't wanted to disobey. That she had bullied him into it,* she thought.

"Steve, help me carry Sam. I'll call ahead and get Meera to bring the truck."

He thrust Beryl into Jade's hand. "It's loaded. If the bear comes back…," his voice trailed off. He didn't need to finish the sentence for Jade to catch his meaning. "Cock it and shoot accordingly. Like I showed you."

"But, I…," she began. The look on Avi's face said he didn't want to hear what she had to say—perhaps ever again.

Steve's mouth was agape at the sight of Jade being handed the rifle, but he didn't say anything. He helped Avi pick up Sam, and together they started walking trying hard not to jostle the injured dog. Jade walked backwards, checking behind her with each step. The rifle butt was pressed firmly into her shoulder with her hand poised to cock the hammer and pull the trigger if necessary. She peered uneasily into the woods surrounding them—listening with every fibre of her being. All she heard though was Sam's occasional, pain-filled whimpers and the men's heavy breathing. After what felt like an eternity but was more like 10 minutes, they reached the clearing where Meera was waiting with the truck—her face was pinched, anxious, and Jade realized, full of anger.

Meera rushed toward them to help get Sam into the bed of the truck. Jade couldn't look at Steve and didn't dare look at Avi. So, she got in the bed of the truck to be with Sam.

"Hold this to his shoulder and don't take it off," Meera said handing her a yarrow compress and taking the rifle.

When Jade tried to speak, to ask if Sam was going to be okay, Meera just turned and got into the cab, slamming the passenger side door closed. The engine roared to life, and they headed back to the centre where Rose and Aaden were waiting for them.

The men carried Sam to the house, and Jade trailed behind. Meera took her by the arm, turning her gently.

"We've got this," she said. *I don't want to set eyes on you right now* is what Jade heard. "Go and have a sauna. It's ready. I'll see you at dinner."

"OK. Maybe…."

"I'm not interested in what you have to say right now, Jade. Just do as you are asked." *Cause when you don't… look at the mess you create.* "Sauna first. Then dinner."

Jade nodded. Tears filled her eyes until the sight of Meera following every-one else into the house was too blurry to see.

29 Moths and riddles

The fierce heat of the sauna did nothing to alleviate Jade's distress. Every time she poured water onto the lava rocks, the sauna scratched its razor-sharp fingernails down her moist back. Every time she closed her eyes she saw the blood-stained claws of the bear ripping open the earth. Sam's whimpers echoed in her mind. Over and over she relived those terrifying moments in the forest until her skin was drenched in sweat. The cold shower that followed, usually a welcome reprieve from the heat, didn't soothe the fire within—she burned white hot with shame. As the water washed the tears from her face, the mental flagellation began: *You think you're better than Steve, but you're not. You're a fucking child that can't see the bigger picture and you almost got Sam killed because of your stupidity. You've got six months to go, and no one is going to look at you the same. You might as well crawl into Aaden's hellhole and die. They won't find you; they won't look.*

She got dressed and walked up to the main house. Still feeling overheated and slightly woozy, she headed for the side deck and the Adirondack chairs that faced the afternoon. She decided to take a moment, to collect herself before seeing everyone. Aaden had the same idea. He was reclining in one of the chairs with his leather-bound journal open on his lap. His eyes were closed, drinking in the sunshine that shone on his face rather than looking at the words on the page before him.

Jade walked over and sat in the matching Adirondack beside him. Too worked up to relax, she sat on the edge of the seat, propped her elbows on her knees, and hung her head. She closed her eyes and exhaled slowly. "Hi," she said. She didn't want to be alone. She wanted to be with someone—someone who knew shame intimately enough to leave her be.

"Are you OK?" Aaden asked without opening his eyes.

Jade took a moment to search for the right words, but "No" was all that came.

"Steve told me what happened. Sounded…intense. Terrifying."

She opened her eyes just so she could roll them. She could just imagine Steve's enthusiasm for being the first person to tell Aaden how royally she had fucked up.

"Yeah, terrifying describes it," she said. Her gaze stayed on the weathered boards rotting slowly beneath her feet. "Is, uh, Sam going to be OK?" she asked, her voice cracking a little at the end.

"Yeah. He's gonna be fine. Meera stitched him up. It was just a flesh wound. She said he was lucky. You all were." Aaden opened his eyes and looked at her with a mix of concern, care, and *what were you thinking?*

Jade tried to say something, but her throat constricted and tears threatened to overpower her words. She swallowed hard and tried changing the subject, "What are you reading?"

"You're deflecting," he said holding her gaze.

"Yup," she said defiantly and repeated her question.

Aaden looked down at his book conceding to the change of subject and touched the page of his book tenderly.

"I saw a moth while I was helping Avi fix the fence today, and it reminded me of something from when…," he stopped long enough to clear his throat, "… when everything went up in flames. I, uh, wanted to write about it while it was still fresh in my mind."

A breeze moved through the trees with a murmured—shhh. It sounded like a primary school teacher asking their class to settle down and pay attention. Jade looked at the trees, noting the way their limbs swayed, the way shafts of sunlight dodged pine needles and branches to get to them. *They're watching and listening to us Jade thought. Like we're putting on a show for them—the deck is the stage, the sun the spotlight.*

"What about it?" Jade slumped into the chair and brought her knees to her chest. She wrapped her arms around them and squeezed—a much-needed buffer between herself and the rest of the world.

"What?"

"While you fixed the fence today, you said you saw a moth. What about the moth reminded you of…?" Jade said. She planned to keep asking questions so she wouldn't be asked any questions.

"I saw," Aaden flicked back a page in his book. Jade glimpsed a drawing and words she couldn't read. He cleared his throat, "A moth. Black and white with patterns on it like some ancient Aztec artwork."

"And?" Jade prompted as Aaden's attention momentarily gravitated back to the sun.

Aaden looked again at his book thinking about how to begin. He sighed heavily, and a pained expression crossed his face as he turned toward Jade.

"Before everything went… up, I was sitting in front of the fire. Listening. Chanting. Just watching the flame. And then a moth came. I don't usually see them in the morning, but there it was. It sat to the side of the brick—just out of the direct heat of the fire. Then it flitted up as though to see the flames for itself before hiding behind the brick again. I watched it go back and forth for what felt like hours, although I'm sure it was just a minute or two." He glanced down at the drawing. "At some point, it noticed me and flew directly at my face. Bopping me on the forehead—you know how they bounce off windows and doors when they're chasing the light?" Jade nodded. "Just like that. Except when it bumped into me, a question popped into my head. A riddle. I was shocked. It bumped me one more time, circled the fire, and then flew off. Like, 'Message delivered. Off to my next job.' I started to think about the question. But the more I thought about it, the more anger I felt. The more shame." He cast a sideways glance at Jade and then kept speaking. "Ashamed about stuff I hadn't thought about in years. And the more I thought about that stuff, the more I felt worthless. I could feel this ball of rock-hard lava in my stomach; it felt as though it was gonna blow. Death by shrapnel from the inside." He put his hand over his stomach at the memory. "Then the moth came back. And the more anger I felt, the hotter the fire in front of me felt, and the more the moth flew in erratic circles around my head. I wanted to swat it, I wanted to run away and cool off, but I couldn't. Because that would've meant I had failed. You know, abandoning my quest. Then the sun came out from behind a cloud and added to the heat. It was…," he blew air forcibly out of his mouth rustling the pages of his journal. He didn't elaborate further—he just sat, remembering. Jade waited for him to continue. She went to touch her stomach where a similar ball of lava sat but changed course at the last moment. She opted to sit on her hands instead.

The movement made Aaden look up at her. She nodded for him to keep going. His face flushed and his eyes glittered with unshed tears.

"Everything became too much. I couldn't take it. So I thought if I went to the bathroom that would be a legit excuse to step away for a moment. So, I put an extra log on the fire and went, but then…," he made a twirling motion with his fingers not needing to finish his story. Jade remembered all too well what happened next. Aaden looked back at his journal and took out a folded piece of paper from between the pages. He handed it to Jade. "Instead of staying with the practices, focusing on them and just witnessing what was coming up, as the

Lady had told me I'd need to do when it got hard, I just kept spinning the story of not being good enough. That the world would be better off if I just died and I didn't have what it took. It threw me into the depths of hell. If I had just trusted her…," he stopped and watched as Jade gently unfolded the paper.

A single line of script was scrawled across the page. The strokes were frenzied and chaotic—nearly illegible. It was as if the words knew that once committed to the paper they would be trapped, remembered, and held accountable.

"It's the last thing I remember doing with any clarity before going to the bathroom—writing down Moth's message…" Aaden closed his eyes and lifted his face back at the sun while Jade deciphered the words.

What are you doing if your ego can no longer feel the heat from the flames?

Jade whispered the words. Speaking them aloud did not unlock an answer regardless of the number of times she said them. They sat in companionable silence; the trees holding their breath waiting for the next part of the scene to unfold.

"Well? What was the answer? Did you figure it out?" Jade finally asked.

"Yeah, I think so. Like I said, I was working on the fence and saw that moth today. Then I saw a bunch of memories string together. Like a slide show, ya know?"

"Did the moth show you the answer?" She smiled to show she was joking. Sort of. Rose talks to birds and trees. Maybe moths talk to Aaden.

"No… The Lady on the Hill did."

"What? Rose? When? Today?" Jade asked each question in rapid succession.

"No. When she came to see me. When I was in the hole."

"How did she show you? What's the answer?"

Aaden looked at her, his eyes locked on hers. "When she came to see me, it was like she was from another planet. I could see her, but she wasn't in the same reality as me. Like, we were in parallel universes. She was untouched by the anger and shame that filled the room. She was untouched by the heat of the summer's day. She didn't resonate with any of the qualities burning me up in that hell I existed in. Her natural state didn't resonate with me. Then, when she walked out the door, it was as though she just dissolved into the light. Like she didn't exist in my reality unless she was in front of me. It was like she was showing me that the heat on the outside was the mirror to the anger on the inside."

Aaden was more animated than Jade had seen him in weeks. He had fully turned to her now and was perched on the edge of his seat. He trembled with excitement. The pieces to his puzzle were starting to fit together; he was starting to understand what he had been through.

"I wonder, now, that if I could have softened in that moment, instead of imploding. If I could have endured long enough to let go and surrender these pieces of me—my hate, my disgust—then the lava ball would have dissolved instead of exploding." He stopped for a moment lost in thought. Then he sighed, "If I had just trusted her; followed her instructions completely, I could have found out who I was if I wasn't identified as being angry if I wasn't ashamed. I could have completed my quest." He said the last part quietly as he sat back in the chair again and closed his eyes. His face filled with sadness before shifting to a more hopeful, peaceful expression.

Jade's eyes squinted and her brow furrowed slightly. She turned over all he had just said, trying to match Rose's dissolving into light with the moth's riddle, but she couldn't.

"So, what's the answer? If your ego no longer can feel the heat of the flames? What are you doing?" she asked.

He turned his head, grinned at her, and then went back to basking in the golden glow of the evening sun. The smile didn't leave his face.

"You're bathing in light…" he said.

A breeze rippled through the trees again. This time, instead of a quiet murmuring, the branches and leaves burst into applause. The ball of shame in Jade stayed though. She put her hand over her stomach and wondered who she'd be without it. She closed her eyes against the brightness of the sun and waited for the bell announcing dinner. She didn't wait long.

Jade jerked upright as the sound of the bell disrupted the quiet. Her face must have flushed with terror because Aaden suddenly looked at her with concern.

"It's going to be OK, you know," he said as he stood and placed the book in his bag. "You might have to eat some humble pie, but you'll survive."

She went to stand up, but her body had other plans. It remained anchored to the spot—refusing to budge. "I'm not very hungry," Jade said trying to buy some time. Anything to avoid what was to come.

Aaden held out his hand to her. His long, artist's fingers (with slightly grubby fingernails she noticed), waggled in the air requesting her hand. She groaned and whimpered, "I don't wanna."

He waggled his fingers again, and she took his hand. His touch was warmer than she expected, stronger. He smiled reassuringly at her as she came to her feet.

"Remember, this place, this centre," he gestured around them, "it's on the earth, but it's not *of* the Earth. Not in the way you and I have come to expect the world to be. It's…," he trailed off looking for the right word. "Rose is human, but she's also *more* than human. We all are. But she remembers where we have forgotten." He looked at her with such tenderness that she had to look down at her feet. "The Lady never gives a directive without good reason. I guess that's why they say better than admiration, is obedience."

Jade nodded. She looked off into the distance trying to draw in as much serenity as she could. She repeated his words in her mind hoping they'd calm the storm within. She smiled ruefully at him, and they walked into the house. This time, Aaden led the way.

They walked into a deafening silence, and for a brief second Jade thought they were the first to arrive. But then they entered the dining area. Everyone—Rose included—was already seated. The tension was palpable, and only Aaden's firm grasp kept her from fleeing the room. Steve looked everywhere and nowhere at the same time, and he squirmed uncomfortably in his seat. He, too, seemed disquieted by the silence. But, Jade thought, it could just be he wasn't accustomed to not talking about himself. Meera didn't look at her, nor did Avi. Only Rose seemed comfortable in the silence. She smiled and gestured to the already-made plates waiting for them, and once they sat, Rose began to eat. Everyone else followed suit.

No one spoke, but their conversation was loud and clear all the same: the sighs, the way people cut their food into tiny pieces so they wouldn't have to open their mouths large enough to eat, the tiny sips of water. Meera and Avi didn't even fight over the tea towel.

Jade made it halfway through the meal before she couldn't take it anymore. She got up, cleaned her plate and left. She heard Meera's chair scrape the floor announcing she was getting up, too. Probably to follow me, Jade thought. But then she heard Rose's voice and Meera's chair scrape again. She didn't know if she was relieved or not. She wanted—needed—to hear that Sam was, truly fine, but she also didn't want to talk to Meera. Not yet.

By the time she got back to her camper, she no longer felt like crying, but the ball of shame remained. She sat on "her deck" and watched the birds have dinner, hoping to catch Aaden walking over to Avi's cabin. But exhaustion washed over her, and she went inside. She stopped short upon seeing a note placed on her bed.

She sat down and opened it.

"Dearest Jade,

It's days like these that are our biggest opportunity. These days are for breaking through who we think we are and taking a step towards who we are destined to be. It is imperative you attend Mantra practice in the morning. I will see you there."

The word imperative was underlined. Twice.

30 Déjà Vu

The next morning Jade woke to the bell beckoning everyone to chant—like it did every morning except Sunday. She rolled onto her back and stared at the ceiling. The word 'imperative' flashed like a neon sign in her mind.

She peeled herself out of bed, hazily pulled on her sweats and hoodie, and quietly walked up the hill to the main house. She was still more asleep than awake, and the misty morning added to the dream-like state she was in. Her shoes stepped on the bare ground to the beat of her heart, and somewhere to the east a bird sang *"Hello darkness my old…"* Jade stopped and listened. From the woods came again, *"Hello darkness my old…"* Friend. She silently answered with a hint of a smile. Friend.

A lone sheep greeted her with a sleepy, hungry bleat as she walked past their night pen.

"Shh… soon," she whispered.

Yesterday felt like years ago. The details were fuzzy. There was only a lingering trace of despair and when she searched for her lava ball of shame, she found only the grumblings of hunger. She wondered how it could've disappeared overnight, especially since it had featured so prominently in her dreams. Still, she welcomed the lighter feeling.

As soon as she stepped foot on the cobbled path, the main house reached out to her on its thread of incense. She breathed deeply and followed the scent into the teaching room. The candles were lit. Their flickering light illuminated people, philosophies, and godly beings alike as the centre's residents readied themselves to chant the morning into existence.

Her eyes adjusted to the soft light and she saw everyone already sitting silently.

A single cushion waited for her next to Meera who had turned upon hearing the door. She patted the cushion; there was no hint of yesterday's rebuke. Everyone else remained facing the eastern altar; their energy drawn inward and bodies wrapped in their meditation shawls, or in Steve's case, a blanket.

Jade sat down on the cushion. Her knees still stuck up at awkward angles, although not as awkward as they used to be. She placed a block under each thigh and allowed her legs to relax and the floor to support her. Meera handed her a book opened to the correct page. Rose began to chant and everyone joined in. Gently, almost lovingly. The sounds of the chant seemed to be coaxing the light over the mountains.

Jade still didn't know the chants well and oscillated between trying to chant along and just listening with her eyes closed. Each time her thoughts drifted to a memory of the day before, she was overcome by a compulsion to sigh, and then a rush of calm would come over her. Each exhalation seemed to be removing the negative thoughts before they could be anchored into a feeling.

A door hinge squeaked, but no one seemed to pay it any attention: no one moved or missed a beat in the chanting. She kept still, waited a few seconds, and then reached out her hand burying her fingers in the warm fur of one of Rose's dogs.

A small smile formed on her face, but she didn't look, she simply allowed herself to soften into the rhythms as they called in the light of day. She could hear each voice if she listened hard enough, but there was a strange beauty in hearing all the voices joined as one calling out to, and welcoming in, the Divine before they greeted each other as individuals. The thought reminded her of something her mother would say. Jade wondered if she was here, too, gathered with all the other honoured beings.

When the chanting finished, Jade opened her eyes to a room pierced with shafts of golden sun streaming through the window. Dawn had arrived.

Beside her, Pebbles was lying on her side and snoring softly. Her paws were outstretched and her pink tongue was poking out between her lips. The sun had turned her black fur into luminous dark chocolate. Everyone was looking from Rose, to the dog, to Jade. They were all smiling, clearly amused at the sight. Rose looked fondly at her pup and with a gentle nod that echoed through the room just as the bell had throughout the forest, signalled everyone to fold their shawls, pack up their cushions, and return them to the shelves at the back of the room.

As Steve walked past Jade, he looked at the dog and smiled. She didn't recoil or bristle at his presence. She could only assume this new reaction was a sign that today was no ordinary day. Jade brushed her fingers through

Pebble's fur again, and the dog groaned. It rolled onto its back exposing a warm belly that was available for additional pets should Jade feel up to it. She did and murmured sweet nothings to the dog as she stroked its soft fur.

Rose walked over to the two once everyone else had left. She looked down at them and nodded compassionately. Jade raised her head and gave Rose an apologetic smile: the kind that speaks louder than words and admits more than a confession.

Rose reached out and touched Jade's shoulder every so lightly as she moved towards the door with Pebbles now at her heels. "Just keep going. Let each wave of grace wash over you. Engage with every task today with full heart, and just—keep—going."

Jade inhaled sharply at the touch. Her mum used to do the same thing—calling that touch her "butterfly kiss". It had been her way of saying: I see you're going through something. Hang in there, kid. It gets better. Trust the process.

Jade nodded. She took a deep breath and exhaled slowly. "Thanks, Mum," she whispered and then stood and gathered her things.

31 Migrations

Jade opened the windows—seeking relief from the hot summer air trapped inside the camper. The heat wave had hit hard and fast rendering all hoodies and sweats redundant until the harvest was done. It was t-shirts and shorts from here on out. The open windows did not affect the interior temperature as the night air outside was only marginally cooler than the stifling heat inside. To make matters worse, the open windows might as well have been neon, all-you-can-eat buffet signs calling mosquitoes near and far to dine at Cafe Jade. Still, she accepted the inevitable inconvenience of itching for the ability to breathe.

Sprawled on the top of her bed, she tried to read *Living with the Himalayan Masters* by Swami Rama in the hopes that reading about residing in the cold mountain passes of India would perhaps trick her body into believing it was cooler than it was.

While she read, the usual evening's chorus faded into the background of her awareness: the crickets recited their evening mantras; a single clapper lazily met the lip of a bell hanging from an animal's neck as it wound down for sleep; the Northern Saw-Whet Owl piped its monotonous call (sounding like a child that only knows how to play one note on a recorder and does so with commitment); the occasional wolf's howl coming from a distance. The sounds used to keep her awake at night but now they comforted her, soothed her.

A high-pitched jingling of thin metal striking thin metal cut through the evening's lullaby making Jade's ears perk up. She stopped reading mid-sentence and listened. The tinkling sound made its way from around the north side of Jade's camper, circled to the south, and announced its arrival with cumbersome scratching on the door. Jade frowned.

She laid the book face down to hold her spot and opened the door. Pebbles was on the deck, sitting politely, tongue lolling out the side of her mouth. Jade looked around for Rose while Pebbles took the open door as an invitation and entered without so much as a backward glance at Jade. Pebbles jumped on the bed, briefly sniffed at her chosen spot, and lay down. She was kind enough to keep her back end off the pillow.

"Well, hello to you, too, Pebbles," Jade said, turning to look at the dog after deciding that Rose's presence was not forthcoming. Pebbles lifted one of her bat-like ears upon hearing her name but flattened it again almost immediately.

"I don't think you're allowed to be in here. Come on now. Let's go!" Jade held the door open and patted her thigh. She kept her voice light and sing-songy hoping to entice the dog toward the door. But Pebbles merely opened one eye, saw that Jade wasn't moving closer, and shut it again feigning sleep. "Come on now," Jade said more firmly. "Rose will be looking for you." She leaned over the bed and hooked her fingers under the dog's collar jingling the tags that had alerted her to Pebble's arrival. Pebbles got up reluctantly and jumped off the bed.

Expecting Pebble's momentum to carry her through the door, Jade removed her fingers from the collar and stood up. Pebbles clearly had other plans, and as soon as she felt Jade let go she quickly turned around and jumped back onto the bed. She resumed her previous position—pretending that the last few moments had never happened—eyes closed, ears twitching.

"Fine. But I'm not taking responsibility when someone comes looking for you. It's all on you, you hear me?" Pebbles groaned in contentment and stretched out on the bed claiming her share. Jade shook her head and chuckled as she shut the door. Then she claimed her portion of the bed, returned to her book, and listened for any sound that indicated someone was looking for her guest.

Jade read until her vision started to blur and she could no longer comprehend the words on the page. Then, and only then, did she mark her spot for the night and attempt to get some sleep. The heat of the day persisted despite the sun having set hours earlier causing her to sleep in fits and starts until, at last, deep sleep took hold. Her dreams were nonsensical—flashes of things she didn't understand mixed with images of her life in Kimberley and life at the centre. Smoke obscured dream-Jade's vision, and her ears pulsed with a heartbeat that wasn't hers. Pebbles scratching at the door to be let out woke Jade up. She rolled off the bed and opened the door for the dog. Silently cursing the animal she fumbled to put on her headlamp.

Despite her grogginess, she noticed that it was late enough for the crickets to have quieted but still too early for the sky to silhouette the trees in the pale light of dawn. She leaned against the door frame with her eyes half-closed—attempting to preserve her sleepiness—and directed the beam from her headlamp at the dog.

Every once in a while the light would catch Pebble's eyes and cause them to glow in the dark. Eerie at first, but a lot easier to track the light reflecting in her eyes than trying to discern her dark shape among the shadows. Pebbles finished her business and started meandering toward the camper when she all of a sudden halted and turned westward. Her ears stood on end and her hackles went up. Her body rigid, Pebbles dashed a few strides toward the shadows beyond Jade's headlamp and barked.

It was her "alert" bark. Her "warning bark". Jade hoped it was a deer moving under the cover of darkness and not the bear from the month prior. "Shhhst! Let's go!" she said in a loud whisper, not wanting her voice to alarm Avi who was likely sitting on his porch. "It's nothing you big galoot. Come on." Pebbles let out a final, indignant woof as if telling Jade and the noise in the woods to fuck off. Then she headed back inside the camper and flopped down on the bed. Jade lay next to her marveling at the dog's ability to go from high alert to dead asleep in a matter of seconds. She hoped to do the same, to sink back into the deep sleep she'd been awoken from. Instead, she slipped between worlds.

Odd noises from the west roused Jade. Trying not to wake Pebbles, she grabbed her headlamp and tiptoed to the door to look outside. She shined her light into the darkness hoping to catch a reflective pair of eyes and quell her curiosity. Had the animal Pebbles heard earlier returned?

Jade stood at the door—half in, half out—listening to the sounds growing closer and louder under the sliver of the moon. She could hear the crunching of sticks and leaves as the animal moved through the woods. She stood rooted to the spot, paralyzed by curiosity and fear; she held her breath and strained to hear.

She braced herself for the return of the grizzly or a cougar but hoped for a deer or an elk. She kept her eyes cast in the direction of the beast and waited for it to come closer. It took a second or two for her to reconcile the foal that came into view with her imagined predators. Jade's surprise doubled when a few steps behind it another foal emerged and then another. As each one came into view, she could see them better and better. They seemed to be bringing daylight with them. Her headlamp became unnecessary, and she clicked it off. The three foals were followed by a fully grown horse with a First Nations woman upon its back. She rode tall, with her back straight, regal in posture; she did not glance in Jade's direction.

As she passed, Jade could see that the woman carried a baby on her back. The infant was swaddled in a soft hide and strapped to a board. The board's petal shape gave the impression of a halo around the sleeping baby's head. Jade watched until the child was out of sight and then turned her gaze to the others that followed.

Most of the women on horseback rode with little children either strapped to their backs or sitting in front of them. The younger children held onto a tuft of mane for balance while the older ones practiced braiding it—the need to hold on was no longer necessary. The men came next. They, too, rode with the ease and confidence that one can only gain from having spent a lifetime on and around horses. There was no indication that they saw her; no acknowledgment of her presence. She seemed to be invisible.

Jade stared at the procession in silent wonder.

Emboldened by their lack of awareness of her, she left the safety of her camper and took a few steps toward the horses and their riders. The world around her felt thin, and the boundary between the past and present no longer seemed to exist. She watched the tribe of families move eastward on their mounts and was fascinated by the way they interacted with each other. She thought of how in the modern world moving house was always so stressful and hectic, but this migration—essentially the seasonal moving house of the tribes—looked joyful, playful, and remarkably calm as the horses meandered over the land.

Unexpectedly, a single horse stopped in front of Jade and looked right at her. It had dark brown eyes flecked with bits of amber and the longest eyelashes she had ever seen. The horse stared at her, assessing her. Then it blinked and tossed its head as though to shake off a fly. The spell broke, and Jade's eyes moved down the horse's neck to the teenage boy sitting astride its back. He was staring at her, too. His wide-eyed expression was a mirror image of her own.

The boy swivelled on the horse's bare back and said something to the man travelling behind him—an elder—their Chief. The man's eyes widened in surprise, and he looked directly at Jade taking in her bare feet, shorts, tank top, and headlamp strapped to her forehead. Feeling self-conscious and inappropriately dressed for her guests, she yanked the headlamp from her head and reached into the camper for a covering. She did not want to turn her back on them—fearing they would disappear. She grabbed the sheet she had kicked to the foot of the bed and wrapped it around her shoulders.

The boy said something to another rider who had just emerged from the trees and was stopped on the other side of the Chief. Similar in age to the first, Jade noticed the family resemblance and concluded they must be brothers. The two teens and the man regarded her with equal parts curiosity and reverence. Jade looked at them the same.

The Chief's gaze scanned his surroundings, taking in Jade's world: the camper, the deck, the prayer flags, and the muddy shoes she had left outside to deal with in the morning. He said something to the two boys in a language Jade did not recognize and dismounted his horse. The boys nodded and smiled. With his back to her, he searched through the raw-hide pack that lay across his steed's rump. He found what he was looking for and turned to Jade holding something in his hands.

His weathered face was framed by two, long black braids that ended mid-chest. His shirt was made out of a thin, light-coloured hide and was covered with a vest made of the same material. The vest, however, was decorated with intricate beadwork. Someone had carefully sewn a brightly coloured pattern of interlocking triangles and squares to create ribbons of colour up the front of his chest. His eyes were filled with wisdom and had a depth to them that she assumed came from leading his people. Or, perhaps it was the reason he was chosen, or born, to lead. His gaze made you want to stand tall and listen. She could see he was a proud man. A strong man. A kind man. He came toward her with the bundle of cloth he had removed from his pack cradled in his large hands.

Once he reached her, he painstakingly unfolded it, peeling away each delicate fold until a poncho-type shawl was revealed. It had been hand-stitched in a patchwork of thin hides and recycled cloth. She let out a small gasp, marvelling at its craftsmanship and beauty. He smiled at her and gestured for her to take it. She hesitated and looked over the Chief's shoulder to the boys on horseback. They nodded at her reassuringly, encouraging her to take it. She turned to the Chief and bowed in acceptance as he opened the shawl and draped it around her. She felt its weight in direct proportion to its honour. *A true gift is one given freely when there is not much to give,* her mother's voice whispered in her head as the shawl settled onto her shoulders.

Jade searched her mind for something of value to reciprocate, something to honour him, his family, and the people of his tribe. She gestured for him to stay where he stood. He responded by pointing at the ground and taking one step back; he smiled at her to show his understanding. She turned and hurried into the camper. In her haste, she caught her foot on the long train of the sheet and stumbled, knocking her shin into the metal frame of the door-step. She glanced at Pebbles. The dog whimpered and twitched its legs—the unexpected jostling of the bed had not disturbed her slumber.

She made her way to the cupboard that held the only thing worthy of be-ing a gift: the ceremonial scarf Meera had given her—her *angavastra*. It was sacred to her. Important. She had folded it into the size of a large postcard and slept with it under her pillow for a week after that day at Ma Labyrinth before she put it in the cupboard for safekeeping. She ran her hand over the fabric and pressed her lips to the blue, silk cloth simultaneously thanking it for its beauty and saying goodbye. Then she hastened to the door hoping the Chief was still there. He was. She stood before him and bowed her head. Then she wrapped the electric blue *angavastra* around his neck.

The Chief put his hands on his hips and puffed out his chest. The two boys giggled at the sight. He threw a look in their direction and then bowed to Jade in appreciation. He returned to his horse and said something to the boys which transformed their giggles into bashful smiles. They bowed their heads in acknowledgment of the gift and to show their laughter was not at her ex-pense. Jade smiled at them; she knew. Satisfied, the Chief mounted his horse and gestured for the two brothers to follow the rest of the tribe. He looked at Jade and her camper one more time, and then he followed his people over the hill towards the morning sun.

Jade jerked awake. Her heart thumped wildly in her chest and tears streamed down her temples soaking her pillow. The camper was bathed in the same soft glow of dawn light that had been in her dream. Overcome with the feeling of seeing and being seen, of there being something more than *this*, she sobbed tears of relief. Her heart cracked open in gratitude. Pebbles, who at some point had left the bed seeking a cooler spot on the floor, lifted her head at the sound of Jade's sobs. She got up, stretched her back legs with each step, and jumped up on the bed. She started licking the tears from Jade's face. Jade grabbed Pebbles and hugged her. The warmth of another body, the humid breath on her face, and the dog's beating heart brought her to this world; returned her fully to the present. Pebbles rolled over so Jade could rub her belly now that the hard work of cheering her up had been accomplished. Jade obliged.

As she sat up to get out of bed, she found the sheet wrapped around her as it had been during her meeting with the Chief. She hopped out of bed and stumbled as pain shot through her shin. She stepped toward the cupboard where her clothes were; she opened the door to see the shelf that usually held her a*ngavastra* was bare. She looked around hoping to see the poncho she'd been given, but it was nowhere to be found. Both objects had vanished. Perplexed but not entirely surprised, Jade sat on the edge of her bed and uncovered her leg to expose a small cut and a bruise. "What the fuck?!" she thought.

Jade grabbed her journal and wrote down the details of the dream into her journal. She wanted to anchor the memory to this world. While she was absorbed in her task, Pebbles scratched at the door wanting out. Jade reached over and opened the door. She watched Pebbles walk out the door and head eastward, following the path the Chief had ridden mere moments before.

Jade wasn't a fan of Meera's French toast or any French toast for that matter. It was something about the bread being soaked in a mixture of eggs, milk, salt, and pepper, and then topped with maple syrup that seemed to give it an identity crisis. The bread didn't know if it was supposed to be sweet or savoury, and it would just sit in Jade's mouth refusing to move. But it was a favourite of Aaden's, and Meera, who was still trying to coax him back to full health with her cooking, had made it every morning that week. Jade opted for a plain slice of bread with butter and chased it with a cup of tea. She was eager to get to the garden for her morning duties. She wanted to finish them quickly so she could find Rose and tell her about the strange dream she'd had.

On her way to the greenhouse, she was delighted to see Rose walking up the drive. Pebbles was at her heel. The pup was wagging her tail and looking very pleased with herself. She gave a woof of excitement as Jade came into view. Rose looked up at the sound and smiled. Jade threw her arm up in what was supposed to be a wave but ended up looking more like a cry for help.

"Good morning, Rose," Jade sang out when she got within polite earshot. Then she bit her lower lip to stall the torrent of words trying to spill from her mouth.

"Good morning, Jade. Did you sleep well?"

Energy surged through Jade and all the hairs on her arms stood up. "Um, do you have a moment?"

Rose turned her gaze towards the mountains before answering. To Jade, it seemed that she was assessing the morning light and weather. Then she looked at Jade with a faint smile on her lips and a guarded yet curious expression on her face. She nodded, "Why, yes. I do have a few moments for you. How may I help?"

32 Messages and Murmurs

Rose feels something in her bones, something she can't yet articulate but is real nonetheless. In the same way, animals sense earthquakes before they happen, Rose senses an unseen change in the frequency around her. Her own earthquake if you will. A shift in the weave of life. There is a *before* and an *after*, but never a *back to normal*. Some look in hindsight at these shifts, these mutant threads, as imperfections in the fabric of reality, but Rose doesn't. She sees the skipped warp threads and knotted wefts as part of a bigger design; the imperfections in the weave of life are the beautiful places that show us what we're truly made of.

Pressure is building in the air. It was subtle, not at all like the pressure that registers on the skin or in the sinuses as a storm approaches. But to those sensitive enough—and Rose was—the pressure was undeniable and her body vibrated with the knowledge that something was about to change. She had seen enough moons to know that change was neither good nor bad, it just was.

She can tell Pebbles feels it, too, which is why Rose had let her out the previous night when she started scratching at the door. It is also why she wasn't surprised that Pebbles hadn't returned until the early morning, and when she opened the door to greet her pup, the dog simply lumbered in and headed to her usual spot to sleep. Rose was curious as to where she had been and what had transpired, but Pebbles's snores started almost immediately. Story hour would have to wait. Rose sipped her tea slowly. She had time. She was patient. She sat and rocked in her chair. Listening. Thinking. Not quite worrying, but not exactly relaxing either.

"Something is coming," she said aloud.

Rose left her cabin and headed toward the centre on her usual route in the morning with Pebbles at her heels. Pebbles was ready for the day, feisty almost, after her early morning nap. Some people read the paper or listen to the radio to gather their news; Rose listens to the birds, to the trees; to the breeze.

She keeps her eyes focused on the ground so that her ears can lead the way—directing her toward those places where the land is speaking. She has learned that the land does not hold back its secrets if you know how to listen for them. After all, Earth is one large organism, Gaia, of which she is a part and gains nothing from concealing information from itself. That does not mean the forest is psychic, foretelling what is to come before it happens. No. That would be foolish to believe. But it does speak of changes, of shifts, and the land's messages are being sung by the birds, whispered by the trees, and carried by the breeze.

Something, something the birds chirp while they nervously forage for food. The trees, usually standing at attention and ready to offer their updates as Rose walks past, are unusually quiet this morning. They are distracted; their energy is turned inwards. Rose cocks her head to listen to the breeze but nothing is forthcoming as though it too is in a state of listening.

Pebbles woofs in greeting, and Rose looks up to see Jade walking—no, striding—towards her. Her head is high and she's waving in earnest. From this distance, she is the spitting image of her mother, and Roses smiles at the thought. *My sweet sister,* she thinks, *just look at your girl.*

"Um, do you have a moment?" Jade asks once she's close enough to be heard without shouting.

Rose notices their usual, awkward greeting has been snuffed out by whatever it is that Jade needs to tell her. She glances toward the mountain before answering and feels an incremental increase in the pressure. *We have almost arrived at the something* she thinks.

"Why, yes. I do have a few moments for you. How may I help?"

Jade begins to speak, and Rose simultaneously listens to her words and the spaces between them. For it is in the spaces where Spirit speaks and wisdom lays. When Jade finishes relaying her dream, Rose continues to listen for the messages that are still echoing. It is like Jade has launched a stone into a lake, and the story is not over until the waters are calm. Jade looks at her. Waiting to hear her thoughts. Waiting to be told what it means.

Rose shifts from listening with her ears to listening with her eyes. She looks critically at Jade. She wants to see how Jade is handling this new experience of reality before she shares her thoughts. Rose detects a spark that was not present yesterday. A layer of protection has cracked, and the light behind it breaks through a single star on a dark night. Jade's light.

Rose opens her mouth to respond but stops. A full-sized Bald Eagle glides overhead and lands on an upper branch of the closest Brother Ponderosa thirty feet away. Its mustard-coloured talons grip the branch as he gently pumps his wings a few times checking to see if his chosen branch will hold his full weight. Satisfied, he tucks his massive wings to his sides for safekeeping. Rose has not taken her eyes off him, and now that he is settled, she bows her head in a gesture of respect to the adult male. The bird mimics her and nods in reply. Jade stands frozen beside her, her mouth slightly agape.

The eagle looks down at them, making sure he has their full attention. Then, the snow-capped descendent of the Thunderbird cocks his head skyward, opens his yellow, hooked beak, and screams to the heavens. Jade jumps; Rose does not. The call Rose understands to be yet another message to layer on top of all the others—the *something* is nearly here.

Rose begins to join the invisible dots—Sherlock-ing her way through the trail of clues. She does not need to solve a murder or discover the secret of the hounds, but she does need to decipher a coded message. Why the Bald Eagle and not the gossiping Crows? Rose looks toward the western horizon and catches a glimpse of a flock of birds taking flight. Why did the Eagle come from the West when he normally goes in that direction at this time? She frowns.

"In what direction did you say the tribe was moving, Jade—in your dream?" An eastbound breeze answers her question before Jade can find the words.

"Um. From the West? They were walking toward the morning sun. So, yeah. towards the East." Jade has not looked away from the bird but Rose now focuses solely on the horizon.

She closes her eyes and opens the one in her mind so that she can see the picture the clues have provided with greater clarity. "Aaaaah," she says softly. "It is time." She looks back at the bird and nods her head in understanding and gratitude.

"Thank you, kind Sir. Be well," she says.

Seeing that his message has been received, the Eagle spreads his wings and takes off. His massive wingspan briefly blocks the Sun as he, too, heads eastward.

Rose watches until the bird is nothing more than a speck and then turns to look at Jade. She is not surprised to see the girl is already scrutinizing her: her eyes are filled with questions; and her brows are furrowed seeking answers.

"He came to give us a message," Rose says matter of factly.

"Which was?"

"Something is coming. Being that it was Brother Eagle, ancestor of the Thunderbird, it's likely a storm—lightning—perhaps a…," Rose trails off as a boom of thunder claps in the distance.

Jade gasps at the synchronicity.

Rose glances westward. "I'm very sorry, Jade, but I must go. Now. Your dream… is important and soon you'll understand why." She puts her hand reassuringly on Jade's shoulder. "I'll have Meera send for you soon." She gathers the fabric of her skirt in her hands and lifts it just high enough for her feet to be able to move swiftly without being hindered. "For now, please run and get Aaden. Tell him I need to see him. Then I need you to water the vegetable garden." Jade doesn't move, dumbfounded by Rose's response to a bird in a tree.

"Go. Now," Rose says urgently. "Run. Tell Aaden that Thunderbird has come."

33 Trees: Forks

Perspective is what sets a reality, and orientation is what gives direction, yet it is your senses, sweet one, that tell you the story. But what you see with your eyes is not the whole, for we see in hums, and we hear in light, our senses are fluid in their ebb and flow weaving a bigger picture. A picture that perceives the unseen.

Time, too, for us, is fluid. So slow and circular, that nuanced changes in our forest blur until unrecognizable, one day we are saplings—the next day stewards of the land, towering memory keepers, gripping Earth, and home to birds. To pinpoint when the change happens is impossible. For change is life's constant, always flowing. Our time spans are measured in forests, not in trunks. We still feel the pounding of the hooves of the migrating tribes of your distant past, rippling echoes through the ground into today's rings.

With time so slow, and witnessing so long, death, to us, is different. Our roots anchor to a world where death and birth are mere shifts from an inhalation to an exhalation. Night into day. Nothing to fear, simply a change in the direction of life-force that pervades us all. We never die, for our memory, our blood surrenders back to the ground from where we sprouted; our final offering, food for tomorrow's life.

Each cycle of your breath is a life of its own, and in the world of dualism, it's the flow of breath that keeps the momentum of the paradigm of time. As the up and down movements of a bird's wings help them to fly forward. Oscillation propels life. Humans must forget, to remember. Fall down into the rich darkness of Earth, to practice standing up to the Divine light of Sun, for it is in Earth Herself where we find the courage to stand up. We should know—you have to root, to rise.

Our breath, too, cycles, but more slowly. Our breath flows in time with the Earth's circling of the Sun.

There is a portal now. A fork in your road sweet one. You stand at it while your body sleeps. One road will be an end and one, the road less traveled——a birth. Life's choices are not measured in right or wrong, for in the path of eternity all roads must eventually join to the One. You have already had many such turns——old souls welcome the maze. For there are many lives within one body; many bodies within a soul's journey; many souls within the song of Creation. You know the one, the birds sing it each morning, to welcome back the light.

34 The Quest

Jade was physically present in the garden, hose in hand, watering the juvenile beans, but her mind kept slipping away to revisit the events from the last 24 hours: the foal, the migrating tribe, the poncho, the look on the Chief's face as he took in her surroundings, the missing scarf, her bruised shin, and the Bald Eagle in the tree. The scream it had given was unlike any sound she had ever heard. And the thunder, her mind whispered. Don't forget about the ominous thunderclap that caused Rose to turn and flee. Then her mind brought her back to the first foal stepping into the clearing. And she was right back where she had started. Like a snake eating its tail, she went round and round but never got anywhere with her perseverating.

She took a deep breath and blew the air out forcibly. She made her lips flap and the sound was loud in the otherwise quiet garden. I need a distraction she thought. Avi walked by in the direction of the main house, and Jade remembered the game he had shown her. Well, it wasn't a game per se—Jade couldn't imagine Avi ever playing games—but a practice. A training exercise for the senses.

"When you water the garden," he had said, "water it with your eyes closed and see if you can hear the shift in sound from when the ground is thirsty to when it has had enough."

Ok, she thought, let's give it a go. She closed her eyes and listened. The sound was muffled: a plonking of water drops on the leaves and silence on the soil. The water sounded low, far away, which Avi said meant the ground's satiation point had not yet been met. She opened her eyes to see if what she was hearing was correct. Yes. The beans needed a little more water. She closed her eyes again, listening intently for the water to change its tune.

"Jade," Aaden said. His voice was urgent.

She opened her eyes at the sound of his voice and spun around expecting to see him in full stride walking towards her. He was not. Aaden had stopped dead in his tracks a few steps into the garden. He was standing like Jesus—palms held upwards, his face looking at the sky. She followed his gaze to see what had caught his attention. Rain? No. Snow? Not exactly. Snow wasn't black.

She turned off the hose and dropped it to the ground. She held out her own hands to catch—she wasn't sure what she was trying to catch. The pieces floated to the ground like feathers. She caught one. They were needles, barely recognizable as such now with their burning red tips and short black tails, but very clearly either fir or pine needles. Jade rubbed her fingers together, and the needle disintegrated. Her mind refused to accept what she was seeing.

"What the…"

"It's ash, Jade. From a fire. The dry storm this morning, the thunder—well, the lightning—it started a fire up in the crown land—to the West. The forest is burning."

Dazed, Jade looked westward and saw a massive flock of black dots moving across the white sky. Moving away from a plume of dark smoke. They passed overhead calling to one another to hurry, calling out to those below to take flight, to find safety. Jade looked fearfully at Aaden.

"Rose needs to meet with all of us in the meditation room. Like, right now. She asked me to come get you."

"OK," said Jade, her legs already in motion before the words had even formed on her lips.

Inside the meditation room, the candles were lit on the altar as though they were going to repeat their morning chanting. Avi, Meera, Steve and Rose were already there. The silence was absolute, the nervous energy palpable.

"Come, Jade and Aaden. Sit down," Rose said as they entered the room. She waited for them to sit and then continued, "As you all know by now, there is a wildfire twenty-five kilometres away. It is up in the Crown land. Now, that might seem like a long way away, but with the prevailing winds and no rain in the forecast, it could easily reach us within a few days—perhaps sooner."

Jade looked around the room. Everyone was responding to the news in the only way they knew how: Meera furiously scribbled notes with her pencil across her notepad. Avi sat motionless and stared at the floor in front of Rose. Steve, squirmed with barely contained excitement. And Aaden looked back and forth between Rose and Jade with a face showing equal parts anticipation and apprehension.

"Anyone who wants to and can leave at this time, can," Rose said looking directly at Steve. *Can't take the hint,* Jade thought. "But, I believe the fire in the Crown lands has come to our door as an opportunity. The impetus for a quest of sorts."

"I'm in!" Steve said. "I'm your guy."

"I don't believe this quest is yours to take, dear Steve," Rose said patiently. Steve settled back on his cushion looking dejected. "Fire can be destructive and lethal, but it is also transformative," Rose said addressing everyone. "It brings balance and ushers in new life. It is a portal for change, and this fire, I believe, has been called forth for Jade."

Everyone turned to look at Jade. Meera stopped writing, and her eyes flicked back and forth between Jade and Rose. Avi nodded—his go-to gesture when digesting new information. Steve looked like he had been sucker punched in the gut. Aaden's face told her he already knew the fire belonged to Jade, and he was simply watching how she was going to respond. Jade didn't know what her face was revealing—she couldn't feel it. She touched her cheek to make sure it was still there.

Rose waited a few moments for the shock waves to settle and then began to issue directives. "Meera, please pack up any essential items we will want evacuated, should it come to that. Steve, I would like you to help Avi tag all the animals in case we need to let them loose in the forest. We need a way for them to be identified as ours. That means our phone number, name, etcetera. Aaden, Jade, please stay a moment longer. I need to talk to you both."

Meera and Avi got up and began walking towards the door. Steve held back, his brow furrowed. He opened his mouth to speak, but before he could say anything, Avi spoke.

"Let's go, Steve. You're with me." He waited by the door, clearly not leaving without him.

Deflated, Steve got up and followed Avi out. He cast one last look at Jade and Aaden and then scurried out as Avi barked his name once more.

Rose watches as Aaden and Jade exchange nervous glances. They are two old souls posing as young adults. Both of them trying to remember something they don't realize they've forgotten.

"Come, closer," she says and waits for them to move.

They scoot closer and adjust their cushions. Rose smiles and then gestures for them to wait quietly for the energy in the room to settle.

The floating wick on the altar behind her dips below the oil takes a sip of water, and crackles in surprise. Aaden's heart is pounding, and he is focusing on his breathing. Although his head is down and his gaze is fixed on a point on the floor in front of where she sits, she can see his t-shirt rhythmically jumping off his skin. Jade is sitting still, straight, unconsciously emulating the woman from her dream. Her eyes, however, are darting from side to side, and she is biting the nail of her thumb. She is also trying to slow her breathing and calm her racing heart.

Rose is well-versed in watching the internal dance people do when old patterns meet new levels of awareness. In such moments, patience is key. You cannot rush. You must wait for people to come to their own conclusions. So, she sits. A minute turns into two, then three, and then time no longer matters.

The wick balks at another sip of water and extinguishes itself in protest. The room fills with the scent of burnt cotton and vegetable oil that invokes childhood memories of deep-fried onions at the fall fair. They must be out of ghee again, Rose muses. Outside she can hear the animals bleating in objection at being corralled earlier than usual and tagged for identification. Finally, Jade makes eye contact. It is brief but speaks volumes. Rose can feel her dear friend Angie in the room with them now, and she wonders if Jade can feel her mother's presence, too.

"Jade…," she begins, but before she can say anything more Jade interrupts her.

"I'll do it."

Aaden and Rose look at her in surprise. Rose shifts slightly on her cushion and waits to see what lies behind her words. Jade shifts uneasily. She knows she's being analyzed, but this time, she doesn't back down.

"I mean, it's not like I have a choice. You said it yourself. This quest has been called forth for me. Why else would I have had that dream?"

Aaden opens his mouth to ask a question—probably along the lines of 'What dream?'—but decides against it.

"I don't know what I'm supposed to do," Jade says to her hands. "But, I just keep seeing that Chief. And thinking about the way he looked around. The way he looked at *me*. And then the Eagle. I mean—what was that, Rose?" Jade looks up at her with confusion and determination warring in her eyes.

"You have a choice, Jade. You always have a choice."

Rose needs her to step forward and accept the quest fully. Not because there is a lack of options, or out of fear of what might happen if she doesn't. She needs to *want* to step forward because she believes that in doing so. Something amazing will happen, something transformative.

"I believe you are right, though." Rose continues. "This opportunity is connected to your dream; it's showing you that you are ready to make the journey, to migrate from the past into the future. This wildfire has come so that you can face, and breakthrough, your own inferno of anger—of self-destruction."

Outside a woodpecker sounds its alarm: Danger! Danger! Flee to safety!

"But what do I do? Sit there and pray while a wildfire starts burning down the forest around me and try not to get pissed off?" Jade brings her knees up to her chest and locks her arms around them. She glares at Rose, but Rose knows the glare is not meant for her. Not really.

"No, not exactly." Rose lightly scratches the bridge of her nose to hide the smile threatening to break through. "You would have your fire in front of you, like Aaden did for his quest." Rose looks briefly at Aaden and the room momentarily fills with the echoing memory of the hell he has spent the last month crawling back from. The hell that she, and everyone else, tirelessly supported him through.

Rose clears her throat, and they all return to the present. "The quest, Jade, is twofold. It works simultaneously on the inner and outer worlds. If you balance one, you balance the other. Do you remember the photo on the altar of the Ancestors? The one with the five fires?" she says directing Jade's attention to the group of photos on the deep windowsill behind her.

Jade looks at the photos, always present in their never-ending vigil over the room. "Yeah. I do. You explained it to me when I was cleaning."

"Well, the quest at your level is a simplified version of that," Rose says. "That does not mean it will be easy. I can tell you that to succeed, you will have to find more faith and courage in yourself than you ever have had to before." Rose pauses and adjusts the fold of her skirt that drapes over her knee. She wants to allow time for her words to sink in, to penetrate the fear that is bubbling just below the surface.

"You need *awareness* and *consistency* of the outer fire in front of you," Rose continues, emphasizing the words hoping they will be latched onto as a life raft when the moment calls for them, "and *purification* and *endurance* of the inner fire. Only by maintaining balance in both the outer and inner fires, through chanting and other practices I will show you, will you be able to create the frequency that will balance both."

Jade's mind buzzes with the words awareness, consistency, purification, and endurance as overhead a water-bombing plane buzzes the house on its way to the fire. The animals—and Avi—erupt with bleats and curses at the unexpected noise. Steve's girlish scream and subsequent string of curses, likely from having been nibbled on by a goat, breaks the tension in the room.

Rose pretends not to have heard.

"And if I can bring balance to my internal fire—my anger—then I will balance the wildfire? It will go out?" Jade asks returning everyone's focus to the purpose of their meeting.

Rose nods, "That is correct."

Rose remembers this moment with her teacher. How she mistook the simplicity of the quest, for ease. How wrong she had been. Rose knows there is nothing she can say to prepare Jade for what she needs to do. She will either fail or succeed. She will either move through this rite of passage as Rose had done many moons ago, or she will fail just as Aaden had.

Jade looks to Aaden. Rose sees that their connection has reached the stage where words are not always necessary. He nods in encouragement and puts his hand over his belly. She puts her hand over hers in reply and nods before turning back to Rose.

"Do *you* think I can do it?" she asks. Her words sound assertive, but her eyes betray her as they search Rose's for reassurance.

Rose knows that Jade is looking for absolutes, for assurances she cannot give her. Instead, she searches for words she can stand behind. "You were signalled out by Thunderbird himself. You have been blessed by the Ancestors of this land who knew the time to migrate is now. They will be with you. We will *all* be with you. But, Jade, only you can do it."

While Jade absorbs her words, the old woman turns to Aaden.

"Aaden, since you have faced your fire before, you will be in the support position, as Avi was for you. To support another is the final stage of your quest." Aaden shoots a glance at Jade and smiles. "You must make sure she has the right amount of firewood next to her at all times. That her water is there. Once a day, you will bring her rice and a litre of Rose and Tulsi tea." Aaden nods and repeats back Rose's instructions making sure he has them down correctly.

"Rose," Jade said, not looking at her but at the picture on the altar behind her, "if the wildfire is the mirror to my internal fire, then what's the fire in front of me?"

"You need something external to focus on physically. You can't see the wildfire, so you must focus on the fire in front of you. It's the same element. You balance one, you balance them all."

"Balance one, balance them all," she repeats starting at the photo on the altar. She looks at Aaden again and then locks eyes with Rose. "I'll do it."

"Remember, Jade," Rose says, "the world is not separate parts that bump into each other once in a while. It is one organism. It ebbs and flows, mirroring and contrasting itself, onto itself, in a never-ending flow of consciousness. Your dream is not separate from the outside world. *You* are not separate. The fact that you had that dream the night before the Thunderbird himself came and the dry lightning started a huge fire is not a coincidence. We can, as most people would, put our heads in the sand, and deny responsibility, but…," Rose leans forward slightly, pulling Jade's attention away from the altar and holding it with a piercing gaze, "you were not born to put your head in the sand, Jade Madden. You were born, like your mother was, to stand up and remember."

Rose's words were electric. Their energy coursed through Jade's body making each hair stand erect and quiver. All at once, Jade felt both unrecognizable to herself and more herself than she ever had before. Rose was right. Jade could see it, but she couldn't quite understand it. Not yet.

It was as if a fairytale had come to life. Dreams crossing into reality, animals delivering messages, balancing elements to save the world. But, she could see that Rose was not making it up. That there is truth behind the fairytale. That's why some stories calcify into myths, like the ones her mother read to her at bedtime when she was a child. The stories are told over and over because at their nucleus a truth lies waiting—dormant—ready to sprout if only someone would remember to give it water.

35 Waxwings and Wapitis

It had been there on and off for the last hour or so. The bird with the black bandit mask. A mask that confirmed rather than hid its identity. Every other bird Jade had seen had been flying east, but not this one. This one had stayed. It flitted between the fruiting Saskatoon bush and the tip of the teepee pole above her head. The canvas of the teepee had disintegrated long ago, she'd been told, leaving its skeleton exposed to the world and a place for the peas to climb in their quest to reach the sun. Back and forth. Back and forth. The bird busied itself eating and singing—if you could call those beeps of high-pitched, monosyllabic buzzy notes singing. It watched her from behind its mask. It was fascinating and irritating at the same time.

"It's a Waxwing," Aaden said when he bought her a thermos of tea. "A Cedar Waxwing, actually. It's medicine is migration—transformation and clear perspective."

"I thought you weren't supposed to talk to me."

"I'm not. But it's too cool to let it just fly by without you knowing what its deal was," he said with a wink.

Jade smiled. "Thanks."

"I'll be back in the morning. You should have enough wood here now to get you through the night—plenty in fact. Remember, before you lie down, set the intention to wake before your fire goes out. It works. I don't know why. It's weird," he added with a slight tilt of his head, "but it works."

"Thanks," she said again as she returned her attention to the waxwing. It had another berry in its beak. It must be nearly full, she thought, this is the 7th berry she'd seen it eat since she'd started counting.

Watching the bird nibble on its purple delicacy reminded her that she was hungry. No. She was starving. She had eaten a piece of bread with butter at breakfast and then had been put straight into preparations for her quest before she'd had a chance to eat lunch.

The collection of wood, followed by a hot sauna and cold shower, and then meeting with Rose to learn the protocols and techniques she'd need for her quest had distracted her from her stomach. But now there was nothing else to pay attention to, except the bird and her outer fire. The realization that she'd be eating only half a cup of rice per day for the foreseeable future, tugged at her, distracting her from the things she was supposed to be doing. Just the thought of rice with a dribble of ghee gave rise to a strong craving for chocolate—almost strong enough to make her abandon her quest and let the centre burn down.

To divert her attention from her stomach, she decided to make her bed while it was still light. She unrolled her mat on the west side of the fire pit so her back was to the wildfire and she was beside the little altar with the assortment of crystals and statues. The photo of the old man sitting with his five fires from the practice room was placed on the altar to give her encouragement. Then, she placed the blanket Meera had given her to wrap herself in and the elk hide Rose had given her on top of the mat. Rose said she'd need the elk's stamina and the interactivity of community. She was to sit on it or lay under it to invoke its medicine. She closed her eyes and brushed her hand across the pelt. She could picture the beast, alive and warm, like that strong, antlered male she'd seen so many months before. She imagined it was reading the air with every strand of coarse hair on its back, pounding its hooves on the ground surrounded by its herd—free.

"Wapiti," she whispered. She has always loved the sound of the First Nations word for the elk. She smiles and mouths "Wapiti" again, enjoying the way the syllables are formed and hearing it echo in her head. A memory of a particularly wet Wapiti music festival brought a sad smile to her face.

While everyone else had clung white-knuckled to their umbrellas and stood under the trees waiting for the summer downpour to pass, Angelica had hiked up her soaked, linen skirt and danced an Irish jig in her bare feet just to make Jade laugh. Jade remembered she had looked like a drowned rat with her long hair clinging to her face. She had been smiling and laughing, her joy contagious. But it had been the sparkle in her eyes that Jade remembered most, that Jade missed the most.

A breeze blew in from the west and brought with it the faint smell of green wood smoke. Jade looked up just in time to see the Waxwing take flight towards the east. It finally decided to listen to the message the breezes had been sending all day and followed the rest of its kind to safety across the river. She looked over her shoulder, checking the source of the smoke, and saw the tops of the Fir trees waving slightly in the air. *Are they saying hello to me or writing their wills on the canvas of the sky?* Her stomach flipped at the thought.

Jade placed another log on the fire in front of her and watched the flames first start to lick the new wood, then char it with its teeth, before devouring it mercilessly. The smoke from her fire did not smell the same as the smoke riding the wind. Hers was comforting and familiar. The traditional scent of fire being liberated from something already dead, not of something being burned alive.

She watched a finely shaped crescent moon rise above the mountains in front of her. Its light was diffused by the smoky haze, and it moved with none of the urgency Jade felt on the ground. Its position in the sky was Jade's only sense of time, and right now it seemed that time had slowed to a crawl.

As night slowly enveloped day, the temperature started to dip, and Jade reached for the thermos of hot tea: Tulsi Basil and Rose infused into hot water. I wonder who thought to do such things the very first time, she mused as the tea touched her tongue. She thought that Aaden had forgotten to put in the rose because all she could taste was the Tulsi all sharp and spicy. But then the aftertaste of the Rose waltzed in, fashionably late to the party and danced on top of the green herb. It made her nose want to inhale the scent trapped in her mouth. She imagined the two flavours holding a standoff within the thermos, each refusing to mingle with the other, and smiled to herself. She took another sip and then another, letting the herb and the flower create personalities and dialogue in her mind, and soon the thermos was empty. "Damn it," she said shaking the empty container, trying to eek out the last drop. She had wanted to save some for tomorrow—to ration her sips—until the plain rice arrived. She sighed. She'd have nothing now, except a small amount of water.

The fire popped and hissed in commiseration as sap seeped from the burning wood. The scent of burning resin filled the air around her, and she breathed deeply. The flames flickered and danced—mesmerizing her while the moon finished its climb and started to glide across the sky. She slowly came out of her reverie as the flames died down, their meal nearly over.

She decided to turn in for the night and began her evening routine. She wrapped herself in the blanket Meera had given her that afternoon and re-cited, syllable by painful syllable, the mantras Rose had instructed her to do. She set the intention to wake before the fire went out, just like Aaden had said, and laid down, lullabied by the breeze and the whirring of a Nighthawk's wings against the darkness as it searched for the easy meal of fleeing prey. She drifted off to sleep wondering when the nighthawk would abandon her, too.

She woke to a pitch-black world. Terrified the fire had died while she slept, she bolted upright. Her heart pounding. "Fuuuuuuuuuuuck," she moaned and mentally began berating herself: you're a failure; it's over; you couldn't even make it through one night. She had just gotten to having the ruin of the centre on her conscience when she saw the bright glow of the coals hiding at the heart of her fire pit. They flickered and spoke softly, kindly, urging her to be gentle.

"Still here…waiting," they said. "All is not lost."

She fed the fire and then went to relieve herself, grateful rather than remorseful that she had drunk the full thermos of tea.

She took a moment to scan the horizon in all directions before lying down again. Only the faint, orange glow in the distant western sky and the fire's light in front of her gave any indication that the world existed. It was beautiful in its own way. If colour had sound they could have been two distant cousins calling out to each other in the darkness.

For the rest of the night, Jade slept poorly. She slept and woke at odd intervals, which was terrible for any sense of being rested for the day ahead, but great for her fire. Finally, she gave up on sleeping as dawn began to creep its way into the sky and she was able to see farther and farther. She was tired, so tried, and hungry. She decided to try and fuel herself with fresh air and her morning chants.

When Aaden arrived mid-morning carrying more wood and a tray with a bowl of rice, she wasn't even all that interested in eating but was grateful for the brief connection of his presence. He handed her a folded shawl that faintly smelt of sandalwood but didn't speak to her this time. He caught her eye and flashed a smile as he took a note out of his pocket and tucked it under the bowl of rice.

As soon as he was out of sight, she took the note and opened it expecting to see the scribble he called handwriting but instead found Rose's elegant hand.

Remember Jade,
The portals of initiation come through the elements.
The human body is born, initiated through water; the human mind is born, initiated, through fire.
In fire, we find enough intensity to seed a new world.
We do not break the mind, but we surrender it.

Surrender it to what? Jade thought. She read the note twice more before she folded it up and tucked it under the old man's picture on the altar. Sometimes Rose's cryptic nature frustrated her. Why couldn't she just say what she meant? Why did she always have to be so ambiguous? Speak in riddles?

She spent the morning and most of the afternoon moving between weeding the surrounding garden and sitting in front of the fire. It was hot. The sun was a fuzzy ball in the sky, but its rays still burned her Irish skin. She started to feel uncomfortable, vulnerable, and exposed. Like Gollum, she skulked from one brief shadow to the next, hiding under the shawl, trying to avoid the light at all costs as the sun crawled across the summer sky.

By mid-afternoon, she was exhausted from all the hiding. She laid down—feeling more dead than alive—next to her fire and asked it to speak loudly when it got hungry. It popped and crackled in reply. *Is this what having a baby is like?* she wondered as she closed her eyes. *Your existence constantly revolving around the feeding of an insatiable beast?* No wonder she was an only child.

When she woke, her thermos of tea had been placed next to her. The Sun was merging with the fire's light in the western sky creating an effect that was end-of-world-eerie.

Was the fire getting nearer? Was it growing? Was it out of control? Or had the forest fire crews made headway taming it? She stared in the fire's direction trying to determine if it looked bigger, brighter. Unable to answer her questions, she gave up wondering, turned to the rice and ate. Finally. She waited as long as possible before drinking her tea hoping that she could use her bladder again as an alarm in the night.

By evening, just over twenty-four hours after having started this crazy endeavour, she felt a rhythm had been established. An animalistic rhythm of sleeping when tired and eating when hungry, of listening to the sounds or the absence of them from someplace beyond her ears. She was strangely content, which concerned her. Wasn't she supposed to be facing her anger? She didn't feel angry. Wasn't she supposed to be facing the intensity of her fire? Whatever that meant. Apart from her sunburned skin still glowing, she didn't feel uncomfortable and *that* realization made her discomforted. Irreverently, she threw another log onto her fire and took out Rose's note from the photo.

She unfolded the note and tilted it toward the flickering light in case it needed fire to reveal its meaning, to translate it into something Jade could fully understand. *The one note to rule them all.* She snickered. The page took on the glow of the flames, and Jade decided she needed to feed it to the fire so that the fire could fully digest its meaning and then tell her what Rose meant. She tossed it onto the coals and watched the ink on the page dissolve into wisps of white smoke. The smoke made pretty swirls in the air that twisted and turned before vanishing. No secrets were divulged, and no messages were given.

"Screw you then," Jade said. Her voice sounded strange to her ears; aggressive. It contrasted violently with the land she sat in.

The flames dimmed immediately at her insult, leaving behind flat, fragile ash across the log as they retreated. She poked and blew on it in apology. She did not beg forgiveness for being crass, but she came close.

When the fire had been sufficiently coaxed back to life, she laid down and closed her eyes after once more asking the fire to alert her when it was hungry. She hoped fires didn't hold grudges. But instead of being awakened by the soft clicks of the fire, or her bladder, she woke to her stomach desperately needing to evacuate its contents. She ran to the edge of her circle, fell to her hands and knees, and threw up. Tea and tiny bits of undigested rice splattered on the ground. She wretched with enough force to startle an owl who called, "Who-cooks-for-you? Who-cooks-for-you?"

She sat back, looked down at her vomit in the firelight, and then looked at the fire itself. It waved at her as it fed on the wood she'd given it earlier. She crawled over to it and placed another log on top, but before it could spark with thanks, she scurried back to the edge of her circle and threw up again. "What the fuck?" she gasped once she finished. She hadn't eaten anything that could make her sick. You don't get sick from herbal tea and plain rice, she thought. "This is bullshit," she said to no one, "fucking bullshit." Her stomach cramped in response, and she puked again. Saliva flecked with vomit oozed down her chin. She wiped at it weakly with the back of her hand and waited for the spasms to pass.

When there was nothing left to offer the ground, she laid down in a puke-free spot on the wood-chipped ground and tried to concentrate on breathing. So far from the fire, she could feel the chill of the night air, and her body started to shiver. She crawled slowly back to her fire's side for its company and warmth and buried herself under the elk hide.

Elk's medicine is endurance, to see something through to the end. She heard Rose's voice telling her in her mind. I guess this is a good time to be cloaked in it then, she thought.

Nausea rolled through her body for the remainder of the night. She tried to drink a little water, but it came back up again before it could reach her stomach. The dashes to the edge of the circle and the subsequent crawling back to the refuge of the Elk left her exhausted. She tried to see her experience from her fire's perspective—was it watching her go back and forth, swear and moan, toss and turn? If so, it seemed unfazed by her distress, focusing on its own preservation—consuming everything in its reach.

She covered her head with the Elk's pelt—hiding from the smoke-scented air and the always-watching moon. For the first time in a long time, she didn't care if she woke up. Then sleep took her, and she dreamed of fire.

36 Trees: Fire

It's working, our friend! It's working! Do you hear our cheers for you on the breeze?

This is what it takes to burn. One must lose all control. All desire to retain the status quo. All sense of ease. One must beg to survive only in whatever way creates the most beauty within. This is what it means to transform into the One.

Wisdom bubbles up from the mantle below us. Every being wants to be a diamond, but no one wants to go through the pressure and the heat to become one.

Sweet caterpillar writhing on the ground in your cocoon of another's skin, this is how wings are formed.

37 What It Takes To Burn

The cool, silent dawn registered more ominous than calm as Jade emerged from under the shelter of the Elk. She blinked a few times. Bleary. Befuddled by the grey light. Then she remembered the fire.

She threw off the hide and crawled to the hearth just a few feet away. It was sleeping. Jade poked it, allowing the cool morning air to wake it up. She fed it splintered morsels of wood until it burst to life once more.

She sat back, relieved and also satisfied with her pyrotechnic skills. She was getting good at this. Steam rose from the dew-covered bricks as they grew hot from the fire. Beads of water formed, danced, and then disappeared leaving no trace of their existence. Fire changes everything, Jade thought. Changes, not destroys. And for a brief second Jade almost understood Rose's message, but then the fire popped and she lost the thought.

The smell of wildfire smoke was worse this morning. There were no birds around to sing the news from the treetops. Instead, the westerly wind carried the day's missives: tales of chaos and carnage swirled through the trees. She scanned her surroundings trying to locate other heartbeats hoping to hear the usual rustling of chipmunks and squirrels in the brush. She was alone. Completely alone. No birds, no animals. Even though she knew there were humans nearby—or at least hoped they hadn't fled without telling her—she felt like the last human on Earth. She looked at the fire: her sole companion.

The night before felt distant. Surreal. Like it had happened to somebody else. She put her hand to her stomach and frowned, unable to understand how she could go from being so ill to being so well in such a short amount of time. Had she really spent the night puking? The puddle of vomit said yes.

Her body said no.

She took a sip of water. It went down without a problem, so she took another.

Don't push your luck, she thought and turned her attention to the morning practices, chanting and meditation, and the rituals: the offering of herbs, rose water, and ghee to the fire. The main mantra was flowing better now; the longer ones, the ones she didn't have to repeat as often, still needed care. One by one she recited them, her voice hovering just above a whisper as though she was trying to coax a wild animal to safety or impart a long-held secret.

Aaden arrived with her meal just before lunch. Again, he didn't speak, but he didn't have to. The look on his face said it all. Apparently, she looked worse than she felt. Looking at him carefully, she saw worry etched into every line and the tight smile he gave her did nothing to assuage her fears.

When the sun reached its apex, she took refuge under her shawl and tried to eat a few bites of the plain rice, more out of something to do than out of hunger. As she nibbled at the parts that had the most ghee and salt on them, she saw, through the sparse lilac hedge bordering the far side of the garden, a van crawled up the driveway.

Jade put the rice down and added a piece of wood to the fire. She wanted her full attention on what was happening. She didn't recognize the vehicle or the driver, but their arrival seemed to set Meera in motion. She spun around and jogged into the house. Then the boys, Aaden and Steve, emerged from the main house carrying things wrapped in blankets.

"Fuck," Jade whispered, and the fire spat in response. "Sorry," she mouthed at the flames. And then turning back to watch the boys she said, "This is bad. Really, fucking bad."

She couldn't go anywhere, or help, or ask questions. The lack of under-standing started to make her body tremble with anxiety. Her mind conjured images of the buildings on fire, the animals bleating in terror, and her still sitting there. The image twisted and everyone clambered into a car and drove away—Rose included—while she stayed where she was sitting in front of the fucking fire.

She jumped to her feet and started to pace the five feet in front of the hearth. She wondered if this was what Aaden felt like when his bed went up in flames. Panic started to rise and her heart began to pound. The blood rushing in her ears drowned out the sound of the boys' and Meera's voices.

She stood over the fire. The heat made her skin itch and the smoke made her eyes water. But, the fire was ambivalent to its effects on her or anything else for that matter. It glowed with self-importance. It didn't care. It just wanted to burn.

Jade heard the van doors close, and she watched as it drove away with Aaden and Steve inside. It disappeared down the drive carrying all the centre's valuables to safety. It wasn't until the sun was well on its way toward the horizon that the van returned. And then after what felt like an eternity after that, Aaden arrived with her thermos of tea.

The moment he stepped into the circle she pounced on him like a big cat that had been stalking its prey from a tree.

"What's going on?" she demanded.

"I can't tell you," he replied looking around to make sure no one was watching. "I'm not allowed to talk to you, remember?"

"I don't give a shit. Tell me what's happening."

The fire crackled between them like a toddler trying to distract its arguing parents.

Jade's hands curled into fists, and Aaden clenched his jaw until she could see a vein bulging in his forehead. "Tell me!" she hissed.

He turned and walked away.

"Fuck you, you weak, spineless bastard," she said loud enough for him to hear, but his stride never faltered; he walked away and didn't look back.

Jade picked up one of Rose's crystals decorating the altar and threw it at the gate Aaden had closed behind him. The crystal hit the wood panelling and landed in two separate pieces on the ground. She had thought throwing something would make her feel better. It didn't. Now she was angry at herself for damaging something beautiful—something that wasn't even hers to break.

She turned to the fire. It looked weak. Pathetic. Barely even a fire. She threw a piece of wood onto it. The fire flared. It still wasn't enough—wasn't hot enough, big enough to match her fury. She added more wood until it stood raging out of control and ready to hurt anyone who got too close.

She walked in circles around the fire, her bare feet making a ring of destruction on the wood-chipped ground. The fire, which had already exhausted its rage and was returning to its polite size, waited for her to do the same. Eventually, she stopped pacing and sat. She was still fuming but the outburst had at least worked up an appetite. She looked over at the tray with her half-eaten bowl of rice and saw another note, the same paper as the last one, sticking out from under the tea towel. She grabbed it, unfolding the paper as she sat back, and quickly read through Rose's note. She didn't understand a word she had read. She swore under her breath and read it a second time and then a third. The fourth time through, she was able to slow down enough to pay attention to the words on the page.

Jade, beloved Self,

Everyone must face their own fire—their own ego—their own mind—at some point if they are going to heal. Some people's fire comes through what you call depression. They create an internal prison and lock themselves inside. Aaden, Jade thought. Others' fire is an outward expression—anger, volatility, outbursts of entitlement and indignation. Me, she sighed. Either way, inward or outward, for the mind to come into balance, the fire must be faced and transmuted away from self-destruction and into fuel for a higher good. Let go of who you think you are—your temperament, the you that holds you separate from everything—and surrender to your essence.

Embody your essence in this moment and you will find peace.

Tat Twam Asi.

She folded up the paper and tucked it into her bra strap. She put a single piece of wood on the fire and gathered her knees under her chin. Rose's words swirled in her head. Anger, fire, temperament, fuel, face… face. "That's it!" she said. She had everything—her seat, her bed—on the western side of her fire. She had been lying between her fire and the wildfire, sandwiched, embroiled between the flames. She needed to face them—not be in them. She scrambled to her feet and dragged everything to the opposite side of the teepee's circle. Now when she faced her personal fire, she also faced the wildfire and the altar, giving her a choice of what to focus on.

She looked up and saw the late afternoon sun was being distorted by black smoke. The gray haze of yesterday was gone. The fire was getting closer. From over by the barn she could hear the animals calling out to each other in fright and Avi and Meera shouting. They were rounding up the animals— likely to trailer them to a neighbouring farm out of harm's way.

"Oh, Shit. This is bad," she muttered, "This is really, really bad." She felt the ground start to spin, her vision tunnel and her thoughts spiralled. She was too late. She was going to fail. The fire was too close. Then, one thought burst through them all: surely Rose would come and get her if she was going to be in harm's way. Right? She had to trust, that if she had not been told to leave the circle, then she still had a chance of success. There was time. She could still do it.

The gate slammed open, and its sound brought Jade back to the present. Aaden came through the opening with an enormous armload of wood. It was balanced against his cheek and went higher than his head. He stopped and looked at the ground as he reached behind himself to kick the gate closed with one foot. His hands—obviously—were occupied.

Without dropping a single piece of wood, he stepped inside the circle but kept his distance from her by walking the long way around to the woodpile.

"I'm sorry," she said softly.

He nodded in response.

"Avi's moving the animals?"

He nodded again.

"It's bad, isn't it?"

"Yeah," he whispered, despite the prohibition. "The Lady, Meera, and Avi are going to be here tonight. They will come and get you if you need to evacuate. Steve and I are going to stay with the Clooneys on the other side of the river." He began to walk away but hesitated before he stepped out of the circle. He faced her and said, quietly, "I believe in you." Then Aaden stepped over the imaginary threshold and passed through the gate and out of sight.

Jade felt as though the sun fell out of the sky rather than set, but in reality, it was the black smoke that plunged day rapidly into night. She looked behind her to the east, hoping to see the moon rise, but there was nothing above the dusty peaks of the mountains. Tonight was the new moon. The dark moon. She hadn't realized how much she counted on its crossing to help her keep track of the night's progress. Without it to watch and the increasing smoke cover blocking all the stars, she was sure to lose all sense of time.

Now and then a distant call of an animal could be heard, but it was always a single cry and not enough to determine its direction. Also, she wasn't entirely sure if she actually heard the animal or imagined she did.

Darkness took over the land, casting everything in shadow before swallowing it whole. It wrapped its arms around Jade and infiltrated her mind. She felt helpless. A failure. Worthless. She considered walking away—facing another court hearing would be easier than facing Rose. She considered walking west towards the flames—give herself over to the wildfire. That, too, seemed easier than facing Meera, Avi—Aaden. She felt little bits and pieces touching her face, her arms, and her legs, and she wanted to crawl out of her skin. She brushed her hands against her legs, trying to get at what was irritating her. Her fingers came back black and grey. Ash. Ash was falling again.

Beyond the immediate silence that surrounded her, she could hear a low rumble like a fully laden logging truck driving the dirt roads at high speed. But it was night. There weren't any logging trucks now. She closed her eyes to hear better. It was the fire, she realized. She could hear the growling of the wildfire.

Her heart started rabbiting in her chest. She needed to do something to stop herself from running away and hurting herself, but there was nothing she could do, but sit, feed the fire—and chant. She got up and pulled the Elk pelt she'd spent the night hiding under to the fire's side and sat on top of it. She grabbed Meera's blanket and wrapped it around her for comfort and the shawl on top of that. She started to chant out loud—repeating the mantra until her voice became hoarse and her breathing laboured—fighting the emotions that swirled like a cyclone inside of her: anger, failure, despair, grief.

Rose's note poked at the soft skin of her breast, and she pulled it out of her bra. She read it again by the light of the fire.

"I'm facing the fire," she whispered to the note. "Now what?"

Words leaped off the page at her: *Let go of who you think you are… surrender to your essence. Embody your essence in this moment and you will find peace.*

"In this moment, Rose, I am nobody," she said. A surge of emotion rammed against the confines of her chest like a caged animal that has found a weak link in its prison. "I have nothing to give, I don't know what to do!" The fire popped and sizzled, and another bolt of energy rammed the cage of her chest creating a fissure. A paw with razor-sharp nails lashed out through the gap grasping at freedom and promising to decimate anything it came in contact with. "Tell me, and I'll do it!" she cried. "Just tell me what to do!" Tears streamed down her face; she was no longer able to contain them. "JUST FUCKING TELL ME!" she screamed as the wild beast sprang free from its cage in her chest and raced westward into the night. Jade grabbed at the earth in front of her to stop her body from running after it. Through her tears, Jade saw that the world around her had disappeared. She was alone. Like she always was. The orange flames before her and the tortured growls in the distance were her only companions.

"*Chant, child, chant…*" a voice from beyond the flames, from beyond her own mind, whispered as sweetly as a mother's lullaby.

She did as she was told. She let go of her fistfuls of Earth and sat up straight. She wiped at the tears and snots with the back of her hands and began to mouth the mantra between her sobs. The tears and sobs lessened. She focused on the words. She surrendered to their flow.

38 Shiva's Tongue

Gently rocking in her chair by the window, Rose sits sipping her tea and watching the westward sky. She is mesmerized by the wildfire, by the trees silhouetted in an undulating red and orange glow, by the pine needle embers dancing through the air and landing delicately upon the ground. She ponders how sometimes destruction, in and of itself, can be beautiful.

With a gentle smile, she casts a knowing glance at her Shiva statue, who sits on His tiger skin watching her watch the sky. "You, the Destroyer, would know all about that wouldn't you?" she says.

Shiva holds his tongue; his silence speaks volumes.

39 Carved Bones and Conversations

Jade sits with her eyes shuttered and repeats the mantra over and over. Her senses no longer seem to function the way they're supposed to, and she is too exhausted to resist when her words whisk her up onto a magic carpet of sound. The night air and the fire before her move in and out of her peripheral awareness—and she is unable to decide what to focus on. She gives up trying and surrenders to the flow of syllables.

The mantra ends, and she starts over. She's lost track of how many times she's done this. She just knows she has to keep going. Despite her lowered lids, she sees… something forming before her. Her eyebrows furrow slightly in concentration, and she squeezes her eyes even tighter trying with all her might to see what it is. It is not the orange glow of the fire but rather a translucent sheath—a veil. It has no beginning. It has no end. She tries to will her mind to see beyond it and fails. The mantras form something akin to vines of light that reach out and pierce the sheath with ease. She lets go of trying to see beyond the veil and directs her attention toward the sounds, the expanding vines. They relax her, soothe her, and at last, they carry her through the sheath to reveal what lies beyond.

A translucent sphere the size of a huge cottage hovers before her. It is made of what looks like intricately carved bone, as fine and as delicate as an eggshell. A narrow bridge extends from the sphere to her feet, spanning a void between them. Up close, she can see the bridge is made of the same material as the sphere, but solid, and the carvings are as ornate as Chinese jade—but white. Everything is varying shades of white.

An apparition forms inside the sphere and then emerges before her on the other side of the void. It is not flesh and bone, but rather a personality pulsing with white and gold light that has been formed by frequency. They regard each other for a moment—she and this thing, this being. Suddenly, a stream of light from the orb reaches across the void to her and floods her with feelings of pure compassion and kindness. The light brings forth the painful awareness of why she has come here, The wildfire. Her wild-fire.

She attempts to step onto the bridge. Earthly words and actions feel infantile and sluggish here in a world that is shaped by the mind alone, but with the intention of reaching this being and pleading with it for relief from the inferno raging inside her, she tries to move forward. An invisible force blocks her way. *You must do things differently here. Send it to me,* she hears in her head. The words are not hers though they echo in her mind. The words belong to the beam of light, and she does not question them.

Jade brings her awareness to the ball of lava that has sat in her stomach for what feels like forever, but in reality, was formed the day her mother died. Filled with despair and self-loathing it has grown larger and hotter and pulsates with a heartbeat of its own. She pauses for just a moment to focus on the mantra and then sends the energy of the lava ball to the orb on a thread of sound—infused with her own beam of, murky, not quite white, light. She focuses on keeping her mind steady, and slowly, her thread of emotion crosses the void and lands at the orb's base. The orb flashes once, nearly blinding Jade with its brilliance, and then begins to drink. It absorbs the thread into its Self the way a tree's roots soak in water from the rain-laden ground. Jade can see her murky light being transmuted in the orb until it is white and pure and sent back to Jade's heart. A circular link is formed between them—a conversation without the need for words. Jade empties every ounce of pain she's had locked away into a silent cry of surrender.

Jade ceases chanting. There is no need for it now. The mantras emanate spontaneously from within her and carry her shadows across the void. The orb's beam of light grows stronger, and brighter somehow, and fills the newly emptied spaces in Jade with white and gold. Jade wants to cry out, but she is incapable of speech. Her chest starts to burn, not in pain, but in compassion. Compassion not just for herself, but for all beings. Faster and faster the loop of light cycles between them until all Jade's pain is neutralized by the orb's compassion and all that remains is Love. Pure, unconditional Love.

In some distant place, she feels warm tears run down her face and drip onto her hands. The orb beckons her closer, but the bridge remains impassable.

She remembers Rose's words. *Let go.* And she does.

With her arms relaxed beside her, she turns her palms towards the orb and takes a step toward the land of bone and light. She lifts her chin slightly, laying bare her heart and throat. She can feel the barrier dissipate, and the sacred syllables carry her over the bridge to the place where silence sings. As soon as she steps onto the bridge, she remembers where she fits, where she belongs and she leaves the world behind.

40 Abraham's Mother

Rose's mind rocks back and forth matching the rhythm of her chair. She knows Jade has what it takes to balance the fire, but the motherly part of her worries it is all too much, too soon. She is still young.

Angelica was young too, she remembers. Not much older than Jade is now. Jade has her fierceness; the thread that can either pierce the worlds and let light into places lost long ago to darkness or incinerate everything with which it comes into contact. Rose can see that as clear as day—has seen it. And yet, she is concerned that this moment is asking too much of her. Back and forth she see-saws from trusting the signs—the dream, the thunderbird eagle— and what her heart knows, to worrying that Jade will break like Aaden did. His hell still echoes through the trees after all.

The room is lit by a single candle, and its flickering lights distract her from her inner musings. It dances as if being fueled by something more than the beeswax, and an almost airless breeze washes over her causing goose bumps to cover her skin. She cocks her head as if she has heard something, but she is uncertain. She slows the rocker and then stops it completely so that she can listen uninhibited by the creaking chair.

Tap… tap… taptap… tap…

Something is playing the metal roof above her head like an arrhythmic xylophone. A note here, a note there. She looks up, trying to see through the wooden ceiling to the sky above. She wants to see who, or what is playing the tin, but her eyes cannot penetrate the timbers.

She looks out the window. An hour ago, Orion had been plotting his course to Sirius across the heavens, but now he was nowhere to be seen. She stands to get a better look. Maybe she has missed him while lost in her musings?

She places her half-drunk tea on the side table and goes outside.

"Sweet Mother of Abraham! She's done it," Rose whispers, as much to herself as to the large Fir that stoically guards her door. Rain splashes on her upturned face and she smiles as it increases in intensity and drums against the tin roof and earthen ground. The sound is delicious.

A breeze moves through her friend's branches and it sounds like an ovation; Rose is showered in little green confetti. She laughs and twirls in the falling needles.

"I know!" she says. "And we *will* celebrate. But, first," she laughs again, "First we must tell her she has triumphed!"

Rose sits on the opposite side of the fire from Jade and looks at her sitting so peacefully, no longer aware of this world for the time being. Her face is tilted slightly toward the sky, and the raindrops falling between the spoked ribs of the teepee, camouflage the tears that streak her face. Her hands rest lightly on her lap, palms up, collecting the raindrops before they can reach the earth—a blessing to drink upon waking.

Rose can't take her eyes off her. Jade's pale skin is alight in the glow of the fire. The rain refracts and reflects the firelight in each droplet as it falls to the earth making Jade look as though she is being showered in tiny falling stars. Rose is immediately reminded of the Willow trees—the Salis—as their golden, buttery flowers cascade to the ground. The memory of the sweet, floral honey smell collided with the charcoal before her. She inhales deeply, and her soul rejoices.

The rain falls steadily and brings much-needed relief to the land. The bricks sizzle; steam rises in the air. There is nothing to do now but wait. Wait for the rain to put out the wildfires. Wait for the dawn to break. Wait for Jade to come back to the earthly realm.

Rose feels a familiar pressure in her chest. Her heart bursts open in gratitude and her eyes well up in response. She gives a soft smile and does the only thing that seems right at this moment: she gently lifts her face toward the sky and closes her eyes.

41 Ground Cherries

Jade sat on the edge of her bed with her legs stretched out in front of her. Groggy from sleep, she stared blankly at her feet as she rocked her neck back and forth working out the stiffness from having slept so long. The black toenail polish she'd put on before arriving at the centre was now just a strip across the tip of each nail. They looked like someone else's feet. Or, perhaps, they were her feet, but she was someone else?

She felt like the night she had seen the Chief, as though she was in a lucid dream. She grabbed a handful of sheet and rubbed it between her fingers just to feel the physical texture of the cotton against her skin. Nope. Not dreaming. A loud thump came from the camper's roof, and she thought a pine cone had probably fallen onto it. Still slightly dazed, Jade looked outside the window to see the trees bathing in a golden glow. Late afternoon light, Jade mused. She had slept the entire day.

She stretched her arms above her head and let out a yawn that seemed like it was going to split her head in two. She shook her head in an attempt to dislodge the sleepiness that still had her thoughts moving in slow motion. She felt marginally better, marginally more alert, and she rubbed her quads to ease their achiness and ground herself in the present. She looked out the window again and began to retrace the events that had taken place the previous night.

She remembered the images of the carved bone sphere and the Orb that inhabited it. She remembered the feeling of unconditional love that flowed from it and into her replacing all the anger and hurt she'd been harboring for so long. Then she had opened her eyes and found Rose sitting on the opposite side of the fire. Rose's eyes had been closed, and she was drenched to the bone as the rain ran freely down her face.

Jade had been drenched, too, although she hadn't felt wet. The rain had filled her open palms, and it looked like she was holding liquefied night. It was then she had realized she was thirsty—unbelievably thirsty—and she drank from one palm and then the other. The water had tasted like heavenly nectar.

"You did it." Rose had said to her with her eyes still closed. "You did it." Then Rose had slowly opened her eyes and met Jade's. Rose's gaze was direct, and as it washed over her Jade experienced the same feeling of Love that the Orb had beamed into her. Rose smiled benevolently at her and looked around at the falling rain. Then she added a few branches to the fire between them before smiling once more at Jade. So much joy had emanated from the gesture that it reached across the flames and wrapped Jade in a hug.

The fire flashed and roared to life between them as Rose's offering was accepted. Red and orange flames, unfazed by the rain, danced in the darkness. Jade watched as the fire showed her its true self: not a beast with a thousand hungry tongues of blazing heat but an entity of illumination that was conscious in its own right.

Jade put her hands together at her heart and bowed to the fire, the same way she had seen Rose do to the rising Sun or the altar when they chanted. Thank you, she thought, for not going out, for waking me up, for being here with me.

Jade had then looked toward the western horizon expecting to see the orange glow of the wildfire. There was none. The sky was pitch-black.

It was only then Jade had fully understood what had happened. They were safe. Grinning from ear to ear she turned to Rose. She *had* succeeded. The threat was gone. Rose nodded and beckoned for her to come and sit beside her. Jade had complied immediately.

"Give me your left hand," Rose said as she sat down, and Jade once again did as she was asked. Jade extended her hand palm down and watched as Rose wrapped her wrist with a thick, red, cotton string. Rose wrapped the string three times and whispered mantras as she tied three knots to fasten it. When she had finished knotting the string, Rose spoke directly to Jade, "For you to remember this moment by. To remember who you are on the inside when you face challenges in this world." Then Rose had squeezed Jade's hand slightly and smiled knowingly. "When it naturally falls off, then it means you have remembered, lets say, digested this chapter and are ready to step into the next." Jade examined the string and ran her finger between the red cord and her wrist. The string was unyielding; its strength was undeniable.

They sat in silence and watched as Jade's fire slowly dwindled. Finally, it went out with a bow and a hiss, and one last swirl of smoke danced in the pre-dawn sky. The silence it left was deafening.

"Go and sleep now, Jade." Rose had said. "I will take care of putting this back in order."

Jade nodded. She had wanted to say something, but words wouldn't form in her head. She stood and her right leg promptly gave out: her leg had fallen asleep. She smiled awkwardly and rubbed her thigh vigorously as pins and needles rushed from her hip to her toes. Once she'd been able to stand without hobbling around, she had bowed slightly to Rose and then stepped out of the circle. Before exiting the garden, she paused to look toward the point in the eastern horizon that would soon be welcoming the sun. Thank you for this new day, she thought. Thank you for this life and this chance.

Jade murmured, "Yes, thank you for this chance," and then she winced. Both legs had fallen asleep while she had been caught up in remembering what had happened. She rubbed life back into them as she tried to recall how she'd gotten back to her camper. That part was lost in a fog. As was how she had changed her clothes or gotten into bed. The discarded pile of wet clothes on the floor indicated that she'd changed, but she couldn't remember doing it.

The dinner bell began to toll calling everyone to the main house to eat. She wondered if Aaden and Steve had returned while she slept the day away. And the animals, had they been returned? Had all of them survived? The thought of finding out what happened to Newton spurred her into action.

She stood up and put her hand on the counter for balance; she felt like a toddler with legs unaccustomed to standing upright. She also felt slightly high, almost euphoric, and her own body felt unfamiliar. She took a step and then another, and while the euphoria didn't go away, the unsteadiness did.

She opened the camper door and tentatively sniffed the air like a bear emerging from hibernation. What awaited her outside the safety of her den? She did not smell smoke, but rather petrichor—the earthy scent produced when rain falls on dry soil. She smiled. Her wordsmith mother would have been proud. Jade closed her eyes and inhaled deeply; she wanted the smell of this moment to be locked into her memory forever. With each breath in and out, Jade wondered what her mum would have said if she were here. Would she have allowed me to spend three days and nights on a quest? Would she have thought I'd succeed? A honk from above interrupted the thought, and Jade opened her eyes in time to see a skein of seven geese flying Westward. She hoped they were returning to their summer home now that the fire was out. This caused her to think of all the animals that had fled from the fire and she wondered at their well-being, too.

Jade walked slowly up the drive and into the courtyard. Illuminated paper lanterns hung from the rafters of the outdoor sun deck and tea lights lined the hand-cobbled path. Each little flame waved at her as she walked past, and it took a conscious effort not to wave back. Jade hadn't expected the outdoor picnic table to be set for a celebration, but it was. Red cloth and matching china painted in sunflowers marked each person's seat. There was only one space not filled—hers.

As she approached the table, everyone turned to greet her.

"Jai ho!" they cheered and clapped; Aaden gave her a standing ovation. Rose was sitting at the head of the table, smiling beatifically, as though her eyes were portals to the Universe itself.

As soon as Jade took her place, everyone started moving at once: asking, passing, reaching, and serving the food. It was chaotic, familiar—wonderful. While they passed plates and poured drinks, Jade took in the setting with eyes that felt like they were seeing it all for the first time.

Glasses dripped with condensation as the iced tea inside met the warm summer night. The pasta was topped with cherry tomatoes and fresh basil, and the colours glowed making the dish almost too beautiful to eat—almost.

"Meera, did you make this pasta from scratch?" Jade asked.

"She did. With my help," Steve said before Meera could respond. "With grain right out of the garden and freshly milled."

"Wow!" Jade said. She looked at Meera, "So fancy!" Her cheeks warmed as she realized all this effort was for her.

She picked up one of the tomatoes and put it to her lips—it was warm and smelled like sunshine.

"Thank you, everyone. Truly. This is amazing and unexpected. I'm… I'm… so grateful." Her gratitude was met with mumbles and nods of acknowledgment—their mouths too full of food to articulate anything coherent.

No one asked Jade about her experience. They either knew better or had been directed not to ask, but the air about the table, the sideways glances, and stolen smiles that were bandied about, let her know that they were all eager to know what had transpired if she was willing to share. Everyone except Rose that is. Rose sat in her usual, joyfully simple state. She ate quietly and watched all her 'children' interacting with one another. Of course, she knew what had transpired. She also knew that the experience was deliciously unspeakable. Not because it was taboo, but because there simply wasn't sufficient language to describe the experience of meeting and transcending the fires. Jade smiled at Rose and then tucked into her meal. That also was deliciously unspeakable.

As dinner slowly wound down, Meera leaned over and whispered something to Rose who nodded in response. Meera turned to Aaden and said, "Aaden, why don't you take Jade into the garden for dessert? I have it on good authority that there's a newly ripened batch of ground cherries next to the greenhouse that has your names on it. Go on now. Steve and I will take care of the kitchen tonight. Avi, can you do the evening animal check?"

Aadan's face lit up like a child who was given free rein on the presents Christmas morning. Steve, meanwhile, looked like he'd been slapped with a wet fish. Someone must have kicked him under the table because he jumped slightly and managed a smile at Jade.

Jade looked at Rose to make sure the berry smorgasbord was sanctioned. She waved them off with an "Enjoy!" and the two of them jumped up from the table and dashed out to the garden before anyone could change their minds.

Aaden and Jade sat side by side on the ground with their knees almost touching. They faced the ground cherries unable to decide where to start. The bushes were low growing and their branches hugged the ground like they were protecting a valuable treasure. Each ground cherry was a jewel about the size of Jade's thumbnail, the colour of imperial topaz, and encased in a delicate, translucent, paper lantern that made Jade think of Dragonfly wings. The cherries shined brightly from the shadows as the early evening light reflected off the lanterns whenever she or Aaden moved a branch.

At first, they moved slowly and carefully, gingerly peeling back the branches to expose the berries. But as their gaze became less appreciative of beauty and more predatory, the paper-like lanterns betrayed the gems they were created to protect. Jade and Aaden smiled hungrily and began to pillage the bushes. Their pile of riches grew steadily and soon the branches were depleted. They thanked the bushes for their gifts and then turned to the task of choosing the first berry to eat. Aaden picked up a cherry and examined it from all angles. Then he tipped the fruit at Jade before tossing it into his mouth.

His eyes rolled back in his head as he savoured the fruit. "Oh my God," he moaned. "What would you say these taste like to you?" he asked once he had finished swallowing.

"Um….delicious?" Jade said, offering the single-word response based purely on his reaction alone.

"Delicious!?" Aaden said incredulously. "What in the world do you mean by delicious? What does delicious even taste like?"

Jade looked at him for a moment and then rubbed at the side of her face as she imagined what he'd say when she told him she'd never eaten one. She scrunched up her nose, "I've never had one sooo…," her voice trailed off as Aaden gasped and then nearly choked on the one he had in his mouth.

"You've never eaten one?" Aaden sputtered once the threat of choking had subsided. Jade giggled. She had expected the incredulity, not a near-fatal reaction. Aaden shook his head and tutted, "No. No. No. This won't do. Today is your lucky day. Try this one." He had carefully selected a large lantern perfectly intact and handed it to her. "OK. Now describe every aspect of it. See how minutely you can break down each sensorial experience of your first ground cherry until it creates a symphony that encapsulates the experience."

Jade had never heard Aaden speak that way. He was usually so matter-of-fact. But tonight he was different, or perhaps, she was different.

"OK," she said. Her voice cracked, and she cleared her throat preparing to string more than two words together. She peeled back the lantern and held the berry in her hand. "It's round, no wait,"—she waved her hand at him to shush him as he had muttered, "Good lord, Jade. It's round?!" She cleared her throat again and brought the ground cherry up to her face for a closer look, "OK. It's slightly oval—is that better?"

"Yes, thank you. You may proceed."

"Firm like a cherry but smaller, like a…" she paused not wanting to say the first thing that came to mind. She furiously searched for a synonym that would be more… appropriate. She settled on, "A baby olive." Then she popped it in her mouth. Aaden nodded at her, encouraging her to keep going.

"Its outer layer is shiny, incredibly smooth, much smoother than I was expecting. And to bite into it you…," she took a moment to position the fruit so she wouldn't choke while trying to talk, "you have to be committed or it just keeps sliding around in your mouth."

"That's it. They're slippery buggers. Keep going… bite into it and tell me what happens."

Jade bit down and a tangy bitterness, so forceful, that it made her eyes want to clamp shut filled her mouth. Just as she was about to make a this-is-revolting-face a complicated sweetness came rushing to the forefront and made her momentarily forget where she was or what she was doing.

"Oh my god. What *is* that?" she exclaimed.

"Right? See what I mean? That. Explain what THAT tastes like…" In his eagerness, he had shifted from sitting criss-cross to being perched on his knees facing her. His hands were supporting his weight as he leaned towards her, and Jade thought he looked like a puppy wanting to play fetch. *If he had a tail, it would surely be wagging,* Jade thought. Images of Aaden playing pretend puppy with small children filled her mind, and she started to giggle. Rather than explain why she was laughing, Jade concentrated on trying to label what was happening in her mouth. But no ordinary label could do justice to the various flavours bombarding her taste buds. This little golden berry was a bouquet of senses.

"It tastes like," she stumbled as the flavour she was trying to capture faded too quickly. She grabbed another one and bit into it. The initial sharpness passed, and she waited for the sweet chorus to come rushing in. "It tastes like, yellow rosebuds marinated in butterfly songs and wrapped in lemon tree leaves."

"And that, ladies and gentlemen, is dessert!" Aaden lifted his arms in triumph as if Jade had just scored the home team's winning goal.

Jade laughed and closed her eyes to savour fully the moment. She only opened them again when it had disappeared into the depths of her being; Aaden was staring at her. Heat flushed her cheeks as she realized that in complete absorption of the experience she had likely looked rapturous. She shifted and reached out for another berry trying to seem nonchalant rather than mortified.

"You did good today," he blurted out awkwardly, and he, too, grabbed a berry and popped it into his mouth. He repositioned himself criss-crossed on the ground and looked straight through her rather than at her.

"Thanks," Jade said, suddenly feeling stripped bare, naked—alive. Only a few berries remained in the pile between them, and Jade was already feeling remorse at having so few left. She wanted to prolong this feeling.

The bell on the hill chimed in the breeze and Jade looked around suddenly aware that the light was fading.

"I gotta go," she said as she jumped up and headed for the gate feeling like Cinderella realizing it was midnight. She was unwilling to witness either of them turn into pumpkins or mice; she was unable to let the chemistry between them simmer a moment longer for fear she'd cross a line she wasn't sure she should cross. Yet.

Aaden looked just as startled by the bell. He scooped up the last of the cherries and followed her out.

Jade stopped halfway to her camper and turned to see him jogging toward Avi's cottage.

"Goodnight!" she called after him with a wave.

He turned to her but kept walking backwards. He was almost at the forest's edge when he hollered with a grin, "It sure was! Thoroughly enjoyable," he waved back at her, as the trees swallowed him whole.

Autumn

42 Call of the Cowbird

It looked slightly drunk as it zigzagged over the page moving its little, black, compartmentalized body from the text to the meticulous pencil sketch of Mullein in Jade's wildcrafting book. Finally, it—the ant—found the valley-sized crease of the book's spine and was able to follow the crease to the safety of Fox Walking meadow. She was sitting among the wild grasses and flowers in the September light.

Jade's routine had changed since the fire four weeks ago, and she liked the rhythm of her days. Steve had taken over the cleaning duties with a few exceptions: she still cleaned and set the altars in the meditation room. He was also fully in charge of the animals. Aaden was back in the garden and seemed to be thriving just as much as the plants were. Avi moved between the two, and Meera remained head of the household. This meant Jade was free to focus on her studies. There was so much she didn't know that the time spent with Rose learning "Nature's ways" was becoming one of the best parts of her days. The other part was Aaden.

She was seeing more of him than ever. The last month they had become close—not romantic—but their connection was like nothing she had experienced, and she looked forward to every moment they could spend together. They had successfully and painstakingly hand-shorn the four Angora goats, and together they had cut the Rye down in the bottom field and made hay stacks for drying the way you see in old English paintings.

Jade put down her pen and surveyed the books sprawled out around her. Each one was opened to a different page. Books on plant identification, formulas for wildcrafting (she hadn't even known something like wildcrafting existed), fungi identification, bird identification, and her favourite, *Totem Symbology of Animals in Western Canada*. The first thing she had looked up was the Grasshopper in honour of her mum's altar figurine. *You are ready to take giant leaps forward in growth and consciousness.* Jade had smiled and nodded thinking of her own leaps forward since she had arrived.

She found it astonishing that most people moved through the world not knowing what half the beings right in front of them were or what they meant. How she had moved through the world not knowing! Now, on her afternoon walks with Rose, she was being asked to name every tree, every bird, every living thing and know what its presence was saying. Just the other day, she'd seen a Nuthatch and Rose had paused under its branch, turned to Jade and waited for her to regurgitate her lessons. Jade had done her best to recall what she had read about this little bird and what it meant. She had taken a deep breath, scrunched up her nose, and closed one eye. Then she began to speak, "Ummm, the Nuthatch. Its totem is to remind us to ground spiritual wisdom to the earthly plain—shown by the way they come down the trunk of a tree headfirst. Also, it is a travelling companion to the woodpecker and helps to anchor new rhythms of life into our everyday existence. The, uh, local varieties include white-breasted and red-breasted. What else? What else? Oh yeah, they excavate their nests rather than build them and will often use old woodpecker nests as a starting point for their own. The Nuthatch will make the holes made by the woodpeckers smaller by using tree resin."

Rose seemed impressed at Jade's knowledge, "Or they will enlarge the holes in trees or river banks to also use as nests." Rose had offered with a warm smile.

Every species was connected in some way as well connected to the trees and plants around them, and it was her task to understand this web. Some days she found learning about all the interconnections fascinating, even liberating, her world expanding tenfold in the sighting of a Blue Jay. But today, after a late night stargazing with Aaden, she just felt overwhelmed by all the layers.

She laid back in the grass and closed her eyes. The fall sun was warm and its midday light pierced her closed lids with hues of speckled blonde. She placed an arm over her eyes to protect them and then allowed her body to soften into the heat just as she'd done in front of the fire. She breathed in the light and let the heat move through her. The air was an intoxicating palette of smells intensified by the heat of the sun. Not one scent was recognizable on its own for they had melded together into a simple fragrance called 'Summer's End'. She took deep, filling breaths over and over until she felt a little woozy. No wonder the ant looked drunk, she said to herself and giggled.

"So, this is what studying looks like to the next generation," Rose's disembodied voice spoke.

Startled, Jade's eyes flew open and she bolted upright. Rose was standing before her perfectly positioned so it seemed like she was wearing the sun as a golden halo.

"I was—researching," Jade said. "Trying to identify bird calls without looking—at the birds."

"A-ha?" Rose replied with a raised eyebrow and a smile. She was not convinced. "And what bird did you identify?"

Jade smiled guiltily and said, "Um, the one that sounds like… crickets?"

Rose chuckled. "The summer Sun often makes one need to hear the 'cricket bird'—especially around midday." Then she picked up one of Jade's open books. "Ah, good. I see you have made it to Magnificent Mullein. May I sit?"

Jade hurried to move some of her books to make space for Rose, careful to keep the pages she was studying open.

"Humans are funny, you know. We have a long list of these plants called weeds. Which is nothing but an itemized list of our ignorance," Rose said as she ran her fingers over the page lovingly. "Weeds are plants we can't control, didn't plan on. They exist in service to the land rather than us." She shook her head slightly in dismay, "Take Mullein for example," she tapped the picture of the tall, single-stemmed herb with fuzzy leaves, "it's one of the most amazing native plants around here. The First Nations of this land smoked Mullein to help dislodge grief in times of loss, and when you look at how it interacts with the land, it only comes up where the land has been unnaturally disturbed. Like when we put the road in," she nodded across the meadow toward the driveway. "The first thing to come back up along the disturbed sides was Mullein." Jade followed Rose's gaze to the bright yellow flowers on either side of the drive. Yellow beacons where the healing in the land was happening. "Mullein's role is to help the land heal from grief, from change," Rose finished speaking and turned her focus back to Jade.

Jade squinted her eyes against the bright sun and said, "So, what you're saying is… that the plants that grow—when we're not planting or controlling the process—are a natural part of the land's healing process. Even if we don't understand its process, the land is always trying to move towards healing?"

"Exactly. Nature, when left alone, is always moving towards balance. Even wildfires are Nature's way of creating balance. The fires reduce the overcrowding of baby firs in the forest *and* give the Pine trees an opportunity for their seeds to sprout." Rose pointed to a patch of densely packed firs with trunks no thicker than her wrist and the lone baby Pine standing among them. It was dwarfed by its elders, but the young pine's long, dark green needles contrasted with the short bright green of those surrounding it making the sapling stand out despite its size. "But we suppress the wildfires out of fear for our homes, and the baby Firs take over choking out the grasses that keep other animals and insects healthy—like deer and elk."

Jade picked a piece of grass; she wrapped and unwrapped it around her finger leaving a pattern of perfect ridges in her skin while she imagined the sequence of events in her mind.

"What comes after Mullein then to help the land as it heals?" Jade asked.

"Well, it depends on what trees are around that piece of disturbed land," Rose said. "Here, on this land specifically, we see a lot of Arnica grow when Mullein's job is done."

"And Arnica's medicine," Jade said. "When it's used as a salve, it helps speed up the process of healing injuries—like sprains and bruises. It supports the healing of damage done beneath the surface."

"Very good! So it's interesting to see the correlation between what the plant does for the land and how the plant helps to balance and heal us as well."

"Because we are part of the land, not separate from it."

"Exactly...," Rose said as she stared off into the distance.

As they sat in silence, the short, guttural, xylophonic call of a brown-headed Cowbird sounded exceptionally loud. Jade looked up to see it perched on the tip of a nearby Fir tree, watching them curiously.

"Mmm," Rose said nodding her head in response to the bird's call.

"What?" Jade asked feeling uneasy all of a sudden. A breeze blew through the meadow causing all the pages of Jade's opened books to flip frantically and the Cowbird to take flight.

Rose turned to Jade and studied her face for a moment before speaking. Then she said, "I am going on a trip for ten days, and I would like you to look after Lola and Pebbles for me while I'm gone."

"Me? Why? Where are you going? I guess I can. Doesn't Avi usually look after them?" Jade searched the ground for the calm she was feeling moments ago.

"Yes, Avi does," she said once Jade had stopped her rapid-fire questioning. "But Pebbles is a sensitive young dog, and she clearly has a connection with you. So, I would like you to take charge of their well-being while I am gone. Can you do that?"

"Yeah, I, uh, can do that for sure. But where are you going? Has this been planned all along? Or is it short notice?" Jade asked feeling her anxiety rise.

"Why all the questions?" Rose asked. "What does it matter?"

"Sorry...," Jade replied, abashed by the reproof.

Rose softened at the apology. "I am going to France to teach there for a few days and to connect with a dear friend of mine who is not long for this world."

"Oh, I'm so sorry, Rose."

Nuthatches and Chickadees sounded their alarms all at once causing both women to look in the direction of the ruckus. Aaden was walking down the path to the well, and he waved when he saw the two women sitting in the grass. They waved back and watched until he was out of sight and the birds had settled.

"I will write down a list of instructions and care for them," Rose said. "Are you certain you feel up to the task?"

"Well, do you think I am?" Jade asked. "I mean, your dogs are, well, like, fur babies to you."

Rose laughed heartedly. "Yes. I guess you could say that. They are my closest companions as I walk this world, but I love them no more and no less than I love every other beast and beauty I encounter." Rose closed the book of plant medicine and placed it on the ground beside her before standing up and brushing off the bits of flora that had latched onto her skirt. "And, I would not ask you to look after them if I didn't think you were the right person for the task."

Jade nodded. "Then yes, of course. I'd be delighted to look after them for you."

"Thank you," Rose said moving once more in the line of the sun so Jade could look at her without being blinded.

"One question though, before you go?"

"Yes?"

"What did the Cowbird say?"

Rose smiled, "What the Cowbird always says...," and she glanced down at the open book of animal totems. "See you after lunch for our lessons and walk."

"Ok. See you...," Jade said as she looked down at the page the wind had blown open. The brown headed-creature with the xylophone's call stared back at her.

43 The Loan of Attachment

Jade picked up the Totem book and glanced at the page—128. *Ha! My birthday*, she thought. The 12th of August had come and gone while she had been sitting before her fire. She realized it after and by then it hadn't seemed to matter.

She grabbed her journal and opened it to a new page. At the top, she wrote "Cowbird", and then sat back, and began to read. She jotted down key phrases that caused her body to flush with energy. She quivered as she read: *Resolving parent and child relationships… parasitic nester, eggs laid in others' nests—brought up by others… issues around adoption… searching for right relationship to parent energy… abandonment…*

Ugh. She thought.

"Hey, Jade!" Aaden called. She looked up to see him wave as he walked back up the path towards the main house.

"Wait up!" She yelled and hastily marked the page with a piece of scrap paper; stacked and picked up the other books; and quickly walked to catch up to him at the meadow's edge.

"How's it going?" he asked when she got closer to him.

His words did not have their usual, upbeat candour. They were weighted. Trepidatious. She eyed him cautiously as she caught up to where he was standing waiting for her. His body was tense, and he looked like he was bracing for her answer.

Jade squinted at him suspiciously, was about to answer fine, but stopped.

"Weird, actually," she said glancing back to the spot in the meadow where she had just met with Rose.

"Oh, yeah?"

"Yeah," Jade said turning back to him. "Rose just told me she's going to France for ten days and that she wants me to look after Lola and Pebbles."

"Um," he said, looking at the ground, then over towards where she had been sitting in the meadow, then to the tree tops—everywhere and anywhere that wasn't her. Jade realized her words were not news to him. She stood waiting for him to speak. Pressure started to build inside her, and she realized she was holding her breath. She forced herself to exhale slowly and be patient.

Finally, after examining the cuticle of his thumbnail, he said "I'm going, too. With Rose. To look after her." He shoved his hands into his jeans pockets which pushed his shoulders up around his ears, and then he looked at her trying to gauge her response.

Jade's face lit up and she grinned. "You are? That's awesome! It'll be so much fun. When you come back, you'll be able to tell me great tales of French people watching, and you better bring—"

"I'm not coming back." Aaden cut her off and looked back down at the ground.

"You're kidding," she said, the smile sliding from her face. "What do you mean you're not coming back? You're committed to being here till next spring. That's what you said."

"Yeah, and I was… committed. But, now, I'm going to go…" his voice trailed off. He looked at her with his blue eyes and she felt the otherworldly connection that she had come to expect between them pierce her soul.

"When are you leaving?" she asked realizing Rose had not given her that detail.

"Day after tomorrow." He dropped his gaze back to the ground choosing to focus on her shoes rather than her face.

Jade took a step back, concerned the ground would crack open between them.

"… And you're not coming back," Jade said matter of factly.

The air between them spat, pleaded, and then sank in resignation.

"I'm sorry, Jade," Aaden said finally. "I've been enjoying this last month, this… thing… whatever it is between us." He took one small step forward, but she took a bigger one back.

"Don't be sorry—go. It doesn't matter. Whatever this is—was," she waved at the air between them searching for the words that would tourniquet the joy hemorrhaging from her body, "It was just a way to pass the time. Have a great trip."

He tried to step towards her again, but this time she side-stepped and pushed right past him.

"I gotta go," she said. She walked away and didn't look back.

Jade flung open the door to her camper and threw the books on her bed. *Totem Symbology of Animals in Western Canada* bounced off the mattress and onto the floor. It landed with a thump and opened to the page she had marked before her disastrous meeting with Aaden. The words *resolving childhood issues of abandonment* jumped off the page before she had a chance to avert her eyes.

"Oh, piss off," she said as she picked up the book, shut it, and threw it back on the bed with the others. "Not fucking interested in karmic messages at the moment."

She felt furious. Betrayed. She'd been lulled into a false sense of security and then—BAM—abandoned once again. She was better off alone. Less chance of getting hurt.

She ran her finger under the red string still wrapped around her wrist. The string Rose had put there, as a reminder, the night of the fire.

"To remember who you are on the inside when the world brings its challenges," Rose had said, *"and when it falls off, it means you have fully embodied the transformation the fire has brought you through."*

"My life is one, big, fucking challenge!" Jade raged as she tugged at the string.

"Try to remember. Try to remember," she chanted. She closed her eyes and attempted to conjure the image of the orb and the carved bone sphere, but her insides were a swirling tornado of emotions, and the image wouldn't stick. Instead, her old three amigos—isolation, abandonment and anger—burst through the door of her mind, jostling for their favourite spots on her mental couch as though they'd never left. She felt as if her mother had died all over again. Tears threatened to spill down her cheeks and her throat ached.

She got up and reached into her clothes cupboard for the pair of socks that kept her letters safe. She didn't read them; she hugged them, socks and all. Then the tears began, slowly at first and then in a torrent. Jade sat at her little table and let them. Her thoughts turned inward, and she was soon staring into the abyss she'd just so recently left behind.

"Jade, love? Are you there?" Meera's voice came through the door of the camper and she gave a few gentle knocks. Jade jerked her head toward the door and gave a startled, "Yeah!" *Fuck,* Jade thought and then repeated, "Yeah, just one sec, Meera. Hold on." She threw the socks back into her cupboard and wiped her face with the towel she had hanging on the cupboard door. She knew it wasn't going to make a difference. Meera wasn't stupid.

Jade opened the door.

"Hi!" Meera said in her usual chirpy voice "Can…," she stopped talking and her face fell as she took in the devastation on Jade's features. Jade left the door open and turned to sit on the bed.

"What's wrong?" Meera asked as she stepped into the camper.

"Rose is going to France for ten days," Jade answered with a sigh.

"And…? What's the problem with that?"

"And Aaden is going with her. To assist her."

"Yes… and?" Meera said still waiting for the problem to reveal itself.

"And he's not coming back…," Jade said.

"Aw, bless," Meera murmured as she sat down next to Jade and put her arm around her.

"It's not… it's not even about him really," Jade forced out the words. She took a shaky breath not wanting to release the wave of tears she was holding back. "And it's… not about. Her. She… she's coming back."

"I know, child." Meera soothed.

"It's just…,"

"I know…," she said again. "It's OK. Just let it flow. Let it go. It's bigger than a boy leaving. He's just the straw."

Jade cracked a superficial smile and snorted, which made snot burst from her nose and onto her top lip but no tears came. Meera grabbed the towel hanging on the cupboard door and handed it to her.

"Grief is not of this world, child," Meera said as she moved the books so she could sit facing Jade leaving a little space between them. "That's what Rose told me when I sat where you are now."

Jade sniffed. "What do you mean?"

"Well," Meera said, "Rose explained to me once that 'Grief is held collectively, but processed individually. It is a seed that is planted in loss and roots through the loam of attachment.'" Meera said it in her best Rose impersonation. "But the seeds," she said, now back in her voice, "are not only of this life. Sure, we experience loss in this life, but the root of it, when we dig, is a longing of the soul that goes beyond this lifetime, beyond this body. Grief is the pain of forgetting. Old souls, like us," she said with a reassuring smile, "when we start to remember the depth and beauty of who we are, we also have to face the depth of grief that we have carried with us. The grief of each moment that passed while we forgot. While we slept. I think the grief, both the personal and the collective," she patted Jade on the leg "is what you are experiencing right now. A grief that is triggered by the present, but is rooted much further back in the past."

"Maybe," Jade said. "It sure feels deep."

"Yup. It sucks," she said. "And it's normal." Meera stood up to shut the door to the camper now that Jade had settled a bit. She then sat back down and continued, "When you start to wake up, you face all sorts of feelings… of memories that aren't from this time. They might be yours, might be another's—it makes no difference to whom the memory belongs."

Jade looked at Meera with her eyebrows raised slightly. "Oh yeah?" she asked, her voice full of doubt. "Like what?"

"Well," Meera said looking at Jade deciding how much to share, how explicit to be. "I've had memories of being burned at the stake; of being flogged in a dungeon; of watching my beloved leave on a ship that I knew would never return; of my child being taken from me before I even laid eyes on her face…" She let her words hang in the air before sighing and returning to focus on the present.

"How do you know it's a real memory and not just a daydream or a…," Jade twirled her hand in the air to whisk the right words into form without having to say them.

"The way the body responds… Well, at least that has been my experience. When I have a memory like that come through, the cells in my body feel the memory as well, feel the trauma. It's not just in my mind. The grief pours forth from the very depths of my marrow. The key, however, is to feel it, to watch it, but not to buy into it, or you will create another hook that will have to be processed next time."

"Crazy," Jade said trying to imagine what it would feel like to be flogged in a dungeon or burned at the stake. She shuddered and realized that maybe she didn't want to imagine those things.

"Yeah. Sooooo…," Meera said trying to turn the conversation to a lighter tone. "I get it, and… it's going to be okay. Try to make the next couple of days while Aaden is still here into pleasant ones. It'll be better for both of you in the long run, OK?" She stood up and made her way to the door. She turned, "And if you need to cry, cry. Use his leaving to bring up, and let go of your grief, but don't grieve him leaving." She looked down at Jade sympathetically. "Do you see the difference?"

Jade nodded slowly as Meera's message soaked in.

"Also, I'm here if you need to talk. And so's Avi. He's a good sounding board and enjoys the process of helping one sort their emotions. Don't tell him I told you that, he likes his gruff, grouchy facade."

Meera opened the door and stepped out of the camper. Jade called out, "Hey, Meera! Wait! What did you want? Why did you even come?" She heard her words come out sounding harsher than she had intended. "Sorry. That came out wrong. I meant to say why did you come to my camper?"

"Oh. No worries. But thank you. Well, a little bird told me to check in when I was heading up to make lunch," she said with a wink.

"Figures…," Jade muttered and stood up. She moved to the doorway and scanned the trees for the potential narc. There, at the tip of a Larch in front of her camper, sat the Cowbird. It didn't even have the decency to try concealing itself.

"Go wash your face, and I'll see you at lunch," Meera said to Jade as she picked up the full basket of greens she'd been carrying up from the garden. "You got this, and you're not alone. Avi and I are here for you every step of the way. OK?"

"OK."

"Glug-glug," chimed in the Cowbird as it flew right over their heads.

"I said OK," Jade called to the bird as it landed on the tree behind her.

Meera smiled and headed up the hill.

44 Do Chipmunks Kiss?

Jade was on her bed watching a chipmunk out the back window of her camper. The chipmunk was hunkered on a branch shelling seeds and stuffing them into the cavity of its cheeks. Its fur glowed in the evening light, and all the blacks, browns, and golds seemed brighter than she thought those colours could be. She was mesmerized by the motion of its tail: it flicked mechanically from side to side while the chipmunk munched in short, jagged bursts of movement. Then a few brief moments of absolute stillness as the chipmunk listened, its cheeks bulging before resuming its seed shelling and mouth stuffing, and the tail flicking movements started up again. The whole thing reminded her of the stop-motion, flip cartoons she had loved as a child.

"Knock, knock…," Aaden said at her open door. He was due to leave the next morning, and she had been trying hard to make their interactions over the last two days ones that would be remembered fondly, even though her chest felt like it had been hollowed out with blunt carving knives.

"Hi," Jade said turning away from the chipmunk. "Come in."

"Ah…best not. You never know when Meera's gonna jump out from behind a tree and say 'No guests of the opposite sex are permitted in your cabin!'" he joked and pretended to brandish a stick in the air.

"Good point," she said giggling at his impersonation, and stood up to follow him outside. They sat down on her little pallet deck with their backs to the camper's door. "You excited?" she asked.

"Yeah," he said, looking slightly embarrassed.

"You gonna go and drink that hot chocolate in Paris and people watch?"

she asked remembering the dinner conversation from her very first day at the centre. She had wished then that the man-boy who wouldn't shut up about Paris would just go to Paris. And now he was, and she wished he wasn't.

"Ha! You remember!" he smiled at her, all tension between them, momentarily, gone.

"Of course," she said. "I remember everything." She looked at him and smiled despite her cheeks flushing and her eyes filling with tears. She blinked a few times and then redirected her attention to cleaning dirt out from underneath her fingernails.

She was in uncharted territory, and she didn't get the feeling he was well-practiced in these kinds of conversations either. They sat in the warmth of the evening sun and quietly filled the space between them with thoughts instead of words. She wondered how much could be said, without looking foolish; what needed to be said, to part kindly; and what should be said, so there weren't any regrets. The *shhhhh* of the breeze through the firs filled the space between them while Jade waited for the answers to her questions to magically appear. They did not. Then something fell to the ground on the deck behind them breaking the moment.

Jade turned around to see what it was and found a pine cone lying on the plywood. She looked up to see its origin and discovered that they were being watched by two chipmunks perched on the edge of the camper's roof. The chipmunks froze momentarily, and then upon realizing she was not going to move, they resumed eating and chattering like they were watching Aaden and Jade's conversation for entertainment.

She returned her attention to Aaden who was now pushing the cuticles back on his thumb. His go-to response when he was nervous.

"What time are you leaving tomorrow?" she asked.

"Before dawn, I believe. We have to drive to Calgary. Rose wants to make sure there is plenty of time to handle any unforeseen delays so we don't miss our flight." He spoke to his thumb, shifting in his seat uneasily.

"OK, then. Well, I guess I won't see you in the morning," Jade said feeling both relieved and sad at the same time.

"Probably for the best. I'm not any good at goodbyes." He stuffed his hands into his hoodie pocket. "Oh!" he said, pulling something out. "I wanted to give you this." He held a small, intricately woven basket made of pine needles in his hand. It was a smaller version of the one Rose had been making the day Jade had visited her home.

"Meera taught me how to weave last fall before you came." He handed it to her. "She said you're supposed to gift your first basket to someone dear to you." He looked sheepish, and now it was his turn for heat to flush his cheeks.

"Thanks," Jade said, taking it from him and holding it carefully in her hands. She examined it, turning it over in her hands to see all the threads link and bind the pine needles into a cord that spiraled around onto itself until it was three inches high. The perfect size for trinkets or jewelry. "It's really beautiful, Aaden. Thank you…," she spoke looking directly at him, taking in his features, and trying to imprint them into her memory. She wanted to remember him exactly as he was in this moment.

He glanced up the hill and then quickly leaned over to kiss her. But, out of habit, she had followed his gaze up the hill, and his kiss landed on her cheek instead of her lips. By the time she realized what was happening and tried to turn back to him, the moment was over, and he was sitting back in his spot like it had never happened.

He smiled awkwardly and winked. "Perhaps one day, when we are not here, we can try that again."

Jade nodded, still trying to catch up with what had just happened—or hadn't happened rather.

Aaden stood up and turned to her. She looked up at him. He seemed even taller from this angle, and she wanted to jump up and wrap her arms around his waist, bury her face into his chest, and beg him not to leave. And as he stood with his hands in his pockets and his shoulders slightly forward—a posture Jade had always found ridiculous in others, but adorable on Aaden—she felt another wave of grief rising inside her chest, and she hoped to make it back inside the camper before the tears came. He pursed his lips and nodded, acknowledging the nothing that had been said. When Jade leaped to her feet, concern washed over his face.

"Take a sip of that hot chocolate for me, OK?" she tried to smile as she said it, but was pretty sure her face looked more pinched than encouraging. She swallowed the sob that threatened to ruin the moment.

"Yeah. Yeah, I will… and, um, I'll send a postcard so you know where I land. OK?" He took a step back, "Tat Twam Asi, Jade Brennan. I'll see ya' round." Then he smiled at her with such tenderness that she almost ran to him, but he turned and walked towards Avi's cabin before she could convince her feet to move. Unable to watch him walk away, she stepped inside the camper, shut the door, and slid down it until she was sitting on the floor with her knees bent and the back of her head resting on the cool metal.

Everything was eerily quiet. Except for the chipmunks. She could hear them chattering back on their branch by her window. She assumed, by the fervour of chatter, that they were recapping tonight's show. And then she wondered, do chipmunks kiss?

45 Devoir du Chien

Jade set her alarm to wake early enough to bid Rose and Aaden a safe journey, but in her haze of anticipation and dread, she somehow set it to PM instead of AM and woke to the alarm call of a Nuthatch instead.

She bolted upright, jumped out of bed, and opened the door to see if the centre's truck was still there, but it was gone. In its place were Pebbles and Lola looking brokenhearted at the end of long leads that had been tethered to the tree outside her camper. Without moving their heads off the ground, they looked up at her with forlorn eyes. *We've been abandoned and left to die from loneliness and neglect. We'll probably starve, too.* Their eyes seemed to say. Although, Jade had seen these two dogs give the same look when they'd been left outside the centre's main door a time or two, so she knew they had a wee knack for drama. Nonetheless, she knew how they felt. Being left behind sucked.

"Oh, I know. I know," she crooned. She walked barefoot over to the dogs; the cold, dewy ground was a rude contrast to the warm, cozy bed she'd been in only a few moments before. They didn't move as she approached, and Jade was grateful. She didn't have it in her to manage bouncy, jumping dogs with tails wagging a mile a minute. She flopped onto the damp ground and instantly regretted the move as moisture soaked through her pyjama pants. Resigned to a wet backside, she stroked their heads and whispered more to herself than to them. "She'll be back in no time. She will. I promise. She's not gone forever." Pebbles gave her hand a soft, comforting lick. Lola didn't move.

Jade saw a Ziplock bag held in place by a rock on the ground between the dogs. She picked it up to see a sheet of Rose's notepaper folded inside.

"Come on, pups. Let's go snuggle on my bed and see what she has to say."

She untied their leads from the tree and guided them into her camper where it was warm and dry. She took off her dew-soaked pyjama pants and got back into bed where the warmth of her body was still stored under the covers. As she was getting herself comfortable with a pillow behind her back so she could sit up better, the dogs jumped onto the bed. They laid down, one on each side of her legs, and resumed their morose disposition.

"Make yourselves at home, why don't ya?" she said. "Mi casa es su casa." She tried to make light and scratched behind the dogs' ears, but they did not register her welcome; they pretended to already be asleep. She gave a half laugh and opened the bag. A faint smell of sandalwood filled the camper. The letter had been written on handmade paper, and as Jade unfolded it, she marvelled yet again at the extra effort Rose exerted in her daily life.

Dearest Jade,

You will find the exact care instructions for my precious fur babies (as you so aptly called them) attached to this note. Thank you for looking after Pebbles and Lola while I'm gone. For anything I may have missed, you can refer to Avi.

I know they are prone to depression when I leave for extended periods so please give them extra affection, but, don't let their grief lull you into thinking they will not go off exploring on their own. They will. Please make sure you know where they are at all times.

Be well and see you in ten days.

Tat Twam Asi

"Ok, then. The boss lady said lots of cuddles. No exploring. Got it?" Pebbles groaned, rolled onto her side, and stretched out her legs. Lola opened one eye, looked at Jade, and then closed it again. She wasn't making any promises. Jade gave them a more vigorous rub behind the ears this time, and the smell of lavender wafted up from their collars. She wondered if Rose used an essential oil for calming their anxiety or perhaps Jade's by extension. The thought brought a small smile to her face as she lifted her fingertips to her nose and inhaled. She felt her nervous system relax a little—shifting from high alert to medium alert. She took a few more deep breaths, drawing in the lavender scent to help get her into the right head space for what was likely to be a difficult day without Aaden or Rose.

Aside from the two dogs that followed her everywhere and hogged the bed while she slept, the first few days could almost be described as normal. If she imagined that Aaden had gotten up early to work on the garden and Rose was doing Rose-like things in her house, she could almost trick herself into believing they were still here—which eased the pressure in her chest.

Avi and Steve were busy building a new resident log cabin. As far as she could tell, they were using chisels and chainsaws more than hammers and nails. She brought them iced Sorel tea each day and was thus able to sneak a peek at their progress in an unobtrusive way. Avi and Steve could have come into the main house for it, but the warm fall days were numbered. Evenings were already starting to feel chilled, and the mornings were cold and damp, so a daily tea delivery was a nice excuse to sit in the long grass and feel the Sun-warmed Earth beneath her without having any other agenda but to sit, drink, and be.

By the fourth day of her dog duty—her *devoir de chien* as Steve kept referring to it—she thought she had a fairly good routine established. She would get up early and take the dogs for a walk on long leads so that they'd be tired and sleep during her morning chanting and cleaning of the altars. Then they came with her to the garden where they ran around and played freely. It was amazing how they had been trained to run the rows between the beds and not across them. Another nap while the humans had lunch, and then back to the garden or a walk around the property on long leads in the afternoon before dinner. They finished the day with another walk after dinner before retiring to her camper for the night. Jade missed her afternoon lessons and walks with Rose, but she also delighted in the break in routines. It was nice to just walk the property without any obligation other than 'keep track of the pups'.

If everything had kept moseying along in the same way, then Jade could have seen how the ten days would have been fine—would have flown by, even. But instead, on the fourth day of *Devoir de Chien,* it all went to shit.

Jade was happily weeding around the last of the spinach while the dogs lay in the shade of the Saskatoon bush having their morning nap when Avi's voice bellowed from across the field at a great distance.

"Jade! Jade! Come quick! HURRY!"

She dropped the bone she'd been using to dislodge the weeds and jumped to her feet looking in the direction of Avi's voice. She saw the old man half running, half limping, and waving his hands above his head at her.

She jumped over the spinach bed and ran to him as fast as she could.

Seeing she was heading his way, Avi didn't wait for her to catch up to him. He about-faced and started running back in the direction from which he'd come—the new cabin.

"Fuck," Jade breathed and found she could run a little faster.

By the time Jade got to the cabin, Avi was braced to lift a huge log at one end. At the other end was Steve. Well, under its other end, Jade realized. His thick leg was pinned under a trunk over three times the girth of his thigh. Her mouth fell open, and when she looked at Steve's face, his eyes locked onto hers; he was terrified. She saw his jaw was locked in pain; his face so red he looked like he was set to explode, and sweat poured down his temples.

"Oh-my-god. Steve!" she said and briefly knelt in front of him. She placed her hand on his foot, a foot that looked and felt like it no longer belonged to the rest of him, and he grunted.

"Jade!" Avi barked. "Come over here. Help me lift this log onto that stump."

Jade jumped up and wrapped her arms around the log a little ways up from Avi's.

"On three. Ready? One. Two. Threeeeeee."

They strained to lift the log, but it only rose a couple of inches—not nearly high enough to get onto the stump. It was too heavy, and as they were forced to lower, Steve yelled in agony as the weight shifted on his leg.

"Shit!" Jade said. She looked at Steve and winced. He looked like he might pass out any second from the pain, and he was making high-pitched whimpering sounds. "Hold on one sec," she said to both of them as she grabbed a shorter stump and rolled it down toward Steve's end of the log so that they wouldn't have to lift the heavy limb as high to free his leg.

"OK. Let's try putting it on that," she said a bit breathlessly.

Avi and Jade wrapped their arms around the trunk, practically hugging it to their chests, and Avi repeated, "One. Two. Threeeeeeee."

Somehow, they managed to lift the giant tree trunk onto the edge of the stump, but the weight of the trunk was too much. It started to crush the bark on the stump's rim and lower back towards Steve's leg.

"Lift! Liiiiiiiiiift!!" Avi groaned between his gritted teeth and shifted his grip.

Jade repositioned herself, too, and lifted with all her might. Avi cried out with the strain; Steve cried out in pain as the weight lifted off his leg and the blood rushed through his veins again. But, they got the log onto the stump, and it stayed put this time. All three of them were panting from the strain.

"Hold it steady," Avi said as he ran to Steve. He grabbed Steve under the arms, slid him out from beneath the log, and laid him down on the grass. "Now, Jade, run! Run and get Meera!"

Jade turned and sprinted towards the main house where she knew Meera would be preparing lunch for everyone, but as she ran past the garden, she stopped dead in her tracks and stared at the gate. It was open.

"The dogs," she whispered. "Oh-my-God. Fuuuuuuuuuuuuuck-fuck-FUCK."

From the field behind her, she heard Steve cry out again in pain. The sound jolted her back into action, and she continued running to the main house.

"Meera… you gotta… come," she panted, "Steve… his leg… under a log. We got it off… but… but he can't walk. And…," she was too breathless to go on. She put her hands on her knees and bent over to catch her breath.

By the time she could finish the sentence, Meera had already untied her apron, grabbed the first-aid kit from the pantry, and was headed for the door. Jade followed her, giving her as much information on Steve's condition as she knew while they walked briskly to the cabin site.

Meera's initial examination of Steve's leg suggested that it was not badly broken if broken at all. Possibly a small fracture. Definitely, severely bruised. The three of them helped him hobble back to the main house and made him as comfortable as possible on the couch. Steve had his eyes closed and was practicing his deep breathing skills to manage the pain. Meera was trying to prop Steve up with a cushion while also on the phone with the X-ray department of the local hospital. Jade seized the moment and pulled Avi aside.

"I fucked up," she said. Her heart was pounding so loudly in her ears that she was surprised Avi couldn't hear it as well, or see it trying to jump free of her chest.

"Excuse me?" he said. "What are you on about, lass?"

"The dogs," Jade started to hyperventilate. "When I ran to help you with Steve, the gate, it didn't close behind me, and now the dogs are gone."

Avi ushered her outside and sat her down on the stone wall. She put her elbows on her knees and rested her head in her hands trying to regulate her breathing.

"I'm sure they'll come back, lass. They usually do," he said soothingly.

"Usually?" she shot up and looked at him. "What do you mean 'usually'?"

Avi didn't answer right away. He looked like he was trying to figure out what to say without lying. "Usually," he repeated at last.

"Oh, Christ. Rose is going to kill me. They're her… her…"

"It's OK. We'll go look for them. First, we'll get Steve sorted, and then we'll look for them together. OK?"

"Yeah. Yeah. OK," she said wiping her eye like it had dust in it.

"Avi, get the truck! We gotta get down to X-ray before it closes at one," Meera called from inside the house before she stepped out and saw Jade crying on the rock with Avi sitting next to her.

"It's a big fright for all of us, darlin'," she said, "but I'm sure he'll be OK. I really don't think it's broken."

"Ah…," Avi started to say but Jade shot him a look that caused him to change course. "I'll be right there. I'll just grab the keys from my cabin."

While Avi and Meera took Steve to the hospital where they got confirmation that his leg was not broken but so severely bruised that he would need a stabilizing brace and a single crutch for a few weeks, Jade did laps around the boundary of the property calling for the dogs.

Avi must have told Meera on the drive because after Steve was settled on the couch once more, Meera, Avi and Jade immediately split up to do a systematic search for any signs of the missing dogs.

"Jade, you go south. I'll call the neighbours to let them know you're heading their way."

"Jesus, Avi. Do you have to shout it from the rooftops and tell everyone in town?" Jade asked.

"Do you want to get shot at for trespassing and then have them complain to Rose when she gets back that students are walking over their property?" he replied sharply.

"No. I'm sorry. I'm just…," she shrugged, not needing to say anything more. Avi and Meera knew.

He nodded acknowledging and accepting her apology. "Then it's best we seek permission, 'cause there ain't no forgiveness around here." He shot a sideways glance at Meera that Jade couldn't read. "I'll head to the pond. Meera, you head down towards the highway. Meet back here in forty-five minutes, OK?"

"OK." Meera and Jade said simultaneously, and then they all turned to their respective directions and headed out.

The search was futile. Dinner was a subdued affair, and Jade just poked at Meera's I-don't-have-time-to-cook-mac'n'cheese. She ducked out while Avi and Meera were fussing over Steve's bed on the couch and retreated to her camper.

She sat down on the pallet step with a defeated thump. Exhausted. Stunned. Emotionally drained. She couldn't finish a coherent thought in her head. How could a day (which now felt more like a year) start so well and end like… like this?

She looked around at her surroundings. The evening light was nothing like

Jade had seen since she had arrived. The sun had turned everything to gold. It was breathtakingly beautiful. How could a world look like this when everything was wrong? Did it have to set up such a stark contrast between how she felt and what she saw? She put her head back and breathed out a loud "FUCK MEEEEEEEEE!" But not too loud, because she didn't want Avi and Meera to hear and come running.

She couldn't sit still and look at the beauty around her while there was still an hour of light left in the sky. She needed to walk, to search. She needed to do something, to feel something—anything—that might temper the inferno of self-judgment that was scorching her lungs and urging her to rip off her skin.

She wrote a note and left it on the pallet deck in the same bag Rose had used and anchored it with the same rock.

Gone for a walk towards the pond, back before dark.

She knew she could get into trouble for walking in the forest at this time of evening without actually telling someone, without taking bear spray, but she didn't care. To be eaten by a grizzly would be a blessing at this point.

She walked and called and walked and called until her voice gave out. She stopped in front of the biggest Ponderosa Pine she had seen on the land. She would need two Jades if she wanted to wrap her arms around its mighty trunk. She stood facing the tree and leaned her forehead against the thick, rust-coloured bark until the connection between the soft skin of her forehead and the unyielding bark of the trunk felt painful. She welcomed the pain and pressed even harder—feeling pain was at least feeling something. She tried to focus on her breath, but all it did was stoke the inferno inside of her until she was completely overcome with anger. It coursed through her, and she felt an inexplicable need to lash out.

"Why!? Why couldn't they just stay where they were? Why couldn't they stay nearby? WHY!?" She demanded punching the tree faster and faster to emphasize every word. "Why did they have to go? Why did SHE have to go?!" She slumped to her knees in a flood of tears. Her hands dug into the loam of needles at its base, gripping the Earth, holding it in place, in case the tree, too, had ideas of leaving. The tree stood unmoved by her outburst. Not a breath of wind, nor a bird dared to disrupt the grief that flowed out of her, down her face, and soaked into the ground. The grief she felt was like nothing she had ever felt before. It came from a deep place inside. Deeper than at her mother's funeral, deeper than her first night alone, deeper than when she told the bees of her mother's passing. A faithless depression pinned her to the ground at the base of the tree, and she was not sure if she would, or would ever want to, get up again.

Fragments of Rose's teachings flitted about her mind, but they were about as useful as a butterfly's wings in a hurricane. She ignored them at first, not wanting to think about Rose in case somehow thinking of her would cause her to know what had transpired. But, the teachings would not be ignored despite being buffeted about by the storm in Jade's head, and she began to listen. Rose's voice was just a whisper, but it cut through the noise: *All the trees are woven together in a web of interconnectedness. They listen through the water; they speak through the heart; and they send messages through the birds; Make a prayer and a promise, Jade. Remember, you offer so you can receive.*

A spark ignited inside of her born from the chemical reaction of despair and determination mixing at rock bottom. As she pushed herself upright, her hand screamed and something slippery oozed between her fingers. She looked down and saw fragments of pine needles glued together by the fresh blood that stemmed from cuts on her knuckles.

She looked the tree up and down—sizing it up—as if preparing to fight it again. She both loved that it wouldn't leave and hated that it wasn't afraid of her rage. She flexed her hand, relishing the pain as she opened and closed them.

"You want my blood? You want my tears?" she said threateningly. "Will they tell you exactly where I'm at? You want me to remember? To believe that you can, I can—*communicate?*" She felt a slight softening at the mere utterance of the word 'communicate' but shook it off. "Then get word to Pebbles and Lola to come home. Make your beloved birds find them and tell them to come home! Here," she wiped her dirty hands down her face covering her palms in tears and smearing her ivory face with earthen war paint. "That's what you want, isn't it?" She smeared her hands over the bark. "Take it. Take all of it. You find them, and I won't give up. I'll believe." She looked around at the silent grove. "That's what you all want, right? For me to believe, for me to *remember?*" She spat out her words and surrendered to another wave of anger and tears, fury and despair, at the ridiculousness of talking—pleading—with a tree, until there was nothing left inside of her and her hand bled freely. Still, the tree did not move. Exhausted, she lay down at the point where the tree entered the Earth. She cradled her head in her arms, and the blood of her knuckles dripped into the soil. She offered one last silent plea to send the dogs home, and for a moment, just a moment, she let go and closed her eyes.

46 Trees: Air

Breathe, dear sister. Breathe. Let the depth of your grief be the channel for your scattered pieces to return home and for the wholeness of your heart to finally be found. Do not lie down, defeated. Instead, sit with us. Let our pulse, the pulse of the forest, entrain you to the drumbeat of Love that permeates all.

Breathe, so that the transformation of grief into gratitude may transpire—for it is the foundation of gratitude upon which wise ones stand. For you, too, are destined to stand tall alongside the humans who have remembered. The humans who are rooted here like us, but do not live earth-bound. They move ever skyward. We call these humans "thank yous" for that is the sound their hearts make with each beat, with each step, as they walk among us.

Where the 'thank yous' walk, the day becomes brighter and the night becomes sacred—never dark. They do not use their feet to run in fear, instead, their movements weave light. Yes. They churn the air into silken threads of light that dance on the wind, tickle our bark, and envelop all in Love. Join the light-weavers, sweet sister. That they are, Tat Twam Asi.

47 Battle Scars

$\mathcal{S}$omething small crawled across her cheek and tickled the tiny hairs near her ear. Jade, still mostly asleep, tried to swat at it but ended up just slapping herself in the face. Hard. Fully awake now, she sat up and opened her eyes finally able to relate to the phrase "slapped awake"; she was surprised to find herself still at the base of the old Ponderosa. She wiped off the fragments of pine needles stuck to her face and wondered if they'd left any indentations— tiny, temporary battle scars. She gazed down at her hand and tried to flex it into a fist. The cuts had stopped bleeding, but her knuckles gleamed in the moonlight with fluid that should have been on the inside. She gingerly wiped away the dirt, and pain shot up her right hand and made her gasp through her teeth. She let it rest on her lap and searched for the rage that had led to her wounds, but she couldn't find it. Instead, she felt calm and connected but also like she had been hit by a truck. She stood up and looked around. The trees were silhouettes against the last light of the day, and the full moon shone brightly above the mountains.

"Mother-fruit snacks," she muttered. Avi and Meera would be frantic that she wasn't back yet. She began to walk back toward her camper, but before striding across the field she turned around to face the towering Ponderosa.

"You got this? Yeah?" she asked.

A breeze whispered through its needles. "Shhhhhhhhh," it seemed to say.

She felt a wave of knowing flood her, and she accepted the fact that she'd done all that she could do. Now it was time to trust. She spun on her heel and ran back to the camper, where she found Avi sitting on the step next to the note with the rock. His eyes were slightly closed and he looked like he was waiting for a bus.

"Oh, fuck," Jade mouthed as she approached him.

At the sound of her footsteps, he opened his eyes, looked her up and down, and nodded to himself. Then he slowly stood up.

"I'm sorry, Avi."

"It's OK, lass. Glad you're back." His white moustache twitched in the moonlight. "Just…ah…take a moment to clean up that hand before you go to bed, and….ah," he paused for a fraction of a second, "wash your face. We'll see you in the morning."

Jade looked down at her hand and self-consciously put it behind her back. She pursed her lips trying to think of something to say.

"Thanks for…," she began.

"You're welcome, lass." He cut her off before she had a chance to say more. Not only had he waited up for her, but he also hadn't told Meera what she'd done otherwise she would have been there sitting next to him. He knew she knew how irresponsible she'd been by being out after dark, and there wasn't a need for a lecture at this time.

"Goodnight," he said stepping off the deck. "Try to get some sleep."

"Goodnight," she whispered as his form disappeared into the shadows.

48 Cougars and Krishnas

Not wanting to see Steve or Meera, Jade washed her hands and face using the tap inside the garden and returned to her camper by the light of the moon. She lay on her bed and closed her eyes. She wasn't trying to sleep, nor was she sleepy thanks to her impromptu nap at the base of the Ponderosa; she was trying to listen. She strained her ears to hear the jingle of tags cutting through the still night, just as she used to listen for the jingle of her mother's keys in the lock of the front door when she was a child so that she could finally sleep knowing everything was as it was supposed to be.

Instead of hearing the familiar snap of the lock on the door followed by keys hitting a counter, she heard the distressed wail of a peacock as it flew up into a tree. HONK -WAp-WAp-WAp-Wap HONK-waaaaa!!! The alarm call was followed by a male voice yelling and cursing. Cursing at what she couldn't tell.

Jade leaped out of bed and grabbed her sweater and sneakers. Sneakers that were once pristine white with a crisp blue line trim and used only for the mall and dinners out, were now creased, sepia coloured and used as slip-on farm shoes. She found herself running up the pathway towards the commotion the same way you run toward a car wreck—as fast as you can while trying not to see what's in front of you. She saw Avi yelling at the night sky. And, if she didn't know better, she would have thought he was drunk by the way he was moving.

"Yah. Hup! Get out of it you stupid cat!" he hurled at the trees before him. "Haven't you ever heard you're not supposed to kill the messenger? We have an agreement!"

"I think that's shoot the messenger, Avi, not kill," Jade said and then quickly apologized for startling him when he spun around with the shovel poised to whack her.

"Dear God almighty, girl! I didn't hear you."

"Yeah. I figured that out when it looked like you were about to murder me. What's going on?" she asked eyeing the flashlight in his left hand and the shovel in his right. She squinted as the light hit her full in the face, and Avi grunted in apology. He shifted the beam back toward the forest and then to the peacock lying on the ground. He pushed the flashlight at Jade's hand; his shoulders slumped and he dropped to the ground beside it.

"Either way it still ends up dead," he said softly from beside the peacock. Jade recognized it as the head male of the flock—Krishna. Avi gently picked up the bird and cradled it as if it were an infant. He slid Krishna onto his lap and spoke, "Hold the light still, lass. Shine it just to the side of us. I want to see what we are working with."

Krishna's big eyes blinked slowly up at Avi. His beak opened and closed like he was wanting to say something but didn't have the words. Either the shock was too much or he had just realized he was safe in Avi's embrace because Krishna didn't try to flee or cry out again.

Avi carefully lifted one wing watching the bird for any sign of pain. There was none. Avi lowered the wing back into place and gently rolled the bird onto its other side. Jade winced and made a hissing sound—the damage from the cougar's jaws was visible on the bird's underbelly. The cougar had attacked from underneath hoping to pull the peacock off its evening perch. Avi gently investigated the extent of Krishna's injuries and was careful not to probe the mass of feathers that were matted together. Jade saw the area was saturated with blood that pulsed and oozed in time with her own heartbeat—a rapid thundering beat that hadn't settled from her run up the path.

"The bite must have hit an artery," Avi sighed as he looked at the gaping wound.

Jade felt paralyzed by the look on Krishna's face. The bird, or so she thought, seemed to have no idea what was happening but also a profound understanding of what was to come. The flashlight began to shake in her hand as the sorrow she felt for the injured bird began to grow.

"Come with me, lass. There's nothing more we can do here tonight." Avi looked over his shoulder, and Jade chased his gaze with the flashlight. While no reflective eyes were peering back at them, Jade still felt that they were being watched. After a few seconds of scanning the darkness, Avi returned his attention to Krishna. He held the bird tenderly and struggled to stand.

He didn't ask for help, and Jade knew better than to offer, but watching as he made his way from kneeling to standing put his frailty on full display.

"Let's sit for a moment with our friend here and let your heart calm and ground back into the land before you sleep."

They walked slowly back to Avi's cabin as though part of a pre-mortem funeral procession. The trees gave way to the moonlight, and Jade saw that Avi's face shone with silent tears.

The old man motioned for Jade to take the folded chair leaning against the wall as he sat in his rocker. The chair's runners squeaked on the wooden porch deck, and if Krishna's body hadn't been in his lap, Jade wouldn't have been able to tell that tonight's vigil would be different from all the others. During the day, bleats would have been coming from the goats' pasture next door, but at 11 PM it was quiet.

She was too rattled to sleep, so she accepted his invitation gratefully. As she walked over to get the chair, she thought she heard something and glanced skyward. The sky was a blanket of breathtakingly exquisite stars. She sat her chair next to Avi's rocker, settled into it, and looked to the stars again. They were so beautiful that she kept looking up at them to make sure she hadn't imagined them or conjured them up in a dream. But, every time she looked over to the ever-increasing limp form of Krishna curled up on Avi's lap, she could feel the heaviness of being awake.

"Avi," Jade said after a bit. And when he looked over at her, she asked, "What did you mean by—'We have an agreement'?" He scratched his head but didn't answer. Krishna moved slightly on his lap seeking the return of the weight of his hand.

"When you were yelling at the cougar," Jade added.

"Ah, yes," he said, realizing what she was asking about. He spoke in time with the slow rock of his chair which gave his speech a slightly disjointed rhythm. "We have an agreement with Nature. We've promised to use no firearms here for hunting so that all animals will have safe passage. But, they cannot come in and take the living for themselves. They may only receive what is offered when Nature runs its course." He looked down at the fully grown peacock dying on his lap. "I suspect the logging out back, the lack of rain this summer———the fire, has pushed the cougar to take desperate measures."

"Do things like tonight happen often?" Jade asked tentatively.

"No." He rocked, thought, and then added softly. "I will talk to the Lady on the Hill when she gets back. The dogs—this...," he stroked Krishna's neck with a hand that was all bones and freckles in the moonlight. "Until then...," his voice trailed off leaving Jade to draw her own conclusions. Avi switched from stroking Krishna's neck to gently stroking the iridescent blue feathers on his body, between his zebra wings, all the while rocking back and forth——back and forth.

Jade looked at the sky again seeking solace and strength from Grandmother Moon above them. She asked the question she'd been wondering for months, "Do you like being watchman? I mean, if nothing ever happens, and if it does, then it's, well...," she stopped talking as she looked at the bird gasping for breath. Avi leaned forward seeming to hug Krishna to his chest as though imparting a secret. The shifting of his weight stopped the perpetual rocking, and he looked at Jade with such seriousness that she had to look away.

"You think nothing is happening unless there's drama," he said finally, and then he continued to look at her without speaking, without rocking.

She had nothing to say to that, and eventually, Avi started his chair rocking again. Jade glanced at him and saw him rub the side of his cheek, then his forehead, and then pinch the bridge of his nose with his free hand. His face softened as if he had come to a conclusion on something, and he took a deep, slow breath. He looked almost longingly out into the darkness and began to speak.

"The Land, She's shy. Only reveals herself when you're patient." The bird let out a small noise requesting Avi's full attention. "Shhhh. It's ok... You close your eyes now. Go on." He started patting the side of Krishna's back as though consoling a baby who was fighting sleep.

Once the bird's eyes closed and its laboured breathing eased slightly, Avi continued.

"She sings at night, the Land does, and it's... wondrous." Avi rocked back and forth a few times and looked up at the night sky as though listening.

Listening to what, Jade couldn't figure out. There were no sounds aside from Krishna's flock mates periodically honking back and forth as if bantering 'Marco!—Polo!—Marco!—Polo!' in their efforts to find each other after the attack; Krishna's laboured breathing; and the crickets. She closed her eyes straining to hear something more.

"Humans make the world about them. But at night, you learn that that's not the way. There's entire realities here, right *here*, lass," he pointed to the ground, "that are not designed around human will. You have to be awake to see it." He paused. Then, "I wish I could have seen that when I was your age. I would have done things differently."

He shifted back from patting Krishna to stroking his neck as if they were having an entire conversation Jade wasn't privy to.

"After the war," he continued, shifting uneasily in his seat as he spoke, "my nights became painful. I fought sleep as hard as…," he sighed and stopped rocking.

"As hard as what?" Jade asked.

Avi looked at her, half smiled and shook his head at the same time. "Some things you just don't speak of lass." Jade looked down again at her feet embarrassed at her naïveté. The silence hung between them until he started to rock once more. She looked up to see him gently nod in agreement with something unsaid. "But since I came here the trees———the land give me something at night to look forward to." He looked at Jade, and she nodded for him to keep going. "At night, I'm part of something. Something that isn't trying to have power over me. Hell, She, the Land, doesn't even care if I'm here or not," he said with the hint of a smile, "but she welcomes me just the same to bear witness. It's brought me peace."

He looked down lovingly at Krishna, and at that moment the bird gasped, his body began to shudder, and his neck twisted at an odd angle as though trying to look away from his own fate. Avi laid both his hands on his feathered friend and started to chant quietly. "*Om tryumbakum, yajamahe…*" rolled off his tongue like a child reciting the ABCs. He sealed it with, "Go now my friend—Tat Twam Asi." The words were barely audible. They didn't need to be, Jade realized, because the words weren't going to be received in this world anyway.

Avi looked up at Jade and a kindness from him washed over her. It was a feeling from him she had never experienced before, like the love of a grandfather she had never known.

"Go now… and sleep," he said. "We'll find those dogs in the morning. This day has nothing more to offer now."

Then, he went back to rocking in his chair and stroking Krishna's blue feathers. The tears in his eyes acknowledging the space this beautiful bird had left behind and the dried blood on his shirt, the only indications that this night had been different.

49 Mapped in Fur

Jade slept through morning chanting and woke up just before breakfast feeling as though she hadn't slept at all. She considered skipping breakfast altogether and just heading to the greenhouses until she could connect with Avi, but the hollow gurgles emanating from her stomach reminded her that she had barely eaten any dinner the night before and her body demanded to be fed before she started her day.

For the first time since his arrival, Jade was grateful for Steve's presence. He was self-absorbed and always tried to dominate the room with his questions and, more often than not, his opinions.

Usually, this irked Jade to no end, but this morning—as he told Meera how the place could be improved, made suggestions as to what she should cook for lunch, and expressed a desire for her to help him have some sort of bath this morning because he was feeling uncomfortable—it meant no one spoke of the missing dogs or Krishna. It also meant that no one noticed, or at least no one mentioned, her hand. She had worn long sleeves this morning in an attempt to hide it, and luckily her shirt had the thumb hole to keep the sleeves in place and her knuckles mostly covered.

"Jade, I'm going to go and get ready for the day. Come out when you're done, and we'll head out. OK?" Avi said as he stood up to bring his dishes to the sink.

"Oh? What are you guys up to this morning?" Steve asked.

"Never you mind," Avi replied. "You focus on getting that leg right. First rule around here is do the work, don't be the work. Even sittin' on that couch I'm sure Meera can find ways that you can be helpful to her, rather than *you* finding more ways for her to be helpful to you."

Jade looked at Meera. She had blushed in embarrassment at Avi's words and wouldn't look up from her plate. Jade had always seen a fondness between Avi and Meera. She thought it had been like siblings but suddenly wondered, based on the hue of Meera's cheeks, if there was something more.

She shook her head to dislodge her train of thought. "I'll be right there," Jade said to Avi as he turned to walk out the door. "Thanks for breakfast, Meera," she said gathering up her dishes and walking to the sink. "Looking forward to whatever you make for lunch." Meera looked up at her. Knowing Steve couldn't see her face, Jade smiled and winked at Meera making her blush even deeper. Jade quickly washed up, carefully dried her hands, and hurried to the door.

"Good luck," Meera called out as Jade pulled the front door closed behind her.

Jade ran down to her camper to grab her old sneakers and change out of her long-sleeved shirt. It had served its purpose for the time being. She fixed the heel of her sneaker—making sure it was up in case she needed to run—and began to do up the laces. She was so absorbed in the memory of buying them with her mother that she didn't hear the jingle of Pebbles's collar. It wasn't until the pup inserted her head under Jade's arm to make her stop what she was doing that Jade noticed the dog.

"Oh My God! Pebbles!" she shouted. Jade grabbed the dog and hugged her a little too tightly which made the pup wriggle out from her grasp. Jade looked around for Lola, but Pebbles seemed to be alone. She heard paws running down the path and looked over expecting to see Pebble's partner in crime, but found Sam bouncing heavily along the ground, still looking like a punk rocker with one shaved side. He had recovered nicely, and as he ran towards them he looked like a lop-sided, fluffy, white cloud.

Pebbles ran over to meet him and assumed a position Jade had never seen her do before. She stood at attention like a four-legged soldier reporting for duty: legs rigid, chest puffed out, head high, and her tail straight out from her body. She was completely still. Sam woofed once and began his inspection.

He started at her nose and then sniffed her up to her ear and down her neck. Then, he repeated the same thing on the other side before returning to the first side and sniffing from her shoulder, down her torso, and finish-ing under her tail. Jade watched with fascination. Sam's nose inhaled the fragrance of each event stored on different parts of Pebbles' body so he could break down the timeline of her adventure. Pebbles didn't move until Sam returned to standing in front of her. When he licked her face, Pebbles' body finally relaxed. She lowered her head and leaned it against his neck. Then, slowly, she turned and walked to the water bowl, drank, and went to lay down in the shade of the tree next to Jade's camper. Sam walked over to Jade. Sadness surrounded him. She could feel it as he approached, and she tried to lean away from him but that didn't stop him from walking up to her and laying his head solemnly on her thigh. He sighed.

"It's OK," she said as she dug her fingers into the thick, white fur on his neck and gave him a loving scratch behind his ears. "She will come back," she tried to reassure him, but neither of them believed her words. He looked up at her with brown eyes that didn't belong to an animal, blinked once, and then turned and walked over to Pebbles. He assumed the same position as her, his eyes said but focused on Jade as if to say, "Now what, boss lady? Now what do we do?"

"Well, there you are!" Avi called out cheerfully to Pebbles upon seeing her as he walked down the path toward Jade's camper. But when neither Jade nor the dogs answered him, he stopped walking and stared.

"Oh, dear," he murmured, picking up the ethereal fragrance in the air just as Sam had from Pebbles' fur. "Oh, dear," he repeated sadly. His shoulders dropped, and he walked over to sit next to Jade.

They didn't speak. They didn't need to. Jade looked from the dogs lying under the trees to the ground in front of her, where she saw a trail of ants industriously moving bits of leaves to their nest under the rotting stump a few feet away. She looked up at the flock of Pine Siskins darting about in the trees around them. There was an air of calm that made yesterday's frantic desperation seem far away. Somehow Jade felt complete despite the silent tears that rolled down her cheeks and made little dark circles on her jeans. Avi sat beside her and sniffed. He wiped his moustache with his handkerchief, and she didn't dare look directly at him to see if he was crying. There was no need. She knew.

"What do they mean?" Jade asked gesturing to the Pine Siskins with her chin.

Avi sighed. "Adverse knowledge. Wisdom. Earth magic. And they're cunning as can be. They get what they want…," his voice cracked a little and he stopped speaking.

Jade kept her eye on the Pine Siskins flitting from branch to branch calling out in their raspy, single-note call that sounded like they had smoked a pack a day for ten years. And then, for no apparent reason, all the birds flew away at once. As Jade watched them fly Westward and disappear into the blue of the sky, it seemed to her that they were tethered together by invisible strands that couldn't leave anyone behind.

Avi slapped his hands against his thighs, rubbed them twice, and stood up. "Well," he said, "I'll go and tell Meera Pebbles has returned." The silence that followed would have allowed him to finish the sentence with words no one wanted to hear, but Jade nodded in acknowledgment of what was said and unsaid. "You give her some water and food and then leave her in your camper for the morning so she can sleep. Likely, she's had a big night. Once you've done that, head to the greenhouse for the morning. OK?"

"OK," she said and stood up. "Come on, Pebbles. Let's get some food."

Pebbles got up and walked slowly towards Jade. Sam got up and followed Avi. Neither dog nor human moved with their usual pep.

Once inside the camper, Pebbles jumped onto Jade's bed. She sniffed the spot where Lola usually slept, and then walked to her side and laid down.

"I'm so sorry, darlin'. I wish I knew what happened." Jade buried her head in Pebble's neck to comfort her just the way Sam had.

"Sleep now," she murmured. "I'll get you some food and water, and then I'll come and get you at lunch, OK?" Jade gave the dog another hug and got off the bed. Pebbles did what Jade now considered her signature move: she moaned, rolled onto her side, and stretched out her legs to push Jade away so that she could claim the bed in its entirety for herself. Within moments, the orphaned pup was fast asleep.

50 Rose Returns

Much to Jade's relief, the last five days of Rose being away were completely uneventful. She didn't think she could take any more uncertainty, and she definitely couldn't take any more death.

Pebbles stuck close to her every moment of the day, and for that Jade was grateful and happy. Steve had started to move around a little more on his crutches but was still basically incapacitated. Jade noticed he had become quieter now, or at least quieter whenever Avi was in the room. She also noticed Meera was becoming more irritated with him and less accommodating.

Jade's mornings were consumed by weeding and watering the gardens. Late September apparently was *not* the end of the gardening season, and the plants still needed constant care. She no longer had free time for studying because Steve's injury meant she and Pebbles spent the afternoons helping Avi with the new cabin. At first, she couldn't see how all the timbers would go together, which made the process of preparing the cuts and notches in the wood seem tediously slow, not to mention back-breaking. But when they started to stack and peg the pieces together, it seemed miraculous the way the cabin sprouted out of the ground. Avi seemed pleased with their progress and gave Jade one of his rare compliments: it would be ready for roof rafters by the time Rose returned, just like Rose had hoped, thanks to her.

Jade was looking forward to seeing Rose. She was also dreading it knowing that she would have to own up to the fact that it was her mistake that led to Lola's escape and, despite Avi's reassurance that Lola would still return, her eventual death. His optimism had faded by the time Rose was due home, and when he caught Jade biting her lip and casting frequent glances toward the driveway Rose would soon be driving down, he said, "The Lady, will understand, lass. If there is anyone who will understand, it will be Her." She had nodded dumbly and went back to focusing on NOT winding up like Steve.

They had finished for the day and were heading back up the hill for dinner when Rose's truck bounced and bumbled up the dirt driveway to her parking spot by the campers. Jade froze in her tracks as a wave of nausea swept over her. Unaware that he was now walking up the path by himself, Avi continued explaining the math behind where to notch a bird's mouth in a two-by-eight.

Pebbles recognized the sound of the truck immediately. She ran past Jade and then Avi only to hit the end of her lead with such force that it nearly ripped Jade's arm out of her socket and Pebble's subsequent whiplash caused Jade's teeth to clack together. Hard. Avi was surprised to see Pebbles try to sprint past him. He stopped and looked questioningly back at Jade. "Oh," he said, following her gaze to the spot in the distance where Rose had parked.

He lightly stroked Pebbles' head to soothe her, "Hold your horses, Pebbles. We'll be there soon enough." Then he turned back to Jade, to soothe her, too. "It's OK, lass. It's not going to come as a shock to her. Meera already let her know. Better to rip off the bandage than drag it out. Come now."

Jade put a hand across her stomach and looked at him like she was about to throw up. Pebbles kept yanking on her lead in an attempt to run forward. She was unable to understand why Jade was not as eager to get to Rose as fast as she was. She managed to drag Jade a few feet and then stopped.

"You can throw up," Avi said, "but that's not going to avoid what needs to be done. Be sincere, be honest, and all will be well." He held out his hand to her, beckoning to her in that gruff, grandfatherly way of his that she had come to know and love. The way that said (without actually saying it) cut the shit, I know it's hard, do it anyway, I got you.

She nodded her head slightly and permitted her feet to start walking. Pebbles danced with delight, weaving in and out between the two of them now that they were finally heading in the direction she wanted to go. By the time they got to where the truck was parked, Rose was already out of the vehicle and talking to Meera. Their conversation ceased, and they turned toward Avi and Jade as they came around the corner of the camper. Pebbles barked excitedly, and when she lunged forward this time, Jade let go of the leash. Pebbles dashed past Avi in a full sprint and jumped up on Rose with such force that she had to brace herself for the impact. Pebbles wrapped her front legs around Rose's waist in a full canine hug and whimpered with excitement. Jade felt tears start to rise as she watched the reunion from a distance. Avi had walked up to the women and greeted Rose with a welcoming smile alongside a solemn nod.

Meera said something to Rose, and Rose looked briefly at Jade before responding with a single word and a nod. Meera and Avi turned in unison and walked up the hill as Rose made her way over to Jade. Pebbles walked next to Rose, her tail wagging with such force that it made her whole hindquarters sway from side to side.

"Hello, Jade," Rose said once she got within earshot.

"I'm so sorry, Rose. I'm so…"

"Shhh, child. It's OK. Come now. Let's sit and talk." She took Jade by the hand and led her toward her cabin. She gestured for Jade to sit on the deck and then sat next to her.

"I'm so sorry, Rose," Jade said again. "They were great. It was going so well. I was on top of everything. And… and then…," she struggled to speak over the lump in her throat, "and then Steve's leg got pinned and I ran to help…"

"Jade," Rose said in a slightly firmer voice, "It's OK." And then she added, "Truly" as Jade looked like she was about to apologize again. Rose looked out into the forest's canopy for a moment before continuing. "The play of the Divine, or the leela, as we call it, has a way of aligning things into a sort of," she paused looking for the right word and settled on "perfection. Yes. That's a good way of labelling it for now. Lola and I, we had a wonderful, perfect, bond." And she smiled at Jade although it was a smile wrapped in sadness. "Lola also had a wonderful connection with you, as we saw from the first day when she sat next to you in the meditation room." Jade wiped her nose with the back of her hand and then wiped the back of her hand down the side of her jeans, and nodded.

"But sometimes, when it is someone's time to go, it is not so easy to leave when the one you love the most is right there with you. Sometimes," she said more softly, "they wait until you are not around so that they can depart. This is what I feel Lola did. She waited for me to go—so she could go."

"And me? How do I fit into this… *perfection*? Why didn't she go when Avi was looking after her?" Jade asked mournfully. "I've had enough things leaving me lately."

Rose looked at her lovingly, "Because it was your opportunity to face your grief, not Avi's." She looked briefly at Jade's hands, and then turned back to looking at the trees, "And it was your test to see what you would do this time. To see if you would respond differently when faced with uncertainty—with death," Rose looked back at Jade with her eyebrows raised inquisitively and also knowingly.

"These events are tests, portals to be moved through, and moved through them you did, from what I hear."

"What?" Jade said in surprise, "I did? I thought I had completely failed because Lola was gone." Jade rubbed her hands self-consciously—gently touching the scabs on her knuckles.

"Lola would be gone regardless, child. It's just that her leaving gave you an opportunity to stand tall and connect to the bigger web of life. And you did that, too, Jade."

"I did? So, I, uh….passed the…uh, portal…. test?" Jade asked looking a little confused.

"Yes, you most certainly did," Rose said as she clasped her hands together as if in prayer. She searched Jade's eyes with her own, "So, tomorrow morning, we are going for a drive. I will wake you when the time comes. Be ready. OK?"

"Where are we going?"

"Does it matter?"

"No," Jade said sheepishly, "but I'm not allowed to leave the centre…" Her cheeks flushed in embarrassment and fear of reprisal if she were to break her promise of staying at the centre.

Rose stood up and shook off a pine cone and some sunflower debris from the chipmunks' latest meals and looked down at Jade, "You can if you are with me. Do you trust me?" she asked.

"Yes," Jade replied without hesitation.

"Then I'll wake you in the morning. Go on up and have dinner. Please ask Meera to deliver my meal to me in my cabin. It's been a long day of travelling."

Rose lightly touched Jade on the head and murmured, "Sleep well, dear Jade, tomorrow will be here before you know it."

Jade nodded.

"Pebbles, Lo-," she caught herself, "Come. Let's go home."

51 Carpets of Moss and Ribbons of Water

The highway disintegrated into a gravel road, which turned into a dirt track that was barely wide enough for the old Ford to crawl along the dark trough along the valley floor. Everything around them seemed to disappear into an abyss of assumptions—was that a tree? maybe; was that a boulder, or perhaps a bear on the side of the road—who knows? Jade could only focus on the area directly lit by the truck's headlights. They drove through the pre-dawn for what could have been ten minutes or half an hour—she couldn't tell, but eventually, they crossed a wooden bridge spanning a river—or so the sign said. Jade couldn't actually see the river. Not long after that, the track narrowed and started to ascend, weaving its way precariously along the edge of the cliff with the river far below them.

Rose had not uttered a word since they started driving, and before that, she had only spoken enough to wake Jade up and tell her it was time to go.

After an eternity of journeying up and then down again, and just as the trees were starting to peel themselves away from the backdrop of the night sky, Rose turned off the road and stopped. She left the keys in the ignition, rolled down the window, and got out of the truck.

"Come with me," she said, her voice barely audible above the noise of the river they had crossed, left far below, and then had journeyed down to meet. Jade watched Rose close the truck door and look at the back seat through the open window, "and could you please grab my shawl from the backseat? It's cooler out here than I expected." Jade nodded in reply, but by then Rose had already turned away, and Jade was left nodding at her back.

Jade exited the truck and closed her door carefully. She walked over to Rose and handed her the tartan shawl. Rose bowed her in thanks and then started to walk toward the din of the water. Jade followed her without a word. They stumbled over current-carved boulders and stepped on stones that had been kissed smooth and round by water that no longer flowed over them before finally making it to the river's edge.

The two women faced the roaring waters. It moved with purpose, tumbled and twisted, ocean-bound, ambivalent to the two-legged beasts standing on its shores.

The morning air danced and swirled around them as though it was a living being darting in to touch Jade's cheeks before flitting away. Its cold touch made her pale skin blush.

Rose tucked her hands into her shawl and put her back to the churning ribbon of water. She lifted her face slightly, closed her eyes, and waited. Jade, hoping to somehow connect to whatever Rose was experiencing, mirrored her stance. For a split second, a neon sign flashed "This is bullshit" in the darkness of her mind's eye, and then the first shaft of morning light touched her face eradicating the neon sign and the darkness with dazzling reds and yellows.

She stood watching the lights shimmering behind her closed eyelids until she heard rocks crunching as Rose shifted her position. Jade opened her eyes and saw Rose had turned back toward the river and was staring at something on the other side. Jade followed her gaze and saw the valley wall brilliantly illuminated before her. The coniferous forest, dark green and looming up from the banks of the river, had their faces turned to greet the morning light. They basked in its golden glow like baby birds with their necks outstretched for the day's first morsel of nourishment from their mother.

Rose moved closer to Jade and cleared her throat to speak above the water's roar. She was so close Jade could smell the sandalwood that permeated her shawl and wished she'd had a moment to brush her teeth before they left. She closed her mouth and focused on breathing through her nose.

"Pictures, paintings, even photos do the river a great injustice. They showcase River's beauty and her serenity. But," she paused for a moment to make sure that Jade could hear her and then continued when she nodded that she could, "But they silence her voice. They take away her song, and River does not like to be silenced. She demands you listen." Rose glanced at the river and leaned even closer towards Jade, "Like a child who is not yet satiated, who has not had enough attention." Rose caught Jade's eye, briefly raised an eyebrow, and tilted her head knowingly. Jade smiled.

"River lures you, drawing you closer to be part of her dance, but when you get there, the sound of the stampede makes you want to run away and seek stillness." Then heeding her own words, Rose turned and walked away from the water's edge. She settled on a spot close enough that they could see the river, but not be drowned out by it. Rose sat down on a blanket of moss at the bottom of a Fir tree and waited for Jade to join her. Eventually, Jade did. But not before glancing toward the sunlit evergreens again.

Rose watches Jade make herself comfortable on Forest's floor. After all these years, she marvels at how mental and emotional growth can change someone's physicality so dramatically in such a short amount of time. Jade was no longer the cowering cat ready for a back alley fight that had arrived ten months ago. In front of her now sits a young woman holding her head high with eyes that are no longer haunted and guarded. Her fingernails harbour a small amount of garden soil instead of being angry stubs chewed down to the point of bleeding.

Jade settles and Rose begins the day's lesson. She hopes, that if it all goes well, Jade will take advantage of the opportunity for growth the lesson River bestows.

"Human emotions are akin to water," she says sounding more formal than is necessary, but she needs Jade to take her words seriously. "They need to flow like Rivers flow because still waters don't evolve. They stagnate. They become a petri dish for imbalance and disease. That is why we must drink from flowing water and not from sloughs." Rose lovingly caresses her old friend Moss beneath her and as she picks up her hand, Moss reaches toward her wanting more. She smiles at the response to her touch and runs her hand over a few more times. "When we are ready to come into right relationship with our emotions, we come to River as our teacher and guide. We sit close to the rushing of her waters and offer her the herbs from our pouches. Then we surrender the shards of our pain to her and allow them to dissolve into her roar and chaos until we are left feeling calm."

Rose notices that Jade is looking towards River as she speaks, and she follows Jade's gaze to the fleeting, white-water peaks breaking on her surface. For a moment she is swept away to the banks of Ma Ganga River as her memory of learning this very lesson rises from the depths. She is with her teacher and Angelica, who looked as young and as beautiful then as Jade looks now, and her teacher's voice joins her own as she says to Jade, "But this surrendering of our emotions to River's waters is only the first stage of her medicine. And it's a stage that can become addictive. The build-up of emotion, the release, the calm. For some, it's like a drug." Her eyes leave the water and bore into Jade's just as her teacher's eyes had bored into hers and Angelica's. She needs Jade to hear her. So many before her have come to this point in their journey———have become enamoured by the water's power to take away their pain—only to be swept away both figuratively and literally.

"Mother River is a wonderful beast, don't get me wrong," she smiles and purposefully strokes the living carpet again returning her focus and Jade's to the forest. "But, River needs to be utilized as an aide—not a crutch or a habit—to help our stagnant waters move once more. Then we must learn to transcend, her pull, create a life that doesn't let the waters get so stagnant in the first place."

The air around them is suddenly filled with the raucous call of Canadian geese. Rose and Jade turn as one to watch the flock swoop down to an eddy nestled into the side of River, drink for a moment, and then continue flying along the dark ribbon skimming the surface the way a lover's finger traces the curves of their beloved's body. They watch the long-necked birds until the last one has disappeared around the bend; a final honk echoes through the morning air but it is quickly swallowed by the voice of the water. Rose leans back to rest her head against the Fir's trunk. She closes her eyes. The energy of her words swirl around them, and Rose waits to see if they land on Jade and take root.

Jade says nothing and hasn't said anything for quite some time. Only when Rose feels Jade shift her seat, in readiness, does she open her eyes and continue with her lecture.

"And this is one of the conundrums of the human experience, yes?" she says with a smile as though halfway through a thought. "The chaos draws you in, but at a price."

Jade laughs, but harshly, and it is more of a 'no kidding' laugh than one of humour. She nods in agreement and speaks at last, "If offering your emotions to the chaos of the water is stage one, then what is stage two?"

"Stage two of River's teachings," Rose says, "is stillness. We must be able to sit next to the River, or in the roar of life, and become the calm in the chaos. We must be able to hear the quiet behind the noise," she looks at Jade intently as she speaks to emphasize each phrase, "to see the Divine behind suffering; perceive the Truth beyond the reality of emotions. This is not about diminishing the value of the human experience, but rather about holding one's experience in the right perspective. It's about allowing our emotions to be a part of our reality but not being enslaved by them or whisked away in their current. Be engaged but Sovereign." Jade has remained impassive until now, and Rose watches a symphony of micro-movements dance across her face as she receives each word. A few words bounce off, some create openings, and others shut her down. Finally Rose asks, "Do you understand?"

"I think so?" Jade says with one eye scrunched and her head cocked to one side. "It's a lot all at once, but I get what you say about emotions building, the release that comes when you finally explode one way or the other, and then hopefully the calm that follows—like a drug." Jade looks bashful, and her just-in-case-devil surfaces and bares its ugly teeth reminding her that he was still there... just in case.

Rose looks back at the waters to take the pressure off Jade. She opens her mouth to speak and then closes it, uncertain how to proceed. A soft push comes from the Fir, and she nods. Of course. She begins to say, "I used to think that living an *authentic life* meant feeling deeply, expressing all my big emotions, and allowing those things to propel my actions. But I was wrong. So very, very wrong."

"What?!" Jade blurts out, in surprise. "Why were you wrong? Isn't it good to feel your emotions? You know... it's your party, cry if you want to and all that?"

Rose laughs. Jade's ability to fuse humor and serious topics of conversation never ceases to amaze her and more memories of Angelica begin to surface. She says, "Yes, it is important to feel your emotions—cry if you want to so to speak—but don't be at the mercy of them. Because," Rose leans forward slightly and locks eyes with Jade. "You are not your emotions." And then she shoots a look straight at Jade's bruised and scabbed hand.

Jade recoils. She crosses her arms in front of her, trying to hide the evidence of her violent outburst against the tree. Her cheeks burn and her eyes flash.

Calmly, Rose leans back against the bark and focuses on emanating gentle patience. She watches the girl with flames for hair process the information she has just been given—her lips moving slightly with half-formed shapes of words before falling away to the next without a sound. Rose notices Jade's body relax, so she closes her eyes and listens to the birds' morning chorus while she waits.

"Rose," Jade says loudly, making Rose wonder if the girl has had to repeat herself a few times to rouse her from an unexpected nap. Rose opens her eyes to see Jade smiling at her. Her hands are now lying palms up in her lap—the only hint of self-consciousness that remains.

Seeing that Rose is awake, Jade asks, "How do you get to experience being this 'calm in the chaos' when you feel *everything*?" She looks towards River as though her torrent of water symbolizes the intensity of her emotions.

"By orientating to the silence within." Rose says with an understanding smile, holding herself back from calling her 'child'. "We call it *Mouna*."

Rose watches as Jade's hand, almost of its own accord, reaches out to the ground to caress the moss tips with her palm. The tips flick back to their original position, and Rose is impressed that the moss is connecting to her. "So… there's a space…Mouna… that exists between feeling an emotion and having it take you—your actions—over?"

"Yes. And that, I feel, is the opportunity you are ready to explore."

"What? Really? Interesting. You think so? Why now?" Jade asked in her usual rapid-fire question way.

"Why not now?" Rose tilted her head to the side.

Jade takes a few deep breaths. "So, is this opportunity like another quest? Like the fire?" she asks.

"Hmmm. No. It's not so much a quest," Rose says. "It's more of an initiation."

52 All In

Jade stands naked at the water's edge and watches the river rush past her the way the past rushes into the future and disregards the present. Rose had gone to Wildcraft Burdock root further up the valley, promising to come back for her when the Sun touched the valley's ridge to the west. Before she departed, she tucked a stray strand of hair behind Jade's ear and said, "When you meet Ma in the waters for the first time, it needs to be a private meeting—just you and Her." The moment was so tender that Jade wondered if Rose was looking at her or her mother.

Now, standing on the banks, Jade didn't feel alone. She felt thousands of eyes staring at her from the shadows in the forest, from the branches swaying high over her head, from the watery depths in front of her. One rock that kept catching her eye looked like an actual eyeball.

She looked down at her ivory torso, flanked by her heavily freckled, sun-kissed arms—that almost looked as though they were tanned—and wondered if, from a distance, she looked like a streak of milk coffee and creme.

She shivered. Even with the Sun climbing diligently in the sky, the cool breeze coming off the water chilled her, and waves of goosebumps erupted all over her skin. She felt self-conscious, vulnerable and—ironically enough—badass standing there with all her bits and pieces exposed to the elements. She tied her hair up in a loose bun and exposed the delicate nape of her neck to the breeze.

She walked to the river's edge and looked at the small leather pouch Rose had lent her. Much to her chagrin, she had left her offering pouch behind in her pre-dawn stupor. She opened the pouch and a fragrance too complicated to isolate into specific plants wafted into the air. Jade breathed in the scents and then inserted two fingers—all the bag's opening would allow—to grab a pinch of the dried herbs within. Then as Rose had shown her, she hung the pouch around her wrist and cupped her hands together around the herbs to keep them safe inside. She closed her eyes and murmured a prayer of thanks to the water's willingness to teach her how to flow; how to keep moving into the unknown. She gently blew into her palms to cover the herbs with the essence of her life force. Then, she opened her hands to the sky and blew the herbs toward the water. The water lapped up the flecks of earth medicine and whisked them downstream and out of sight.

"Tat Twam Asi," she whispered. The words fell almost involuntarily from her lips, as the last speck vanished from her sight. Self-conscious, she looked around to make sure no one heard.

Across the waters, she caught sight of an Osprey perched atop a tree that had long ago been shattered by lightning. The bird shook its wings and let loose its high-pitched call of accelerating beeps. To Jade, it sounded like an Osprey version of a wolf whistle. She smiled, blushed, and tried to resist placing her arms in front of her body for modesty. Then the Osprey swooped down to the river and plunged its talons into the flowing water. With a mighty flapping of its wings, the fishhawk rose from the water with a meal gripped in its talons and continued on its way—unknowingly following the same path as the Geese and herbs.

Jade had watched the bird with awe. The way it had launched itself into the frigid water was full of purpose and without hesitation. It bolstered her into action. She walked away from the water and looked for the largest rock she could find to store Rose's pouch. She didn't want to lose another thing that belonged to her. Once she was certain the pouch was safe, she walked back to the river—determined to conquer the water and her emotions. She took a deep breath and spread her arms out like wings for balance. Then she curled one bare foot over a wet rounded rock, then the other, and tottered into the swirling water. With each step, her feet felt like they were on fire. Rocks poked the tender soles of her feet, and she stumbled her way along until the water reached her ankles. She glanced down and beneath the crystal-clear water, her feet were bright red. They had stripes of white and blue from the water reflecting the sky above, and they looked beautifully distorted like the Picasso paintings she had studied at school. She lifted one foot out of the water and saw a perfect pink line marking the water's depth. Submerging it again, Jade realized her feet were already numb. The intensity of the water overpowered any emotion and all her senses; it forced her awareness into one concrete thought: keep going.

She waded into the current and felt the river's power push against her thighs and threaten to sweep her away with one false step. She gasped as the water reached her abdomen and wished that she could flap her wings and lift straight up out of the water like the Osprey. But instead, she had to lower her arms into the current as a ballast.

With chattering teeth, Jade took one final step and stopped. She had reached the place Rose had directed her to, and she was submerged from her belly button down. Carefully, on unfeeling feet, Jade turned in the water to face upstream. Her lower body alternated between feeling the excruciating burn of the cold and being completely numb.

Jade repeated Rose's words, psyching herself for what was to come next: "Submerge yourself three times. And then come out and sit on the banks until the sun and the air dry you completely."

"OK. I can do this," Jade said. "I can do this." She focused on the shimmering leaves of a trembling Aspen upstream that was diligently holding the river bank from falling into the waters. She drew in a large breath and dunked herself. One, she thought, shooting up out of the water, and gasping in shock. Still keeping her eye on the tree for stability, she dunked herself again. Two. And then, as she dunked her body into the water for the third time, her eye caught sight of a red bird taking off from the river's edge. Her shift in focus from the tree to the bird made her lose her balance against the current. Her foot slipped as the rush of water started to pull her backwards, and a shot of panic surged through her body. Instinctively, her arms shot out and she made giant sweeping strokes pulling the water past her until she was upright against the current once more. She stood, leaning slightly forward, and breathing hard; she was confused. How many times was that? she thought. Two? Three? Three, she decided and headed toward the shore trying to run out of the water and away from the river's tantalizing suggestion that she should follow the Geese and the Osprey.

Sitting on the large rock, she tucked her knees under her chin and hugged them for comfort. She could feel the air licking her skin and the sun trying in vain to penetrate the icy shell that enveloped her. She shivered uncontrollably as her body attempted to warm itself. She placed her forehead on her knees and focused on trying to catch the breath the river had taken away from her. The bun on her head came loose, and her hair tumbled down over her shoulder. It was familiar against her skin, and she wished to be Rapunzel so she could wrap her dry hair around herself in a cocoon of warmth.

Unbidden, Rose's instructions replayed in her mind: submerge yourself three times….

I did, Jade thought. And now I'm sitting here cold, wet, and miserable. A little Jade-sicle.

The sun's rays set alight the leaves on the Aspen she had kept her eye on as she submerged herself, and they waved at her on the breeze. It made Jade think of the annoying neighbour they'd had. Always "you-hoo-ing!" across the fence trying to catch her or her mum's attention to passive-aggressively remind one of something about something they'd forgotten to do.

She looked from the Aspen to the river and back to the Aspen again. The words "submerge yourself…," were carried on the breeze and danced around her—catching one strand of hair after another—until her dry hair was blowing in the same direction as the flowing water.

"No. Nope. No way. You've got to be *fucking* kidding me," Jade roared.

The wind picked up and whipped around her naked body lashing out at her with equal vehemence.

She tucked her head back down against her knees and tried to hide. Her body recoiled at the thought of returning to the icy water. She couldn't do it. She wouldn't. Panic started to rise in her chest and her mind quickly proposed alternative scenarios to save itself. Don't go back in, tell Rose that your hair dries quickly. Don't go back in, tell Rose you thought she had said your body, which meant, not her head. Don't go back in, tell Rose you hadn't understood that she meant *all* the way.

But she had understood. It's the fucking definition of the word "submerge": put completely under water.

"For fuck's sake," she muttered.

Jade sighed, stood up, and once more tied her hair up in a bun on top of her head.

"Thanks," she said sarcastically to the Aspen tree. "Thank you very much. You've been so helpful." The annoying neighbour just shimmered in the sun and waved.

Jade stomped to the water's edge trying to ignore the cold. She was less reverent, less in awe of this sacred initiation now that she knew what was about to happen. But her steps never faltered. She was filled with fire and stormed into the river as any determined, tottering toddler would swinging her arms for momentum.

Her indignation carried her into the water until it was up to her belly button. Then she turned, glared at the Aspen, and gave the tree two middle fingers. She took a deep breath, pinched her nose, closed her eyes and dropped below the surface.

As her face went under, her jaw locked shut and her teeth ached at the instant and overwhelming brain freeze. She pushed off the river bottom with legs she couldn't feel and burst through the surface. Although her lungs were gasping for air, she didn't allow herself recovery time. She forced them to inflate and immediately went back under. The fire of determination coursed through her and radiated outward battling the cold. Cold that had stripped her awareness of having skin and left her an exposed mass of muscle. Cold that sought to find its way to her vital organs. Cold that wanted to convince her to head downstream with all the others who had come to Ma River for salvation. She shot up out of the water, gasped, and without opening her eyes went under once more. She screamed her refusal to submit and surfaced for the last time. Close to hyperventilating and shivering uncontrollably, Jade pushed her soaking hair from her face and glared at the trembling Aspen. For the briefest of moments, the leaves stopped waving and stood eerily still. Jade turned her back on them and strode from the river like an Amazonian woman returning home from battle. Victorious. Invincible. Mythical.

53 Success in Limbo

Jade lay across the large, warm boulder in nothing but her underwear, while the breeze dried her body and the sun, warmed her bones. They worked together to dry her thick hair into matted streaks of cooled lava. While the sun climbed and then peaked in the sky, she sat by the river's edge and listened to its roar. It was deafening and the forces at work inside her urged her to walk away, to retreat to a quieter spot. A safer spot. She refused and stayed where she was but allowed herself the protection of her clothes.

She thought about her mother: what she would say about all that had happened to her since she'd left? The thoughts turned to wishing. Wishing things were different; wishing her mother was here; wishing she could share her life with her; wishing she could see her grow. Thoughts of her mother faded and thoughts about Aaden took their place. He had left just as she felt she could open up to another person again.

Love. Loss. Love. Loss. It defined her life. It had brought her here. To this spot. And at that thought, the river's voice became louder than the voices in her head, and the tears began to fall. Her body shook with the severity of her sobs. Eventually, the sobs turned into sniffles and the sniffles turned into silent despair. She'd sit quietly for a moment or two and then another voice in her head would echo and the tears would start a new. Before long, she'd be shaking with grief all over again. The water goaded her into letting it all go, and once she'd done so, it became a raucous, cheering crowd that cancelled out her howls. Then, as the tears streamed down her cheeks, the river shifted to a sibilant hushing of comfort and knowing, soothing her until she had emptied herself and fallen into the deep silence Rose had spoken of so often. The one found just beyond the senses.

By the time Rose returned riverside at the promised time of the sun touching the western ridge, Jade was exhausted from the day's efforts. Rose sat next to her on the boulder and gave Jade an appraising look—likely noticing the dried tears and snot, the red-rimmed eyes; hopefully noticing the calmness that flitted just below the surface.

"Success?" Rose said finally.

Jade nodded and looked at the river.

"You had to do it twice, didn't you?" Rose asked with a cocked eyebrow.

"How did you know?" Jade asked surprised and suddenly embarrassed. She thought she'd been alone. That Rose had left.

"Because at my first meeting with River I, too, had to do it twice…," she spoke while looking at the river water as one might an old friend. "Something about offering your head. While it is absolutely necessary, it is also subconsciously terrifying." Rose smiled at Jade.

Jade nodded. Rose had nailed it perfectly—subconsciously terrifying. She waved a matted lock of hair as proof, "Yep. But, I did it."

"Yes, you did. You know, it took your mother two days to do it." Rose said with a chuckle. "She wasn't as honest with herself as you were. We all could see that her hair was too dry to have been submerged underwater, but she swore she had completed the task. The next day, at lunch, she walked in wet hair. She sat down and ate without a word. It was only later than she confided in me that she had gone out early that morning and had hitched a ride to the waters to submerge herself. Again. Fully this time."

Jade laughed. "Sounds like mum," she said.

Rose nodded in remembrance. "She was a wild one your mother—and I loved her. Oh, I loved her so much." A small smile crossed her face at the memory before she looked up and was snapped back to the present. "Now," she said looking at the sky and then the trees across the river. "Let's get you back to the centre and set up for your retreat."

"Retreat? I thought the bathing in the river was the preparation for an initiation?" Jade said returning Rose's herb pouch.

Rose bowed her head in thanks before returning the pouch to her medicine bag. "It was," she said patiently and stood up. "The initiation happens during a nine-day silent retreat."

"Oh," Jade said.

"I did tell you that before I left this morning."

"Apparently, I have selective hearing today," Jade said sheepishly looking up at Rose.

"Today…?" Rose teased with a smile. "Come on, let's go."

The drive out of the valley and back to the highway seemed to pass by much more quickly than the journey in this morning. Despite the fading light, Jade could still see all the different trees living side by side. Each one doing their part to hold the valley walls in place and stop the earth from tumbling into the river that snaked along the valley floor. Jade wondered if the river knew it was headed, eventually, to the ocean, or if it just knew it needed to keep moving forward without any inkling of its destination. Maybe the river felt purpose in the movement, and that, in and of itself, was enough. Maybe it just trusted an unseen force, an elemental God if you will.

"You did good today," Rose's voice derailed Jade's train of thought. "Rest now. Tomorrow we continue." Rose's words were like an incantation, and Jade realized she was on the verge of sleep. She let her eyes close and her body relaxed. The truck's slow plod on the dirt road soothed her, and she fell asleep. She woke briefly—barely registering the waking world—when Rose ushered her into her cabin and pulled the covers up over her clothed body.

The next morning Jade stepped out of her cabin to see that Fall had arrived. All at once. In one night. The same field that had greeted her for almost a year was filled with a new sense of wonder. The sudden morning chill had transformed the fine, summer-kissed alpine grasses into threads of golden steam rising from the Earth. Everywhere the land had managed to hold its green was now adorned with diamonds of dew.

The sky above Jade was a blank canvas of mineral blue, and as Dark Eyed Juncos punctuated the moment with their morning trill, she imagined the sound being painted on the dawn sky like a sonogram. Each bird's song criss-crossed until the abstract called *Morning's Song* was finished.

Across the valley to the East, dark clouds concealed the mountain tops. Jade took in the panorama before her. The two scenes—here in the field and there in the land beyond—seemed so different from each other, yet were only a valley apart. If the land itself could run such contradicting stories, then maybe it was not so surprising that she, too, felt like a contradiction standing on her doorstep in a sort of limbo between who she was and who she was becoming.

54 Nine Nights of the Mother

Jade walked into the main house expecting to see Meera darting around the kitchen, Avi drinking his morning tea sitting in the old green chair by the window that looked out at the cloud-kissed mountains, and Steve laid out on the couch with his leg up—eating. But the room was empty. She listened for the sound of others in the room next door… but nothing, not even the hum of the refrigerator greeted her. A single piece of paper sat on the counter. She moved over to it and saw that it was a note, and it screamed at her in all caps.

JADE

EAT THEN MEET ROSE IN GARDEN

STEVE

Why was Steve writing me notes? she wondered. Her stomach answered for her, *Don't worry about it*, it said. *Just eat. Please, god, eat.*

Savoury tapioca had been left on the stove for her, and she eagerly dug in. She was thankful to be eating alone as she used her finger to unceremoniously wipe the bowl clean. She took her cup of black tea to Avi's seat and watched the clouds play on the mountain peaks as she sipped. Finally satiated, she cleaned up after herself and went to the mudroom. There she changed into the Fall boots Meera had left for her and headed to the garden.

The two remaining peafowl were enthusiastically pecking at the ground devouring the cat food that had been strewn about. Sargent Tibbs, despite having her own food kept scooting around in an attempt to get some for herself. The peafowl weren't keen to share their favourite foods and kept a wary eye on the cat burglar. To look at the birds, she never would have been able to tell that their head male had been brutally murdered a little over a week ago.

As Jade neared the garden, she saw Rose sitting at the fire pit facing East. The peas were gone now and the trellis was bare, thus the normally hidden fire pit and sacred circle were exposed. Jade walked around the fence to the entrance, and just as she was about to call out in greeting, she saw that Rose's eyes were closed and her body was completely still—statuesque. Jade noticed her body seemed to be buzzing at the edges as if absorbing and offering energy to each of the different plants around her. Jade wondered if Rose was engaged in some sort of morning fauna update, and smiled at the thought.

Jade removed her boots and entered the circle. She sat facing West, just as she had when the wildfire had threatened to consume the centre. She made herself comfortable, and imitating Rose, she closed her eyes.

At first, Jade heard nothing out of the ordinary. The morning was as quiet and peaceful as it usually was. Then the quiet fell away, and Jade realized she could hear all sorts of different sounds: the bees across the garden; the sharp flick of a grasshopper jumping from one plant to the next; a murmured conversation of leaves rubbing against each other as a bird briefly landed and then took off near the grasshopper's spot. She opened her eyes to check her ears and saw a Mountain Bluebird take flight with the insect in its mouth. She made a pouty face to acknowledge the grasshopper's demise and then smiled when she realized she was experiencing nature on a level she'd never been before. She closed her eyes to see what else was going on around her, and for the briefest moment, she thought she could hear the soft flicking of the Gazania daisies, fanning out their striped petals to greet the morning sun.

She allowed her skin to soften, remembering that Rose had taught it was the fastest way to opening her heart, and felt herself dissolve into a gentle witnessing of all the happenings taking place around her. Jade felt a beam of sunshine on her face that hadn't been there before. She had become accustomed to the morning sun warming her back, so this light on her face caused her to open her eyes. Rose was looking at her inquisitively and with the utmost kindness.

Not long ago, Rose's direct gaze would have made Jade self-conscious and she would've looked down in shame wishing the ground would open up and swallow her whole. Now she simply stared into Rose's eyes and waited. They smiled in unison—welcoming the joy of the moment and acknowledging the growth.

"Yesterday, I mentioned that I felt it was time for you to retreat and you asked me why. Why now and not earlier." Rose started speaking very matter-of-factly as though the day's preliminary pleasantries had already been exchanged. "Well, if you had retreated when you first arrived, it likely would have felt like a banishment. It would have felt isolating. It would have felt like you were living in the prison cell you had avoided by coming here. Why not mid-summer after you had settled? I can see you are about to ask that. Well, to retreat takes great trust. Trust in your surroundings, and most importantly, trust in yourSelf. You needed time to find your footing here, to create relationships, to witness others moving through challenges within themselves and come out the other side, for your inspiration." Jade knew she was talking about Aaden's hell and the connection they had nurtured before he left. "With all you have experienced, with all you have been through, you are not the same person who arrived here in early Spring. It is my hope that you see that about yourself and that you will welcome this experience as an opportunity. An opportunity to step forward, to integrate, to retreat into a chrysalis and emerge as a butterfly." She paused for a moment but did not look away from Jade. "Who are you? Who do you want to be? You have to decide, Jade, on the qualities your butterfly will emerge with." And then, as if they'd rehearsed it, an orange butterfly with white dots danced around Rose's head weaving an imaginary crown. Jade watched the butterfly for a moment admiring its grace and beauty and then continued.

"Retreats like this are a gift, Jade, but they are not always easy. I am telling you this not to set you up for difficulty, but so that as you experience the different waves of consciousness, you will be able to remember my words just like you did when you met your fire. You will remember that you are not alone." She paused and nodded at the Cedar Waxwing who'd been waiting to offer its high-pitched buzzy endorsement of Rose's advice. Jade was instantly transported to her first day at her fire and her and Aaden's whispered conversation. She started to silently recite the waxing's medicine—*clear perspective, gratitude, gentleness, transformation, consciousness*—just as Aaden had taught her.

Rose seemed to hear Jade's thoughts and waited until she had finished her recitation before continuing, "Every tree, plant, animal, and insect knows you are here. You have, I believe, glimpsed this." Jade nodded as she stared into the ashen pit remembering the experience she had had in this very spot—when creation Herself rushed to Jade's aide when she cried out.

"In this retreat, you must invoke the Divine Mother in the form of Durga. She will be with you and protect you from re-identifying with the shadows. When engaged in the proper manner, Durga will protect you like a Mother and allow you to anchor fully into a new dimensional perspective, or a new way of moving through this human experience if that's simpler for you to understand at this moment." Rose pulled a piece of paper from her pocket and placed it in her lap.

"I have written a list of preparations for you to do before you move into the cabin this evening at dusk. Tonight is the new moon, and this cycle happens to be closest to the fall equinox making it an optimal time for a retreat." Jade looked up at the sky half expecting to see a sliver of moon in the west, but it had already surrendered to the day. Rose reached across the firepit and handed the papers to Jade, who took them but didn't open them. "I have also written out your daily schedule for the next nine nights."

Rose smiled at Jade, looked around at the garden, and then began to speak again. "For a retreat such as this, it is important to think of it as a cycle—a progression of sorts. Stage one is the emptying, which you started at the river yesterday. But you will need to go deeper, and the first three nights will help you to do that. Stage two is receiving or filling, and stage three is integration. The Divine Mother will be with you the whole nine nights, but she will be in the form of one of her three aspects: Kali, Lakshmi, and Saraswati."

Rose scanned Jade's face checking to see that she was receiving her words. "River helped you start to let go. Now, Ma Kali will aid you. She will help you cut the threads that hold you down; help you to let go of all that is no longer needed." Rose waited a moment and then nodded in encouragement. "Remember, Jade, holding onto your grief is not an act of love. It is an act of attachment—an attachment to things and people that no longer exist in the form that you have known them. Just because we do not see someone with our eyes anymore does not mean that they are gone." She glanced over to the entrance of the circle as though acknowledging someone standing there. Jade looked, too, but found only onions and bolted broccoli. Rose pointed to the papers in Jade's hand. "Pray for Ma Kali to be with you as you do the practices I've listed."

"The next three nights are dedicated to Ma Lakshmi. Having emptied in the first three nights, you beckon forth the abundance of light to fill the creases in your mind that are ready to step into fullness. The last three nights are offered in reverence to Ma Saraswati as we come into the wisdom and the integration of the transformation that has taken place.

"The Mother cannot leave you, Jade," Rose said as she stood up and flattened the creases in her skirt. Jade looked up at her; Rose was beautiful. The morning light shone through the loose strands of her grey hair and her body seemed to glow. "When you emerge after nine days, my body will be waiting for you. But, if you need me while you are secluded you will find me in your heart. Bring your awarenesses to your breath, and your mind to the Name and you will find me there. OK?"

Jade nodded, her eyes a little wild around the edges, and said, "OK." Rose pulled out another folded piece of paper and handed it to Jade. This one was sealed with red wax. A Dragonfly had been stamped into it, and Jade ran her finger over its smooth edges wondering what secret was held within.

"On the tenth morning, open that," Rose said handing it to her, and then walked away before Jade could answer or ask anything more. She didn't look back. Not that Jade had expected her to turn and wave. But still, she couldn't help but watch as the Lady on the Hill weaved her way through vegetables that seemed to lean towards her ever so slightly as she passed, just in case she did.

55 Trees: Either

In silence, you learn that the heart is your single, unceasing, sentiment of devotion for life.

It is the signature of your soul, and like bird's wings, it flutters the breeze and creates ripples, motifs that tap against our bark as coded messages of dots and dashes. Dots and dashes telling stories heard beyond the ears; songs sung beyond the voice. For it is in silence that Truth speaks. It is in silence that Ma's song can be heard. And once your soul hears Her, words become superfluous.

56 Origami Flowers and the Scent of Medicine

Jade tucked the wax-sealed note into her pocket and turned her attention to the papers Rose had handed her. There were four. She quickly scanned the headings of each page and saw they were labelled: *Retreat Preparations, Day One, Day Four,* and *Day Seven*. One page for each phase, she thought, and then opened the first one, gently, like reversing an origami flower and began to read. She paused at the four, underlined words telling her not to read ahead—which, of course, only made her *want* to read ahead. *You're not a toddler,* she thought. *Control yourself.*

The first task was to create four smudging bundles—one for each stage of the retreat and one as a gift to the light bearers, the unseen guides on the path.

Easy enough, Jade thought, and she set to work. She got scissors, string, and a basket from the greenhouse and wondered what medicine she would like to invoke in her bundle. Meera's voice—the one she used when giving instructions—popped into her thoughts. *If you know the teaching you wish to invoke, then you will know the herb you need to work with. If you don't know what you wish to invoke, then sometimes the plants will lead you to them. Understanding will come in hindsight.*

Jade ran down the list of medicinal herbs that Meera had taught her. She was surprised not only at how many she had committed to memory but also at how many of their teachings she could recall. Nothing from her mental list jumped out and said "Pick me! Pick me!" so she decided to feel the plants, to let them call to her, rather than seek them out herself.

With her gaze soft and her heart open she perceived the Marigolds reaching out to her—their energy determined to be recognized—and their heady smell enveloped her. She didn't need smothering, so she simply murmured a gentle good morning to them as she moved past. Then she felt the strength of the Sunflowers. Face-sized blooms sitting atop thick, green poles that reached for the sky, yearning to be as close to the sun as possible. But next to them, instead of feeling empowered, she felt small. She trailed a finger lovingly up the stalk of the nearest sunflower and gently stroked the yellow petals she could reach. Then she thanked them for shining so brightly and kept scanning the garden for a voice that would bring solace.

On the edge of the rock wall, a shrub sat low and formed a perfect circle. It was a humble plant, not too flashy, and she wasn't sure why it caught her eye, but it did. Soft, almond-shaped leaves that were a subdued, greenish hue invited her to touch them, and in turn, she was bathed in gratitude. *Mother Sage, powerful in purification and cleansing,* Meera's voice echoed in her mind.

"Bingo," Jade said. She knelt before the shrub to ask it permission to be included in the bundles she needed to make. She took a pinch of dried herbs from the pouch on her hip and sprinkled it clockwise around the plant. Meera had yet to quiet in her mind, and her lesson and demonstration at Ma Labyrinth was on repeat in Jade's head: *First, we offer. Then, we ask. Lastly, we listen. If the answer is a 'yes', then we receive with gratitude and seal it with another offering. If the answer is 'no' we leave alone and move on.* A Raven passed overhead and chirped a single purred note, which felt like an announcement to its forest friends, that the process of Jade's initiation had begun.

Jade moved her hand in and out of the Sage plant, caressing the stems and automatically removing dead leaves and weeds to keep the plant healthy. She hoped her hand could let her heart ask what needed to be asked and would hear the answer without getting her mind too involved. Back and forth her hand went, waiting to feel which stems—if any—would like to be part of the bundles. With each *yes,* Jade felt a little rise of energy in her chest, and she knew that piece of the plant was willing to aid her. She snipped it just above the bottom leaves to ensure it would grow again next year. Finally, she had all she needed, and she sprinkled another pinch of herbs in gratitude, stood up, and continued her search. She moved like a blind woman, smelling, sensing, and feeling her way through the garden to find the next plant that would bring her closer to her Self.

Somewhere, between the Pumpkins and the Paddy Pans, she stopped. The familiar scent of Mother Lavender reached up and held her in place.

She remembered how Meera had told her: *Lavender's purple flowers spark intuition, but its true medicine is for healing the heart, for softening grief,* and then how Meera had smiled lovingly at her. Briefly Jade smiled to herself at the memory———then she scrunched up her face trying to recall what else Meera had said about its medicinal properties. She knew people used the flowers to turn fibre green—which she thought was weird, why weren't they turning clothes a purple or lavender colour? She muttered to herself, "As a herb…as a herb it's…it's….yes! It's used to help refine one's state of consciousness. Lavender works with the nervous system to slow the overactive mind, to calm the perpetual swirling of thoughts, and to anchor one's consciousness in grateful calm or tranquillity." She did a little victory dance for nailing the recitation. She looked around to see if anyone had heard only to find a Chickadee in the lowest branches of the Fir was watching her. It seemed to nod its approval before flying away.

Jade knelt before the Lavender plant, inhaled deeply and felt her whole being slow down. She opened her pouch and offered her herbs. With its spirit already singing yes, she clipped four stems and placed them next to the Sage. After sealing the harvest with gratitude and more dried herbs, she stood up and looked around the garden once more.

The many different plants, flowers, herbs, and trees all seemed to welcome her presence, but there was only one plant beckoning her to come a little closer and take a look. She did.

Jade examined the patch of grass that had called out to her. She didn't recognize it right away and thought it might be Sweetgrass. But, after careful consideration, she determined that its stems were too thick and the blades too wide. She ran a few blades through her hand and it sliced through her skin making what felt like a paper cut at the base of her index finger. She snatched her hand back, confused. Why did it want to be part of the bundle if it was going to cause her pain? She brought her face closer to the plant, and as the blades tickled her cheeks, she caught the sweet smell of lemon. Ahhh, Lemongrass, Jade thought. And on the heels of naming the plant she received its message: *Everything in life can hurt you if you engage with it carelessly.* Too late, she realized she'd been asking for information before making an offering and proceeded to sprinkle a healthy dose of herbs around her base. Jade knew that even with her new-found experiences and perspective of the land, the old shadows of depression and despair still lingered. Perhaps the Lemongrass's medicine was an acknowledgment of that, and so she requested it to be part of her bundles. As she asked she felt her heart lift a little and could feel the energy of the plant reach out to her with permission.

Once permission was granted, she cut four thick, red stalks. The air was instantly infused with the sweet smell of citrus, and Jade felt a little lighter. She carefully held the blades of grass and then lovingly placed them next to the Lavender. Feeling complete with her collection, Jade looked for a spot in the garden to sit and assemble her bundles. The blue and purple Salpaglosis' and salmon pink Strawflowers caught her eye and the area they were in was partly shaded, which made it just right for the task she needed to do.

Jade sat half in the sun and half out relishing the perfect fall weather. Then she emptied her basket of its contents. The Sage, Lavender, and Lemongrass were separated into four piles. She made sure there were equal amounts of each plant in the piles before binding them in the yellow and red string that was used specifically for creating smudging sticks. As she wrapped each bundle from stem to tip, she let her thoughts of the upcoming retreat float in and out of her mind. She was mindful to wrap each bundle with an intention for its existence, and in this case, she mused over what kind of butterfly she would like to become.

Once all four bundles were wrapped, she returned the basket, scissors, and string to the greenhouse, and then paused. In her excitement to get started on the retreat preparations, she had forgotten about her everyday tasks. Her mind raced as she stacked her list of to-do's that would be left undone during her retreat. Soon, the list towered higher than the mammoth Sunflowers and her heartbeat quickened. She resolved to find Meera or Avi and give them all the information they'd need while she was occupied with turning into a butterfly as soon as she completed Rose's list.

She stood just outside the greenhouse door and opened Rose's instructions, a little less reverently this time.

Avi has prepared the Sauna for you. While sitting in the heat, turn your mind toward internal reflection. It will take time for all the chatter and movement of your mind to calm. Be gentle with yourself in the heat and the subsequent days. Do not worry about your current duties, the list of to-do's, the things you don't want to forget. They have already been addressed. Let go of the outside world, Jade, and start to journey within.

Aaden's voice echoed from the depths of her subconscious, "The Lady never gives directive without good reason…I guess that's why they say better than admiration is obedience." Jade smiled and headed toward her camper leaving, or at least trying to, all her worries behind.

57 Liquified Mind and the Drip of the Drum

Jade stared down at her feet and tried to focus on slowing her breathing. In and out. In and out. *It shouldn't be this hard*, she thought. *It's fucking automatic after all*. And then, she added begrudgingly, *but maybe not so automatic in 85°Celcius*. She closed her eyes and tried to soften her skin but the intense heat of the sauna was hell-bent on pushing her body into fight or flight. *I'm either going to sweat to death or combust*, Jade thought. She tried for a while—much longer than she probably should have—to figure out which one would be worse.

"Fuuuuuuuuuck," Jade moaned as the sauna's heat overwhelmed her. She sat back and rested her head against the sauna's hot wooden wall. Of all the saunas she had had since she arrived at the centre, she could never understand why some days they were relaxing, and some days they were unbearable.

Today, her mind refused to settle; it just kept recycling the ever-expanding to-do list for the garden, over and over. She had to keep reminding herself that she wasn't reneging on her duties. She had been instructed to be here; she had been instructed to let go. To let *all* of it go. Breathe in. De-sucker tomatoes. Breath out. Harvest and freeze green beans. She leaned forward, propped on her elbows, and hung her head. "Fuuuuuuuuuuuuck, I forgot about to put away the curing garlic," she said.

Eventually, the heat became too much for her to think about anything else, and her to-do list turned to liquid. Sweat trailed like tears down her body, accumulated at the edges of safety—her nose, her chin, her nipples—before letting go and dropping to the floor. Plonk. Plonk. Plonk. Each drip sounded like a slow, ceremonial drumbeat marking the moment a to-do admitted defeat and surrendered.

With her mind no longer able to dwell on the present, it slouched back into the past. She could feel her old mindsets, her old ways of being, coming to the surface—drawn out of her by the heat and the steam. She watched the sassy comments bubble to the surface of her mind, the snide retorts, the sarcasm that veiled her vulnerability. She witnessed it all—each memory, each flicker of a scene, each echo of a conversation—with equal parts compassion and embarrassment as they seeped like toxins out of her pores until she couldn't watch anymore. She jumped out of her seat and went outside.

She stood naked with her hands arms crossed and her head tilted toward the sky. She drew in deep, shaky breaths of cool air and let the gentle, fall breeze lick the sweat that continued to pour down her body. She surveyed the trees in front of her—the Firs and Pines still fully green, the Larches turning golden, and the Birches beginning to undress for winter—and contemplated the ease in which they could just let go until she felt chilled and goosebumps covered her skin. The trees shivered in the breeze and more leaves fell. Jade returned to the heat.

This time, she focused her mind on the mantra that Avi had chanted and taught her when they worked together in the hot afternoon sun. His voice became louder than the other ones in her head, "It's a sweet song…," he had said when he taught it to her "…it vibrates at the speed of the human potential. But don't worry about that, lass. Just let the energy do the work for you."

She freed her mind to swim in the melody of Avi's song and her body to swim in the steam of sweat. She added her voice to his, repeating the words over and over—*sitaram sitaram sitaram*—until her heart rate slowed and her skin dissolved into the strength and the tenacity of the heat. It was spontaneous. It was blissful. It was divine.

Jade stood in the shower outside the sauna and watched the shadows lengthen. She felt the water sluicing over her body but not its temperature. Was it warm from the day's sun, or had the shadows from the trees kept it cold? She neither knew nor cared. All thought had been left in puddles on the sauna floor. Soundlessly, she scrubbed her skin with soap that smelled of lemongrass and was embedded with poppy seeds. The soap made her skin sing as the seeds exfoliated the old layers from her body. With each rinse, she felt the water wash months, years, and even lifetimes away.

58 Under the Eye of the Universe

Now dressed and carrying a small bag of essentials, Jade started to walk down to the cabin she had been assigned for the retreat. She held Rose's first note of instructions in her hand as she walked. The paper had softened and moulded to her hand from the heat of the sauna. She looked up to see Grandmother Moon—a silver sliver etched into the sky hanging just above the mountains.

Jade started down the old Elk trail but stopped halfway down as the sharp scent of tree sap permeated the cool air. She looked for its source and saw a newly split pile of wood next to the path waiting to be stacked. Breathing deeply, she hoped the smell of the sap was embodied with as much selfless wisdom in death as it was in life. After getting her fill, Jade continued along the trail until the smell of pine was replaced by the smell of woodsmoke coming from the cabin she'd be calling home for the next nine days. Someone had already lit the fire to ward off the chill of the evening, and she was eager to get inside.

There was no porch on this cabin, but the roof overhung the front door giving ample shelter to the stack of firewood that lay against it. She stepped inside and found a small table against one wall with a single chair tucked against it, and against the opposite wall, a twin bed. The distance between the two was about five feet. Opposite the front door was a tiny fireplace and next to it, sandwiched between fireplace and bed, was a bedside cabinet. On top: a posy of Marigolds and a piece of folded white fabric, inside, shelves for her to unpack her things into. The far corner of the room had a ladder that led up through a hole in the floor to a loft.

She wanted to take a peek, but before that, she busied herself with setting the altar on the table: she lined up the four smudging bundles, placed the picture of her mother and Rose by the river to the left of the statue of Shiva that was already there, and then lit the candle that was also already there. Jade stepped back and looked and thought: *first we offer…* "Offer what?" Jade almost said aloud, and then remembered this was nine days of silence. She remembered the flowers she'd seen upon entering the cabin. She clipped a Marigold bloom from its stem and placed it in front of the candle. She closed her eyes and sent a silent prayer asking to be guided and protected throughout the nine nights; then she opened her eyes and looked at the candle. She liked how each of the forms the candlelight touched looked richer, alive almost, when bathed in its soft golden glow. A great sense of calm washed over her when her eyes landed on the photo of her mother and Rose. They looked out at her joyfully, eyes twinkling, and she thought she heard them laughing.

With her offering and intentions finished, Jade sat on the bed and looked around, more carefully this time. The cabin was beautiful and cozy. It had been constructed with hand-chiselled timbers, and the walls were clad with pine wood panelling. The small wood stove was made of cast iron and had a squirrel embossed on the side. Upon it sat a cast iron kettle that had a steady little stream of steam to humidify the room.

She climbed the ladder to the loft above and found a double bed, but Jade decided to sleep downstairs on the single. It would be easier to stoke the fire in the night and she wouldn't kill herself trying to climb up and down a ladder in the dark. She knew from experience she wasn't the most alert at 3:00 AM. So many times over the summer she had missed the step off the porch of her camper when she went outside to pee at night. The jolt always made her more awake and harder to go back to sleep. She also liked that sleeping downstairs meant she'd be able to see the trees better during the day and the sky at night through the two, huge, east-facing windows. Star gazing on a moonless night would maybe be as good as going to the movies.

Jade laid down on the pillows, imagining what the night sky might look like—wishing for shooting stars—and thought the windows on either side of the door looked like eyes and the middle window of the door looked like a nose. I'm looking through the eyes of the Universe she thought. Or, maybe the Universe is looking at me? The idea made her feel a bit like a goldfish in a bowl. She was being watched by the forest, by the sky, by the moon, and by the Divine itself. But, she told herself, if she was not willing to be seen by them, then she was not ready to be initiated.

Jade turned her head to the side to look at the folded fabric next to the flowers. She sat up and carefully opened up the folds. Out of the white shawl, a string of wooden beads fell onto her lap. She reverently felt the little round beads—each secured with a knot and sent a silent "thank you" to whoever spent hours making it. She put on the beads over her head making sure the tassel was behind her neck, just as she had seen Meera wear hers, and wrapped herself in the shawl. The shawl was satin smooth and the way it draped over her shoulders felt like folded wings.

Still wearing the shawl and beads she unpacked her small bag of essentials. Taking out the sock with her mother's letters, her clothes, Rose's notes—her directions and the one with the wax seal—her brass grasshopper, her journal, and the pine needle basket Aaden had given her. She placed the grasshopper, her mother's letters and basket on the altar and put her clothes away. Then she looked at Rose's notes. The directions she placed on the altar in Aaden's basket. All that was left was Rose's sealed note. She once again examined the wax seal and stroked the perfect dragonfly wings with the tip of her finger. *On the tenth morning open this.* She frowned comically and put her head back pretending to cry at the ceiling—to entertain herself as well as whomever was watching from outside—and knew this note would need to be kept out of sight. Looking at it every day was not a torture she was willing to subject herself to, so under her pile of clothes it went. She looked around. There was nothing else to do.

She glanced over at her mother who seemed to nod at her, encouraging her to take the next step in her journey of self-discovery. Jade smiled, took a deep breath, and nodded back. Time to get a move on.

Perched upon a silk cushion, embroidered with golden dragonflies flitting around the fabric attempting to find their way out of the seams, she sat on the floor facing the windows and beyond that, the evening sky, putting the warmth of the fire behind her. She closed her eyes, and began to practice one of the first mediation techniques Rose had taught her when she started her formal studies—so she could quiet her mind and ground herself.

Now that she was suddenly facing a lack of anything to do—in the cabin specifically, but also within the centre itself—her mind was chaotic. Unfocused. *Almost* Schizophrenic, she thought. She watched, fascinated, as it swirled untethered. Lights danced in the darkness of her mind, and from those lights, Past and Future appeared strolling drunkenly, arm in arm, down an old, cobblestoned English lane. Past Jade brandished her umbrella as though fighting an invisible monster, and Future Jade twirled hers lackadaisically as she rambled on about all the great things she'd be doing. Maybe she will go to school to be a naturopath and learn more about the way Nature's herbs work with the body, or maybe Chinese medicine, acupuncturist, or become a counsellor, so she can help people the way Rose, Meera and Avi have helped her—suddenly there were so many options she was interested in.

Jade was entertained by them far longer than she should have been. But when they started on the third round of the same old monsters and the same odes to tomorrow, she finally brought her awareness to her breath. Past and Future Jade looked startled at the sudden breeze and opened their umbrellas in anticipation of rain. A gust of wind swirled around them, picking them up, and carrying them away a la Mary Poppins. Present Jade settled down to watch the kaleidoscopic light show her mind was putting on. Oranges and pinks swirled, blues flickered and greens seeped in around the edges of her mind.

She watched and wavered and watched again, and finally understood why it would take nine days of seclusion to let all of these energies exhaust themselves before revealing who she was ready to be.

Finally, the light show started to dim and her mind got quiet, she opened her eyes and realized the Moon was no longer watching her through the window. It was late—10 pm, way past her bedtime as far as the centre was concerned. She peeled herself off the floor, noting how much easier it was to sit compared to when she arrived nine and a half months ago, and after blowing out the candle and stoking the fire, she crawled into bed, laid under the eye of the Universe, and waited for sleep to arrive.

59 Nine Nights: Letting Go

Sleep stood patiently outside in the still, cold night waiting for its turn to come in. The heat of the fire made the interior not exactly stifling, but warmer than was necessary or comfortable for sleep. Two flies took to the air, and they used the heat of the room to fuel their unbridled desire to tango, to buzz, to swirl, and to scream at the injustice of their existence, like toddlers on too much sugar—indignant that the remainder of their lives would be confined to this very room.

Jade tossed and turned and tried every trick she had to draw her awareness away from the chaotic buzzing of the flies. She was not sure how long it took before it happened nor did she notice, but eventually sleep snuck in and took her by the hand to a land beyond.

She woke the next morning feeling out of sorts. The Sun was about to appear over the mountains, and the Universe's eye, which had watched over her as she slept, now framed a beautiful dawn. The distant mountains created a smoky line across the horizon splitting Heaven from Earth and creating a platform for rose-gold clouds to sit upon. Jade stayed in bed and watched, awestruck, as the clouds turned pink and then morphed into orange. The colourless expanse of the sky turned a pale, baby boy blue, and then, finally, the sun began to show.

As the sky brightened, she noticed two trees through the windows watching her wake up—a Larch and a Fir. One, a deciduous liberal signalling it was time to take off its clothes by setting itself alight in gold. The other, an evergreen conservative who would only consider going naked as a final act before death. Every needle on their branches looked crisp and defined in the dawn light. Larch and Fir stood silently—at least Jade assumed silently as she could not hear them from inside the cabin—watching her watch the sunrise; ~~an~~ odd couple content to be part of the moment.

With the outside world fully illuminated, Jade stood up to start her day and realized she was bleeding. Five days early. *Better than late* her mum used to say. Jade sighed. *Early still sucks, though,* she replied to the voice in her head and set about cleaning herself up. After that unexpected start, she ignited the fire which had gone out in the night, made a cup of herbal tea, and sat on the bed with Rose's 'Day One' note in her hand. She opened it carefully and began to read.

Blessed Self,
As you embark on your first nine-day retreat in Silence, I offer these pages to you as a guide and talisman of support. You read the first one yesterday preparing for today. Remember, do not read ahead.

Read only the note you need, and for today, that is this one—Kali. Leave the one titled 'Day 4' until the first day of Laxmi and the note titled 'Day 7' for the first day of Saraswati. This is of the utmost importance.

The first three days of Kali are for letting go. Do not be surprised if you start to bleed, no matter where in your cycle you are. It is normal for the body to bleed and to reset in big initiations like this.

"Now you tell me…," Jade mouthed.

As you move through your days, here is a list of approved tasks that will help you integrate the energies of the retreat and stay focused throughout the nine nights.

Jade skimmed the list of activities: mantra meditation, walking Ma Labyrinth, laundry, cleaning, and attending (from a distance) the fire ceremony they were planning on doing each day at 5 pm to support her retreat. Her attendance was completely optional———only if she needed it.

Someone will bring you a meal each day at noon, and they will make sure you are not ill. Otherwise, we will leave you in peace.

There will be times when you think this retreat is worthless, and there will be times when you will never want to reenter the talking world. Be aware that these feelings can change in an instant and also occur multiple times a day. Witness the swings. Watch them, but do not engage with the internal narrative they may bring. Do as I have writ-ten, and you will move through with ease. Trust this truth.

Burn one-third of your smudging stick each day—when you choose to do this is up to you.

Be present with each moment. Yes, every single moment. Keep your toolbox of aware-ness, witnessing, and gratitude, in hand. These will bring you back to your sensibilities if you spiral too far out.

May the Grace of the Divine beings be with you always.

Tat Twam Asi.

Jade stared at the letter and then reread it. She felt uneasy. What the hell was she going to do for nine days of... nothing? The "approved activities" list she could do in one morning if she needed to. What was she supposed to do for the other eight-and-a-half days?

She looked out the window and stared at the trees surrounding the cabin. To the human eye, they were pillars of stillness. Yet, the trees were con-stantly moving, growing, reaching toward the light in ways indistinguishable from moment to moment but undeniable from year to year. She wondered if she would ever be able to live like a tree—witnessing everything, trusting fate completely—for the trees could not pick up their feet and move if they were bored and looking for something else to do. She shook her head to clear her thoughts. She was not a tree. She had feet and free will and free thoughts, and at this moment, not even an hour after she had awoken, just the thought of having nothing to do for nine days had boredom all ready to kick down her front door.

"You will think this retreat is worthless...," echoed in the silence, and Jade let out a sigh to rival all the others she'd ever given and looked over her approved tasks once more. She decided to return to the Dragonfly mat and start her day with a silent chanting practice. As she tried to repeat the simple words over and over, she found it to be a completely different experience than when she chanted out loud with everyone in the morning. She hadn't realized how much the act of speaking the mantras aloud and having other people chanting around her, kept her mind from wandering and helped her focus.

Frustrated, and annoyed that only twenty minutes had passed, Jade decided to clean. Not because the space needed it, but because she did. She found a bucket, cloth, soap, and a short-handled broom under the table and got to work. She pulled out the bed frame and the bedside table and swept and mopped each corner. She picked up three dead flies and wondered if two of them were the dancing and buzzing fiends from the night before. She wiped every surface, every windowsill and lovingly cleaned each object on the altar until not a speck of dust or fly poop mark remained.

At noon, Meera arrived carrying a tray of rice and vegetables just as Jade was trying to wash the windows, which were getting progressively more streaked while Jade was getting progressively more frustrated. They didn't speak, but as Meera looked around to see the whole place dismantled and being thoroughly cleaned, she smiled. She placed the tray on the table and left without a word. She returned ten minutes later with a bottle of vinegar and a stack of newspapers that she left by the door.

It was mid-afternoon by the time Jade finished cleaning the main floor and the loft above. The windows gleamed thanks to Meera's vinegar and newspapers, the surfaces were spotless, and if she needed to, she would seriously consider eating off the floor. She felt inexplicably satisfied. To sanctify the space, she burned the first third of a smudging stick and watched the smoke twirl and waft in the shafts of sun that streamed through the window. The bed was bathed in sunshine and seemed to invite Jade to put her feet up and bask in its warmth. She did and promptly succumbed to a nap.

She woke in time to have a shower and make a cup of tea before the sky turned to salmon pink and then faded to black. She decided not to stoke the fire before getting into bed, opting instead for an extra blanket she had found in the loft. She welcomed its weight as she nestled into her bed and watched through the window frame as the forest changed before her. First, it glowed brightly with dust motes dancing through shafts of light, and then, slowly, the shadows grew until Larch and Fir were lost in the darkness. As the sun retreated below the horizon, stars appeared one by one and watched over her slumbering body bearing witness to the completion of her first day.

On the second day, Jade focused her energy on cleaning the area around the cabin. She started in the space directly outside her front door and then moved in expanding concentric circles. She picked up each twig, each leaf, each pine cone that had fallen to the ground including a sprig of golden Larch needles that were so perfect they begged to sit alongside her bundles on the altar.

With each circuit she tried to hold her mind completely in the moment without straying to the past or the future—it was harder than she realized it would be. But, as she moved, she felt an orb of energy being created around the cabin—a dome of cleanliness—and again, she felt the satisfaction of a job well done.

While she was at the rear of the cabin cleaning, someone must have come by, for when she returned to the side with the door, she found a thermos on the doorstep and a tray of food beside it. Jade sat in the long grass with a cup of Meera's delicious chai and listened to the last of the crickets and their continuous muttering of high-pitched prayers. As she listened, Jade took tiny sips and sought to identify each flavour. Regardless of whether or not she named the correct spice—cinnamon, cardamom, star anise, and a few other ingredients she was uncertain about—Jade savoured each one.

Time seemed to slow down once early afternoon hit. Each moment stretched like taffy, and it was difficult for her mind to manage. Jade sat outside and surveyed her morning efforts. She frowned when she saw some leaves and sticks had sullied her perfect landscape. She scurried to pick them up and then returned to her spot in the grass. Rose had said to bring her awareness to the moment, so she tried to take in the natural world in as much detail as she could to pass the time. She tried to count how many rapid *chits* a squirrel called out in alarm—fourteen seemed to be the average. She tried to figure out which birds were within earshot—closing and opening her eyes to ensure accuracy. She even tried to follow a line of ants hoping it would lead her to where their nest entered the ground. But, try as she might, she still felt separate from it all. And that separation pushed her frustration to the surface, until she wanted to scream—but couldn't. So she walked.

She walked in circles around the cabin unconsciously treading the same path as the morning. She ranted in her head. She raged. Unable to break the silence, she punched the air with her fist and gave lame karate kicks to get her energy moving. Finally, she resorted to handstands against the side of the cabin hoping a new perspective would give her some insight. It didn't.

Exhausted by the day's efforts Jade showered again and got ready for bed. Then, as she was casting anxious glances towards the mountains—not wanting to miss the light show on their peaks—she remembered she had yet to burn her smudging stick for the day. She sat on the step and watched the smoke curl and twist around air currents she couldn't see until the last third—tomorrow's third—was left. She stubbed it out and placed it inside a perfect half-circle sheath of bark that lay beside the woodpile. She picked up the bark and carried it into the cabin. A perfect smudging stick holder for the altar. She placed it next to the Larch needles, blew a kiss to her mum, and crawled into bed. She watched the light fade, and before the first owl could ask "Who cooks for you?" she was asleep.

Day three. Jade woke up to heavy cloud cover that soon gave way to rain. She stared at the ceiling not wanting to be part of this retreat anymore. She spent most of the morning sitting in bed, dreaming of ways she could skip out on the next seven days, without losing face. She read the 'this is going to be hard' pep talk on the second page of Rose's note until she had it all but memorized—and used every last ounce of self-control not to devour the last two pages of instruction. Out of desperation, Jade piled several cushions on top of one another and then placed her mum's photograph on top. This way she could sit in bed and have a mental conversation with the young version of her mother, who unfortunately, if Jade stared at her long enough without blinking, just nodded encouragingly.

Eventually, Jade dragged herself out of bed to do some laundry with the hope that the rain would help rinse the grime from her clothes and perhaps from her mind, too. She was grateful to be in the bathroom when Meera brought her meal; she couldn't face anyone and wasn't sure she'd be able to hide the struggle that clouded her face.

The sun appeared in the afternoon, but it did nothing to help Jade's mood, which had shifted from general malaise to low-grade panic. She didn't know how to be with herself. She felt nauseous as the reflux of potential failure bubbled up from her stomach. She tried to lie down but had too much physical energy to sleep. At the same time, she felt too lethargic to read or do anything constructive. She felt paralyzed. So, she sat and she stewed, and she watched a story form inside her head about who and what she really was. She could see it, she knew Rose had warned her about it, but no matter how many mantras she chanted, no matter how much she witnessed the thought forms, no matter how much she tried to redirect the negative into a positive pep talk, she still felt like a needy child who failed at everything and was tolerated rather than liked. She started to count the hours until the fire ceremony at 5 pm, where she might not be able to talk to anyone, but at least she would be with others.

As soon as she heard the bell announcing it was time to join the fire ceremony, she jumped off the bed and started to walk up the hill. With each step she took, she felt more and more expectant that the uneasiness inside of her was going to dissipate once she was around Rose. She came around the side of the greenhouse and the fire ceremony preparations came into view. Jade stopped in her tracks, unable to take another step forward into the energy-filled garden.

Steve was sprawled on a chair (still incapable of getting down to or up from the ground) and was being his usual loud, obnoxious, chatty self. Meera was arranging the flowers on the altar, and another woman—one Jade did not know—was standing to the side like she wanted to help but didn't know how. Two children, who likely came with the new woman, were running around the garden in circles pretending they were aeroplanes. She couldn't see Avi, and Rose didn't seem to be anywhere. Jade stood rooted to the spot trying to figure out a way to go into the garden without engaging with the chaos. She didn't want to be with Steve or the newcomers; she wanted to be with someone who would make her feel better. Meera or Avi would understand how she felt, but it was Rose she needed. She kept watch from the greenhouse, undecided and gnawing at her lower lip, as Steve pointed from his throne, trying to direct the new woman on how to place the mats around the fire pit. Jade winced at his, 'I have so little self-worth I need to tell you what to do to make myself feel better,' voice. She didn't want to be alone, but she didn't want to be with them. Meera smiled warmly and beckoned for the woman to come closer. She obliged, and Meera began to teach her the proper way to decorate the fire pit with flowers while Steve started to direct the children on where to sit and what to expect.

"Lonely", she mouthed. "I'm so lonely." Her eyes filled with tears and the scene before her became a blur. Not wanting anyone to see her or see her crying, she turned around and returned to the sanctity of the cabin. She burned the last third of her first smudging stick and asked the sun to take her loneliness the same way it had taken the day—without a second thought.

60 Nine Nights: Treasures and Symphonies

Jade opened her eyes as the sky was just beginning to brighten. She tingled with anticipation for today was the day she could read the next page of Rose's letter. She threw off the covers and jumped out of bed as if it were Christmas morning. She grabbed the letter from Aaden's basket on the altar and dove back into bed, burrowing under the covers for warmth. Before opening it, she made herself stop and take a few deep breaths. She needed to draw this out and make the excitement last. She examined the paper. It was the same thick, handmade paper that Rose always wrote on. The corners and seams were still crisp having never been unfolded—until now. It reminded her of a promise that had never been broken or a secret that had never been told. Clean, uncompromised, virtuous. She gingerly unfolded the paper and began to read. Her eyes raced over the words, scanning top to bottom but retaining nothing. She took another deep breath, went back to the beginning, and started anew. *Savour each word*, she told herself, *there are three whole days to wait until any new ones come our way.*

Beloved Self,

As I write this, I am imagining the first three days have been… trying. I remember feeling terribly lonely the first time I did this retreat. So lonely. I remember trying to think of ways to sabotage myself to get out of the rest of the retreat. I look back on it now fondly and know it was all part of the process.

We must all travel through the tunnel of loneliness to find the sweet light in being

Jade folded up the letter and placed it back on the altar for her mother and Rose to keep safe. Tossing aside her usual morning routine of mantras and cleaning and still in her pyjamas, she took the second smudging stick outside. There she lit it, adding just a little of her breath to the herbs to get them started and then proceeded to walk around the cabin taking the same route she took on her martial arts tirade from two days prior. Then she stopped, spun around, and walked in the opposite direction. This time, instead of punching the air trying to expel what was inside of her, she walked holding the smoking stick as a bouquet in front of her, as though a bride and offered silent thank yous with each step. She only paused when something beautiful caught her eye: a perfectly formed piece of grass with a single droplet of dew poised at the tip of its delicate seed head reflecting the morning sun or the empty casing of a cicada affixed to the side of a fir. She left the grass but plucked the cicada shell gently from the bark and examined it closely in the palm of her hand. It was intricate, fragile, and precious, and Jade could envision the moment the cicada had disconnected from its shell but still clung tightly to it. After all, the casing had protected it for so long.

She spiralled outward in circles from the cabin until a third of her bundle had been offered in gratitude, and with the cicada's casing still in her hand, she went inside. She returned the smudging stick to its bark cradle by the altar and placed her morning's treasure at the foot of Shiva alongside the sprig of Larch. The needles and the cicada's casing greeted each other. They were the same golden honey hue that sang of being plucked at the exact moment of transformation. She stepped back and took in the beauty before her. She wondered what it was about the colour that seemed to speak to her so strongly, but the thought dissolved before it was fully formed. She turned her attention to completing her daily routine of mantras, laundry, and meditation.

The bell echoed through the air, and the sound caught Jade off guard. She hadn't realized it was time for the fire ceremony. She crept up to the garden, close enough to hear the mantras but far enough away that should wouldn't be seen. She followed along, chanting in her head while being bathed in the voices of those that cared about her, and whom she cared about in return. She sat there with her eyes closed, feeling the connection that went beyond the physical. It was amazing the difference a single day could make. Yesterday she was paralyzed with loneliness; today she felt bathed in love with no contact from anyone. Rose's note flashed "*Even if you don't feel like you let go of anything, know that you have, it is these moments that are defined as magic.*" Jade smiled to herself—*they sure are,* she thought, *they sure are.*

Jade woke on the fifth morning and felt something around her had shifted in the night, but wasn't quite sure what. She looked out the windows and saw it was between the dawn and sunrise. A little flock of Crossbills were on the branch of the fir welcoming her to another day as they ate its seeds for breakfast. She smiled sleepily at the rain of seedless cones as they fell to the forest floor, and turned her thoughts inward.

She put her head back onto her pillow and stared up at the ceiling, waking up bit by bit, trying to discover what was different about herself. She used her big toe to scratch at an itch on the opposite ankle and stopped. She felt like where she ended and the blankets began was blurred, that the boundaries between 'self' and 'other' were softer. She wiggled her toes. The air beneath the blanket, rather than being empty space, felt denser somehow. She raised her hand in front of her face and wiggled her fingers. She felt like she was *touching* the air not just moving through it. Her mind filled with memories: Rose sitting at the River stroking the moss that moved toward her hand; Rose walking through the garden and the plants following her; Rose listening to the trees as the branches rustled in her wake when moments before there'd been no breeze. Jade's eyes widened in surprise and sudden understanding. Rose wasn't moving through empty space, she was moving through space filled with…*filled with what?* Jade thought. *Energy* she decided on. *It's got to be some sort of energy.* Each action was connected to something else. No movement could occur without energy being transferred out as little waves of communication. *Is this what Rose's everyday experience is like?* Jade marvelled. *Constantly moving through the air like it's water? Sending and receiving ripples of energy—silently communicating with everything around her?*

Elated at the discovery, Jade wanted to harness this new level of awareness. She threw off the covers and decided to do a longer meditation after her morning mantras. She shivered. It was chilly in the cabin, but she thought she might be shivering with excitement as well.

She wrapped herself in the shawl that had become somewhat of a comfort, the way a child keeps his or her blankie close by, and took a moment to enjoy the way it felt: the silkiness against her skin, the weight of it on her body, the sense of protection it gave her as it draped down and covered her head, neck, and shoulders. She took the string of wooden beads, the mala, into her right hand and held them the way Rose had shown her for her fire quest, and she wondered if she would get through the whole practice today before her hand cramped like it usually did about halfway through.

She closed her eyes and started to repeat the words she had been taught. Her tongue moved slightly in her mouth formulating the shape of each word so that when she heard them in her mind they were clear and precise and perfect.

When she brought her awareness to the left nostril over the right one, a calming, cool breeze rushed over her as though someone, somewhere, had briefly opened a door to show her the way out. She felt the tension in her body and softened her skin until the tension flew away on the breeze and her body stayed, anchored in place by the words she was repeating. She moved on from her nostrils to check in on her tongue only to find it plastered to the roof of her mouth as if it were glued there by a glob of peanut butter. She almost smiled at the image of what she'd look like de-peanut-buttering her mouth, and her almost smile made her tongue relax and her jaw, which she hadn't known she was clenching, unclench.

The syllables continued, and the words took on a life of their own. Just as it had happened at the fire, the mantra was now in perpetual motion emanating from inside her. The beads kept their gentle rotation in time with the silent repetition of the seed sounds. Each one capable of sprouting a new beam of light within her. Her mind watched them cycle on their own. A proud parent being left behind on a concrete path.

The momentum was constant and comfortable, and she felt her body spontaneously move—she leaned back, her chin rose the slightest bit, and the tips of her ears grew a little. Her body was a semi-inflated balloon that was being slowly filled with light, and as her creases unfolded she felt as though she was easing herself into a warm bath.

A well of energy sprang forth from within, and she wondered how long she would be able to stay here soaking it all in. She watched the words continue to cycle, and she lost the beginning and ending of the mantra. She took to emphasizing different words and marvelled at the kaleidoscope of shifting frequencies. The words spiralled away from her only to bounce off some invisible construct of self and echo back. Over and over the words went back and forth until the two forces cancelled each other out, and she realized the words had stopped and her beads had fallen to the floor. The silence in her mind was deafening.

She opened her eyes and looked around. The sun was bathing the forest before her in a radiance that could only be described as ethereal. The constant, low-grade anxiety she had come to think of as who she was, had somehow shifted. Her fluttery insides had stilled into a deep well of... the only word she could come up with was contentment. She put her hand over her heart to feel her chest rise and breathed deeply. She tried to fill herself with the feeling; etching the soft, deep calm onto her soul; committing it to memory to be recalled later as medicine.

She moved slowly trying to hold her awareness to the feeling of her morning practice while she had her morning cup of peach and ginger tea, she went outside and sat on the ground. She rested her back against the cabin's shingled wall and once more closed her eyes. She softened almost immediately. She could feel herself calibrating—entraining to—the forest before her, and in turn felt the forest unfolding its edges, opening, and inviting her to join them.

As she sat listening to all that was happening around her, she realized she was thinking of the trees and animals as equals, as "people" in their own right. And she understood why Rose always wrote their names with capital letters and addressed them with reverence.

She could, if she didn't try too hard, almost pick out each tree's different energy as though they were people standing in front of her. She listened with her eyes closed and watched, as a symphony of Life swirled around her painting her skin with frequencies that existed between sight and sound. Each Junco chimed as a triangle, each Raven a cowbell, and every Nuthatch a clarinet. The breeze made the Firs into violins and Ponderosas into cellos. At some point, an elk bellowed in the distance sounding like a tuba—which made her smile. Sun beams weaved in and out of branches and moved up and down on the wings of birds keeping the beat and unifying the musicians as only the great conductors can when they move their arms and bring the music to life.

The symphony ebbed and flowed, started and stopped, and then quieted into a lullaby until the Sun disappeared behind the roof line above. The bell tolled loudly calling the residents to the evening ceremony, the symphony had consumed most of the day. Jade opened her eyes. The trees and grasses were the same as yesterday, but she wasn't. Something had shifted. She turned to find a tray of food beside her and began to eat.

Jade hoped that the sixth day would start in the same vein as the fifth, but it didn't. She woke feeling flushed and agitated—a sense of being watched had permeated her dreams. Old patterns and habits momentarily took hold as she hid under the covers. She felt vulnerable. Exposed. Trapped. Terrified. Her imagination had a man, a predator, looking through the window at her salaciously licking his lips. But, when she peeked out from beneath the blankets, she found a chipmunk perched on the Universe's windowsill cleaning its tiny hands with its even tinier tongue as it watched her through the glass. Jade gave a silent snort of laughter at her paranoia and tried to slowly prop herself up to get a good look at the chipmunk without scaring it off. She had just about completely uncovered her head when the chipmunk froze and glanced into the trees. Once, twice it sniffed and then scampered off out of sight. Disappointed, Jade sat up in bed and rubbed her eyes. She looked in the direction the chipmunk had, toward the South, expecting to see a squirrel on a nearby branch, when her breath caught in her throat. A black bear was walking slowly, lazily toward her cabin; its sizable weight swaying from side to side. The bear stopped and looked around scenting the air.

She wondered if he could smell her through the walls, and then wondered if it was, in fact, a he. She glanced sideways at the door handle and wondered if it was worth locking, but decided to stay where she was. It was half the size of the grizzly that had charged her, but her heart didn't know the difference. It was beating rapidly, and the pounding in her ears made it difficult to focus on anything else. She resorted to regurgitating all the facts she had learned about black bears since arriving at the centre: masters of adaptation, they give birth before emerging from hibernation, and their symbology is of intuition, introspection and protection. The bear seemed oblivious to her existence and didn't even glance at the cabin. It was more interested in the little red Kinnikinnick berries hiding among the golden grasses. Slowly, after nibbling on the tiny, red morsels that they ate for intestinal worm control, she watched its enormous backside meander down the hill. He paused only once, stood up on its hind legs to get a look at something, and then continued on his way. The bear didn't look back. She craned her neck to watch him go until he was consumed by the thicket of Snowberries at the bottom of the valley.

The remainder of the morning was spent see-sawing between being excited at seeing a bear and terrified of going outside in case it hadn't really left and was just waiting to jump out from behind a tree and attack her. She had to remind herself, multiple times, that all the wild beasts—bears and cougars included—had been here the whole time, they just hadn't shown themselves to her. She also kept repeating Avi's wise words: "If it's destined, not a damn thing you are going to be able to do about it, so step forward and keep going."

Still, she stayed close to home.

Meera came with her tray of food at lunchtime, and by then Jade had completed all her chores and practices and had reread all of Rose's letters just in case she had missed an approved indoor task. She hadn't. The only approved activity she had not yet done was Ma Labyrinth.

She sighed and looked down the hill. The same hill the bear had walked hours earlier that morning. Jade bit her lower lip. She knew she needed to walk her. She could feel Ma Labyrinth beckoning and could hear her calling. She could also feel the fear of stumbling upon a bear having an afternoon nap in the middle of the day. *If it's destined, lass….*broke through the indecision, and Jade made a determined face, put on her shoes, and closed the cabin door behind her.

Jade walked slowly down the Elk path, turning every few feet to gauge how far away she was from the safety of the cabin. Eventually, she stopped at some invisible boundary of perceived safety to decide if Ma really was calling to her. She revisited the conversation she'd been having on the walk down: go back and pretend it never happened, or step forth and accept whatever may come your way.

I'm no chicken, she thought and decided on come what may. She fixed her eyes on the valley below and started to walk. Every footfall ignited a wave of pops. Tiny little firecrackers went off left and right and only stopped when she stopped. She frowned and took another few steps—Pop! Pop! Pop! She kept still—nothing. Forgetting all about the bear, she crouched down and waited. The tiniest twitch caught her attention, and she found herself eye-to-eye with a large, brown grasshopper clinging to a strand of summer-kissed grass that lined the path. Jade gave the insect a fond smile and let her energy marinate in thoughts of greeting before sending her message to it….him…her? Once again she realized she didn't know how to tell the difference. When she stood up, the grass came alive again—Pop! Pop! Pop!—as numerous grasshoppers jumped around announcing each of her movements.

"The grasshopper tells us to take giant leaps in life," her mother had said having found Jade as a child playing with her brass grasshopper. Jade smiled at the memory and felt, just for a brief moment, that her mother was standing next to her. *I'm leaping, Mum. I'm leaping,* Jade thought.

Walking with the grasshoppers distracted her from her fear of marauding bears, and before she knew it, she was at the entrance of Ma Labyrinth. She thanked the grasshoppers (and her mother) for their companionship and took in her surroundings.

Here in the valley, the air was cooler than at the cabin. And it was still. So still, she didn't want to breathe and disturb it. The Larches had already put on their autumn finery, and their golden needles contrasted beautifully with the dark evergreens of the forest.

Ma lay peacefully in the clearing soaking up the beauty surrounding her, bathing in the afternoon sun. Jade's eyes followed Ma's lines as they undulated over the ground. She knew they all led to the centre, but she was no more successful tracing the path to the Rose Quartz this time around than she'd been when she first walked Ma. *It's life,* Meera's voice popped into her head out of nowhere. *Ma moves up and down because life is filled with ups and downs. Each rock touches the one on either side of it showing that the moment-to-moment of everyday life is what creates the path of reality. Those things, in and of themselves, create a beauty that is to be discovered, or perhaps, recovered.* Jade smiled, and she caught the whiff of Meera's chai as her voice went silent in her mind.

She offered Ma a single, deep purple Oregon Grape that had caught her eye among the yellow and burgundy leaves. It was, like Ma, bursting and ripe. Jade removed her shoes and delighted in the feel of the cool ground beneath her feet, and then she walked. She kept her head down and focused on the path, following the turns back and forth as it moved her bit by bit toward the centre. Her eyes roved over the trinkets and sentimental offerings others had left behind, and as she walked past she wondered about their previous owners. Were they happy? Had they found their bliss? Did they get their answers? She saw a few rocks out of place—perhaps a deer had knocked it with their hoof or a dog or coyote had shifted it in their play. But without a second thought, Jade reached down and lovingly returned the rock to its position before continuing on her way.

As she walked, Jade reflected on the first time she had walked Ma with Meera. How she thought it was stupid and a giant waste of her time. The Jade she was then was barely recognizable to the Jade that slowly and purposefully walked Ma Labyrinth now. She had felt the shifts—some had been subtle, others had been seismic—but couldn't exactly label them. However, she knew in her heart of hearts that she was not the same person who had arrived at the centre in the Spring. And, as she turned to the Rose Quartz, she thought, *who am I now?*

A single offering tucked in at the base of the Quartz caught her eye. Her heart quickened before her brain registered what it was. Gingerly, she picked it up between her thumb and her index finger and placed it in her hand. She held her breath in case moving it would cause it to disintegrate. It didn't. Instead, the object sat perfectly in her palm: a round, honey-coloured lattice casing of a ground cherry. The gossamer lantern, despite having been exposed to the elements for who knows how long, had retained its form, its beauty, its memory of hot, summer nights. And she thought of Aaden. Oh, how she missed him. His laugh. His quick wit. His smell.

She stood cradling the delicate lantern in the loose cup of her hand and held it against her heart. Memories washed over her, and she wondered what he was doing at that moment—perhaps he was sipping coffee and eating a *pain au chocolat* just like his grandmother had described. She felt him, even though he was thousands of miles away. Could he feel her, too? She hoped so. Jade blinked a few times and came back to the present. She asked Ma if she could take the lantern and place it on the altar in the cabin. The breeze in the trees whispered: *We were keeping it safe, for you.*

61 Nine Nights: The Elders

The next morning Jade woke just before the sun breached the mountain tops. Wanting to savour the moment of Rose's day seven note, she slowly got out of bed, walked the five feet to the altar, and stood looking at its components in the morning light. The photo, the note, Aaden's basket, and the Shiva statue all felt important, but it was the treasures she had collected in the last three days that felt profound. They were all the same hue—honey and harvest—and they held her eye the way the Sun does just before its rays sink beneath the horizon.

She took Rose's note from Aaden's basket and retreated to the warmth of her bed to read the last page.

Beloved Jade,

Integration is the final three days of your retreat. Let time fall away. Let the forest guide your every move.

During these last three days, there will be no human-made food delivered—just herbal tea and water. If you feel called to eat, eat! But, your nourishment will come from the Land—small amounts of berries, the tips of fir, the pitch and seeds of pine. Foods of this nature will sustain you.

On the tenth morning, you may open the wax-sealed note.

May the Divine beings be with you always, and may you be ever Skyward.

Tat Twam Asi.

No human food for three days? She had grown surprisingly accustomed to her one meal a day of rice and vegetables. But this?! While her mind searched for the right words, her stomach didn't have to, it grumbled in protest.

Exactly, she thought, *we're gonna be hungry.*

She wouldn't suggest it if you couldn't do it, Meera's and Aaden's voices echoed inside her. Intellectually, Jade knew that Rose only asked of her what she knew she could accomplish, but… and this was a but with a capital B—three days without any food except for some berries and pine seeds? Somewhere, in the primal part of her brain, Jade felt she was standing on a melting cornice looking down into a chasm of starvation.

She grabbed her journal and started to make a list of all the things she knew she could eat that could be found in the fall. Lambs quarter, Watercress, Oregon Grapes, Juniper, Kinnikinnick, Fir and Ponderosa cambium. *Only in extreme cases,* Avi's voice murmured in her head, *'cause it will likely kill the tree, or at least damage it enough that it will take a long time to recover.* Her stomach gurgled, *This could become an extreme case*, she thought.

Jade imagined the lack of food would make her want to keep a low profile for the next few days, content at the thought of whiling away her time in and around the cabin, journalling, drawing, and dabbling in a bit of poetry. But the seventh afternoon was unseasonably warm and the bright blue sky lured her outside. So she decided to take a walk down to see Ma Labyrinth again. On her way there, she was struck with the need to relieve herself, and in her search for the perfect spot—not too exposed and with a good, sturdy tree to reach out for balance—she stumbled across a small and very happy shrub of Oregon Grape. She explained her hunger and asked it to share its berries. Then she dusted the plant with herbs from her pouch, and when a slight breeze blew, she saw the prickly leaves turn away and expose their small, thick-skinned, juicy, purple orbs. She took this as permission and thanked the plant profusely for providing her with nourishment. She was careful not to harvest more than half the berries in case another hungry creature needed food or she needed more tomorrow. The tiny berries burst in her mouth with a flavour punch well beyond what their tiny packaging promised. She hoped the handful of berries would carry her away from hunger's whine for a few hours. She closed her eyes to better savour the flavour, and while she tried to stay in the present moment—witnessing the way the flesh of the fruit burst when she bit into it, the tang of the juice against her tongue—she was momentarily lost in the past. *"That! Explain what THAT tastes like…"*

She rested quietly on the side of the hill, and softened, utterly content in the silence. Silence—it used to be so scary, so overwhelming—was a close friend now. She had become so accustomed to the silence, comfortable with it residing within her, she wondered what the point of speaking out loud ever was. She realized the silence was not devoid of communication, but that it was in the silence that she could finally hear what was being communicated, by people, by the Earth—by her own soul. It was a whole new world hidden within the old one like Russian dolls stacked one inside the other. The doll on the shelf looked complete and alone until it was split in two. Then, lo and behold, another one, one more beautifully designed, more refined, lay nestled inside.

The warm, fall sun danced along her exposed skin and she felt nourished inside and out. She walked down to Ma with a slight skip in her step, listening to the birds sing, watching the grasshoppers leap from grass to grass, and keeping a wary eye out for bears.

The eighth morning Jade busied herself with laundry and foraging for more berries. She found another stash of Oregon Grape and a few Kinnikinnick, and she ate a handful of Blue Spruce fir tips as well. They were so aromatic and she could feel their frequency being absorbed by her whole body, not just her stomach. The feeling was wild, and she wondered if that was how food was supposed to be consumed—as a full-body experience.

She spent the afternoon sitting against the Larch tree by the cabin with her eyes closed so she could listen to the symphony of the forest without distraction. The first day of her fast she had not calibrated to the listening state easily. Her body had been loud with gurgling protests as it tried to reorganize itself with the lack of food, and she couldn't hear anything beyond her uncomfortableness both in mind and body. It was the difference between trying to focus on studying in a room cluttered with boxes that needed to be gone through and organized, versus a room that was orderly, sparse, and clean.

But that afternoon, while she could hear the forest's symphony, she could also hear what sounded like a single flute playing out the back and out of tune. The flute of expectation. It played a wistful tune of hoping for something special to happen. Being able to hear the song of the forest was no longer enough. She wanted more. Something miraculous or (even more) profound to occur as she neared the end of her retreat. And each moment it didn't happen, she started to feel that perhaps she had missed it, that somehow she had failed. Frustrated, she opened her eyes and glowered at the trees, accusing them of withholding payment for all the work she had done. She turned away from the ever-stoic stewards of the woods and went inside the cabin, awash with shame and rejection.

On the final day, Jade still felt the sharp edge of entitlement digging into her ribs. She cleaned the cabin, as thoroughly as she had on the first day, and despite the lack of food, she felt energetic, clear-headed, and calm. She was surprised to find cobwebs in the corner, dust on the rungs of the ladder, and as she cleaned the altar, she thought she could feel different notes of energy coming off each item. She sat and focused on each component individually and then took note of any feeling or mental change inside of her. Remarkably it was like its own little symphony and depending on where she rested her attention she could change what she experienced inside her. It was like forest listening on another level, not just feeling or hearing the frequencies, but directly experiencing how each 'note' changed her reality inside. She spent the rest of the day walking through the forest with her newfound superpower, experiencing each tree, each bird, and each rock from the inside. She was *in* the picture, not just observing it.

By the evening she decided to take some time to reflect on the last nine days. They had been beautiful, boring and brilliant. She took Rose's sealed note from its hiding place under her clothes and rubbed the dragonfly emblem. *On the tenth day… open it,* Rose's voice echoed inside her. *That's tomorrow,* she thought.

She tucked the note behind the photo on the altar, making her mother and Rose the gatekeepers to whatever was inside. *Tomorrow,* they whispered from behind their youthful smiles. And with that Jade crawled into bed and looked out at the sky above. There was a star that came up over the mountains close to the moon. She frowned. *Too bright to be a star, it must be a planet,* she thought. If she only knew which one. She tried to connect to it the way she had the objects on the altar, but all she felt was calm and maybe a little watched. She decided if the star wanted to watch her that was fine, but she wanted to try and sleep so morning could come sooner.

Sleep came quickly, left in a hurry, and then knocked again like a dog that was always on the wrong side of the door. She couldn't get comfortable enough to relax and tossed and turned. She was too hot, and then she was too cold. She didn't want to sleep past the moment just before dawn, when the trees are outlined but the Sun has not yet lit up the sky. Each time she woke, Grandmother Waxing Moon and that same planet were there watching her—*not yet,* she could hear them say, *not yet. Sleep a little longer still.*

Finally, Jade gave up on rising early, and at the moment of capitulation, she watched her body fall into a deep slumber. Her mind, however, had other plans, and it went wandering through the woods, Fox Walking barefoot, until she found a moonlit path she did not recognize leading towards Ma Labyrinth. But when she got to the clearing where Ma Labyrinth should be, Ma was nowhere to be found. In her place stood nine, huge, grandparent trees rooted in a perfect circle.

Jade knew Larch, Pine, Fir, Alder, and Cedar, but the other four she did not recognize immediately. She hadn't seen them at the centre and therefore had not studied them like the others. Their trunks were massive columns that silently vibrated as if they contained enough energy to power the world.

She worried she was supposed to do or say something to honour these ancient guardians, but before she could decide what that something was, thin, silver threads of light began to slowly move toward her from the tips of their needles and leaves. She looked over her shoulder to see if she could run if she needed to, but she was surrounded. As the thousands of strands got closer, she could sense that the light—the Trees' energies—were not malicious. The light was… curious, kind—wise.

The threads of light reached her body and stopped just out of arm's reach. She tried to comprehend what she was seeing and finally landed on fibre optic cables that were somehow sentient. Each thread was tipped with a tiny eye, and that tiny eye was examining her closely. All at once, the fibres started to weave a webbed matrix of light that formed a transparent shell around her. She reached out to touch it and found that the shell was, smooth, delicate, and strong. It would not let her reach through it, nor did it shatter when she tried to kick it with her foot. One time, she may have felt trapped, and panic would have overwhelmed her. But, here she felt safe and familiar. Once the shell was complete, she felt almost at home.

Jade watched as the trees retracted their silver threads of light. She expected the lights to return to the centre of each tree, but they didn't. Instead, they reached all their threads toward the tree to their left. Thousands of threads connected one tree to the next turning the circle of Elders into a huge tornado of light moving around her in a clockwise direction. Then, in one single voice, the Elders began to chant, speaking directly to Jade inside her head and filling the space around her with the energy of their words.

You're here! You're here! You have remembered to be. Welcome back; welcome home. We celebrate with thee. Let go! Let go! Remember once more, who you are, who you'll be, when reborn from the seed at your core.

As the Elders' voice swirled around the inside of the shell, she felt her rigid form start to soften and her hands started to tingle. She looked down at them and saw they were dissolving. Her feet and legs had already disappeared; she was nothing more than a torso hovering in a shell made by Trees. And still, the panic she expected to feel had not taken possession of her senses. That is not to say it wasn't there. It was. It was just fluttering at the edges of her consciousness, waiting to be called upon.

Between the tornado and her shell, Jade saw something different emerge. It was easily identifiable against the swirling silver due to the orb's pink hue;

it started to float towards Jade. A form stood in the centre of the orb, and Jade recognized it almost immediately. Rose. Rose had come to save her. Jade tried to call out but no words formed. Instead, a single beam of pink light threaded its way toward Jade and attached itself to the matrix of her shell.

"I'm here," Rose said. "You're safe, dear Jade. Keep your eye on me, and let go. Skyward. Tat Twam Asi."

The thread of pink disconnected itself from the shell, but Rose's orb remained in place hovering in the space between Jade and the Elders.

Jade watched unblinkingly (and unbelievably) as Rose's form dissolved into a single point of pink light. Simultaneously Jade's body continued to dissolve until her mouth no longer opened and her eyes sealed shut, but each time she lost a sense, she felt more loved, more loving, more———Love. Until she *was* a single spark of pure Love. And the form, any form, in which she existed was irrelevant, and so she let go.

Jade didn't know if the spark of Love that was *her* hovered in this state for a moment or a millennium—for time didn't exist here———nothing existed here until she remembered the pink light of Rose and the clockwise tornado of light holding the space for her transformation.

The change started slowly. Imperceptibly at first and then faster and faster, Jade's shell began to spin counterclockwise creating the illusion of stillness all around her. A stillness so complete—so full of potential and life—that nothing was missing, nothing was needed. Jade thought she could stay forever, but the Elders had other plans.

Light, the colour of Harvest Moon grass, erupted from the single point of *her* that still existed and rained golden lava onto the ground. Where the golden lava fell, the shell cracked open and a tiny something sprouted and grew filling the space Jade's legs and spine once occupied. The tiny something did not stay tiny for long. It grew bigger, thicker, stronger. She felt herself growing skyward while also delving into the Earth below, anchoring into the warm, fecund soil that would not let her fall.

From where her shoulders once were, multiple limbs sprouted, branched, and reached toward the heavens, expanding the confines of the shell in an attempt to touch the brilliance of the stars before suddenly softening and arching gracefully toward the ground. Red light—the exact shade of her hair—burst from what was once her forehead and covered her newly formed limbs. A sudden tremor raced through her body, and the fiery red flashed and turned the colour of fresh, wildflower honey. She tingled all over until she was cloaked in little golden flowers.

She grew and grew until the force of her new form shattered the shell the

Trees had cast and the little golden flowers swirled in the air. The smell of them—honey and incense—was intoxicating and brought Jade into a state of bliss. She breathed deeply. The flowers stayed suspended in the air, and Jade wonder if gravity lived inside tornadoes. It was only when the Elders slowed and then ceased their spinning that the flowers came to rest where her feet once stood.

Everything was still. Nary a leaf nor a needle moved making it seem that her transformation had stolen the breath of the world. The Elders were still in their circle, but they no longer seemed to be towering over her. Then she saw Rose. Rose was standing alongside the Elders and had her hands over her heart. She was smiling despite the tears running down her face, and she looked so small no longer surrounded by her pink orb.

Jade tried to smile but the gesture only showered the ground in flowers again. And that's when Jade realized she was not standing in front of the nine Elders but was rooted in the middle of their circle. She had become a Willow tree.

Jade tried to speak, to ask what she was supposed to do now, but instead of hearing her words, the melodic sonnet of a MacGillivray's Warbler filled the air. The little bird hopped along Jade's branches, tickling her, distracting her, and delighting her with his song. "*Hello darkness my old...*"

At the last note of the bird's song, the Elders set themselves alight. They shimmered with golden light that made Jade think of yellow diamonds. The wind started to blow, and the trees erupted in applause. Jade bathed in their light and rejoiced.

Opening her eyes, Jade sees she is lying in a single shaft of golden Sunlight. The Larch and Fir she had dubbed the old (not to mention odd) wedded couple, watch her expectantly. A MacGillivray Warbler perched at the tip of the Larch joyfully announces a new day, or perhaps—a new world. "*Hello darkness my old...*"Friend. She smiles and sits up in bed. As she moves her body begins to tremble as the energy and memory of her dream course through her. Jade starts to laugh and sob simultaneously as her heart overflows with wonder and remembrance. She looks down at her hands; and turns them over in the morning light, half expecting to see patterns of bark up her arms instead of skin.

Her mother's smile catches her eye from across the room, and she remembers the sealed note she is allowed to open this morning. Jade tosses aside the covers and jumps out of bed. Grabbing the photograph in one hand and the sealed note in the other, she dives back under the covers before the cold of the morning can catch her. For a moment, Jade thinks about stoking the fire but chooses not to. She won't be in the cabin for much longer.

Jade looks at the photo and kisses it. *Thank you, thank you, thank you,* she thinks at the two women contained within the frame. They simply smile back.

Carefully, Jade removes the wax seal from Rose's letter and places it on the little table next to the bed. She has plans for that little dragonfly to join the Larch needles, paper lantern, and brass grasshopper. She takes a few deep breaths, and then unfolds the note with care. Inside are seven words written in Rose's precise penmanship.

Willow Jade.
Ever Skyward. Tat Twam Asi

Winter

62 Postcards and Inhalations

Time slows and nearly stops as Rose's words wind their way into the deepest curves of Jade's mind. *Willow Jade.* She reads the words silently and then mouths them, feeling the circular completeness of the word willow. She likes the way it opens and then closes, holding the seed sound of love—the /l/—gently in its core. She looks at the word jade and thinks about its meaning. Found deep within the Earth, jade is an anchor, a rock-solid support system for the gentle willow. She likes it. The contrast. That juxtaposition of the two. The wholeness.

"Willow Jade," she whispers and feels herself simultaneously sit straighter and fill with light upon the hushed sounds. They are the first words she has spoken in ten days.

So engrossed in her new name, she doesn't notice Rose standing at the door holding a tray of food with Pebbles leaning against her leg. Pebbles—tired of being ignored—scratches at the door. Willow Jade looks up, waves, and gestures for them to come inside. Rose says something to Pebbles, and the dog gives a mournful glance toward the bed before she curls up like a fox on the doorstep. Willow Jade chuckles softly; she knows Pebbles is just biding her time.

"Good Morning, sweet Willow Jade," Rose says. "How are you this morning? How did you… sleep?" She puts the tray of food gently on the foot of the bed and then sits on the chair at the table with the altar. The sweet smell of warm cardamom coming from the bowl on the tray fills the room. For a brief moment, Willow Jade closes her eyes and inhales deeply. She soaks in both the sound of her name coming from Rose's lips and the bouquet of spices coming from the tray before she registers that Rose is waiting for an answer.

"Oh. Um, I'm fine… great," she says with a smile. "Thank you." Her voice sounds foreign to her ears. "I had the craziest dream…"

There is no need to elaborate, Rose, after all, had witnessed the whole thing. Rose smiles back at her, looks out the window and then she turns back to scan the room.

"Snow is coming," she says after a moment. "You should stay in this cabin for Winter instead of moving to the main house. I think you will like the quiet. Yes?"

Willow Jade nods. There is no need to fill the space with extra words.

"Good. That's settled then. Break your fast with a small amount of Kheer, and then, when you're ready head to the sauna. Avi has prepared it for you. Follow that with a bucket bath. There's no rush. Then come up to the main house once you've completed those tasks and check in with Meera as to where it would be best for you to put your energies."

"OK," Willow Jade reaches for the tray of food and pulls it onto her lap.

A red-tailed hawk screeches overhead. *Step into the flow and integrate the blessings,* Willow Jade automatically recites as they both instinctively duck their heads and lift their eyes out the windows to see him soar over the cabin.

Rose stands up and smiles. It is the same wide smile as the one in her dream. "Willow Jade," she nods approvingly, "It feels so good to be able to call you by your true name now that you have discovered it yourself. You have set a wonderful foundation. What you do with it will be your next journey."

"Thank you—Rose," She says, her voice still quiet and careful so as not to disrupt the stillness of the room.

"Tat Twam Asi," Rose says as she steps off the front step and closes the door. Willow Jade watches as Rose pats Pebbles on the head signalling to her it is time to move on.

Tat Twam Asi Willow Jade mouths, unable to bring sound to the words.

Walking into the main house, Willow Jade expects to find Steve on the couch and Meera in the kitchen—everything the same as how she left it. But nothing is the same. The couch is gone, the dining table has been rotated to give more space for the living room, and three chairs are now situated close to the fireplace.

Meera is seated in the middle one with her feet up on a rock placed in front of the fire. The rock is clearly positioned so that people would give the fire a wide berth. She gives herself a week, max, before she trips over it and lands on her face. She smiles at the thought. Meera is knitting and mumbling to herself with such concentration that she doesn't notice Willow Jade come in.

"Hello," she whispers with a smile.

"Oh my word, Jade!" Meera says throwing her needles onto the chair beside her and standing up. She stops just short of a hug and looks at her without another word as though she can suddenly sense the surrounding silence and doesn't want to pierce it. Instead, Meera puts her hands over her heart and smiles like a mother seeing her daughter in a wedding dress for the first time.

"My heart," Meera whispers without stepping forward. "It's not Jade anymore, is it? The Lady said you have done well. But, I didn't think I would be able to see it for myself. You are glowing!"

Willow Jade looks down at herself unable to see any difference. As far as she can tell she looks the same as she's always has—although, maybe cleaner.

"Wait till Avi sees you," Meera fusses stepping forward and holding Willow by the shoulders at arms' length. "Do you want a cup of tea?"

"Oh, yes, please. And, you can call me Willow Jade, or," suddenly feeling like a double-barreled name might make a bigger bang than needed. "I guess, just Willow for short, if you want, or if you're in a hurry," she adds with a smile and a slight shrug of her shoulder.

"Willow Jade it is then," Meera says smiling. "Or Willow...," she adds mimicking the shoulder shrug. She holds up the Rose Tulsi and shakes it in Willow's direction. Willow shudders, "Oh, god, no! Anything but Rose Tulsi. Every time I smell it or think about drinking it, I see only wildfires."

Meera laughs. "Of course. That's how I feel about Chamomile. How 'bout licorice?"

Willow nods and takes a seat at the kitchen counter. She smiles to herself, recognizing that she has come full circle, once again joining Meera for tea at the counter in welcome.

"Where's Steve?" she asks looking around the room.

"Oh, he's gone," Meera says filling the kettle with water and placing it on the stove. "His mother and two siblings came to pick him up just over a week ago now." Willow nods remembering the woman at the Fire ceremony; the children playing aeroplanes. "His leg needs to heal, and it will take quite some time. This is not the place for such a journey. Better he comes back when he is well-bodied and able. Winter here is hard on the bones at the best of times. We may not see him for months...," the kettle whistles cutting her off.

Willow merely nods. She does not need to waste words.

Meera hands her the licorice tea, and Willow takes a sip. It is sweet, refreshing, and slightly silky against her tongue.

She catches Meera staring at her and smiles back as they drink their tea in comfortable, companionable silence. Between sips, Willow listens. The air between them is filled with joy and wonder, contentment and gratitude, surprise and pride———and love. So much love.

"So, where can I put the rest of my heartbeats today?" she asks lowering her empty cup to the countertop.

Instead of replying, Meera squints at her as though trying to remember something. Then as if bit by a tiny bug, she leaps up and says, "Oh!" before scampering upstairs without another word.

Willow watches with two parts amusement and one part curiosity.

One minute and then another passes as Willow sits, listening to Meera opening and closing drawers, shuffling objects around, and muttering incoherently.

"Ah-hah!" Meera exclaims then comes down the stairs with a spring in her step and a broad smile on her face. Willow looks at her, eyeing the object in her hand.

"Here. This came for you about halfway through your retreat," she says placing a postcard on the counter in front of Willow.

Willow doesn't want to touch it at first. She just stares at the rectangular piece of cardboard with a glass pyramid on the front. The image was unmistakable: Le Louvre. Paris. She attempts to stare through the glass of the pyramid at the words written on the back, but her transformation over the past ten days has not granted her X-ray vision.

"Well? Aren't you going to see what it says?" Meera asks. She speaks quietly, but the energy behind her words could have knocked down a building in a single blow.

"No," Willow says, partly to tease Meera and partly because she wants to sit with this feeling of anticipation until she is alone and can meet the message without being watched. She has been dreaming of postcards from Aaden for weeks, but with one sitting in front of her now, she feels exposed, unprepared for disappointment from expectations she doesn't want to acknowledge are there. She knows she won't be able to hide her feelings from Meera, so they will both have to wait.

"OK," Meera says clearly disappointed, but shifts gears seamlessly to activity coordinator mode and says, "Well, then to start with, um… you can finish stacking the pile of split wood out back. By the time you finish that, it should be lunch. Then, this afternoon we will go through the canning and organize what needs to be eaten first and take stock of our winter supplies." She stops speaking, sighs, and then adds, "I know it's only been ten days, but it feels much longer. It will be nice to have an extra set of hands again."

Willow smiles and gets up to wash her mug. It feels good to know she has been missed as much as she missed them.

Willow stacks the wood, repeating a Shiva mantra with every movement to forget the postcard in her pocket. It doesn't work. She doesn't get far before the thought of what Aaden has written burns a hole through her coat and into her mind. Sighing, she sits down on the unstacked pile of wood and takes the postcard out of her pocket.

The sky above the old museum is summer-day blue. People are walking here and there across the courtyard while others are standing in front of the glass triangle having their picture taken. Willow examines the glass monument critically. It is a beautiful contrast to the enduring heritage of the stonework. *Modern meets yesterday*, she thinks. *It's just like Aaden—a quirky old soul in a young, handsome body.* She slowly turns the postcard over and reads what is written on the other side. It is only when she sees so few words that she realizes she had been hoping for thousands of tiny letters crammed into every available spot on the card. But instead of Aaden's usual stream of conscious ramblings—the ones she had come to adore—it simply says:

"Jade. The people-watching is fantastic. You should see it for yourself!!"

And underneath those twelve words (she counted) was an address in Paris. There was no closing. No name. No 'I miss you'.

Jade reads it 3 or 4 times before she feels eyes on her. She looks up to see Avi staring. Her cheeks glow red as their eyes meet.

"No one ever sends me postcards," he says with a hint of a smile under his moustache. "Must be nice."

She smiles in return and nods. "It is."

"Meera sent me out to tell you lunch is ready, lass."

"I'll be right there," she says standing up and returning the card to her back pocket.

"Are you talking to me? Or the card?" Avi asks nonchalantly, but he doesn't wait for an answer. If he had, he would have been waiting for a long time. She doesn't have one to give.

"Have you figured out what it means?"

Willow looks up from her lunch and gives Meera a puzzled expression, wondering if Meera wants to know what the message on the postcard means, because that's what she has been thinking about as she eats the rest of her Kheer for lunch.

"Your new name? Willow," Meera clarifies.

"Oh!" Willow says with a spoonful halfway to her mouth. "No, um, I haven't had a chance to look it up yet."

"Do you want me to tell you?"

"No, it's OK. I'll look it up later. I'm just kinda sitting with everything right now. The whole experience was—big."

"I bet," Meera says with a nod. "Mine definitely was, and Avi's was too, wasn't it Avi?"

Avi nods in agreement and then jerks his chin towards the window. "Snow."

The three of them sit and watch in silence as the world slowly turns white before their eyes.

And in the space of a meal, Winter arrives.

Winter at the centre was not black and white; it was pristine and filled with treachery. First winter, as Meera lovingly referred to it, and then nagged on about, was when the sudden drop in temperature and the first blanket of snow lit a fire under everyone to get the last of the winter chores done. Then, winter annoyingly oscillated between snow, mud, frozen mud, snow, frozen mud, and more snow until *second* winter, announces itself by a week of -30 Celsius, then warming enough to make the drive an ice rink—followed by more snow on top all the way to first spring.

Winter is something Willow has always looked at as something that needed to be escaped, and for the past eighteen years, she had done just that. She had escaped into books, into movies, into warmer climates. But this winter— nestled in a cozy cabin when she wants to be alone or at her spot at the fireside with two people she had grown to trust, appreciate, and love when she feel like company—Willow Jade savours every moment.

She soaks in the way they engage in playful banter, the way only a family can. She relishes the way they dream, reminisce, and tell stories—some true, some fantastical, and some she feels have just enough of both in them—that they seem to whisk away the hours and devour the fireplace logs in their wake.

They share personalized poems and letters instead of gifts for Christmas, words and sentiments that ensure laughter, cheers and even a tear at the heartfelt offerings. They busy themselves cooking Christmas dinners and dis-tributing them to the neighbours in every direction before returning home, and like any typical family gathering, eating far too much themselves. They fail to stay up past 10 pm on New Year's Eve but enjoy a whole day fireside with Rose telling stories of her past and weaving tales for the future to start the year off right.

Despite the shorter days, she is as busy with her daily activities as she was in the garden's high summer. But, it is a different kind of busy. It's a nourishing busy. A cup filling busy. "Winter is an inhalation, whereas the business of Summer is an exhalation," Rose tells her on one of their afternoon strolls. Willow embraces the pine needle basket making—she has made one for Aaden for the next time she sees him—the rug weaving, and the candle making.

Then one day, while walking down to her little cabin, after a hearty lunch of lentil cottage pie and listening to her footfalls crunching lightly upon the crisped snow, she stops at an unexpected sight in the freezing temperatures. A Robin sitting on a fence post is watching her. It is close enough that she can almost reach out and touch it. She doesn't try, although the internal debate is contentious. The Robin's red-bellied presence speaks of new life, that Spring is on its way, and that soon—*too soon* Willow thought—it will be time for her to move on, to leave the nest, and to breathe the next breath of her journey.

63 Tat Twam Asi

It's March 15th. The day she impatiently longed for the first four months, hadn't given much thought to as she became more involved with life and study—and Aaden, during the following four months, and now has been dreading for the last four as she finally feels at home within herSelf and the centre. Many months ago, she wrote this date in her journal with the words EMANCIPATION DAY followed by more exclamation points than anyone ever needed to use. Spring Jade would have been ecstatic that March 15th has finally arrived; Winter Willow is not.

Willow's final lunch is a quieter affair than usual. She is used to Meera and Avi chatting about logistics as they eat, but today there's a mournful silence in the air, only breaking with wistful sighs and quiet coughs.

Willow focuses on trying to finish her bowl of Kitchari without bursting into tears. Silently she chants her Ram mantra focusing on each syllable hoping it will stave off…

"Do you have a highlight?" Meera asks breaking Willow's train of thought. "From your year, I mean?"

Willow rests her spoon for a moment on the side of her bowl, being careful not to let it clink. She finds so many sounds unnecessary now and wonders how she'll manage out in the 'real world'. She can't think of any one thing without emotion welling up, so she attempts a half smile and shrugs.

"Avi," Meera pokes, "Do you have a highlight of Willow's time with us?"

"Well now," he says with an air of amusement and pauses mid spoonful. "When you ask that, the first thing that comes to mind is Willow's firey determination to learn how to shoot. You just wouldn't take no for an answer."

Willow sees the slightest smile curl at the corner of Avi's mouth. "I'd never seen that in a lass before," he adds.

"Mine is how you cared for Aaden," Meera says with a nod. "That was really somethin' darlin'."

"Yes, yes that sure was," Avi says in agreement.

"Ah, thanks," Willow says "You, both, um…"

Perhaps seeing that Willow is going to crumble into tears Meera reaches down beside her feet to retrieve something out of her bag.

"Here," she says fumbling for a second or two and then finds what she's looking for. Willow watches Meera slide a bookmark across the table towards her with a sad smile on her face.

Willow picks up the bookmark and looks at it closely. It is old and slightly frayed on the corners, but the artwork of an old Willow tree by a river is beautiful. She turns it over and finds a handwritten note dated 1969.

"Willow asks you to bend with her into the path of retrieval. Follow the labyrinth's trail, connect with the power of wisdom and the rhythm of your soul, and return to your ordinary world strengthened. You will find that your awareness of your purpose is stronger and your intent cannot be broken by the spell of another's will." Celtic Oracle of Avalon by Katherine Torres, Ph.D.

"New Moon magick, creativity, fertility, female rights of passage, inspiration, emotion, binding. Healing, protection, love divination, Love."

Willow looks up at Meera.

"My grandmother wrote that and gave it to me when I left home, way back when. I've carried it everywhere with me all these years. But it seems fitting that it's yours now. I want you to have it." Meera speaks quickly and quietly, and her face looks more flushed than normal.

"Really? No. I can't." Willow says, but she finds that as she speaks the words she is holding the bookmark closer to her heart, incapable of letting it go.

Meera smiles seeing her grip the bookmark tighter.

"Thank you," Willow says. "I love it."

"You're welcome," Meera replies her eyes becoming bright with emotion.

"Ahem," Avi interrupts, wiping his moustache with the kitchen tea towel. Willow can see Meera wants to reach out and snatch it away from him but has opted to sit on her hands instead. Willow suppresses a smile. *Oh, god. I'm going to miss them,* she thinks.

"I, ah, made a little something for you, lass."

Willow can see that Avi is blushing as he puts a piece of rolled cloth on top of the table. It's tied at its center with a piece of sinew holding a single Peacock feather in its knot. The thoughtfulness with which Avi has prepared his gift causes a lump to form in her throat.

"Thank you, Avi," Willow says. She reaches out to receive the bundle, but something is off. It takes her a moment to realize that the string Rose had put on her left wrist at the fire is gone. She pulls her hand back and rubs the place where it has been all these months.

Rose's words wash over her. *When it naturally falls off, then it means you have remembered, let's say, digested this chapter and are ready to step into the next.* Willow smiles briefly and then pulls Avi's bundle toward her. There is something hard inside the soft canvas wrap. She hasn't expected anything from either of them, especially since they didn't even do gifts at Christmas. She starts to unwrap it like a child on Christmas morning.

"I found this piece of blown-down Willow after a storm on one of my walk-abouts a few years back. It's been sitting in my cottage ever since. Makes a mighty fine doorstop. I've been saving it for the right occasion and the right winter. And I believe, this is the right occasion and winter. Thought you might like it."

Willow carefully unties the knot and unrolls the fabric to reveal a set of hand-carved, wooden utensils.

"Oh my God, Avi, I love them!" she squeals pulling the spoon from its hand-stitched pocket. She dips the spoon into her kitchari eager to try it out. The wood feels smooth and warm against her lips, and there isn't a sound to be heard as she scrapes it clean with her teeth.

Avi smiles.

"And it doesn't even make a sound when I eat!" Willow exclaims and smiles back.

"Thank the gods," Meera mutters as Avi sits back in his chair—satisfied.

Willow pulls out the fork and the knife and admires the same care and attention to detail he has put into each one. "These must have taken you hours and hours, Avi."

"Aye, they did. But sometimes time is all we have to give."

"I love them," she says. "I absolutely love them." She smiles at him, a smile that says *and I love you.*

"I stitched the case for them from an old skirt I'd had from many, *many* moons ago," Meera says pointing at the canvas fabric that has intricate hand-painted dandelions on it. "I thought it was time to put it to better use."

Willow runs her hand over the stitching, fingering the seams and the perfect lines.

"It's incredible," Willow says. "Thank you so much." She looks at both of them as they exchange a look of satisfaction, and Willow thinks, not for the first time this winter—*this is what it feels like to belong to a family.*

"Right! Now. Better go and get your things, darlin'," Meera says standing up to take her bowl to the kitchen. "Your aunt will be here soon to pick you up. Time for you to step into the future… and…," her words catch before she can finish and they trail off into the mournful silence that still hangs in the air.

Willow walks up the hill to her old camper and stands on the pallet deck that has not yet been cleared from the last snowfall. She places her backpack on the ground and leans it up against the old tin wall she used to call her 'prison cell'. Off to the side, in a protected patch, the single yellow and purple crocus stands swaying slightly in the breeze.

"Ah, friend," she says as she crouches down in front of it. "You have come to bid me goodbye! Thank you for being with me, for showing me how to bloom and shine when the world is cold and asleep."

She stands up and looks around at her 'prison cell' and smiles. The colorful banners flap in the breeze and the evergreen limbs of the trees seem to wave in her direction, and as she takes in the scene, something catches her eye. It is the Northern Flicker that woke her up each morning. Clinging to the trunk of the Fir, it locks eyes with her, bangs its beak against the bark of the tree three times, and then flies away.

"I won't miss that," she says aloud, then thinks, *Actually, I will. Just not on the weekends.*

A bark interrupts her musings and Willow turns to see Pebbles, Avi, Meera, Rose, and her Aunt Carole walking towards her.

Avi holds out his arms and wraps Willow in a hug. She rests her head on his chest and breathes him in. This taciturn old man had shown her kindness and sternness; he had shown her what it meant to be dedicated and to be OK with what is.

"Where are you going to go now? Do you know?" he asks with a teasing, grandfatherly smile. He already knows the answer. He just wants to hear her say it. Again.

"*Oui, monsieur,*" she smiles and shrugs coyly. "I might travel for a bit. Ya know. See the world—find my place in it."

Meera and Rose look at each other and smile.

"You will always belong here, sweet Willow Jade…You can always come home. Remember that," Meera says, wrinkling her nose and blinking as she speaks in an attempt to hide her feelings with the possibility of an oncoming sneeze.

"I know, and I'm counting on it," she replies. She spreads her arms wide and embraces Meera. "Thank you," she whispers so only Meera can hear. "Thank you for making me clean the floor."

And then she turns to Rose.

They look at each other the way people who love each other do, when it is time to leave, to move on, to fly. Willow opens her arms and takes a tiny step towards Rose. Rose instinctively takes a half-step back, but then something in her face changes, and she moves forward to embrace Willow.

Willow hugs Rose tightly and almost lifts her off the ground just as she used to lift her mother, but she stops as Rose exclaims, "Oh, my child, careful! I'm an old woman!"

Willow puts her down her eyes become glassy and her voice throbs with emotion.

"Thank you, Rose, for, everything. I… I am…."

"Tat twam Asi," Rose says with a slight bow, interrupting Willow—not out of rudeness, but kindness—she knows.

"Tat Twam Asi," Willow replies. "Tat Twam Asi." With her hands together at her heart, she bows to the three of them. "Thank you," she repeats.

"Tat Twam Asi," they say in unison, delighted to hear the words finally fall from her lips. Willow takes a photo of them with her mind: Avi with his arm around Meera who's silently crying and leaning her head against his shoulder; Rose standing slightly apart from them with the sun silhouetting her body giving her an otherworldly glow; Pebbles at her side, tongue lolling.

Willow's heart swells with gratitude. She was one of the lucky ones. She is sandwiched between the love that stands behind her and the adventure that lies ahead. She turns to her aunt.

"Hey," she says, a bit shyly.

Carole looks slightly confused like she doesn't recognize the person standing in front of her. "Hey to you, too, kid," she says after a moment. Then Carole pauses. She looks Jade up and down taking in her scruffy boots, well-worn jeans and hoodie, and clear, bright blue eyes. "You look great!"

"So do you," Willow says, not quite knowing what else to say after a year without superficial chit-chat. "It's nice to see you."

Willow turns and swings her backpack onto her shoulder in one fluid motion. Carole's eyes widen a moment. Willow knows what she is remembering—the Hunchback of the winter prior.

"Well, this is me," Willow says adjusting the shoulder straps so that the bag can sit up a little higher. She gives them one last smile and as she turns to start down the hill to the waiting car, Sam appears beside her. He had escorted her in, and he will now see her out. She reaches down and scratches behind his ear. "I was hoping you'd come to see me out, bud. Thank you for saving me."

"Come back and bring Winter stories to feast on, OK?" Meera calls out as Willow heads down the drive.

Willow raises her hand above her head and gives them a thumbs up, but she doesn't dare look back. She knows if she does, she may not leave.

Voices murmur behind her, and then Carole's voice catches on the breeze, "… my sister always spoke of miracles, but, well, I'm a lawyer, and I deal with facts. And the fact of the matter is, this is a miracle. I am so eternally grateful. Thank you."

Willow smiles as she walks and thinks about all she's learned: the lessons Rose and River shared with her in the fall; the way Avi meets and comforts death; the way Meera nourishes the present with care and attention. She thinks of the way the birds sing for the trees and the way the trees cradle and protect them in return. She thinks about the wisdom shown to her by the orbs of light that reside just beyond what her eyes can see. So many things have helped her to remember who she is. They are all here, she can feel them, vibrating like a nucleus of bees, huddled together, quivering, patiently, carefully, entraining her to the memory of each moment.

She can hear her heavy-breathing Aunt Carole walking a little ways behind her now. She is talking to Sam who has turned back to get her, but Willow still can't bring herself to look back.

She inhales deeply, breathing in the forest, breathing in the land. *Thank you*, she thinks, as she walks down the drive. *Thank you* she thinks as her footfalls pick up the chant. Right foot: *thank*. Left foot: *you*. Right foot, left foot.

A breeze races through the trees and a fine mist of snow rains down on her. The snow sparkles like diamonds and the breeze sounds like applause.

"Thank you," she whispers one last time as her aunt hits the button to unlock the car and pop open the trunk. "Tat Twam Asi."